ON THE SEA

NAVAL ALTERNATIVE HISTORY

Edited by
JAMES YOUNG

DEDICATION

To absent comrades.

FROM THE DESK OF ARES ONE LAST TIME (AS RELAYED TO YOUR EDITOR...)

The sea. Purview of my brother Poseidon. Constructed by Zeus to provide you with sustenance and beauty, yet clearly not a place mortals were intended to inhabit. Its denizens possess the means to consume you without warning. The very environment snatches the breath of life from your lungs. The storms that lash its surface and the tides which moves its contents possess power beyond your comprehension. So of course, some idiots amongst you said, "Let us go there upon that blue expanse to conduct warfare. Combat that will be, of course, the same as the killing and mayhem we can get up to here, just with a higher chance of drowning!" Alas, none of the tales in this volume are from a time when drums beat, slaves rowed, and ships met in a crash of rams. No screams of dismay as idiots discovered armor doesn't float, *I* have no power to save even the bravest warrior from drowning, and sharks do not pick sides.

Instead, this volume begins with the flap of sails as Dragon Award winner Sarah Hoyt postulates a dire turn of events for Portugal and the Royal Navy in "For Want of a Pin." Behold the power of illumination and inspiration in "Martha Coston and the Farragut Curse." Learn that violent, sudden death is not limited to saltwater in Imadjinn Winner Daniel Kemp's "Damn the Torpedoes." Remember a different *Maine* in Rob Howell's "Far Better to Dare." Find out that "dreadnought" is a misnomer as Joelle Presby and Philip Wohlrab bring you two very different tales of the alleged "War to End All Wars." The Fates and I have always found great pleasure in the new and inventive ways mankind finds to kill each other. It's especially pleasing when the scalding, burning, and shredding takes place under a funereal shroud of coal smoke intermixed with the roar of escaping steam.

Of course, the above should not be taken to mean my joy fades when the bloodshed takes place under clear skies. As your editor can attest from past experience (see *Violent Blue Yonder*), I am ecstatic when I think of mortals throwing themselves at one another across Zeus' domain. This fervor grows exponentially when the aerial clashes are combined with battles on the ocean like some martial combo platter. Whether deciding naval clashes between empires ("Skyrockets in Flight") or helping forge unlikely alliances ("Corsairs and Tenzans"), fellow fans of these things you call "carrier battles" will find plenty to entertain here. Almost as a dessert, William Alan Webb adds a "what if" involving a certain debacle at Savo Island in "Five Meters Forward." I still remember poor Atropos had to go through two pairs of scissors in the original timeline. The look "Ms. Fate With the Scissors" would have given me if I'd indulged Webb's solution might have made Medusa's gaze seem benign.

Speaking of things that could give Atropos a hand cramp, fans of the so-called "Cold War" will be glad to see Sidewise Award winner Eric Swedin return with another story from his *When Angels Wept* universe. Between Swedin and Sidewise Award finalist William Stroock ("Atlantic Flash"), readers will understand why Father sent Prometheus to the eagles. Not even I, a god who loves a good burning, can abide by slaughter of that level. After all, no use being a god if all your worshippers are circling the stratosphere. Fortunately, much like calmer (or is that luckier?) heads prevailed in the timeline readers are familiar with, *On the Sea* wraps up with three stories where mortals don't go on the divine pyre. Justin Watson ("Decision at Cam Ranh") and your editor ("Mr. Ford's Cats") provide sequels to the universes they visited in *Violent Blue Yonder* and *Thin Red Tales*, while Jan Niemczyk provides his third "Last War" story to round out the volume.

In the end, whether you're a landlubber or a trusty shellback, *On the Sea* has plenty of instances of what might have been if dear Athena had not gone whining to Father about my brutality. These stories go great with grog, seafood, or whatever you decide to have for a short interlude of entertainment. Just don't consider what those crabs' ancestors probably dined on or how much those steamed prawns probably resemble an engineering section after the boilers burst. I, for one, am going to grab some wine and enjoy watching the *Lexington* and *Amagi* duke it out in a timeline your editor did not see fit to add to this. I will never understand mortals' fascinations with *Tomcats*.

--Fin

CONTENTS

FOR WANT OF A PIN

Sarah A. Hoyt

Dear Albina,

I write to you not knowing if my letter will ever reach you, though I suppose I can send it back with the part of our English escort that will be going back before we reach Madeira.

However, the reason I write is to relieve my feelings. Truth be told, I might as well be writing in a diary, but I feel as though I left our conversation incomplete on November 15 when I rushed to you to procure a pin to secure my hem which had torn.

It was the most absurd fix, since Mama had already had all our household packed, and who knew where the pins might be, and we were supposed to tell no one we were leaving or where, even though everyone must have seen we were packing.

What a ridiculous time.

Of course, as I told you then, the purpose of it all was to

get us aboard these fifteen ships, which among them will transfer the entire royal court to Brazil.

This sea travel business is not as much fun as you'd imagine. The ships smell of fish and unwashed clothes and never stop swaying. And we're piled in like cattle.

I know Papa isn't a nobleman. But as one of the secretaries of the regent, charged with His Highness's correspondence, you'd think Papa would have secured better berthing for his family. No. I'm in a cabin which I share with five other girls, the whole cabin smaller than my dressing room at home, and the whole smelling strongly of salted cod. Mama is lodged similarly, and I know not where Father eats or sleeps, or if he does. It seems every time we see him, he's either running after His Majesty, jotting down things in sheaves of paper, or else being rowed away in one of the boats, to take a message to someone, usually one of the English captains in the ships escorting us. This makes sense, I suppose, since Papa speaks fluent English, learned from his English mother, but all the same, it's very painful not seeing him at all. It's as though I've lost, at one moment, Lisbon and my whole family. And when I ask him when we'll get to Rio de Janeiro or how we'll live there, all he does is shake his head at me.

———

Her name was Maria Francisca Joana dos Santos e Leal, but her whole life, she'd been called Joaninha or, more often, "a menina" since she was the only girl born in the family in many a year, and the only daughter of her parents.

She was named after her English grandmother—well, almost, as her grandmother had been Frances—from whom she'd inherited the blue eyes, and a dimple on her left cheek when she smiled.

Her eyes were such an unusual color in Portugal, that even without the dimple she would have been considered beautiful. Since she also had considerable natural beauty, her whole life she'd been used to having people defer to her, or go out of her way to make her happy.

Only now it had all gone wrong. People wouldn't listen to her, or stop behaving in the most absurd ways.

It had started early in November. She'd heard the conversation at first, not knowing what it meant. Oh, she understood the language well enough. Her grandmother had ensured she knew English almost as well as Portuguese. It was the content that made no sense.

The gentleman in the study with Papa was an Englishman she recognized, a tall man with the reddish tan of a fair man who spends much time in the sun. He was dressed in a uniform that Joaninha didn't recognize, and people called him "Commander" or "Milord." To include Papa, even though it sounded like they were friends, and Joana could hear the clinking of port wine glasses.

"Is there nothing we can do to convince him to take action, instead of this vile, revolting submission?" Milord asked.

"Nothing if we can't convince him that the French mean to depose him," Papa said.

"But does he not care for his country?" Milord asked, his voice sounding shocked in the way British people spoke when they found something outrageous. "Does he not care for the kingdom of his ancestors, and the people who are his responsibility? Does he not care if they're making French subjects and kept under the boot of the beast?"

"I used to think he did," Papa said. "Now, I'm not so sure. I've started to suspect the Regent cares for the country only as a possession. And as a possession, meant to add to his glory, he doesn't want it taken from him. Nothing else matters, nor what conditions are put upon that possession."

Papa walked to the window.

"The sad thing is that the Regent will do anything rather than risk losing power and the chance to be John VI one day," he continued. "And besides, what precisely can we do? And what does it matter to you if Portugal falls with the king in it or not? Is it not bad enough that we fall, with no plan to defend ourselves from the French? That the French will add us to their empire and resources?"

"It would be bad enough," Milord said, and again there was the clinking of the port decanter being opened before he continued. "But the thing is the French will get their real objective, which is your fleet. With your fleet, Bonaparte can make true his plans for invading the British Isles, which have been out of reach since Trafalgar."

"But I don't understand how the king can prevent their doing that. Soult has been marching towards us, since the king's first tender of surrender, and he will be on us too soon for—"

"No," Milord said. "Listen, Leal: if we can but convince him to escape, ahead of the French, on all of the Portuguese fleet, or at least all that's currently seaworthy, to Brazil, and establish his capital in Rio, it will not only—"

"Brazil! A wilderness, halfway around the world?"

"Yes, listen, it will put the entire fleet out of the reach of Bonaparte, and it will—from the prince's perspective—allow him to keep the crown of the kingdom. Even should Bonaparte crown one of his puppets to rule over Portugal, the prince will have a chance of recovering the kingdom someday." He paused a second. "Particularly since we English can then be supplied from Rio and continue the fight. Now what we need to understand is how to make him agree to this."

Joaninha hadn't been, exactly, listening in. Well, not precisely. She'd been walking from the music room to the parlor, and on passing Papa's study, had walked very slowly and caught that much.

Yes, she knew it was bad manners to listen in, but the fact was that she was fourteen and bored. Yes, there was war, and everyone said Soult would come to Lisbon and kill everyone. It was said he had done very horrible things in Spain as he marched his way through. There were stories of villages pillaged and entire nunneries "disturbed," though Joaninha got a feeling that meant more than that the nuns had been told horrific tales.

But there had been war since she'd been aware of the talk of adults, and of worried whispers in the corners of drawing rooms and parlors. It was normal, and therefore boring. Sometimes news came of some city taken, of people killed, of many dead.

Mama or Eufemia, Joaninha's nurse, would exclaim and cross themselves, and Mama or her nurse made her pray for the safety of some city or other, but Joaninha never saw war, never saw anything distressing.

Life in Lisbon was interesting, and sometimes enlivened by uniforms, both Portuguese and foreign, but she was protected, kept inside, made to learn her needlework, and say endless prayers. It was boring. Thus, she didn't understand what Papa's visitors were talking about, but still, it was interesting to listen to them.

Milord's words stayed with her, and she reasoned that if the king went to Brazil, her father, as one of the royal secretaries, would also go. She'd heard of Brazil, mostly in shops. Cacao which made the sweet chocolate that Joaninha drank for breakfast every morning came from Brazil, as came the dark, rich coffee Papa drank. Pineapples came from Brazil, too. And her friend, Albina, had a very funny pet monkey that an old uncle had brought from Brazil. It wore red shorts, and could dance when Albina played her piano.

The idea of living in a land of such wonders colored her dreams. Meanwhile, Papa looked more worried and harassed every day, and it was three days before Joaninha found herself alone with him in the parlor before dinner, and ventured to ask, "Papa, if we go to Brazil, may I have a pet monkey?"

Papa had gone white. "Who told you we might go to Brazil? Who said anything?"

"I don't know," she said. "I heard something. I just thought I'd like to have a monkey and—"

"You must not, under any circumstances, speak of going to Brazil, Joaninha." The indulgent smile that Papa normally gave her when she was vague and silly didn't materialize. Instead, Papa looked as stern as Joaninha's confessor did when she told him of overhearing things or sneaking a sweet from the kitchen. "Don't speak of Brazil. Don't even think of Brazil. You could ruin us all. Amelia, Amelia, come and tend to your daughter. She could destroy us all."

Mama had come, all alarmed, and even she wouldn't be kind to Joaninha, or allow her to explain that she'd just been talking of Brazil because she might have dreamed—

Instead, Mama had been as stern as Papa or Joaninha's confessor and told her it would be a sin to say anything about Brazil, even in other contexts. She'd ended by yelling, "Brazil doesn't exist," and locking Joaninha in her room, which Joaninha thought very odd.

Then things had gotten stranger.

Two days later, Joaninha woke up to a house full of relatives. Normally, she lived with Papa and Mama, Eufemia, her nurse, Mama's maid and Papa's valet and any number of servitors and drudges she barely noticed.

Oh, she had family enough around, beyond those people. Her aunts lived in the next street, grandmama and grandpapa—on Papa's side—next door to the aunts, and there were other relatives and cousins all over Lisbon.

She liked some, didn't like others, and was usually amenable to being taken to visit them on Sundays or for long summer weeks. There were really no cousins her age, and all the cousins were boys, so her society didn't vary much while visiting. But the aunts gave her sweets and her grandparents petted her much.

There had never been an occasion—at least not in her remembered lifetime—that the entire family came to the house. Her two maiden aunts, Eugenia and Miranda, her married uncle Miguel, and his wife and their two infant sons whom she could never tell apart, and her widowed uncle Manuel and his sister-in-law Mariana, who helped him look after his three sons, Rui, João and Joaquim, ranging in age from fourteen to three, and all very naughty, Joaninha thought.

But they were there when Joaninha woke. She was already alarmed she'd woken on her own, and not been woken by Eufemia with a tray of hot chocolate and toast.

She'd dressed herself all anyhow, and caught back her curly hair, before opening the door to her room, to what seemed to be an impossible scene.

The house was full of relatives and luggage.

No one had noticed Joaninha. She'd stumbled around, amid people arguing and talking and gathered they'd all been there all night, since shortly after Joaninha had gone to bed, Joaninha gathered, and they'd brought with them baskets and bags and some very large travel trunks called *Baus de Porão*. Joaninha had always thought them very romantic, since their whole name indicated they were built to travel in the hold of a ship. But it was bewildering to be barely able to move for the press of them.

What was stranger was that all of the house servants and most of the family were packing, taking everything they could reach and stuffing it willy-nilly into more of those hold-trunks. Mama, who never did any housework for herself, was wandering around distractedly and picking up anything small enough: a clock, a candlestick, a piece of unfinished embroidery, and putting it in an open trunk.

She was talking to Papa, who stood by, "Very generous of you, I'm sure, to include my brother," she said. Her brother was Widowed Uncle Manuel.

"Look," Papa said, sounding just a little exasperated. "We were told we could bring twenty people. They might have to make themselves useful, but the Regent is not so cruel as to expect us to leave family behind."

"My sister in Coimbra..."

"Ah, no, Amelia, don't you see that's impossible? We could send word to our family in Lisbon and have them all come in the dead of night. No one need know outside the house. But your sister would have to have known earlier, and to travel—"

"Yes, I know. Poor Almerinda. I shall pray for her."

Joaninha wasn't sure of understanding this, but then she didn't understand any of it. Not only was everything being packed, it wasn't as they'd packed before when they went to Sintra for the summer. No. Things were packed without rhyme or reason.

She'd wandered to the kitchen, unnoticed, to find the cook, Maria, being besieged by Joaninha's two evil cousins, João and Joaquim.

"Maria, if you please," Joaninha said, overwhelmed by the strangeness of the morning, and trying to speak loud enough to be heard over the brats, "Maria, I would like some breakfast."

Maria was the cook, whom Papa had once said was "as large and majestic as a galleon under sail." And though Mama had rebuked him and he'd said he'd never say it where Maria could hear him, Joaninha could never forget it, and had always thought of Maria that way. She looked more like a galleon now, with the two boys, one attached on either side, each yelling, "Biscuits, biscuits, biscuits." As she turned, the boys, holding onto her skirts, turned with her, like lifeboats on a galleon. "Oh, Menina," Maria said. "Let me get you something. These two brats— We all forgot, didn't we?"

And like that, Cook had gotten chocolate and toast for Joaninha.

Which was the beginning of the problem. Because João and Joaquim had been upset. "Why do you get her things but not for us?"

While Joaninha ate, they'd thrown themselves, time and again, at Maria's skirts and apron, while the cook ignored them and... Well, she seemed to be packing hard-baked goods and jams into a trunk, so the madness continued even here.

Just as Joaninha got up, Joaquim threw himself at her, grabbing her skirt and screaming, "Make her give us biscuits."

Joaninha went over against the wall with the impact of the boy, and heard her skirt tear.

She hadn't cried in years, but suddenly she found herself crying, "Oh, oh, oh, my skirt."

The cook had emerged from her labors only long enough to scold the boys, but it was obvious she'd do nothing about the tear.

Holding the tear closed, Joaninha ran to find Eufemia. When she couldn't find her nurse, she tried to tell Mama she needed a needle or a pin to fix her skirt. Mama paid no attention, and Joaninha ran down the hallways to her room, but all her other dresses had been packed, and she couldn't find either needle or pin.

Taking a deep breath, unable to get anyone's attention, she decided she'd go to Albina for a a pin. Sure, she'd caught the implication that no one was to leave the house. But Albina was just two houses away. If Joaninha ran quickly, down the back garden and over the wall, no one would see her go and detect her coming.

Whatever was happening—and she suspected it was the trip to Brazil, she couldn't be expected to travel with a torn skirt. It wasn't even decent.

And she was right, and went and returned with no issues, to find the house in the same uproar.

Joaninha was sure they'd be going to Brazil, after all, even if Papa didn't seem too sure and said things like, "We'll be unpacking it all again in a week, and then watching all of it getting seized, robbed, and destroyed by the French." She'd told Albina all of it, and also how Mama had said they'd have to leave Lisbon, anyway, because otherwise Mama and Joaninha might get killed or worse.

Joaninha had heard this before. When she'd gone to Albina, she'd tried to make a joke of the worse, which was just the sort of thing Mama said, but Albina said, "It is not funny. You know Etienne, and you know the stories he tells."

She knew Etienne, or that is to say, Joaninha had seen him once or twice from a distance. His family was French, and they'd escaped the revolution. And she knew Albina loved him. Or at least, Joaninha thought that explained why they had somehow arranged to exchange notes by hiding them in between two stones in the garden where the two friends often walked.

The notes were the stuff of high tragedy and undying love, and Joaninha had enjoyed immensely hearing them read and envied Albina— three years older—her grand love affair. But this was real. The house being packed up was real. Fearing the "worst" was real. Things being so confused that Joaninha couldn't find a pin was real. Things being so confused no one prepared her meals or listened to her was real. And her possibly having to leave everything behind to go to Brazil or staying in Lisbon and enduring whatever it was the French would do was real.

Whether the stories Etienne told were real or not was open to discussion. After all, he'd been born in Portugal, and Joaninha knew he'd never even been to France, much less remembered the revolution. And besides, "Where did he ever tell you any stories?"

"Oh, we meet sometimes. I go to MM mass, and we sit way at the back, where we can talk."

The conversation had thereafter turned to this exciting intrigue, and Joaninha forgot all about Brazil. Until, of course, they embarked.

It hadn't been too bad, at first. It was new, at least. Her relatives had been dispersed among the boats, with other people of scant importance. And it was a relief to get away from Uncle Manuel's bratty sons.

The thing was that no one was paying her any attention. The girls she roomed with were all older and two of them were married. They talked and laughed in ways that made no sense to her, and often she thought they might as well be speaking a foreign language. Which was why she had started the letter to Albina. But finding a place to write in peace was difficult, and she didn't want anyone reading over her shoulder. Besides, she found she really didn't have much to say to Albina other than describing her intolerable situation, which in turn seemed to make it more intolerable.

So she'd folded the letter inside her missal, which was one of the few things she'd been allowed to carry with her, and instead had gone up on deck. One of the good things about this disturbed situation and Papa and Mama not being anywhere near nor paying any attention to her, was that she could wander about at will.

She was sure if Mama were aware, she would tell her the ship wasn't safe, and that on deck she'd meet rough seamen who might take liberties. No one had, though, and she couldn't spend her life confined with other people. On deck, there were many people, sure, mostly seamen putting sails up and pulling them down, and doing who knew what. However, as long as she stayed out of their way, she could walk and look out at the sea. On deck, no one bothered her or tried to ask her questions, or made jokes over her head and laughed in an irritating manner.

She was walking on deck, inhaling lungfuls of the clean sea air that didn't smell of fish and human misery, like the confined spaces downstairs, when she heard Papa's voice. "Joana! What are you doing here? And alone?"

"Just walking, I—" She was so shocked at being called Joana and not Joaninha she couldn't find her words.

"Never mind that, girl," Papa said. "Go find your Mama and your nurse. We're moving to the *Marlborough*."

"The British ship?" she said, turning around enough just to catch a glimpse of the frigate, a flutter of sails to the west, tinted by the setting sun.

"Yes. Mister Graham and I have some things to discuss, some plans to make, and he's offered to lodge my family and myself. At least your mother and nurse, and Leticia, your mother's maid, will be able to look after you."

———

Traveling between the ships was exciting. They all piled into a little rowboat, like the boats the fishermen rowed in the villages around Lisbon. Joana sat with her Mama, with her nurse and Leticia following in the next boat. After them came a train of other servants, and enough of her luggage that Joaninha wouldn't be living with two dresses and only a missal for reading material.

"Now, Joana," her father had told her. "You must remember we'll be the only family onboard, and that many of these sailors haven't seen any women or girls in months. You must remember that you're a good and religious girl, and you must not give your mother and I any worries."

Now, thinking about it, as the boat tied up to the much bigger ship, and she was helped up a rope ladder, to emerge onto a deck filled with young men in uniform, Joaninha didn't know whether to laugh or cry. Laugh because it was utterly ridiculous. It was Albina, not Joaninha, who'd exchanged notes with a boy! Boys had never even noticed Joaninha, other than smiling at her. And besides, she would be too shy to even talk to one of these young men, who all looked so grown up and busy.

She had an impression of tallness, of hair that sparked in the sun, of beards and of amused light-colored eyes. She'd never be able to talk to one of these young men, even if Mama or Nurse gave her a moment alone to do so. And they wouldn't. Besides, why would any of these young men want to talk to her?

———

His name was Jonathan Winter. She didn't remember how they'd started talking. It had started with smiles, proceeding to casual greetings, proceeding to comments about the weather and when they'd arrive. And somehow it had become normal, within a week, for them to find a corner of the busy deck, where—because others were busy and intent on their work—they could go unnoticed and talk.

There was no grand passion of the kind that Etienne had talked about to Albina, mind. They weren't that sort. And even had they been, what future could they have, being of different countries and aboard a ship headed to a distant land of coffee and monkeys?

"I've heard it's very savage," Jonathan said. "Little more than farmers in a vast wilderness."

"I wonder how we'll survive!" Joaninha said, picturing herself as a farmer's daughter, digging for onions and milking cows.

Jonathan laughed, as though he knew what was on her mind. "Well enough," he said. "I wager. With the entire court and the Portuguese king present? They will arrange things to be comfortable for you and those with you. It just won't be like Lisbon."

"You'll be there?" she asked. "You'll go, too?"

"Only for a day or two, while we unload," he said. "Half the English ships will turn back next week, with Admiral Sir Sydney Smith. Mr. Graham will command the rest of the way. They reckon there isn't much danger when we are so near Madeira and out of the sphere of influence of the continent. It's unlikely the French will catch us."

Joaninha felt a pang. "Perhaps," she said. "Lisbon is captured and utterly burned, now." She wondered, even if she ever finished the letter to Albina, whether Albina would receive it, or even if Albina was alive.

"I doubt it is burned," Jonathan said. "Sacked, probably." He paused. "All the same, I'd give something to see the look in Marechal Soult's eyes when he saw that the Portuguese fleet evaded him and the king was gone."

———

The majority of the British ships had turned back to supply the English troops in the peninsula and to try to win back Lisbon. To the last minute, as men were being transferred between ships, and much communication going on by lifting flags on masts and poles, with each new pennant hoisted making people aboard another ship rush about, Joaninha feared that Jonathan might leave with Sir Sidney Smith, after all.

It was good having someone to talk to, someone who appraised her of what was really going on. Many things that she had heard from Papa in his study now made sense. Jonathan told her, for instance, that the regent had hesitated before making the decision to move the whole court to Brazil. Before that he'd tried to surrender to France, and had ordered his troops to oppose no resistance. It was only when Sir Sidney Smith—whom Joaninha had identified as "Milord" who had talked to Papa in his study— had shown him a copy of a French gazette that talked of the deposition of the Portuguese monarchy that the Regent had made up his mind to move the whole court.

"He's not a very brave man, your regent," Jonathan had said. "But perhaps no man is when his whole family and kingdom is threatened."

It made Joaninha feel very grown up to understand what was going on at last. It made her calmer at the prospect of sailing into the strange tropical land that awaited them. So she watched the ships turn back, relieved that Jonathan was on deck and not going back with them. Of course, she didn't expect anything to happen between them. Certainly not a romantic relationship or even a lasting friendship, but for now, he was an anchor of sanity in a world gone mad. Because Father was still very worried, still going between ships, or closeting himself with Mister Graham late into the night and discussing who knew what.

"We'll be in Madeira in a week," Jonathan said. "We'll make port and resupply. I think until we pass it, your father won't be wholly calm. I mean, it is still possible for the French to catch us. I don't think they will, mind you. Napoleon is no sailor, and his navy are all incompetent, which is why we've trounced them again and again, but it is remotely possible the French will catch us, or perhaps ambush us, before we're past Madeira. After that, it's very unlikely. It is too far for them to sail at venture, trying to catch us.

"Mind you, I think this is too far and so did Sir Sidney Smith, or he'd not have left. But I think your father is one of nature's worriers. He worries about everything that the Regent should worry about and doesn't."

"Yes. He was always like that," Joaninha said, with a little pride at her hardworking, conscientious Papa, even if she had an inkling it wasn't the best way to be.

————

The knock came in the middle of the night, in the cabin she had—gloriously—all to herself. That it seemed luxury, even though it consisted of a sleeping berth and barely enough space to sleep in, told her how cramped she'd been in the other ship.

"Miss! Miss Leal!"

She was sure it was Jonathan's voice, and she wondered what he was doing knocking on her door in the middle of the night. He'd said his father was a clergyman. And surely he knew that Joaninha's father would kill him if he tried any gross impropriety such as entering her room while she was alone.

But she got up and opened the door a crack, positioning her foot so he couldn't push his way in, and she could scream the ship down if needed.

But Jonathan was very pale and seemed not to see her, even while staring at her. "Miss, there are ships sighted. They came from Madeira. We think they are French."

She clutched at her nightgown. "They are? Are you sure?"

"Not yet, but we'd like you to remain below decks. Your father wants every one of our guests to stay below decks. Perhaps they don't know who we are. Perhaps they won't try to give chase."

The truth is, Joaninha thought, *fifteen Portuguese ships-of-the line of and three English ships will have little chance of being mistaken for anything but the Portuguese fleet carrying the royal family and escaping the French.*

She wanted to ask Jonathan if there were more French ships than the combined Portuguese and English force, but he'd already left. She heard his feet clamber up the steps to the deck.

"Menina," Nurse's voice called, and Joaninha saw her, a bulky woman in a nightgown and wrapped in a dark shawl. "Menina, your mother says to come to her cabin to pray."

————

Mama's cabin was crowded, and as Mama called the rosary, the three of them repeated the prayers mindlessly. Or at least Joaninha repeated them mindlessly, while she tried to hear for sounds from above. Was that a boom as of a cannon firing?

She knew it probably wasn't, but she couldn't help hearing every creak as a scream, and every clack as a boom. Aboard ship that meant she was in continuous alarm.

Through the night and into the morning, they prayed, until Joaninha must have fallen asleep while praying.

She woke up alone in Mama's cabin. Scrambling down the narrow corridor to her cabin, she encountered no one and heard no sounds. All the sounds—other than the ship's ubiquitous noises—came from above. Was everyone on deck?

Dressing quickly, she ran up the stairs to the deck, where indeed everyone was.

Mama and Papa stood together. Papa was looking through binoculars and sometimes saying something to Mama. Nurse and Leticia were just behind them, looking worried, and sometimes talking to each other.

"Miss Leal," Jonathan said, coming up from behind her. "I wouldn't worry. There's only ten of them."

"But they're French."

"Yes, they're French, but they're far fewer than us."

He'd gone away, then, because there were message flags to hoist and to interpret, and orders to be relayed. As she watched him move astern rapidly, Joaninha thought that perhaps he was right, but perhaps not. Sure, the Portuguese fleet alone was fifteen ships, and there were four English escort ships. But she doubted very much the Portuguese ships were armed. She'd once read that sometimes when they were being chased, ships would throw cannonballs overboard because the balls weighed too much. She doubted the ships loaded down with courtiers had the ability to carry also the cannonballs. She very much doubted it.

She stood by her parents, staring out and trying to pray.

I fear it will fall on deaf ears, she thought.

"How could they have known we were coming early enough to plan and send out an ambush?" her father said. "After all, they have a small navy, and they couldn't have moved it that fast."

But none of it seemed to matter, as someone shouted, "They're hoisting flags demanding our immediate surrender, our handing over of the ships and the royal family."

"And what do we do?" someone else shouted.

"We fight, by God," said a voice she thought was Mr. Graham's.

————

It was both very fast and agonizing slow, the ships approaching, gliding over the water, wind impelled.

"We can't really run," Jonathan said, in one of the few moments he managed to stop by her. "We can't run without leaving the Portuguese fleet and the royal family utterly unprotected. To run is to surrender. And they can't run, the ships loaded down as they are."

The French ships circled the fleet. The English ships fired, the noise horrible and confusing. Powder and smoke were everywhere. Joaninha thought that it was silly firing at the French ships, because all the men were visible, and they'd all climbed the masts, where the cannonballs couldn't injure them, unless a mast itself was brought down.

And then the French ships returned fire, and hell on Earth erupted. Amid the smoke and the smell of gunpowder, there was now the sudden cracks and explosions of cannonballs, or worse, of charges shaped like bars with a bulge at each end that whirled through, cutting things or breaking things.

Someone shouted the ship was taking in water. She realized she was huddled against coils of rope on the deck, and couldn't see Papa and Mama, much less Jonathan through the smoke. There were screams of people, and she wondered if any of them had been hit and was, perhaps, dying just inches from her. But she couldn't see them, and every instinct told her to make herself small and unobtrusive, like a hunted creature.

She wondered, as shouts redoubled and the ship listed, if she'd go down into the cold dark waters, and die like that, forgotten.

It seemed to go on forever before it stopped. It stopped very suddenly, without warning.

Now there were shouts, but they were close at hand, and she opened her eyes enough to see that the ship was full of fighting. French sailors had boarded. There were sword fights everywhere, and suddenly, out of the smoke and the confusion, Jonathan emerged. "Get up, Miss. Your papa has one of the boats, and he's going to try to make land in Madeira."

It was a mad scheme. Joaninha wondered at it. After all, Papa was no sailor, and she didn't remember his ever having rowed a boat, not even a pleasure boat on the lake in the park. And the island of Madeira was no more than a nebulous grey streak in the distance.

"Come, Miss."

"We'll never make it," she said. "And Papa—"

"Come."

He half-guided her, half-pulled her through the deck. She slipped a couple of times, and realized she was slipping on blood. She tripped over the bodies of men who she was sure were dead. It was a scene she wouldn't have believed outside her nightmares.

Nor would she have believed being lowered onto a boat with a rope under her arms, while all around her battle still raged, some ships—she couldn't even tell which, as night had fallen—still fired on each other in flashes of sudden illumination. It seemed to her even the water was angry, tossing the little boat around while she and Mama and Papa and Leticia and Nurse huddled together in the cold and damp.

Papa rowed. But the land seemed no closer. They did get away from the battle.

It was sheer luck a fisherman's sailboat rescued them. He took them to the house of a local gentleman, and it was days—mostly sleeping, taking trays in her bed—before Joaninha could get up and find her family.

The house was large, and what she could see of the gardens and the isle was a riot of flowers.

Mama and Papa were sitting outside in a sort of terrace. They both looked pale and Papa was saying, "The Kingdom of Portugal is no more. The north has been offered to the former regent as a fiefdom of his family, the Braganzas. The central part is given to Spain. And the South goes to France, giving them good ports from which to sail. And of course, the fleet."

"But—" Mama said. "How did they know where and when to ambush the escaping fleet?"

"Some damnable spy in Lisbon. Etienne something or other. He got word of the escape, or possible escape two weeks before we left. Family had escaped the revolution, but they were still French, you know?" He saw Joaninha then. "Hello, Joaninha. Don't worry too much. The French will need a man who can speak many languages and write in them." He smiled, a pale smile. "We'll probably go to England when the French invade. Not much chance of England holding out now."

But Joaninha did not, could not move. She'd gone very cold.

For want of a pin.

ABOUT SARAH A. HOYT

Sarah A. Hoyt was born (and raised) in Portugal and now lives in Colorado with her husband, two sons, and a variable number of cats, depending on how many show up to beg on the door step. She has over 40 -- the number keeps changing -- published novels, in science fiction, fantasy, mystery, historical mystery, historical fantasy and historical biography. Her short stories have been published in Analog, Asimov's, Amazing Stories (under a previous management), Weird tales, and a number of anthologies from DAW and Baen.

To learn more about Sarah A. Hoyt and read samples of her work, visit http://sarahahoyt.com

MARTHA COSTON AND THE FARRAGUT CURSE

Day Al-Mohamed

"My signals will prove a valuable auxiliary for the Navy and the night would lose half its terrors at sea, when in the darkness and through the storm, ships could talk to each other."

Martha Coston would have regretted those words if she had not believed them to be true. She didn't bother with field glasses as she gazed up at the night sky. Faint shimmers of light reflected off smoke as they floated downwards, remnants of what had been her pyrotechnic display. Martha's lips were set in a tense line. She was grateful that none of the other observers noticed the expression on her face in the darkness. Tonight had been a success. No, the truth was, tonight should have been a success. The darkness had been illuminated by the explosion of dozens of signal flares. Fired high above the waters of the Potomac in Washington City, they had burned a brilliant clear green for at least ten seconds. The first Coston Night Signal.

However, rather than exclaim at her success, Martha heard the men from the Navy examination board mutter misgivings and doubts and questions. Of course, none of the officers aimed any of the questions at her. She was, after all, only a woman. Granted, she was the woman who had created the flares, but they found that fact inconvenient. Even in this dreadful time of war, with the very nation divided against itself, and urgency, like a dog nipping at their heels, they were unwilling to alter their preconceptions. It didn't matter that the Secretary of the Navy had invited her to be present when the board tested the signals. All that mattered was that she was a woman and therefore anything she did was suspect.

Martha retreated back to her lab at the Potomac Yards with their words echoing in her ears. It wasn't really a lab. The Navy hadn't been convinced enough to give her an actual lab. She worked in a tiny shed not far from the waterfront. No assistants, no chemists—it was just her, on her own, every day. It had taken her more than ten years to perfect the plans and produce a finished product. But that was meaningless unless she was able to sell her night signaling system. Martha had invested every cent she had, and several she didn't, into this project.

She sighed and leaned against the rough wooden wall. It creaked ominously. Perhaps she should go to Europe, find out if the British or French would be willing to invest in her Coston flares.

She tucked an errant strand of hair that had escaped her bun back behind her ear and rolled up her sleeves. The Aldens had agreed to keep her sons for the evening, so she might as well take advantage of the extra time. Besides, she had an idea for a new additive to her signals.

Martha walked over to the small desk crammed into the corner of the room. Papers and books were neatly stacked on and around it. There was a clear sense of order. Martha sighed again. Her husband would have had them tumbling in piles with crumpled and stained pages all over the lab. She missed him desperately, and as her two boys grew older, she missed him even more.

Martha narrowed her gaze and her attention. She flipped open a journal and skimmed down until she found her latest notes. It would be a long night. She had a new recipe for her flares. These would burn hotter and brighter, and if her calculations were correct, they might even be unquenchable by water. She would show those *vazey bantams*. She would create something so remarkable that they couldn't ignore her. Step one: calcium.

"Mrs. Martha Coston?"

Martha looked up from where she was putting large cow bones into a vat. A naval officer stood at the entrance to her lab. She nodded, not stopping what she was doing.

"How can I help you?" Her words were curt.

She knew she was being rude, but right now she didn't feel like being polite in the face of potentially more ridicule.

The older man removed his hat and ducked his head to enter. "You may not remember me, but you were a friend of my wife's, Susan Marchant?" He wrinkled his nose and added without thought, "What is that smell?"

Martha stopped what she was doing. Ignoring his question, she wiped her hands on her apron and answered him with a question of her own. "Mr. David Farragut?"

"Yes, ma'am," he said.

Martha stoked the fire under the vat. As the slurry heated, the smell that rose was indeed terrible. She used those few moments to gather her thoughts. Martha knew all about Flag Officer David Farragut. The entire country knew about Farragut. He had failed in an attack on New Orleans. It had destroyed almost the entire Union fleet and resulted in the death of his foster brother, Captain David Porter. In fact, every military endeavor he attempted during the last three years of the war to preserve the Union had ended in failure. Some even whispered that he was cursed.

"Susan was a very good friend," Martha responded cautiously, "I am sorry I could not attend her funeral."

She ducked her head, unable to meet his gaze. The truth of the matter was that she had been unable to afford the journey to New York. Through her own ignorance and "the duplicity of others," what savings she had as a widow had been taken from her. As it was, she was currently living with friends and reliant on their charity for both herself and her boys.

Martha swallowed back tears. She wasn't sure if they were for herself or for Susan. "I'm sure it was very beautiful."

Farragut gave her a small sad smile. "You are kind. I am here to ask for your help."

Martha gestured to a bench, the only seating other than the chair at her desk. "The boiling will take some time. Please sit."

Farragut shook his head. "I prefer to stand."

He paced back and forth as if readying himself, and the words began to flow. "The West Gulf Blockading Squadron is tasked primarily with preventing Confederate ships from supplying troops. These blockade runners are often coming in from neutral ports such as Nassau and Cuba. Outbound ships carry cotton, tobacco and other goods for trade and inbound ships are bringing in guns and other ordnance."

Martha exhaled slowly, hiding her impatience. She was well aware of General Winfield Scott's Anaconda plan. The Union navy was to create a blockade to extend along the Atlantic and the Gulf of Mexico coastlines and up into the lower Mississippi River. The newspapers reported often on its failures.

Martha sat down in the chair and watched him pace. "And you need my help how?" she prompted.

Farragut kept talking as if he hadn't heard her question. Martha pursed her lips, her irritation rising.

He continued, "We are failing in our task. With 3600 miles of coast and more than 200 river mouths, inlets, bays, and channels, it is impossible to stop all maritime trade. But the fact that these blockade runners can fly past us in the dead of night outside of major trading ports is an embarrassment."

Farragut stopped pacing. "I need something to tip the balance."

He took her hands in his intensity. His fingers felt warm against her own cold skin. He glanced down and she could see him taking in the white scars that decorated her knuckles and the backs of her hands. She pulled her hands away and yanked down her sleeves.

He took a step back, his back stiff, his words formal. "I'm sorry, Mrs. Coston."

She gave him a rueful look. "When working with incendiaries, one will get burned. It is not a matter of if, but of when and of how badly." She flexed her hands, feeling the tightness against her skin.

"Surely you have men to do the research?"

She shook her head dismissively. "We hear much of the chivalry of men towards women, but it vanishes like dew before the summer sun when one of us comes into competition with the manly sex." She paused, and smiled to take the sting out of her words before continuing. "I am perfectly capable of running my own lab, Mr. Farragut."

"My apologies. I did not intend to offend. I have the utmost faith in your abilities, and I saw your accomplishments just this night. That is why I am here...asking for your help."

She felt her annoyance dissipate. All that remained was a hollow feeling in the pit of her stomach.

"To me, it was a most bitter thing to find in that lofty institution, the Navy," she said, "men so small-minded that they begrudged a woman her success."

"Then you understand. Mrs. Coston, we need each other. I need the success that your signals will give my squadron, and you need a real-world success for your invention."

"Mr. Farragut—"

"Don't give me your answer tonight. Just...please, consider it. We can discuss it further tomorrow afternoon."

———

Time flew over the next three months. Farragut had asked for 400 flares, but that had been just the beginning. Martha had been hard-pressed to complete the task, but she had found a manufacturer, procured the necessary ingredients, and began production of the Coston Signal Flare. And since that time, Farragut's squadron had achieved unprecedented success. Her pyrotechnic night signal flare and code system allowed Farragut's navy vessels to communicate quickly and easily with each other by night, and firing of the flares in the path of the blockade runners made it easy to track and then trap them. Three months expanded to six months, then eight, then ten. And then things started to go wrong.

"I need to come on to your ship." Martha was abrupt and to the point.

She glared at Farragut as he, once again in her tiny lab, paced back and forth, his steps heavy with worry.

Farragut reeled backward as if he'd been struck. "Absolutely not."

Martha didn't flinch. "I have examined the signals at the design phase. I have checked with my manufacturer in New York. I pulled some of the signal flares off the railcar delivering them to you. The only place I have not tested their efficacy is when you are underway."

"I cannot allow—"

"Because I'm a woman?" Martha cut him off.

"You know that's not true," Farragut snapped.

"Don't lie to me. It is very true."

At the stubborn expression on his face, Martha sighed and softened her tone. "In the last ten months, you have intercepted more than 300 blockade runners. Mobile, Alabama was the largest cotton port in the world, and the last large Confederate port, and you successfully stopped all maritime commerce. That made you a hero."

"Yes," he said through gritted teeth. "Some fool hero."

"And now?" Martha prodded, like the way her younger son would play with a loose tooth. "Tell me again. Tell me what is happening."

Martha knew she had to get him to say the words out loud or he would continue to try and ignore what had become an increasing problem in the last few weeks.

"And now they aren't working. Some of the signals fizzle; some don't even light." Farragut started pacing again, his steps faster and faster. "You know all this. Blockade runners are getting through because my ships cannot communicate to each other."

"Which means we have to do something," she finished. Her words fell like stones into water, their import rippling out in a way that felt almost physical.

Farragut ran a hand over his face. "The men are right. I am cursed." The words were muffled, but understandable.

"You're not cursed, David," Martha said. "But we do need to understand what is happening and, regardless of propriety, I am the only one who knows the recipes concerning how to mix the chemical compounds to create the bright burning signals. I need to board the *Hartford*. I need to test the flares."

"War is no place for a woman," he snapped.

"War is no place for anyone," she countered. "David, let me discover what is wrong."

Farragut growled in concession. "Do we have a choice?"

Pregnant silence was his only answer.

———

Martha Coston walked across the spar deck towards the small room where the flares were stored. Thankfully, she didn't have far to go. The USS *Hartford* had dropped anchor for a few hours before their final approach to the mouth of the river just outside of Mobile, Alabama. Martha considered herself lucky they'd stopped. She'd wanted to take advantage of the opportunity to check her signal flares one last time.

Martha pulled her cap further down over her head and kept her face averted from the faint light emanating from her shuttered lantern. She was dressed like a navy officer, but it would not take much for anyone to discover the ruse. She shifted the heavy leather bag containing her testing kit on her shoulder. Inside, there was the faint clink of glass as the vials of chemicals jostled each other.

On her right, in the shadows, squatted a row of 9" Dahlgren smoothbores. Each required a crew of sixteen and a powderman to fire. She couldn't help but note the shape of the powerful guns. It really was a brilliant design. The smooth curves equalized strain and concentrated more weight of the metal in the gun breech where the greatest pressure of expanding propellant gases was. The result was a strong, maneuverable cannon that was much less likely to explode from pressure.

Martha reached out to touch one of the guns, but pulled her hand back and gave herself a mental shake. This was a distraction; she needed to focus on her mission.

The sounds of water splashing against the sides of the ship and the snapping of the lines against the mast seemed to fill the air. For a full ship, the night was eerily devoid of human sound. The *Hartford* was a sloop-of-war with a full complement of 302 officers and sailors, but tonight, she'd seen fewer than half a dozen men. And so Martha only barely stifled a very feminine shriek when a voice rasped out of the darkness.

"You should know the ship well enough to not be using that lantern."

Martha squinted through the dim light to better see the speaker, but she recognized him immediately. There were only a few black men who served on the *Hartford*. It was Landsman John Lawson. She remembered him from her frantic half-hidden days on the ship. Regardless of the worn and frayed state of his naval uniform, he always seemed to carry himself with a confidence that made him memorable.

"It's bad luck," he added in a hushed voice.

She nodded, ducking her head lower as she passed. So many things were bad luck on a ship.

His eyes narrowed. "My apologies, but I do not recognize you, sailor."

Martha felt the air on her neck go icy. "Checking...for the admiral... important," she mumbled thickly so her words were almost unintelligible. Her pace increased as she sped across the deck and away from Lawson. The whole time, she could feel his gaze on her retreating back. She would have to be quick before Landsman Lawson thought too much about what he had seen.

Of course, Farragut had no idea of Martha's current whereabouts; nor did the skipper of the *Hartford*, Captain Drayton, nor Farragut's own Chief of Staff, Captain Jenkins of the *Oneida*. Martha rolled her eyes at the thought. Captain Jenkins was a pompous little man, and was very much like the naval officers she remembered from that night so many months ago in Washington. He would have had a fit if he knew she was aboard the ship, dressed as a man. Even Farragut—*David,* she corrected...sometimes it still felt awkward calling him by his Christian name—was still trying to persuade her to leave. The only reason he wasn't with her now was because he thought she was "resting" in his cabin until she could be returned safely to Union territory.

She knew David and his officers were likely poring over maps and determining how best to maneuver their ships to address the incoming wave of blockade runners. It would be especially now if they did not have any working signal flares. They had become the cornerstone of their strategy. At the thought, Martha felt her teeth come together and grind in anger. Even before getting on the ship, she had checked and rechecked her formula. It was perfect. All the tests over the Potomac those months earlier had just reinforced her feelings. She knew they worked.

She'd even pulled a few flares from the last batch of kits to be delivered to the *Hartford*. Red, white, and green, these three colors allowed the Navy to have a full code. Every single one had burst bright over the water, flared to life, and then drifted down. So what had happened? Why weren't the flares working anymore on Farragut's squadron? Was it water? The fuses?

Martha opened the storage room door, frowning at its unlocked state. It needed to stay locked, or any fool with a flame could blow them all sky high. She slipped inside the storage room and closed the door behind her. Martha felt secure enough to lift the cover on the lantern, granting greater illumination in the cramped storage room. Shadows warped and danced and under her feet she could feel the thrum of the *Hartford's* engines as she idled.

In the last week alone, at least a dozen blockade runners had made their way through to Mobile and no doubt more were doing the same for Wilmington and Galveston. Even with Farragut's success of the last few months, the cities remained central ports of call, with ships arriving every day from Great Britain, providing arms and supplies by way of Cuba.

Martha wound through the various crates and boxes. Finding the crate she was looking for, she set down her bag and firmly grasped the lid. She lifted and slid it off, grunting in exertion. Maybe she should have asked for assistance from Landsman Lawson or simply had Farragut bring her a box of flares for testing in the comfort of the cabin. Doing this on her own was not only ridiculous, it was dangerous. She yelped as a nail caught her hand, dragging through the flesh of the underside of her palm. Martha glared at the offending nail. She pulled out her handkerchief and awkwardly tied it around her left hand. While the cut wasn't deep, it bled messily. It would have to wait, though; her thoughts were already on the signal flares.

The testing had to be done in secret. Martha had decided that someone had to be purposefully damaging the flares. She did not want to risk the possibility that whoever was sabotaging Farragut would suspect that she was on their trail. She paused and rolled her eyes at the thought. Perhaps "on their trail" was a bit much. Martha felt melodramatic—like one of the heroines in a Victorian novel—for entertaining the idea. But she had to examine every possibility. Farragut had agreed to use the flares. Like he'd said, they needed each other. They would only succeed if they both succeeded. He wouldn't sabotage himself. But he also wasn't a popular man, especially after his failure to take New Orleans and the loss of so many ships with so many lives. And of course, there was the Farragut Curse.

Martha leaned into the crate, this time much more cautious of wayward nails, and brushed aside the loose straw. Dust rose and she stifled a cough. Below was a smaller wooden box. She lifted it out and set it on the ground. Retrieving the lantern, she set it down beside her, careful to keep it well clear of the box and any errant straw.

Pulling a small knife from her pocket, she pried open the box lid. Inside was a full set of colored flares. Red. White. Green. All carefully labelled. She picked one up and examined the strip of tape and paper that wrapped the flare. In the flickering light, it was difficult to see clearly, but she thought she could detect marks on the tape.

She peeled back the casing to better view the multiple layers of gunpowder, the chemicals in between that added the various colors, the central fuse, and the incombustible layers in between that kept the signals separate. She shifted to get better light, careful to keep the combustible ingredients well away from the heat and flame of the lantern.

What was that? Martha frowned and used the knife point to pry out one of the incombustible layers. It was clearly damaged. The gunpowder and chemicals would all ignite together. She didn't need her testing kit to see the damage. It was clearly visible. This collection of chemicals wouldn't hurtle into the night sky as a flare. It would explode.

Suddenly, Martha didn't feel like a silly Victorian heroine anymore. She had proof of a saboteur. "No, that can't be right." She reached into the wood box for another flare. She had to be sure.

Martha started pulling at the tape, engrossed in her examination. Strontium nitrate for color, potassium perchlorate for a rapid burn, magnesium... She only looked up when a burst of air came through and her lantern flickered.

"You! Halt!" The voice was low and threatening.

Martha froze.

"You move and I'll put a bullet in you."

Martha didn't even dare breathe. She heard the sound of boots getting closer. Boots. That meant it had to be an officer.

"I can explain," she said breathlessly, turning. "I just need to see Flag Officer F—"

A large hand wrapped itself around her upper arm and yanked her to her feet. "What a surprise! Mrs. Coston." Another set of fingers wrapped around her hand holding the knife and squeezed.

Martha's gaze travelled up and up. "Captain Drayton?" Martha's tone was a whistle of air. He was big man, not only tall, but graced with broad shoulders and a barrel chest. She tried to remember everything she knew about Drayton. He had been with Farragut since the war began and was the well-respected, if not well-loved, captain of the *Hartford*.

Martha tried to pull her hand free, but Drayton's grip tightened even more. Martha let out a soft cry as pain shot through her hand and the knife fell to the floor with a dull thump.

"Let go of me!" She hated hearing the bite of fear in her voice.

Drayton released her hand and reached down and picked up the knife, slipping it into his boot. He paused and picked up the opened flare. Powder spilled across the floor.

"Careful!" Martha hissed, her eyes going to where the lantern sat. "If you do not care for the lives of the sailors on this ship, at least have care for your own."

Martha stilled as she realized that Drayton had addressed her by name. A chill wrapped itself around her heart and her throat tightened. She licked her lips that had suddenly gone dry.

"Ah, Martha. I can call you Martha, can't I? Yes, I know all about you and your new invention." His voice was liquid, completely unconcerned, as if he were telling a story rather than talking about actual lives.

Drayton tossed the half-opened flare into the far corner of the room. "I was there that night. I saw your test and I knew what it would mean for the war. Did you know I was Superintendent of Ordnance at the New York Navy Yard? I—"

"How did you do it?" Martha interrupted, her words sharp.

She didn't want to hear his story about his past. How he had almost destroyed her project. She wanted to know about the present. "I checked on the signal flares every step of the way. From the mixing and manufacture all the way to their delivery into the holds of each ship."

"And here you are."

"Where else would I be? You are ruining my work!" Martha's voice rose as she renewed her struggle.

Drayton's hand was like a vice. Outside the storage room, a board creaked as someone passed. Was it Lawson?

"Keep your voice down," Drayton snarled.

He yanked her close. She could smell his breath, tobacco and onions.

His lips brushed her ear. "Don't you know? Having a woman on board is bad luck."

"I'll scream," Martha said, desperation edging her words.

Drayton's smile widened. "That's bad luck, too."

He raised his hand, a pistol in it. Martha opened her mouth to scream. He brought it down, and everything went black.

———

Martha woke slowly. Her head ached and she had the urge to retch. There was a rocking motion and water lapped against wood. She exhaled slowly. She tried to put a hand to her head, but discovered they were tied in front of her. She blinked. She was in a small rowboat. There was a dull scraping sound that caused Martha to wince in pain as it ran aground.

"Good evening, Mrs. Coston," Captain Drayton said as he hauled her to her feet.

This time, Martha did vomit. She wasn't sure if she was more embarrassed at the action or more satisfied to see Drayton leap backwards to avoid it.

She stumbled as he jerked her out of the boat. Water and mud swirled thick around her ankles. She could smell the brackish water. No doubt they were at one of the many small inlets or coves that dotted the coastline.

Drayton walked at a quick pace, half-dragging her behind him. She dared a quick glance back over her shoulder. She could see nothing out in the water, but she could hear the *Hartford* just faintly and smell the coal from her furnaces. Ahead of them was nothing but the dim outlines of beach and grasses and scrub forest.

She blinked slowly; her vision was fuzzy and blood pounded in her head. "Why didn't you kill me?" The words seemed to rebound in her head, and she winced, stumbling again.

Drayton didn't slow his pace. "I am not a monster."

"You're a spy."

"No, madam. I am a saboteur."

They reached the building, a small wooden affair just barely out of sight of the water. Drayton opened the door and stepped inside. He threw Martha forward into the blackness. She grunted as her shins came in contact with a hard wooden frame and, unable to catch herself, she fell forward onto the mattress of a bed. Martha coughed at the flurry of dust and dirt that rose around her. The world spinning around her elicited a groan, and she fought down another bout of nausea.

Silhouetted by the faint light of the crescent moon in the doorway, Drayton lit the candle on a pocket lantern. Martha could now see the details of the tiny one-room cabin. It had a dirt floor, the bed she was on, a couple of chairs, a table and little else. She noted a lack of windows.

"You'll be safe here."

She squinted up into the light. "And how will you explain my absence?"

At that, Drayton laughed. "A better question might be, how will Farragut explain your presence?" He shrugged. "A woman with delusions of adequacy. She fell overboard."

Drayton hung the lantern on a hook by the door, and set down a bag on the floor. It clinked as bottles inside it shifted. "Provisions. I'll send someone in a few days."

Martha wanted to respond with something clever and scathing, or perhaps just launch a physical attack and try to get past Drayton, but her thoughts felt as heavy her winter woolen dresses and the blackness at the edges of her vision warned against sudden movement.

He then turned hard eyes on her. "This is not your fight. This is not your place."

Drayton closed the door behind him, and the wooden bar across the outside slammed home with a finality that unnerved Martha. She drifted in and out for some minutes. She couldn't sleep. She knew that would be a disaster. With effort, she sat upright and leaned against the wall. Her stomach rebelled at the movement. Perhaps women truly were not cut out for war.

She'd heard variations of that phrase so much over the last year, even from David. And now he would fail. And her signals would fail. And she would lie here, maybe even die, miles away from her sons. Martha choked on a sob. Her thoughts tasted like copper and acid on her tongue.

It is my own fault I didn't suggest sabotage to begin with, Martha thought wretchedly. She took a couple of slow deep breaths, trying to ignore the pain shooting through her skull. She paused and then took a few more.

"I am not going to die here. I am not going to let that odious man win."

Martha's words were barely audible over the sound of the waves, but just saying them aloud made her feel better. Gathering her legs under her, Martha stood. The room swam and, unbalanced, she promptly fell back onto the bed. Martha cursed inwardly.

Maybe if her hands were free? Martha struggled with the rope that bound her wrists, attempting to work the complex knots, but her movement was limited. She flexed and straightened her fingers, feeling every scar and burn. She put her teeth to it and bit down over and over, chewing like a dog with a bone, to no avail. It was just too tight.

She sighed and leaned back. She needed something to cut the rope. Martha half-laughed as she remembered the bag Drayton had left—a bag of food and water.

A bag with bottles.

Not trusting herself to stand again, Martha slid from the bed and scooted across the dirt floor. With her hands in front of her, it was easy to open the bag and pull out one of the bottles. She eyed the deep olive figural bottle. Drayton had given her a bottle of whiskey. Yes, it would do nicely. She said a quick prayer of thanks that Drayton had not just given her water in a standard Union-issue canteen.

Using one of the chairs for balance, Martha levered herself up to a standing position. She wobbled for a second, but remained upright. Lifting her leg, she brought her boot down on one of the bottles, smashing it. Dropping to her knees, she picked up the largest piece of glass and started sawing away on the rope.

Her hopes buoyed as she felt the cords begin to fray and release. Martha next turned her thoughts to the door. She ran her hands over the frame, testing its strength.

"I just have to figure a way out."

She leaned against the thin wooden door and pushed. It creaked and swayed, but didn't give. Maybe a little more force? Martha took a deep breath and launched herself at the door. She hit it with all her weight, and immediately she saw sparks dance in front of her eyes. She fell to the ground retching, hands clasped on her head. Oh, that was very much a poor idea.

Minutes passed, and as the pain receded, Martha stood and readied herself to try again. She took several steps back and, dropping her shoulder, ran at the door. She closed her eyes tightly and waited for the impact.

It didn't come.

The door swung open, and Martha staggered and would have fallen if two strong arms had not caught her and set her back on her feet. She squinted into the darkness. With almost no moon, it was nearly impossible to see.

"Landsman Lawson?"

"Yes, ma'am," he said, giving her a half-salute.

"I don't think you need to do that," Martha said. "I'm not an officer and you're the one rescuing me."

He hesitated, and then grinned.

"I reckon that's about right," he said, handing her a bloody handkerchief. "I found this and thought you might like it back."

Martha took the small square of cloth and stared at it dumbly. It was just a faint piece of white in the dark.

"You knew?"

Lawson shook his head.

"No. But I did know you weren't a sailor," he said, then offered her his arm. "If I may? You look like you might need some assistance."

The man nodded back towards the shore.

"I've a boat anchored up by the point," Lawson told her.

Landsman Lawson's words swirled in Martha's mind as she tried to put together the pieces.

"I don't understand. How did you find me?" she asked.

"I followed."

They treaded carefully towards the water. Martha's limbs were slow to obey her, and she leaned heavily on Lawson. Out in the bay, the engines of the *Hartford* still thumped gently in the night.

She frowned. "Why would you follow Captain Drayton?"

"I was following you," he said, his voice low. After a moment he continued, his voice dropping even lower. "I'm with the Black Dispatches."

Martha's head snapped up. She immediately regretted the sudden movement as Lawson seemed to appear as two separate men. She closed her eyes and counted to ten.

"You're a spy," she said with conviction.

"I am a spy," he repeated amiably.

"So you know Captain Drayton was a saboteur."

"No. We thought Flag Officer Farragut was the traitor," Lawson said. "He was born and raised in Virginia. His wife was from Virginia. He had too many ties to the Confederates and too many losses in battle for us to ignore."

Martha opened her eyes, grateful that now she was facing only a single Lawson.

"And Captain Drayton?" she asked.

At the question, Martha thought she saw the corner of Lawson's lips twitch upward.

"Captain Drayton, you discovered," he said. "I knew he had a brother in the Confederate army. Now we know he is working with the Rebels. But what I do not know and what I very much want to find out is—who are you? And what are you doing aboard the *Hartford*?"

———

"It's unbelievable." Captain Jenkins said, pouring himself a glass of amber liquid. The alcohol sloshed around in the glass, catching the light.

"And yet, it is true," Martha replied.

She herself felt the need for some liquid fortification, but didn't ask. It wasn't appropriate for a lady. Then again, none of this was appropriate for a lady. Of course, she'd already destroyed a full bottle of similar liquor. Martha squelched the urge to laugh. She did not want to be seen as a hysterical female.

"I'd best go see to Captain Drayton," Lawson said. "I have no doubt some of my superiors in Washington City will have many pointed questions for him."

He slipped out of the cabin, leaving Martha with Farragut and Captain Jenkins. The silence grew long.

"Drayton has no doubt sent a message notifying the blockade runners," Martha said, looking for something to break the silence.

Farragut had been at his desk the entire time, staring at the maps.

"You are correct," the admiral said.

More silence.

"And we will not wait nor try to stop them," he said slowly, drawing out each word. "We're going to take Mobile."

Captain Jenkins choked on his drink. "What?" the man asked.

Farragut rubbed his hands together.

"Oh yes, Captain Jenkins. Call together the other captains of the

Squadron. We have many plans to make and very little time to make them in."

"Yes, Sir," Captain Jenkins said, springing to his feet immediately.

"So what should I do?" Martha asked.

"Find a dress?" suggested Captain Jenkins at the door to the cabin.

Martha glared at him.

He shrugged in response.

Farragut was pulling out another map.

"You've done your part, Mrs. Coston. You discovered the source of the Farragut Curse. Rest well and tomorrow, God willing, you will see us victorious."

Martha prickled slightly at the dismissal, but it wasn't like battle plans were her strength.

"Thank you. Goodnight, Mr. Farragut."

"Goodnight, Mrs. Coston."

Martha yawned and headed back to her cabin, but she had no plans to rest. She'd ask Landsman Lawson to bring her her signal kit and powders. Perhaps there was something she could do that might make a difference. She'd also have Lawson see if the ship's cook had any bones.

———

The sun rose sluggishly over the Mobile Bay as the Union fleet moved in from the Gulf of Mexico. The ironclad monitors sailed parallel to the wooden ships. They would take the brunt of the fire from Fort Morgan. Martha winced as the sound of cannon fire exacerbated her headache but, rather than wait in the cabin, she dressed and came out onto the deck. She'd even, as suggested by Captain Jenkins, put on a dress.

Martha had expected some animosity from the crew at her presence, but their attention was elsewhere. They were all looking out towards an ironclad that seemed to be pulling away from the rest. Faster and faster. The ship was flying across the water. It was the USS *Tecumseh*. Her smokestack belched large black clouds of smoke as she left the rest of the squadron behind. Martha hefted the leather bag that held her testing kit on her shoulder more securely and walked to where Farragut and Captain Jenkins stood.

"What the hell is Commander Craven doing?" Farragut's words were low and fierce.

Martha followed his gaze to the ironclad USS *Tecumseh*. The ship was steaming forward to attack the Confederate CSS *Tennessee*. However, now Martha could see why the sailors had all stopped in their duties to stare. Even to Martha's untrained eye, she could tell the Union ironclad was headed directly across the massive minefield that blocked the entrance to Mobile bay.

The air was heavy, as if the whole world was holding its breath. Could they make it through? There was a muffled boom and water, wood, and other detritus sprayed high in the air. A torpedo had gone off under her hull.

Martha watched in horror as the water surrounding the ship bubbled and the large ship quickly sank. It took only two minutes. She could hear the sailors as they talked to each other softly, desperately scanning the water for men. But only bodies floated up from the wreckage. She put a hand to her throat at the horrific image. There were no survivors. The murmuring from the crew of the *Hartford* grew louder, matching their fear. The Farragut Curse had struck again.

Martha looked back at Farragut. He was ashen under his tan.

Captain Jenkins growled, "We have to pull back."

The Confederate cannons of Fort Morgan and Fort Gaines at the entrance to the bay boomed, like an ominous thunder. There was a crash as one of their shells slammed into the wooden sloop USS *Brooklyn* that was now unprotected without the *Tecumseh* to block the fire.

Martha felt the *Hartford* leap forward as the coalmen added on more fuel. Smoke from the ship's stacks and from the Dahlgren guns filled the air as the Union ships answered the vicious fire.

"We can't pull back," Farragut replied.

"You need to go forward," Martha said, walking up to both men.

"What?" The question came from both men. One was incredulous and one was questioning.

Captain Jenkins's nose wrinkled. He leaned toward her and sniffed.

"What is that stench? Animal fat? Bone?" he asked, aghast.

Martha ignored him. Her attention was on Farragut.

"You need to be first. The *Hartford* needs to be the first ship through the torpedoes. You have to prove to them that the Farragut Curse is no more."

Farragut stared at her as if she had gone mad.

"I think I can help us cross the minefield," Martha said.

Martha looked out over the bow of the ship. Dark water swirled ominously. She pulled out a flare from her pocket.

"Calcium. From the boiling bones." As if it explained everything.

"What good is that going to do us? A signal flare won't work during the day. If you are so desperate to prove the worth of your flares, wait until night," Captain Jenkins said with exasperation.

She locked the brand-new calcium phosphide flare into the pistol and took a deep breath. It really did stink. This had to work. She looked at Farragut.

"Let me help. Trust me."

He nodded once and took a position beside her.

"You're both mad," Captain Jenkins murmured.

"Be ready," Farragut said over his shoulder to Captain Jenkins.

The captain stomped back to the helm and took the wheel of the *Hartford*.

"Ready!" he said, with the air of a man doomed to death.

Martha took aim and fired the flare into the water in front of the *Hartford*. There was a hissing and bright light bloomed ahead of them. The water shone bright blue and everything below the surface was visible.

"There! And there!" Farragut pointed. "Torpedoes!"

Farragut called for changes in direction. The ship turned, cutting neatly through the water, slipping past the deadly incendiaries.

"How many more of those do you have?"

Martha's expression was tense. "Enough."

Farragut looked at her as if he wanted to ask a question, but then stopped himself. He turned back. "Captain Jenkins, order the men to signal the squadron. Follow me!"

As the *Hartford* steamed ahead, Martha saw her incandescent signals blazing below the water, highlighting the underwater bombs. This was it. This was her moment, her success. One by one by one, the other fourteen ships followed the *Hartford* through the mine field.

"Damn the torpedoes! Full speed ahead."

ABOUT DAY AL-MOHAMED

Day Al-Mohamed is an author, filmmaker, and radio host. She is author of the Young Adult novel Baba Ali and the Clockwork Djinn, editor of the anthology Trust & Treachery, and is a regular host on Idobi Radio's Geek Girl Riot with a listening audience of more than 80,000 listeners. Her latest novella, The Labyrinth's Archivist was just released from Falstaff Books. In addition to speculative fiction, she also writes comics and film scripts.

Ms. Al-Mohamed's recent publications are available in Fireside Fiction, Apex Magazine, Sword & Laser, and GrayHaven Comics' anti-bullying issue You Are Not Alone. Two of her films were recently shown on local Virginia cable television, and her award-winning Civil War documentary, The Invalid Corps, recently sold to Alaska Airlines and made its broadcast debut on Maryland Public Television in December 2020.

She is a Founding Member of FWD-Doc (Documentary Filmmakers with Disabilities), a graduate of the VONA/Voices Writing Workshop, and sits on the Board of Directors for Docs in Progress. Her short story, "The Lesser Evil" was nominated for the WSFA Small Press Award for Best Short Fiction of 2015. However, she is most proud of being invited to teach a workshop on storytelling at the White House in February 2016. She presents often on the representation of and importance of disability in media, including for the National Bar Association, at New York Comic Con, and at SXSW.

Ms. Al-Mohamed holds a Juris Doctor and a Bachelor's degree in Social Work from the University of Missouri-Columbia. Ms. Al-Mohamed is a strong believer in community. She proudly serves as a Flotilla Staff Officer (FSO-IS) in the United States Coast Guard Auxiliary and as a Commissioner for the Montgomery County Commission on People with Disabilities. She lives in Silver Spring, Maryland with her wife, N. Renee Brown, and black lab guide dog, Gamma.

DAMN THE TORPEDOES

Dan Kemp

JULY 4, 1863

Vicksburg, Mississippi. The Gibraltar of the South, and the spot where Grant captured that decisive river town, forging America's inland waters into the chains that would divide and bind the Confederate States of America. For that, David Dixon Porter's Western Gunboat Flotilla had to make his famous nighttime run past Vicksburg's artillery But what if the great Mississippi, the Father of Waters, had been less hospitable to the invader, and that Gibraltar had held longer? Where would that bend the Arc of Ares? Here the story bends in the space between one man on the water and another ashore.

———

APRIL 7, 1863
YOUNG'S POINT, LOUISIANA

Newly promoted Rear Admiral (Acting) David Dixon Porter looked over at Major General Ulysses S. Grant calmly. "I'm not terribly concerned. When the time comes, we can certainly punch our way past Vicksburg again. No more digging canals across the bends. No more backwater creeks. If it wasn't for our friend Sherman, I would have lost five gunboats up that creek in Steele's Bayou."

Grant winced. Several recent operations, like much else in this accursed region, hadn't gone well.

Porter carried on. "But the *Arkansas* is destroyed, the *Tennessee* was never completed, and what was left of her was put to the torch. There's no Rebel navy left to bother with here. From the land, there simply aren't enough heavy cannon along the water in that town to stop us. There's fifty guns, at best. Probably closer to forty."

"Didn't you tell Gideon Welles in Washington that 'a finer system of defenses was ever devised' regarding Vicksburg a while back?"

Porter smiled tightly. "You know how this is done, Sam. You make the task seem impossible, and then your superiors as high as the Navy Secretary in the President's Cabinet are even more impressed with you when you succeed."

Grant puffed at one of his omnipresent cigars. He liked Porter well enough for a sailor, but they were rather different men and they had clashed in the past. That was stressful at times like this, and so his cigars would keep at bay the headache he felt building. He knew the habit might one day kill him, but it wouldn't kill him today, and so he didn't much care. "You're certain you can do this?"

"We've done it before. My brothers and I did it last June."

"I know William left for the New York Navy Yard command. I keep forgetting you call Admiral Farragut your other brother."

"Yes, that's what happens when you grow up together. Regardless, the shore batteries weren't a factor when we fought the *Arkansas* in July, either."

"Kept you from going in there after her," Grant snorted.

"She was doomed, anyway, on account of her own awful engines," Porter scoffed. "You can't take whatever steam engine is laying around from powering a cotton mill or a river scow and throw it in a brand-new armored warship, then expect any good to come of it. Particularly with the currents in these parts much of the year."

"Makes sense, I suppose."

Porter continued. "We have one advantage in passing that I have not yet mentioned. They have a blind spot on their near shore."

"How so?"

"The glacis of protective dirt around their ten river batteries is built up and outward to protect the guns, as one would expect," Porter explained. "But they are at least forty feet above the river's level to clear the buildings at the shoreline. Some of their batteries are at the blufftops two hundred or more feet up, so they can defend the land side, as well. That means they can't depress their tubes enough to hit by the near shoreline."

Porter sipped at his drink, for talking is thirsty work, and continued, ticking off his plan on his fingers. "So first, we go at night. Second, we start out at the western shore for the sake of noise. Third, if we're spotted, we simply steer to our port side, hug the eastern shore instead, and get below their elevation."

Grant, though an infantry officer by trade, had distinguished himself in Mexico two decades before by getting a borrowed howitzer up into a church steeple and firing downward. *Porter's got a point about elevation and depression,* he mused. His Army of the Tennessee was running out of options, and he knew his leadership had been criticized from afar in Washington. Still, after a campaign laced with setbacks, his enthusiasm for another gamble was limited. "We're wagering a lot on this."

Porter smiled confidently. "I'm more worried about the river current than the artillery. It's running four knots this time of year. It will help a dash past the Vicksburg batteries, but none of the river ironclads have the engine power to fight back upstream on their own this time of year, not quickly. Maybe two knots of headway, at best. We only get to try this once."

"Once should do. We just need the Army across the river, and the best ground for that is to the south of Vicksburg."

"I'll see you down there, General."

———

APRIL 8, 1863
VICKSBURG, MISSISSIPPI

An adjutant opened the door to Lieutenant General John C. Pemberton's office. "Sir, we have an officer reporting in."

"Who?"

The adjutant fought the temptation to shrug. "An artillery lieutenant from Texas. Never seen the young man before."

Pemberton sighed. "Send him in." The amusing foibles of junior officers might provide some entertainment from the drudgery of his command, whipsawed as he was between Jefferson Davis in distant Richmond and Joe Johnston relatively nearby in Jackson, Mississippi.

The younger man entered, and Pemberton was favorably impressed.

His uniform was a cut above what was usually seen: a nice dark gray wool, and well-tailored, but instead of the Austrian-knot gold braid on the sleeve that had slowly become the Confederate regulation for officer rank, the coat bore the prewar rectagonal shoulder boards now considered a Federal hallmark. Red background, one bar, yes, still a first lieutenant of artillery, but now atypical for their growing army. The boots were clean and freshly blackened; the scent of polish was just barely detectable, though there was a knife hilt conspicuously sticking out from the inside top of his left one. But while most young officers took pride in swords, usually as ornate as they could afford, this one wore only a Colt revolver in a crossdraw holster. *No pretense to this one*, Pemberton thought.

"First Lieutenant Matthew Bradshaw reports to the commanding general, sir!" The salute was crisp and the voice confident.

Pemberton returned the salute, trying hard not to smile. First impressions being what they were, he actually liked this one so far, but he still had to play his role in the garrison leadership drama as old as war itself. "Lieutenant, why are you here?"

"Well, sir, I realize you are a busy man, and I thank you for your time," the young officer began. "I don't know much of military etiquette, and my service to this point has been rather distant from the action, but I recall one of my classes told me I should call upon the senior officer present when traveling through his command."

Interest piqued, and Bradshaw being more interesting than the latest supply numbers for the moment, Pemberton waved the junior man to a chair. "Please have a seat, Lieutenant. You're just passing through?"

Bradshaw complied. "Yes, sir. I'm attempting to make it to Hood's Texas Brigade in the Army of Northern Virginia."

"That's a long way from here, Lieutenant, and you have much further to go," Pemberton noted. "Should you make it that far, you'll find General Hood has risen to division command with that army's churn in leadership." Pemberton kept his demeanor professional. He had begun the war in the Virginian forces himself, but been shoved out, at first southward, then westward.

"Yes, sir. Living out there at the time when Texas declared for the Southern cause, I was commissioned in their state forces and was eventually placed at the San Antonio Arsenal as an inspector of contract ordnance."

That tells me someone either has faith in your abilities or wanted to park you where you could not do much harm, Pemberton mused as the younger man continued.

"That lasted roughly a year and a half, until it was recognized we had more ordnance inspectors than we did ordnance for us to inspect. I was the junior officer of the inspection staff. Those senior to me seemed very happy to spend the war in the Arsenal, though I admit a couple of them are too old to be doing much else. Anyway, it was very firmly suggested I pack my bags and go elsewhere."

Pemberton *harrumph*ed a bit. "They didn't even give you orders? Merely threw you out on the road in front of the gate?"

"No orders, sir. I was merely told to vacate the Arsenal and, I quote, 'seek an assignment closer to the sound of the guns.'"

That seems suspicious but also what one can expect out in these parts.

"Virginia seemed reasonable," Bradshaw continued in a rush, misreading Pemberton's silence. "I'm originally a Virginian, from a bit north of Emporia, if you're familiar with the eastern part of the state."

Pemberton chuckled. "A good bit familiar. I was assigned to Fortress Monroe in Hampton Roads twice, and my wife is from Norfolk. She's...the reason I am standing here on this side of the lines."

Don't know what possessed me to share that last tidbit, Pemberton thought. *Guess I'm warming up to this fellow a bit.* Being a Pennsylvanian by birth made him an aberration among Confederate officers and Pemberton knew superiors, peers, and subordinates alike disliked him for it. He left that private resentment go unvoiced to the younger man.

Generals are supposed to seem a little remote and godlike to junior officers, after all.

"Ah, you understand," Bradshaw replied. "Thank you, sir. So yes, I felt I should perhaps check in on my relations there before getting further involved in this war. I made it here to the river by horse and by rail."

Bradshaw's expression darkened.

"Of course, with the Yankees across the river on DeSoto Point where the rails end, I had to get off and seek another route. Paid a local with a mule-drawn wagon. Fortunately, a boat was available once I finally made it to the river. I swim fairly well, but not that well."

Pemberton nodded with a smile at the small joke.

"The Vicksburg, Shreveport, and Texas Railroad was a wonderful asset, especially when it still came all the way to DeSoto Point."

"I was told the Yankees were trying to dig a canal across the point to avoid your position here."

"It didn't go well. Trying to drain a swamp with teaspoons, really. But our old friends in blue still move up and down the far shore. They do have pickets over there, watching us."

"Yes, sir. Maybe someone will bridge this end of the river one day once all this is over. As for the railroad, their use of 'Texas' in their name is false advertising, and someone should complain about it. That line only started in Monroe. West of that, the travel had been far more questionable."

"The rail service on the Southern Railroad to Mississippi's capital at Jackson is far more regular, and once you make Jackson, it's easier to get eastbound from there. But this is where your obedience to the ideals of military courtesy might have done you in, Lieutenant."

Finally, Bradshaw truly betrayed his inexperience. His eyes widened a bit, the question in his tone readily apparent as he merely replied, "Sir?"

"I am always short of artillery officers here. While I might not be able to formally commandeer you if you are a Texas state officer, I could certainly still put you to work if you are willing to cast your lot with us here."

Bradshaw had a look of honest hesitancy. "Sir, I wasn't planning on staying here for long. I do appreciate your offer. I had hoped to make it home first and then to the main theater of the war."

"I understand, but hear me out, Lieutenant."

Bradshaw nodded, at first seeming to talk as much to himself as he was to his new commanding general. "While I am short on field experience, I did have an excellent instructor on the subject of gunnery at the Virginia Military Institute, one heavily experienced down in the Mexican War. Major Thomas J. Jackson. I figure you know him, but by a different name."

That got Pemberton's attention. "You served under Stonewall Jackson?"

The younger man shrugged. "If one counts four years of instruction at VMI as serving under him, yes, sir."

Pemberton looked toward Bradshaw's hand, and the junior officer noticed the gesture. "Don't look for a class ring, sir. They are not an established tradition for us the way it is for you West Point men. I believe '48 had the first ones, and I recall '56 did, but I was '58. Ten dollars in gold was a lot of money for most of us, so we never bothered. I did have the money saved in case we had voted upon one, but then spent it after graduation traveling west. It funded the beginning of my surveying apprenticeship after I found myself in Texas."

"Surveyor? Quite an adventuresome profession."

"Yes, sir, and I made enough money at that to afford my traveling companion." He patted the holstered Colt. "It's a wild country out there, and one should not face it unarmed."

Pemberton nodded sagely, indulging the younger man. "Yes, Lieutenant. When I was a younger man, I fought all through that country. Heavier arms are always advisable."

"I wasn't going to carry my rifle in here on a brief social call, sir. That might have been considered rude, so it's downstairs with my baggage."

The older officer smiled. "A lieutenant with a long gun. I always said there was no accounting for Texans."

"I was a Virginian first, sir."

"So were Stephen Austin and Sam Houston. No man can say they aren't Texan."

"Quite true, sir."

Pemberton waved affably. "Now this isn't that unpleasant a kidnapping. While your commission may be state militia, there are already Texas artillerymen in my force here, never mind Mississippians, Arkansans, Louisianans, and Missourians."

"Quite a collection. Out of curiosity, which Texans, sir?"

"Waul's Texas Legion, a rather odd self-contained combined-arms force. They might be the shape of things to come, but right now that uniqueness is a disservice because they don't fit yet. They're certainly a wild bunch, as one would expect."

"Texans do tend to be that way, sir. And perhaps you're right, and now I'm counted among them."

The older man grinned a bit. "Lieutenant, I'm a general. Generals are always right, even when we're wrong, unless we lose."

Pemberton gestured towards his office window.

"That aside, it gets stranger out there. I have numerous Tennesseeans after the loss of Memphis. A few Kentucky men are among them, some that drifted this way after the losses at Forts Henry and Donelson, or the lesser actions along the western tip of that state."

Bradshaw nodded as Pemberton continued.

"Alabama is certainly represented, and then I have Georgians a-plenty, including their artillery, since the first two brigades of General Stevenson's division is from Georgia. There's artillery from Louisiana and Mississippi in their support, and a couple batteries all the way from Maryland and Virginia."

"Virginia makes sense if I don't think about it too hard, sir, but Maryland?"

Pemberton shrugged. "It's been that kind of a war. I think they're from that lower bit of Maryland that's more like Virginia, but I haven't had the time to find them and inquire."

"Sir, when I was at VMI, we did have some Maryland men." He sighed. "I do wish I had a chance to see home one more time."

Pemberton nodded kindly. "I do understand, but realistically there's a whole lot of the war going on between here and there, and you might not make it, anyway. Never mind the hazards of the journey; several of my peers favor impressment to a degree that would have shamed the Royal Navy."

Pemberton went to the map on his wall and picked up his sword with which to gesture.

"Now let me paint the strategic reality."

He pointed towards the Gulf of Mexico.

"With the loss of Memphis and the loss of New Orleans, there are only two choke points left keeping any of the Mississippi River under anything resembling our control."

The blade's tip moved up to their current position.

"We're the northern point of what is still our length, while Port Hudson below us on the Louisiana side is the southern."

Pemberton looked at the junior officer, his face somber.

"If we lose here, we lose the River, and the Confederacy loses access to Texas, Louisiana, Arkansas, and whatever of Missouri was ever reliably on our side. We have a lot of supply coming from that Trans-Mississippi West, plus what comes from the blockade runners that use the Texas or even the Mexican coastlines."

Pemberton fixed the lieutenant with a level, steely gaze.

"The only good news is that General Gardner down at Port Hudson has it worse than we do. He's closer to the main elements of the Union Navy, the big blue-water ships with even bigger guns."

Bradshaw sighed; the younger man was at a loss. "Control of the water shaped by control of the land around that water. A reverse of the way it normally goes, so much as I know anything at my age."

Pemberton nodded. "Wisdom from the mouths of babes, as it says in the Good Book."

The lieutenant nodded. "I do take your point, sir, and with that in mind...I accept and will stay."

———

Young's Point Anchorage
10 April 1863

Porter gathered his commanders and explained the plan.

"I'll be up front, in *Benton,* with Lieutenant Commander Greer in command, obviously. The tug *Ivy* lashes on to me. From there, Walke in *Lafayette.* Walke, the *General Price* lashes on to your starboard side for shelter. Owen in *Louisville,* Wilson in *Mound City,* Hoel in *Pittsburg,* Murphy in *Carondelet,* then transports, and Shirk in *Tuscumbia* bringing up the rear. Then the transports, and Shirkin in *Tuscumbia* bringing up the rear."

Porter regarded the *Tuscumbia*'s master.

"Shirk, you have the job of herding the transports, *Forest Queen, Henry Clay* and the rest. If this is going to be worth the effort, they have to make it through with us."

There was a chorus of "Yes, sirs," and Porter continued.

"Everyone tows a coal barge. Once we're south of Vicksburg, we won't be able to get more until the city falls and the river is open. Not to admit to a lack of faith in the Army," there were chuckles at that, "we don't want to run out of fuel before General Grant makes that happen."

"Towed astern, sir?"

"No, tied alongside your port beam. Maybe it will stop a shell meant for you."

"Aye, aye, sir."

Porter continued. "We go through in completely darkened conditions so the darkness will provide concealment. Save your ammunition for the main batteries on Walnut Bluff north of the city, and the city itself. The lower batteries aren't worth the effort of shooting. No one fires until fired upon. With a bit of good fortune, we won't have to fire at all."

There were grim chuckles at that. No man trusted Fortune at this point in the war.

"The next thing we need to worry about is noise. First, and easiest to prevent, there will be no dogs barking or chickens clucking," Porter said, then further explained. "All animals are to be put ashore, with no exceptions. With luck, you can reclaim your favorite dogs later, but for now, we need quiet. Second, divert your exhaust steam into the paddlewheel housings."

"How, sir?"

"Your engineers will know if you don't," the admiral replied. "We don't need any noise from the relief valves or other plumbing escaping above decks. That sound will carry like Hell across the water, even in the dark, and we don't want it drawing fire."

He paused a moment before continuing as he looked the group over.

No one's mutinied yet, at least, Porter thought before continuing.

"As for taking fire, yes, our armor arrangements might not be the best for an all-round fight. Remember that your stern armor by the paddlewheels is thinner and we may take hits from behind. Stack your stern decks with wet hay bales, logs, anything that will give you an extra bit of protection. If you lose your paddlewheels, we can't stop to tow you, especially under fire. No matter what, keep going."

———

THE RIVER BATTERIES, VICKSBURG
SAME DAY

There wasn't a lot of paperwork involved in changing over Bradshaw's commission from the Texas state militia to the "regular" Confederate forces, such as they were. The legalities and paperwork requirements in an army born in wartime and with no permanent regular establishment could be politely described as fragile, especially so far from Richmond. It was merely entered in the Army of Mississippi's orders book that "Bradshaw, Matthew N., first lieutenant of Artillery, is received by this command by order of Lieutenant General Pemberton."

That afternoon, Bradshaw was out walking with his new keeper, Captain Philip Davis. Davis ran the staff, such as it was, for Colonel Higgins, commander of the loosely organized "river batteries." An experienced gunnery officer, Davis was a heavily built old sergeant from the pre-war Army. The former NCO didn't seem to mind the younger man much, and certainly didn't object to having another junior officer about to put to work.

For his part, Bradshaw had the starry-eyed enthusiasm of a junior officer combined with the hard and knowing gaze of a man who'd made a living looking at the lines of land. But the river, The River, the Mississippi...the Father of Waters by many names...it shaped the task of defending the city far more starkly than the land side of town. Bradshaw quickly sussed that out as both men sat atop a cannon revetment while its crew was off finishing their after-lunch chores.

Davis pointed northwest, up the bend of the river. "We put little picket boats out to give us some warning, usually at night. They see anything, it's flares, maybe a bugle or two to sound the alarm. Then there's piles of tar-soaked cotton bales along the water's edge. Those get lit on fire to make enough light to hopefully fight by."

Bradshaw nodded. "Seems straightforward enough."

Davis was picking a bit of his own meal out of his teeth, while Bradshaw stood and got down behind the gun, eyeing its sector of fire. He then walked over to another gun, and back. "Sir, I have a question regarding the elevation adjustments of the battery."

Davis grunted a bit. "Go on."

"The northern batteries shoot from Walnut Bluffs down a long length of river north of DeSoto Point, then covering the bend down to the base of those bluffs. Wide range of elevation needed to cover that change in range."

"Not as much as you might think, but yeah."

"These other batteries to the south of our positions merely shoot across its width."

"Right."

"Well, this battery is supposed to help close down the river, correct?"

"That's right."

"The fortification is built wrong for it, then."

"How do you figure?"

"I'm a surveyor by trade, and it's a slope problem."

Davis stretched and climbed off the parapet. He pointed out at the river, still swollen by spring rains flowing from as far away as Minnesota or even the Dakota Territory. "The guns are here, and the river is right there, Lieutenant."

Bradshaw climbed up next to the massive rifled Brooke, eyes at muzzle height. "Sir, if we depress the muzzle enough to hit any part of the river closer than mid-channel, the shell won't clear the glacis slope in front of the firing aperture. And if we're shooting anything with a contact fuse, then that would be a serious problem when it contacts dirt six feet off the muzzle."

Davis climbed up next to him. "Damn. You're right. Engineers or the hired labor got carried away and made the parapet too thick. Shit, how did we miss this?"

"I'm no expert, sir, but I do know survey work and slopes. Usually when surveying for artillery, we tend to fixate on shooting things far away and not things up close or beneath us."

Davis was quietly furious. "We should have thought of this, and we don't have the time to dig all this out right and change the design. We had that problem when the *Arkansas* came out and fought, but that fight didn't last so long as to make it 'important.'"

Bradshaw was confused for a moment. "The state has troops here, surely, but—"

"No, no, not that state, I mean the ironclad ram that was named for the state," Davis explained. "Came out and thrashed a Yankee flotilla back in July of last year before sheltering here under the guns."

"Ah. Forgive my ignorance, but I was in western Texas at the time and the news out there isn't exactly regular. And where is she now?" Bradshaw had never contemplated a naval career, but he had read enough to know that warships were almost always "she."

The older man winced. "Mechanical failure a couple weeks after that when supporting an attack to retake Baton Rouge," Davis replied with a shrug. "She was then burned and scuttled to keep her out of Federal hands."

Bradshaw shrugged. "Might have been better off to let them have her and waste their time and money trying to fix up the wreckage."

"Goddamned Yankees don't need any of our shithouse ironclads, not that we have any more of them left. They have those damned Pook Turtles."

"What's a Pook Turtle?"

"Looks like a barn full of cannons on a raft, only the barn is thick iron and shooting holes in it is some work. Named for the fellow who designed them, or at least one of them."

"But I take your meaning as we can actually shoot holes in one?"

"Occasionally. *Mound City*, they're all named after river towns, it got knocked out up a river in Arkansas last year. A hole got shot in one of its boilers and the whole crew got steamed like Gulf Coast shrimp." Both men shuddered at the horrific thought.

"And that was the end of it?"

"Oh, no. Yankees cleaned her out, patched the steam system and recruited a new crew, mostly artillerymen from the Army."

My goodness, the smell, Bradshaw thought, shuddering again.

"Grim business. But the risk of being steamed afloat might seem a better deal than dying from something else in the mud."

Davis paused for a moment, and Bradshaw could see the man was still vexed about the cannons' angle.

"It's been slow going for them either way. We got the main river blocked here, so they tried floating them through Steele's Bayou north of us a couple weeks ago with the springtime floods."

"Did that work?"

"Not so much, well, really for either side. Turned into our infantry fighting their single-file line of ironclad gunboats that were stuck in Deer Creek."

Bradshaw saw the man's expression briefly darken.

"If Colonels Featherstone and Ferguson had moved a little quicker, we could have captured a couple of them ourselves, or at least knocked a few out for keeps. We were back here on our guns, of course, but there were some sappers forward with the infantry cutting and dropping trees across the creek. The idea was penning them in like you trap wild hogs. The creek was narrow enough for them to get down, but not wide enough to turn around."

"Sounds like a good trap. Then what happened?"

"Sherman got his boys there in time, more than Ferguson had, and ran our folk off. Damn shame, too. We could at least have blown up and burned a couple of them Pook Turtles as to even the odds since we lost the *Arkansas.*"

"So the major problem is that they have ships and we don't," Bradshaw noted.

"Nor as can we get more. The Yankees hold Memphis and New Orleans, as you probably heard, and the only roadblocks left on the Mississippi are us here and another clump of us to the south at Port Gibson. Little clump in between at Grand Gulf, but there's no boatyards left capable of building anything that size, and even if we did, there's no iron to clad it."

"Enough timber will still stop a cannonball—" Bradshaw mused.

"Lemme cut you off right there before you go getting any more VMI smart feller ideas," Davis snapped, firmly but not all unkindly. "We don't have enough of the right kind o' timber to build a boat. We don't have the engines to move it if we did, and we don't have enough extra guns to put on it to be worth building it in the first place. You play poker?"

Bradshaw smiled a bit. "I have been known to wager a bit on the turn of a card, yes."

"Ah'ight, lemme put it this way: the Yanks got three kings or so ridin' out on that river, and all we got is a pair of twos to hold 'em off," Davis summed up. "And they're gonna call our bluff on these bluffs one of these nights."

"And the only cards we are holding, meanwhile, are these guns along the waterfront, correct?"

"Right," Davis nodded.

"We need to think of something else, then."

"Great, since you already caught one mistake we made, you get to have the next big idea."

"What are the river guns in total? I've been making notes as we go, but I counted one really old eight-inch Columbiad gun, then a British Blakeley that's about a seven-and-a-half inch. God knows what either of those are doing here."

"We couldn't be too particular in what we asked for," Davis replied, "and it's not this is like Charleston or Savannah where there were pre-existing defenses from before the war to get by with. Forts there are older than this whole town."

Bradshaw nodded, seeing the logic of the predicament. "Yes, sir, I get it."

Davis went on. "Two Brooke rifles, one seven and this one, a one six-and-a-half. Yeah, it's a six-point-forty-four, but six hundredths of an inch doesn't really matter. Usually, I just call them Big Brooke and Little Brooke, and we don't keep them so close as to not mix up the ammunition.

"Wise."

"Glad you think so, son, but I've been on cannon crews since about the time you were born," Davis responded, his sly smile belying any possible taken offense.

Just because you've been doing this a long time doesn't mean you've been doing it correct, sir, Bradshaw thought, keeping his face passive as Davis began gesturing around at the defenses.

"Anyway, then there's three 42-pounders and ten 32-pounders. They're old guns that got rifling cut and bands added, so we don't know what we can expect out of them before they give up. The Louisiana battery has an eighteen-pounder done the same way." Davis shook his head. "Makes weird whistling noises, some say, but I'm a little deaf after all this time, so I couldn't tell you. Then two more 32 smoothbores."

"Anything else modern?"

"We have a British Whitworth," Davis said, nodding at Bradshaw's assessment of the old ordnance. "Twelve-pounder and a breechloader—it's with the Louisiana boys. All steel, high velocity, good rifling. Way of the future, I think. Give it another twenty years, I think most new guns will go that way. The British have a lot of engineers working on the subject."

"Where in the name of Hell did they get that?"

"Bought it, I reckon," Davis shrugged. "Louisiana units from down around New Orleans aren't hurting for money the way the rest of us are. Same reason they eat good. If they can't get it out of the supply system, they just go out of pocket and buy from what the blockade runners get in, even with New Orleans being in Yankee hands now. Don't know what it will do to a ship, but we've got it."

"That it?"

"To fight warships? That's about it. We had to beg for what we've got since Charleston and Savannah were both begging for heavy guns, and that's where the British blockade runners mostly come in."

The two men kept strolled back down the hill and through the ordnance yard. Davis pointed at the scrap pile. "We have a couple Parrott guns the Yankees left us when they retreated back from Chickasaw Bayou last December. Well, they left a lot of junk guns and we have some junk of our own, but we have these two, no, three Parrotts. All burst."

"They do have an unfortunate tendency to do that. Most single-layer cast-iron guns do."

The younger man grimaced.

"When we were proofing guns at the San Antonio Arsenal, we learned to pull the primer with a long, long lanyard because we blew up more than a few ourselves," he explained. "But these...these burst at the muzzle. We could cut them short then."

"To what end?"

"Puns are the lowest form of humor, sir, but ignoring that, we could turn them down into mortars."

"Why would we do that?"

"Remember what I said about the dead space our batteries couldn't depress to cover?"

"Yes?"

"We lob the rounds high and short, and they come down from above into the dead space the longer guns can't depress enough to hit."

Davis looked thoughtful for a moment. "I don't know why we didn't think of that."

"Perhaps too close to the problem, sir."

"Now who's making bad puns?"

Bradshaw smiled. "Guilty, sir. The only question is how. There's no arsenal here."

"No, but there's a couple private foundries that could do the work," Davis allowed. "The Reading Brothers had a contract to do 12-pounder Napoleons, bronze ones. Even made some three-inch rifles in bronze."

"A bronze bore isn't going to hold the rifling long."

"I know that and you know that, but we've got to get by with what we can make most of the time," Davis noted. "The important thing is that their lathe will fit a 20-pounder Parrott, at least well enough for a muzzle cut and recrown. Good fellows, considering they're from New Jersey."

"Excellent point," Bradshaw allowed.

"Paxton could do it, as well. He's also doing Napoleons. A.M. Paxton."

Davis paused, as if considering his words.

"Well, he's really doing lathe and finish work on other people's castings, including the Reading Brothers."

"What's the A.M. short for?"

"No idea. Never asked him."

"Don't suppose it matters, so long as he can do the job amongst the other demands on his time," Bradshaw replied.

It didn't take long to get the Parrott stubs into wagons and dispatched to Paxton's shop, with a note giving directions for the cutting and recrowning to be done "as soon as practicable."

When that business was handled, Bradshaw looked at Davis. "Now that I thought of the mortars, what else can we do?"

Davis shrugged thoughtfully. "We could have made some more of those torpedoes as sank their *Cairo*, but it wouldn't have worked."

"Why didn't we do it, and why wouldn't it work?"

"We aren't fighting on the Yazoo or the Black anymore. Out here on the Mississippi itself, the river's current is too strong and would rip them out. Even worse this time of year, since the spring rains for most of the continent eventually drain through here. Same reason we never tried putting a chain across the river like the one at West Point."

Bradshaw was a bit incredulous. "Somebody actually suggested it?"

Davis nodded with a smirk. "One of the West Pointers among the Georgians was doing the math based on the Great Chain across the Hudson from the Revolutionary War. Apparently, their first-year cadets have to know how many links were in it."

"Speaking as a VMI man, West Pointers can be odd ducks," Bradshaw noted. "There's just so damn many of them though, and you can't help but end up serving under a few of them, I suppose."

He chewed on the inside of his cheek for a second.

"Being realistic, sir, if we had enough iron as to forge a chain like that, we could have built another ironclad gunboat instead."

Other soldiers were puttering around the ordnance yard on various labors, and a few were listening, even if technically they weren't supposed to be.

"Is it worth trying to build another ironclad?" one of them asked. That earned him a withering look from a nearby NCO.

"As Captain Davis said earlier, we don't have the iron for it, even if we had the time," Bradshaw said, making clear his displeasure at the interjection. The NCO nodded slightly as he continued. "On the other hand, it can't be that hard to put some barrels of gunpowder into the water on a rope."

Davis shook his head.

"It's not, but the hard part is not losing them afterward. You want the barrels where we put them, not washed down to Baton Rouge or wherever."

"So we don't put them in the water until we need them?" Bradshaw mused.

"How do they get out there fast enough then?"

Another of the soldiers chimed in, making the same NCO look almost apoplectic.

"Y'all know what a planer board is?"

Captain Davis shook his head.

"Not really," the senior officer noted. "I didn't have much truck with moving water before all this. At least not like this. Back home, it was little creeks and a couple of lakes. Been in a couple coastal forts before the War, and the ocean there doesn't move like this, either."

The NCO, a grizzled old Tennessean with red artillery sergeant's chevrons, decided to join in at that point.

"I grew up in Memphis, and we used to get catfish lines out off the shore that way," he said. "You put a raft out on a rope, but with angled boards. That will use the current of the water the way a sail uses the wind. It will pull out into the channel and stay there."

Bradshaw nodded. "Then guided by the tension of the rope and the pull of the current, and along that rope, we space out the torpedoes."

"Where do we get the torpedoes?" the NCO asked, now interested.

"If we have the gunpowder, any empty barrels will do," Davis replied. "At least, that's what we use for fougasse over on the land side of the defense, and I think they build the same."

"There's got to be a dozen or so we can find in some warehouse or trash midden around here," the NCO said.

Davis shrugged, looking thoughtful. "We got plenty of gunpowder. A lot of it's not great, but we've got plenty of it."

"We don't need the good stuff," Bradshaw mused. "It wouldn't take much to blow a hole in a boat, I reckon."

"Well, like I said, we got a lot of that kind."

A trip to the garbage dump turned up two dozen empty salt-pork barrels, the thirty-gallon size used by the Federal commissary arm. The pork in them had been spoils of war at some point. Another trip back to the ordnance yard netted a wagonload of the not-so-good black powder, coarse-ground for cannon.

Bradshaw noted that the two eavesdropping soldiers were the ones having to do much of the dirty work at the bottom of the barrels.

On one hand, we don't want soldiers always poking into officer business, he thought. *On the other, that's a really good way to kill good ol' fashioned initiative.*

"Well, while they're doing that, let's figure out the fuses," Davis said, squinting into the rising sun. "I can't imagine we've got too long before the Federals come with the way the river's rising."

"What fired the torpedo that sank the *Cairo*?" Bradshaw asked.

"Electrical," Davis said. "And we don't have the electrical gadgetry left to fire these."

"Would have been useful if we did," Bradshaw bemoaned.

"Doesn't matter, we have plenty of artillery fuses and are making more," Davis said. "Friction primers on a long string would do. Contact fuse in the top, maybe."

"Why not both, sir?" Bradshaw asked.

"Fair," Davis allowed. "Let's go see how things are going outside."

The two men took a leisurely stroll the couple of hundred yards to where a mixed bag of carpenters and artillerymen were working amongst a cacophony of saws, hammers, and cursing. Sawdust covered the grass where the crews scrambled to assemble three new Parrott carriages, redesigned for their employment as mortars. As the civilians, privates, and sergeants cut and hammered on their task, Davis and Bradshaw stood in companionable silence.

"We need to figure out the mortar firing table," Davis said, snapping his fingers at the revelation. "Tarnation."

"I don't have the slightest bit of experience with mortars, sir," Bradshaw replied. "Other than some test firing at VMI once under Jackson."

"How are you with calculus and geometry as subjects?" Davis asked, raising an eyebrow.

"Better than most, but hardly top of my class," Bradshaw replied worriedly.

"That means you've got a leg up on me," Davis replied. "Let's get to work."

Three hours later, as the sun had risen high in the springtime sky, the two men regarded the firing tables they had worked out. A mess of elevation and range numbers written in large text to make it easier to read in low light, the tables didn't look like they were fit for a textbook, but would work well enough in a firing pit.

"Can we test-fire this?" Bradshaw asked.

Which is a polite way of saying I don't do math well under pressure and we should probably make sure I don't inadvertently put the shells long onto the far shore, he thought, hoping his concern didn't show on his face.

"I already asked Colonel Higgins when I went to the latrine," Davis replied. "We're cleared for three registration shots, at the same time as the battery test-fires on the point over there."

Bradshaw looked at his superior, a silent question on his face.

"Gotta make it blend in so we don't spoil the surprise," Davis explained. "There's still a fair bunch of Yankee pickets in those woods, even after they stopped digging Grant's ditch across the point."

"Well, we have to get the tubes back from Paxton, or this is for nothing."

Thankfully, the Yankees did not come that night. The delivery of cut-down tubes came the next morning, so that afternoon about the same time, the last mortar shell splashed in the river more or less where Davis and Bradshaw calculated. Both men agreed that was as good as they knew how to do.

Now we wait, Bradshaw thought, regarding their preparations. *Our duty is all we can do, so let's hope it is enough.*

Benton was not the true flagship of the Mississippi Gunboat Flotilla. That would be the sidewheeler *Black Hawk*, which retained much of its civilian interior and was not heavily armed or armored. She made an excellent floating headquarters.

Unfortunately, she has the life expectancy of a snowflake in a blast furnace if put under heavy fire, Admiral Porter thought, watching as men moved items from the sidewheeler to the vessel that would be his flagship in the upcoming run.

Originally a civilian salvage vessel before being taken into US Navy service and converted into a casemate ironclad, *Benton* was not the toughest ship in the Mississippi River gunboat flotillas. But what she lacked in protection, she made up with in space for Porter, his subordinates, and all the other necessities of combat command. Her two-and-a-half inches of iron plate armor, backed up by two feet of wood, had proven sufficient to this point.

An admiral must be prepared to lead from the van, Porter thought, nodding as his flag lieutenant reported that the *Benton* was prepared to receive him aboard at his leisure. *Can't remember if that was Nelson or some other Limey, but its true for brown water just as much as blue.*

Porter's decision would not be one he would regret for long.

Sergeant Thomas Lynch of the 1st Louisiana Artillery had been the sergeant in charge of the picket boats for some time, and thus knew many of the sights and sounds of the river at night. Thus, despite the best effort of Porter and his captains, the unfamiliar sound of darkened ships still gave the man several hundred yards to react to the Union encroachment.

"Light the bales! Ships coming down the channel!" the experienced NCO shouted. He fired a pair of blasts from his double-barreled shotgun to emphasize the report. It would be his first and also final act of the battle, as a near-miss cannon shot from the *Benton* would blast him and his two companions out of their craft, making it to shore later. With that, what history would call The Battle of Porter's Run ensued.

Bradshaw, in the company of a carpenter and the man's young daughter, glanced at his watch as he heard the distant booming of cannon. He glanced at his watch and noted the time as 11:16 PM. Giving his respects to his hosts, Bradshaw joined many of the other men in the area rushing to their position as the batteries opened up along the river's edge starting at Walnut Bluff.

Well, glad we got that extra day, he thought grimly. *Now to see if anyone is able to hit anything, even with the bales and other lights.*

In the end, he was unsurprised that there were no clear indications of damage on either side. The Union vessels, for their part, seemed to keep their fire measured as they came south through the initial Confederate defenses. The distance being what it was, it took most of an hour for the action to reach Bradshaw's position south of the Point.

"That's it! Get them in the water!" Bradshaw said, slapping his impromptu torpedomen on the back as he sighted the *Benton*'s dark form. With a heave, the planer board buoy went into the water, and the early summer current caught it easily. Rope ripped off the coil, taking a string of a dozen pork-barrel torpedoes with it out into the darkness of the Mississippi River. Two docks to the south, the action repeated. Two dozen packages of unknown and unproven lethality now lurked in the dark water.

Peering into the dark, in the light of the burning cotton bales and the ships' return fire, Bradshaw saw the Federal ironclads moving toward his side of the river and into the stretch of water they'd guessed at. The lead Federal vessel seemed to pull to port, moving to the dead zone he'd discovered on that first day.

Always nice to know one is not an idiot, Bradshaw thought grimly. He pulled a box of Lucifer matches and lit the torch he'd prepared. Waving it back and forth, he signaled Davis up at the mortar position.

Wave, wave, Davis thought, marking his subordinate's motion, *wave... drop!*

Davis turned to his borrowed Tennesseans.

"Fire!" he screamed, and the three mortars let fly almost simultaneously.

Ballistics is a fascinating subject, all of it predicated on Isaac Newton's work on gravity nearly two hundred years earlier. Simply, it is the mathematical expression of the idea that what goes up must come down. Everything between is merely a question of angle and velocity dictating when gravity will return the launched projectile to the surface. That has underpinned the gunner's art since black powder was first harnessed for warfare.

The twenty-pound shell was intended to go fast and very flat by the standards of Civil War-era artillery when fired, as once intended. From a mortar, it instead launched upward on a steeply looping parabola, tipped over nose-first, and fell out of the sky while picking up speed. It was nowhere near the speed of sound as it descended faster and faster, its path horrifyingly visible to its intended target. Justifying every bit of "Stonewall" Jackson's careful instruction in gunnery back at VMI, the shell hit the *Benton*'s upper deck.

Unfortunately for the Union, that deck was not armored well; nor had it been reinforced, compared to the casemate's rear. The projectile punched right through the wood. An upward cone of wood splinters immediately opened the butcher's bill by taking two crewmen's heads off. The passage was enough to set off the contact fuse, and it exploded as it passed into *Benton*'s gun deck. The resulting shrapnel and fireball killed several crewmen, wounded more, then found one of the ready racks of *Benton*'s own ammunition. The resulting explosion, and then the next sympathetic detonation touched off by the expanding fragments, blew the *Benton*'s casemate superstructure sky-high. Moments later, cold water rushing into her hull found her red-hot boilers and those decided to join in the fatal celebration of thermodynamics.

Federal pickets had watched Vicksburg from the Louisiana side since early in the campaign. The sound of the guns woke the sleeping troops, and they moved from their bivouac sites down their worn-in pathways to their observation posts. The first of them arrived just in time to see the *Benton*'s loss. One of the more poetic men among them would later liken the eruption to as if the "Father of Rivers had angrily flung a dinner plate full of men and coal up from his providential table."

Aboard the *Lafayette*, second in line, the explosion in front of them caused the helmsman to jerk the wheel hard to the left in surprise. She nosed to port, edging past the slowing, slewing wreck of *Benton,* a position which silhouetted her against the flames. Now an easy target in the half-light, a shell from the seven-inch Brooke rifle punched through her casemate side at a gunport. It was a survivable hit on its own, only knocking out a cannon and starting a fire on the gun deck. The fire, however, made the vessel even more of a target, and four more hits quickly followed. One of these was to her bridge, stunning the crew there and preventing them from bringing the rudder amidships. The out-of-control vessel then blundered onto a pork-barrel torpedo, whose dual fuses worked to perfection. Poor gunpowder or not, the resultant hole and destruction of her rudder sent the Union ironclad careening into one of the Vicksburg docks. Her exposed top deck was no protection from downhill fire, and *Lafayette* was soon gloriously aflame.

"Stop shooting that one, she's finished!" Davis shouted futilely at the distant gunners pumping rounds into the blazing Yankee vessel. He turned to the trio of mortars, barking instructions as the two burning wrecks revealed the other advancing Union vessels. Straining to be heard amongst the cacophony of fifty other guns, Davis gave range and elevation, then dropped his arm for another volley.

Two falling shells went wide left and the other a little long, doing nothing but inconveniencing the fish. The third shell came down wobbly and blew up above decks on the *Louisville* in front of her pilot house. That was enough for the somewhat rattled petty officer at her helm to jink to the right, bumping into another salt-pork barrel full of black powder. This time, only one fuse functioned, proving Bradshaw's prudence. Unlike the unfortunate *Lafayette*, the *Louisville*'s luck held as the weapon detonated against the coal barge lashed to her side. The unmanned vessel started to flood as coal tumbled out the massive hole, but the damage wasn't enough to stop the ironclad's southward run.

This left *Mound City, Pittsburg,* and *Carondelet* in the mortars' killing zone, along with a couple transports. The transport *Henry Clay* was hit by the next mortar volley, the shell murderous among her embarked soldiers but unable to inflict a laming wound. The *Pittsburgh*, struck after another two volleys, suffered damage that was barely noticed by her terrified crew. Another two volleys saw the *Carondelet* struck on her bridge, with the resultant explosion and casualties causing the vessel to briefly careen out of control. Proving that redundancy did not equal certainty, the ironclad cheated death when it bumped a barrel that failed to blow.

Damn Yankees are hitting back hard, Davis thought, watching as one of the distant ironclad's sides rippled fire that silenced some of the Confederate guns.

"Faster, boys, faster!" Davis shouted at his flagging, exhausted mortarmen. "We've got to cripple more of those bastards!"

It was at this point that the Fates proved they were equal opportunity arbiters in the Western Theater. A design flaw in many Parrott rifles was that they were prone to failure, as evidenced by the mortars' previous careers. Back in distant Washington, Henry Hunt, the artillery commander for the Union's Army of the Potomac, was already advocating for the Parrott gun's replacement due to their often lethal unreliability. Hunt, having scoured numerous action reports as well as conducted testing, had discovered the Parrotts' unreliability was exacerbated when the weapon fired at high elevation.

Mortar fire, by definition, was delivered at high elevation.

Bradshaw, having just stepped out to grab another lantern, had just reentered the firing position when a gunner pulled the lanyard on Gun Three. It burst at the rear of the tube, sending wrought-iron splinters scything outward at a thousand feet per second. Several men in the revetment went down from shock or fragmentation. One good-sized chunk caught Bradshaw in the thigh, punching deep into the muscle and nicking the femoral artery. It hurt bad enough, he involuntarily screamed from the white-hot agony.

Oh, God, please don't let me be unmanned, he thought, reaching down in desperate assessment. Relieved to find that the fragment had not, in fact, rendered him a eunuch, Bradshaw became concerned as he started to go numb.

Shock. I'm going into shock.

One of the Tennessee gunners ran over to him, covered in the blood of one of his mortally wounded comrades.

"Sir? You all right?"

"Hell no, I'm not. Get me a tourniquet before I bleed to death, Goddamnit."

While the first scurried to the wooden chest marked "Hospital Supplies," one of the wounded men looked at Bradshaw with wide, pained eyes.

"Sir, are we winning?" the man asked, hearing whoops from outside.

Wrestling the wide leather belt around his thigh with help from the somewhat terrified, blood-splattered private, Bradshaw shrugged in darkened revetment.

Lucky none of these lanterns caught fire when they broke, Bradshaw thought. *Thank whatever angels were looking over us.*

"I don't know. We hit two of them, that's for sure."

"More'n that, sir," someone said, the man's voice barely carrying loud enough for Bradshaw to hear him. "One of those bastards is still burning on the docks."

Davis ran into the revetment out of the dark, holding a lantern. "Bradshaw, that you?"

"Yes, sir!"

"One of your damned Parrott guns done blew up again."

"Yes, sir, I noticed," Bradshaw snapped.

The glass lenses of the old riverboat lantern could only magnify the candle's light so much, so it took a moment for Davis to see the blood staining Bradshaw's uniform.

"Ah, Hell. You gonna be all right?"

"Not sure, sir. If someone can get me to a decent surgeon, I might be. I'm in no shape to walk it myself. But with your permission, I'm going to pass out now."

————

The Louisiana shoreline
The morning of the 17th

What was supposed to be the grand arrival of Porter's force was less impressive than anyone wanted. Only *Mound City* was untouched, by some miracle, her bad luck quota having been met earlier in the war. Sailors were patching holes and pumping out flooded compartments while others carried their wounded and dead ashore.

None of the ship captains or their officers were in any condition to take over. All were in shock, some were among the wounded, and some of the wounded weren't guaranteed to make it.

Having taken stock of the situation at the shore, Grant looked around at his staff.

"We're going to have to get word to Admiral Farragut down south. We still have this army on the wrong side of the river from where we need it, and I don't know if what's left of this," he waved back toward the river, "will get the job handled. We'll have to bring Farragut north."

"Sir, he doesn't have much of a force north Port Hudson. The Rebel guns there stopped most of his ships and boats. I think he's got his big ship, the *Hartford*, and a little one, the *Albatross*."

Grant sighed wearily. "That doesn't matter, because the Rebels don't have any ships for him to fight. I just need a senior naval officer who's alive and can organize the river crossing for me since Porter no longer can."

Snapping his fingers, he took a notebook from an aide and began to write.

Admiral Farragut,

I have the sad duty to report the death of your foster brother, Rear Admiral Porter, under the guns of Vicksburg before dawn this morning, the 17th. The Benton hit a submerged torpedo and their artillery did the rest. The survivors of the Gunboat Flotilla, boats and men, will move south to meet you and make a unified command once they are able.

The transports we counted upon did not pass Vicksburg from the north in the strength he had hoped. While I cannot technically order you to do so, I humbly request you bring such strength as you can find up the river so that the Army of the Tennessee may cross the Mississippi, capture Vicksburg, and avenge Rear Admiral Porter and his men.

Respectfully,

U.S. Grant.

"That should do."

He folded the paper, then handed it and the notebook back to his aide.

"Get that on a packet boat south to the *Hartford*. Whether he comes up or not, they were family, so Farragut still needs to know as soon as possible."

"Cavalry down the shore may be faster, sir."

Grant shook his head, patting his pockets for matches, then fishing for another cigar. "But less certain. There's still Rebel cavalry and assorted bushwhackers out there, too. That message has to get through."

"Will Farragut be able to get enough force up here? There's still Port Hudson blocking the lower river."

Grant shook his head. "He's north of Hudson, and that was the bottom end of the problem. Even without most of his force, there's enough small craft, barges, and whatnot between here and there to get us across. Not all at once, but we don't need to get across all at once. So long as we stay in the blank spaces away from Grand Gulf or Port Hudson, there's no enemy fortifications in the way. Once we get a lodgment on the far shore, and it doesn't matter if it takes us a whole week to cross, since they don't have a navy left to interrupt us."

"Do any of us know how to organize all those boats? Or find all the ones we will need?"

"I trust an angry Farragut to make that happen for us," Grant replied. "Even if misfortune befalls him, as well, some of Porter's surviving officers can still be of service once they rest a bit. But one way or another, this army will cross that river and do what needs to be done."

————

APRIL 18, 1863
ABOVE PORT HUDSON, LOUISIANA

The packet boat found the flagship USS *Hartford* early the next morning. Once the "Permission to come aboard" ritual was passed, the note went from hand to hand until it was carried into Farragut's quarters with his breakfast coffee. The admiral opened it, read it, and a fury overtook him. Spilling his mug, not even yet fully dressed, he ran for the main deck. Farragut turned to the officer of the deck and fairly screamed in rage. "FULL STEAM! RAISE FULL STEAM! DAMN THE TORPEDOES, WE'RE GOING NORTH!"

————

So that was it, then. By their combined efforts of stripping every ferry, barge, pontoon, and river steamer between Vicksburg and Port Hudson, Farragut still got Grant across the Mississippi River at the sleepy little undefended town of Bruinsburg in time to drive on Joseph Johnston's positions at Jackson. After winning there and securing his rear, Grant then turned on Pemberton in Vicksburg. Vicksburg's defenses were enough to back him off and prevent a successful assault.

The Siege still occurred, though the devilishly inventive Lieutenant Bradshaw watched the rest of it from a hospital bed, fortunate to not only have retained his manhood but also both of his legs.

The Confederate gunners still had fight in them. Captain William Pratt Parks, commanding the so-called "Arkansas Battery," had been making life hard for Sherman on the Federal right flank. Parks had figured out the Federals' signal code, dismounted his guns, and lowered them into concealment. When the City-class "Pook Turtle" USS Cincinnati *came in to clear out the Arkansas Battery on May 27th, at first, they couldn't find it. Parks then remounted his guns and sank the* Cincinnati. *It still changed little. She was later raised and put back into service, much as the ill-fated* Mound City *had been earlier in the war.*

Pemberton still surrendered on the Fourth of July. History flowed on like the Mississippi River. Sometimes you can remove a different piece or two from the board, but the game still ends the same way.

———

Afterwords and Acknowledgements

Special thanks go out to my new Facebook friend, Civil War artillery reenactor Phil Davis and also to Greg Biggs, president of the Clarksville (Tennessee) Civil War Round Table.

And this one is in memory of longtime Civil War enthusiast Philip Schreier, the director of the NRA's National Firearms Museum. Phil went up ahead to join the advance party on 29 December 2025.

ABOUT DAN KEMP

Dan Kemp is a former member of the Army's 101st Airborne Division who partly reinvented himself as an author of military thrillers, military science fiction, and alternative history. His primary body of work is the *Athenaeum Inc.* military thriller series at Cannon Publishing, which began as "a thinly veiled *Kelly's Heroes* ripoff." Thus far, Dan's short stories have appeared in anthologies at Raconteur Press, Bayonet Press, and in two military alt-history collections for James Young. He sincerely promises the rest of the Norwich Mafia he will properly use that expensive master's degree and write that urban warfare book someday, just as soon as people stop yelling at him for more *Athenaeum* sequels.

Where You Can Find Dan

LinkTree (i.e., one stop for everything): https://linktr.ee/daniel.g.kemp

FAR BETTER TO DARE

Rob Howell

The Flying Squadron rounded Punta Maisi, daring the Spanish fleet in Santiago de Cuba to come out and face it. The squadron's sailors stayed close to their posts, eager for the call to general quarters. The Caribbean danced under the bright morning sun, mirroring their excitement.

No sign of that excitement appeared on Captain Arthur Crenshaw's face, but, like many of the sailors, he had hoped to fight this battle a decade ago.

But maybe this is the right time. The Bulgarians broke free of the Ottomans a month ago. The Austrians overextended themselves in Bosnia. And of course, Theodore Roosevelt finally won. Yes, this will be the morning, and maybe 1908 will be remembered as the year when the monarchies of Europe finally start to die.

"Captain," said an ensign as he pulled a stadimeter down from his eye, "range to *Texas* 420 yards."

"Thank you, Mr. Thompson. Mr. Aitken, please be so good as to ask the engine room to give me another turn on the propellers."

"Aye, sir," responded the helmsman. He twisted the crank on the engine order telegraph.

This was not the first time Crenshaw had made that order. He loved this ship, but she was the oldest in the squadron and often struggled to keep her station, even when following her sister ship.

He peered through his binoculars. The USS *Connecticut* led the squadron, where Rear Admiral Robley D. Evans flew his flag. Behind

"Fighting Bob's" flagship steamed the *Kansas*, sister to the *Connecticut*, and the *Texas* trailed her. Crenshaw's command was the last of the capital ships. However, two armored cruisers trailed her, the *Pennsylvania* and *West Virginia*, as did the refrigerated supply ship *Culgoa*. Three divisions of torpedo boats escorted that line, with one in front and one to each flank.

"Signal from Flag," reported Lieutenant Pope Washington, the signal officer.

"Yes, Mr. Washington?"

"The *Delong* has sighted the Spanish fleet, bearing two points to starboard at 27,000 yards. Admiral Evans's compliments to all and the squadron is to increase speed to twelve knots and proceed in line on a heading of 200."

Crenshaw nodded. *Good: we can pin the Spanish against the Cuban shore.*

"Thank you, Mr. Washington. Acknowledge."

He turned to the helm.

"Mr. Aitken, please increase to twelve knots and stay on station behind the *Texas* on a heading of 200."

"Increase to twelve knots, aye. Continuing to stay in line with the *Texas* on a heading of 200, aye."

The ship shook uncomfortably as it followed its sister. Even these moderate seas hampered both of them. The two battleships ahead of them sliced through the waves and wind with a smooth, quiet grace, despite each displacing more than twice Crenshaw's command. The *Connecticut*-class battleships were the pride of the U.S. Navy, but Crenshaw was exactly where he wanted to be. She might wallow under him, but he had loved this ship since the first time he had boarded her as a shiny new cadet.

Crenshaw patted the steel of the bridge armor. *The girl that stole my heart. She's has been waiting for this dance, too, especially now that she's adorned with the new, longer six-inch guns added in last winter's refit.*

"Sound general quarters, " Crenshaw continued. "Bosun."

"Aye, Captain?"

"Note the contact time and date in the log."

"Aye, sir. 9:47AM, December 8th, 1908, contact reported by torpedo boat *Delong*."

The older man's phlegmatic response eased Crenshaw's tension. Nielson had been a coxswain on this ship during Crenshaw's first cruise, and he had followed the midshipmen after that eventful trip.

I've never asked why he wanted to stay with me, mused Crenshaw, *but I'm damn glad he did.* He blinked back to the moment and looked at his executive officer.

"Mr. Bronson, be so good as to order the main and intermediate batteries loaded with armor-piercing shells."

"Aye, aye." Commander Amon Bronson, leaned down to the voice tubes.

"Signal from Flag direct to us, sir," added Washington.

"Yes?"

"The Admiral would like to know our maximum speed in current conditions."

Crenshaw glanced over to Bronson, but decided to give a nervous midshipman fidgeting on his bridge something to do. "Mr. Howell. Would you be so kind as to consult with Commander Morris? I need to know how much more speed our lady will give us, should we need."

The midshipman, son of Crenshaw's first section commander, nodded and ran off. The captain glanced at Nielson, who smiled slightly.

"Captain, another signal from Flag. The *Delong* reports two *Espana*-class battleships, three armored cruisers, and six smaller vessels."

"That matches our reports of the entire Santiago de Cuba squadron, sir," added Bronson.

"Thank you, Commander. Nice of them to join us, don't you think?"

"Yes, sir. They must have laid a patch when someone saw us." Bronson's beloved handlebar mustache quirked above his smile.

Lieutenant Washington continued, "The Admiral's compliments, and we are to focus on the armored cruisers along with the *Texas* and *Pennsylvania*. The *West Virginia* and the *Culgoa* are to slow and stay out of range."

Crenshaw's eyes narrowed. *The* Connecticut *and* Kansas *were built to fight ships like the* Espanas, *but so were we, at least at one point. The Spanish are supposed to have more ships in the Caribbean, including two more* Espanas. *If we have to fight the rest of the Spanish fleet before we can repair the* Connecticut *from any damage they take today, we're going to wish people had listened to President-Elect Roosevelt's call for a bigger stick these past ten years. It would certainly be nice to have the* Minnesota *and* New Hampshire *here instead of half-built in their shipyards. Or if the Spanish hadn't sold their Pacific possessions to the Germans so they could afford their Fleet Plan of 1903.*

He looked out from his bridge impassively. *But none of that matters now.* "Acknowledge the order."

Midshipman Howell rushed up and saluted.

"Commander Morris's compliments, sir. He believes he can give you four more knots, maybe even six, though if you wish to remain at that speed for long, he requests the release of all backup coalers from their other duties."

"Thank you, Mr. Howell." Crenshaw turned to the signals officer. "Mr. Washington, please inform Admiral Evans we can guarantee him sixteen knots." Then he turned to the bosun. "Mr. Nielson. Would you please assemble parties to serve as coalers?"

"Aye, Captain." He blew a complicated pattern on his pipes, and trumpets echoed throughout the ship in response.

"Thank you." Crenshaw turned back to the midshipman. "Mr. Howell. Now be so good as to see if Lieutenant Boyd has all that he needs."

Howell turned, but before he could run off, Crenshaw spoke mildly. "Mr. Howell."

"Huh?" The boy turned.

"Mr. Howell, what are you supposed to do when receiving an order?"

Howell's eyes widened. "Uh, acknowledge it."

"Now." Crenshaw paused. "Would you be so good to speak with Lieutenant Boyd and see if he requires anything?"

"Aye, Captain." The midshipman saluted and hustled from the bridge, his cheeks burning. Crenshaw could forgive the boy failing to acknowledge one order properly as he went into battle for the first time, but not two. Now Nielson's face held a grin.

Crenshaw stared back with twinkling eyes as he remembered the bosun beating Cadet Crenshaw over this ship's original six-inch guns for exactly the same offense.

I think he went easy on me. He sure didn't beat me like he did the two idiots I stopped from lighting their recently "acquired" Cuban cigars near the coal bunkers when we were moored in Havana. Lit cigars near coal dust? I think I'd rather one of the Spanish battleships hit my ship with a full broadside.

His humor faded as the *Texas* relayed more signals.

"Flag to Torpedo Boat Division Two. Advance and make ready for a run. Torpedo Boat Division One is to move a point south and cover our left," reported Washington.

Crenshaw nodded. *Makes sense. Admiral Evans will undoubtedly send Division One in later, but he's smart enough to make sure we don't get any nasty surprises. On that topic...*

"Mr. Washington, would you be so good as to detail a yeoman to monitor Torpedo Boat Division One? I want to know immediately if they signal anything."

"Aye, aye, Captain."

The spotter in the crow's nest called down. "Enemy in sight! Sailing at bearing 285, approximately fourteen thousand yards."

"Bosun, be so good as to note that in the log. Please also note which lookout spotted them first."

"Aye, aye, sir." Mr. Nielson added the note as Midshipman Howell rushed back in.

"Mr. Boyd's compliments, sir, and he requests you make more speed so his gunners can open fire sooner."

The bridge crew chuckled.

"Very good, Mr. Howell. I'll do my best to oblige him."

As Crenshaw and Bronson trained their binoculars westerly, straining to see the Spaniards with their own eyes, a series of booms wafted over the sea.

"The Spanish have opened fire, sir," commented Mr. Bronson.

"Already, sir?" blurted Midshipman Howell.

Crenshaw raised an eyebrow at him.

He blushed and stammered, "I, er... I mean, it seems a long way away."

Crenshaw nodded. "It does, Mr. Howell. However, the Spaniards designed the *Espanas* to fight at longer range than our *Connecticuts*. Their twelve-inch guns can reach well over twenty thousand yards—"

"Twenty thousand!"

"Yes, Mr. Howell."

"But, sir, even the twelve-inchers on the *Connecticut* and *Kansas* can only get to—" the midshipman paused, "—nineteen thousand, I think."

"You're correct, Mr. Howell. And that's about the farthest our ten-inchers can reach, as well. I shouldn't fret, though. Have any of their shots connected?"

The midshipman glanced out the window. "No, sir."

"It's deucedly hard to hit a target at that range, and I doubt Spanish gunnery is as good as ours. Fighting Bob knows what he's doing. I doubt he'll order us to open fire before we get to ten thousand yards or so."

"Sir, word from the spotters," said Lieutenant Bronson. "Two of the armored cruisers are *Princess de Asturias*-class. The last has three stacks."

"The *Reina Regente*?" asked Crenshaw.

"Probably."

"Who are their cruisers firing at?"

"Looks like the *Kansas*."

As if to answer, a large splash rose near the *Kansas*. She sailed through it, ignoring it as if it were but a pleasant, light rain on a summer day.

"A clean miss, sir."

"We'll focus on the *Asturias*. They're older designs, but the *Regente* only has 5.5-inchers instead of the 9.4s on the *Asturias*."

"Aren't they supposed to have torpedo tubes?"

"So do we, Mr. Bronson. So do we. I assume they're loaded if I need them?" Crenshaw smiled slightly.

"They are, Captain." Bronson returned the smile. "And, of course, all guns report ready and loaded with armor-piercing."

"Excellent. Our ship is a credit to her captain." *A stupid joke, but every little bit helps.*

"That she is, sir." Bronson's mustache quirked again. "That she is."

Lieutenant Washington reported, "Captain, orders from the Flag to the main body. All ships, make sixteen knots."

"Acknowledge." He turned to the helmsman. "All ahead full, Mr. Aitken. Our lady's wanted this fight since she was commissioned. Let's not dawdle."

"Aye, aye, sir," answered the helmsman with a grin.

"Range to the lead *Asturias*?"

"Ten thousand yards," replied the executive officer.

"Lay in the main batteries and the starboard six-inchers."

"Aye, aye." He hesitated. "Captain..."

"I'm aware the six-inchers will be at their maximum range, but we'll close that soon enough."

"That's true," Bronson agreed.

"Signal from Flag. Open fire at nine thousand yards."

"Acknowledge." Crenshaw stared at the lead *Asturias* intently through his binoculars as the squadrons closed on each other.

"Range to lead *Asturias*, nine thousand yards," reported Ensign Thompson.

"Thank you, Ensign. Commander Bronson?"

"Yes, Captain?"

"You may open fire. Alternate single fire with the main batteries, if you please."

The executive officer passed on the order, and the four ten-inch guns, set *en echelon* in dual fore and aft turrets fired sequentially. Staggering their fire meant the main guns fired a shot every six seconds or so. The ship shuddered from each shot's recoil, but not as much as if all four fired at the same time. The three six-inchers on the starboard side joined in, sounding sharp and tinny in comparison to the ten-inchers.

Crenshaw stared at the results. "Looks like the forward battery went high and the aft battery missed to their starboard."

"Agreed, sir."

The second round of fire was much better. Crenshaw might have the oldest ship in this squadron, but her sailors shared his love for her.

Best trained crew in the Navy.

And it resulted in a shell taking off a mast of the *Asturias*.

No real damage, but that'll make them think, especially coming on only our second shot.

"Signal from Flag to Torpedo Boat Divisions Two and Three. They're to advance to flank and run at the *Espanas*."

"At the *Espanas*? What is Fighting Bob thinking, sir?" asked Bronson.

The Bliss-Leavitt Mark 2 torpedoes the torpedo boat destroyers carried had a maximum effective range of 3,500 yards. However, their warheads were much more effective against smaller ships like the armored cruisers, not the battleships.

"Apparently Admiral Evans believes those reports about the light armor on the *Espanas*, especially below the waterline." Crenshaw nodded to himself. *And now our orders make more sense.*

The five smaller ships of Torpedo Boat Division Two swooped in under the twelve- and thirteen-inch projectiles from the battleships. Evans had timed their run perfectly. The Spanish torpedo boats changed course to meet them, but the Spanish battleships and cruisers had already aimed their secondary batteries on the American capital ships. Shifting aim would take time, allowing the torpedo boat destroyers to get closer before taking fire.

The lookout's cry broke Crenshaw's contemplation. "Sir! The *Kansas*!"

Crenshaw turned his glasses ahead. A Spanish shell had taken off the rear mast on the *Kansas*. The loss did not impair her in this fight, though, and in return, one of her twelve-inch rounds took off the aft turret of the lead *Espana*. The Spanish ship trailed smoke, but she responded from her fore turret and splashed two more rounds on either side of the *Kansas*.

In the meantime, Crenshaw's gunners had found the range and began pounding the lead *Asturias*. They landed at least three hits on her, including one that took a chunk off from her bow.

"That's it, lads!" cried the bosun.

"Mr. Nielson, I'd appreciate if you would keep your attention on your duties."

Nielson grinned back. "Aye, Captain."

"Mr. Bronson. Please pass on to Lieutenant Boyd my compliments. Inform him Chief Boatswain's Mate Nielson approves of their accuracy, but that I think they can do better."

Bronson smiled broadly as he opened the voicepipe. "Aye, aye, sir!"

Two Spanish shells exploded alongside them in quick succession and wiped the smiles off their faces.

"It seems that *Asturias* would like us to pay attention to her."

"Indeed, Captain."

Nielson turned from his speaking tubes.

"Damage, Mr. Nielson?" asked Crenshaw.

"We've lost two of the starboard lifeboats. The two marines on the one-pounder between them were killed. Sergeant McDermott is sending replacements to see if they can put the gun back into action."

"Thank you." Crenshaw lifted his binoculars. Smoke surrounded the *Reina*, but the second *Asturias* had found the range on the *Texas*.

"It looks like the *Texas* decided that the *Reina* was the greater threat."

"Yes, Mr. Bronson, and she's paying for that decision."

"It's not like Captain Blandin to make a mistake like that."

"He didn't make a mistake, Commander." Crenshaw's eyes turned frosty. "The *Reina* is not as much a threat to us, but she could have hammered Torpedo Boat Division Two. He took a chance."

Crenshaw hid his wince as a 9.4 inch shell landed on the *Texas*. *Right on the bridge. He paid for that decision with his life.*

"Mr. Bronson, please be so good as to shift fire to the second *Asturias*."

"Sir, the first one is still firing at us."

The captain turned his binoculars to her. "Yes, she is, but only from the forward turret, and I think the *Pennsylvania* can deal with her. Besides, the second *Asturias* clearly has better gunners, don't you think?"

Bronson nodded and passed on the order. Firing the main batteries sequentially instead of as a salvo not only kept the ship more stable; it allowed the gunners to shift their aim while barely losing their rhythm. Crenshaw estimated they lost only about fifteen seconds.

They were fifteen seconds well spent, too, as the first shot from the forward turret landed only ten yards ahead of the second *Asturias*, making it shudder and slow from the concussion.

"Mr. Neilson, is Chief Williams still the fire captain on Turret One?"

"He is, Captain."

"Please pass on my compliments to him and his crew. That was a fine first shot."

"Aye, aye, Captain."

Crenshaw turned his binoculars to the *Connecticut* and *Kansas*. Both looked to have taken more damage, but neither seemed hampered. They still comfortably made sixteen knots and all of their main batteries continued to fire.

And doing a fine job. Both of the *Espanas* trailed smoke, though they looked mostly operational.

He then returned to the torpedo boats. Division Three found itself in a melee with the Spanish torpedo boats, and they swirled around each other. As for Division Two, its third ship had taken several hits and was sinking at the stern. However, the other four had a clear path and looked to be about ready to launch their fish.

Yes! The Caribbean is an American sea, not some damn European monarch's fiefdom.

His ship punctuated that thought with another round from the forward main battery. Crenshaw watched its flight, and kept his face impassive when the round hit directly above the waterline amidships of the Spanish cruiser. It opened a hole in the cruiser, which listed almost immediately.

The rest of the bridge was not so restrained. That was why it took a moment for him to realize Lieutenant Washington was yelling at him.

"Sir! Sir!" Washington waved a hand. "Captain Crenshaw! Signal from Torpedo Boat Division One."

Crenshaw lowered his binoculars. "Yes, Mr. Washington?"

"Another Spanish squadron in sight bearing 170. About twenty thousand yards from the torpedo boats. Several larger ships, though no confirmation of classes."

"Acknowledge and pass that on to the Flag."

"I believe the Flag has seen the notice, sir."

"If Admiral Evans wishes to chastise me for redundancy while I ensure he knows of an enemy fleet, he is welcome to do so, Mr. Washington."

"Aye, sir."

"What do you think the Admiral will do, Captain?"

"Well, Mr. Bronson, it's a pickle, there's no doubt. We've got the Santiago squadron on the ropes, but we need time to finish them off. We can't do that with another squadron engaged with us."

As if to confirm Crenshaw, a torpedo exploded against the lead *Espana*. It staggered out of line. However, the other *Espana*, for the first time, landed a solid hit immediately aft of the rear turret on the *Kansas*. She did not fall out of line, but the twelve-inch shell had clearly damaged her engines, and she slowed.

"Flag to Torpedo Boat Division One. They are to do their best to keep the southern Spanish squadron at bay."

"The division acknowledged," reported Washington. The signals officer paused. "Sir, they report two more *Espanas* and at least two more armored cruisers, along with another division of torpedo boats."

Crenshaw nodded.

At that moment, two 9.4-inch shells hit the *Texas* in quick succession, one amidships and one on the stern. She immediately starting listing as a huge plume of black smoke mushroomed over her.

"Bosun, get the life..." Crenshaw's eyes narrowed, and he swiveled his binoculars from the *Texas* to Torpedo Boat Division One. He hesitated.

"Sir?"

"Yes, Mr. Bronson?" He glanced over at his executive officer, who was staring at the two *Asturias*.

"Looks like the *Pennsylvania* has found the range. She's hit the *Asturias* at least twice."

"Excellent." Crenshaw nodded firmly. "Mr. Nielson, be so good as to get the lifeboats launched. All of them. Use all the ensigns and midshipmen. This is a good opportunity for them to get some experience."

"All of the boats, sir?"

"*All* of them. Make sure they're fully crewed. Use the cooks and carpenters and whoever we can spare. Take every person not manning a crucial post or serving as a backup coaler." He hesitated. "And captain one yourself."

"But—"

"Nielson! Do as I say. Get those boats launched and save all you can from the *Texas*."

The older man narrowed his eyes.

Crenshaw pounded a railing. "Mr. Nielson, I'll thank you to carry out my orders. Unless, of course, you'd rather me to prefer charges of insubordination?"

"No, sir," he snapped. "I'll carry out your orders. Sir."

"Thank you, Mr. Nielson."

The bosun twittered his pipes, then stomped off the bridge, dragging Midshipman Howell and Ensign Thompson with him.

"What are you planning, sir? We'll likely need some of those boats ourselves," asked Lieutenant Bronson after Nielson had left with the cadets.

Crenshaw glanced at his executive officer. "Let me know the moment the boats are clear. In the meantime, why don't you take the signals station? While I think Mr. Nielson is perfectly capable, I think we should at least have a junior lieutenant in charge. Don't you agree?"

Bronson cocked his head and glanced south at the torpedo boat squadron, who had accelerated and turned towards the new arrivals. "Aye, sir. I do agree." He went to the signals station. "Mr. Washington, I relieve you."

"Mr. Washington," added Crenshaw.

"Sir?"

"You'll be the ranking officer of all the lifeboats. However, I urge you to do as Mr. Nielson suggests. The Bosun helped me immensely over the years, and I hope he will do the same for you."

"Uh, yes, sir!" The bewildered young man left the bridge.

Crenshaw stared out at the battle, responding curtly when needed but saying nothing else for the next ten minutes.

"Sir, the boats are clear," announced Bronson.

"Thank you, Mr. Bronson."

"Second Spanish squadron sighted," reported the lookout. "Range approximately fourteen thousand yards."

"Excellent." He turned to the helm. "Mr. Aitken, bring us about on a heading of 170."

"What?" asked the startled helmsman.

"Bring us about, lad," said Crenshaw gently. "The torpedo boats would like some company. Smartly now, let's not waste time."

Aitken glanced at Bronson, but the executive officer merely glanced back blandly. He turned the wheel.

***

"What the hell is Crenshaw doing, sir?" snapped Lieutenant Holden.

"What do you mean, Mr. Holden?" Admiral Evans looked over.

"I don't think he's taken a hit, but he's turned his ship to the south."

Evans whipped up his binoculars and studied the situation. "Please send my compliments to him and request his status. Has he taken any damage?"

"Crenshaw reports no significant damage."

"In that case, please inform him that he should return to station immediately."

"Aye, aye, sir."

***

"Sir, message from Flag," reported Bronson.

"That was quick. Fighting Bob's people are paying attention."

Bronson smiled. "His compliments and he requests our status. Have we taken damage?"

"Let him know we have taken no significant damage."

After a moment, "In that case, he requests we return to station immediately."

Crenshaw turned his glasses to the *Connecticut* and smiled. *Fighting Bob's probably looking right at me at this very moment.*

"Sir, how would you like to respond?"

"Hmmm. What was that quote by Teddy after he won?" Crenshaw thought for a moment. "Ah, yes. Send back, 'Far better is it to dare mighty things, to win glorious triumphs, even though checkered by failure than to rank with those poor spirits who neither enjoy nor suffer much, because they live in a gray twilight that knows not victory nor defeat.'"

Bronson chuckled. "I haven't been a signals officer in several years, sir, but I'll give it a go."

"I have complete faith in you, Mr. Bronson."

"And if he makes a mistake, I'll help the commander out," snapped Nielson from the hatch as he entered the bridge.

Crenshaw turned, startled. "Mr. Nielson, what are you doing here? I ordered you off my ship."

"She was my ship years before you came aboard, sir." Nielson stood before the captain, chin thrust out and eyes narrowed.

Crenshaw stared at the man for a long moment. "That she was, Bosun.

That she was. You're right, as usual." He motioned. "Take your place, then."

"Aye, Captain!"

———

"Are you thinking what I think you're thinking, lad?" mused Evans.

"What was that, sir?" asked Holden.

"Nothing, Lieutenant. Has he responded?"

"He's starting to, but it's apparently a long signal and his signals officer is surprisingly slow."

"Indeed?"

"Sir, he sends back, 'Far better is it to dare mighty things...'" Holden paused. "Sir, he sent back the opening to President-Elect Roosevelt's victory speech."

"Damn him," whispered Evans.

"What shall I send back, sir?"

"Damn him," repeated Evans.

"You want me to send back *that*?" Holden's eyes widened.

"No, Lieutenant." Fighting Bob thought for a moment. "Tell him, 'Congratulations on finding your Fort Fisher.' Sign it 'Gimpy.'"

"Gimpy, sir?"

"You don't think I know what the boys call me? And I earned that limp over forty years ago. I'm proud of it." His frosty eyes glared at the Lieutenant. "I said 'Gimpy' and I mean it."

"Very well, sir."

———

"Signal from Flag, sir."

"Well, Mr. Bronson?"

The executive officer smiled. "He says, 'Congratulations on finding your Fort Fisher' and signed it 'Gimpy.'"

Those on the bridge chuckled, then sobered as they remembered just what Fighting Bob had gone through in that battle. That his leg had not been amputated had been a miracle, though he never walked right again.

"Mr. Bronson, send to Evans, *'Non sibi sed patriae.'*"

———

Evans did not hear the response as he had turned his eyes back to the Santiago de Cuba squadron. The damage to the *Connecticut* was not superficial, but she was still in the fight. Two twelve-inch rounds landed in quick sequence on her target, and the *Espana* started to smoke heavily and listing to starboard. Evans could see crewman start to jump off the side and boats getting lowered.

"Please ask Captain Osterhaus to switch fire to the other *Espana*. Let's finish her off, quick as we can, then eliminate the armored cruisers."

"Aye, sir."

"Sir, the *Texas* is starting to settle."

"I see that, Mr. Holden. Looks like they got most of the crew off her, though."

"Aye. And she put paid to the *Reina Regente*."

"Yes."

The Santiago de Cuba squadron had been defeated, but with the other squadron here, Evans had to annihilate it or have them at his back while he fought the new ships.

Which Crenshaw knew.

———

"Heading 170, sir," reported Aitken.

"Excellent. Make all speed possible directly at the Spanish line."

"Aye, aye, sir."

Crenshaw turned to Nielson. "Be so good as to inform Lieutenant Boyd to cease firing with our main batteries. He may continue firing with any intermediates that can range the Santiago squadron."

"Aye, sir." Nielson's eyes turned wary, as he wanted to ask why send someone for an order that could be communicated via the voicetubes.

Then the captain continued, "Also, you are to have him turn the rear battery forward. Then prepare all relevant stations for firing both turrets forward."

Nielson eyes cleared with understanding. He snapped to attention, saluted, and went off.

"Both batteries forward, sir?" asked Bronson.

"It's what our lady was designed for, is that not correct?"

"Well, yes, but the concussion caused by firing ten-inch guns will cause immense damage amidships."

"I know, Mr. Bronson. I was a cadet in '99 when we tried it the last time."

"Then—" He thought about it. "Of course, sir."

A shell exploded a hundred yards to port.

"It seems the Spanish of the second squadron have noticed us."

"That they have, sir."

"What's our range to the lead *Espana*?"

"Eleven thousand yards, sir."

"Let me know when we are ten thousand yards away."

A sudden relative silence filled the ship when the last of the rear intermediary guns stopped firing.

Nielson returned. "All set, sir."

Crenshaw nodded. "Thank you." He turned his glasses to the scattered remains of Torpedo Boat Division One. Only one of its five ships appeared to remain intact, and judging by its position, it had already launched its torpedoes. Of the rest, one had turned over and two others listed heavily, belching smoke. Another wallowed as its crew abandoned ship. It looked that all they had accomplished was to put a torpedo into one of the Spanish armored cruisers. It had fallen out of line, but that left the two *Espanas* and the rest of that squadron.

"Range to lead *Espana*, ten thousand yards, sir." More shells exploded, rocking the ship.

"Gentlemen, we're about to lose our hearing. Make such decisions as you see fit conforming to helping our lady attack the Spanish."

"Aye, sir."

"Mr. Bronson, please retire to the port torpedo battery. Fire at the first available target."

"But sir—"

"The time for signals has passed, Mr. Bronson, and it's unlikely anyone either here or there will hear me order the launch. Be so good as to make sure you use them well."

"Aye, aye, sir."

"Mr. Boyd," ordered Crenshaw through the voicepipe. "Open fire. Continue sequential fire from the main batteries."

The gunnery officer's response came in the form of the fore turret firing.

Everyone on the bridge anticipated the aft turret's shot, but even so, the concussion and sound was far greater than they expected.

Crenshaw shook his head to clear it. As he did so, he could sense his ship protesting at the strain. *She doesn't feel right!*

Nielson jumped over to the helm, where Aitken had barely kept control of the wheel. He pushed the helmsman out of the way and corrected the ship's course, just before the aft turret fired again. He twisted her back again, and again on the next shot. Crenshaw raised his binoculars to watch their shots fly at the Spanish.

Without the aft turret, we'll be little threat, but if I turn to open my broadside, I'll be a much easier target.

Another shot landed far to the port of the Spanish battleship.

———

"But we're still outnumbered, if the reports from Torpedo Boat Division One are correct," muttered Evans.

"It seems so, sir. The Spanish have essentially destroyed that division. Only one of the ships seems unhurt, and it has already launched its torpedoes."

"Any damage?"

"Maybe a hit on one of the *Asturias*."

"Any little bit helps." Evans sighed. He turned his glasses to Crenshaw's ship. "He's firing both turrets directly forward."

"I thought they determined that did too much damage to the ship with the concussion amidships? And doesn't it hurt her range some?"

"Crenshaw seems unconcerned with the prospect."

A shell landed on the *Connecticut*, but fortunately, it was four-incher and it bounced off the armor. Still, it drew Evans back to the fight in front of him.

———

Crenshaw watched as the first eight shots went wide, left or right, as Nielson struggled to get control. Then, however, he got a feel for the effect as the concussion torqued the seven-thousand-ton warship in a way her shipbuilders had not properly accounted for. Each correction took less as he anticipated the shot.

And that steadied the batteries.

The ninth shot hit immediately in front of an *Espana*. It ripped a small hole in the bow, which enlarged as the Spanish battleship slammed forward at eighteen knots.

The Spanish captain turned the *Espana* out of the line, not only limiting damage to her bow, but exposing three of its main turrets at Crenshaw. His ship might be damaged, but she still could bring six twelve-inch and ten four-inch guns to bear.

Boyd's crew put two six-inch shells into her side as she turned, but that did not prevent the *Espana* from unleashing a broadside at Crenshaw's ship.

A four-inch shell went through the starboard midship's six-inch gun casemate. Another four-inch shell went straight through the aft funnel.

Worse was the twelve-inch shell that went through the casemate of the forward starboard six-incher. It completely destroyed the gun, sending the barrel flipping over the remains of the bow. It lifted the entire foredeck in a storm of teak and steel that showered the bridge as the ship drove straight through the cloud of debris at almost seventeen knots.

One chunk of steel shattered the bridge window, and a shard of glass ripped through Crenshaw's thigh. He screamed, but then pulled out a handkerchief and wrapped it around the wound. *I guess I'll be the next "Gimpy."*

He put his binoculars up again just in time to see a ten-inch round land on the port midships turret of the *Espana*. It exploded in a gout of flame, and the *Espana* turned away.

"Shift fire to the next *Espana*, Lieutenant Boyd," he shouted into the voicepipe. He yelled the order several times until he could see the turrets swivel.

More shots exploded around his ship. The two *Asturias* had pulled out of line to expose their 9.4-inch guns, and their shots landed all around him.

Good—at the very least, we've managed to get them out of formation. And we're only about three thousand yards away now. Maybe we can give them something else to think about.

"Mr. Nielson, turn to heading 200, please." As Nielson turned the wheel, Crenshaw yelled the course change into the voicetube to Lieutenant Boyd.

The turrets swiveled to match their targets as they turned, and Crenshaw watched intently. *Now!*

There was a double thump in the ship as Bronson launched two torpedoes at one of the *Asturias*. The midships and aft port six-inchers, heretofore without targets, also let loose. At least one struck the *Asturias*.

Unfortunately, the Spanish cruiser's crew was just as sharp. A 9.4-inch exploded along the port side of the ship. It did not fully penetrate, but struck right where the port torpedo tubes had been.

Goodbye, Commander Bronson, thought Crenshaw. He saw another six-inch land in the corresponding spot on the *Asturias* and refocused on the battle.

Now if we can just score a hit or two on that other Espana...

As if by request, he watched as a ten-inch shell landed on its second turret. When the smoke cleared, one of the two twelve-inch guns it contained pointed up at an odd angle and smoke came from it.

But smoke also came from the forward turret, which had not been hit. Two twelve-inch shells rose in his direction.

He watched impassively. *One's going to miss to our port. But the other...*

His lady had been incredibly innovative in her time. She had been a place where American shipbuilders had honed their craft. Lessons learned building her would make every other American battleship better, including the *Connecticut* and *Kansas*.

Among those lessons was the need for heavier topside and main deck armor.

———

Crenshaw's done some damage, Evans thought. *And they're out of formation. He's given us at least a half-hour.*

At that point, the twelve-inch shell landed on Crenshaw's ship. A bolt of fire stretched up from her. A secondary explosion rocked her. Then a third one snapped her in half, cracking the superstructure and flinging the bridge away. Seven thousand tons of steel and flesh sank into the clear, perfect blue of the Caribbean almost in the blink of an eye.

All but one person on the bridge gasped as Crenshaw and his lady died almost in an instant.

But not Evans. He had already turned back to the Santiago squadron. Both *Espanas* were now clearly out of the fight. The only ship with any fight in it was an *Asturias* armored cruiser, but that ended soon enough as two shots from the *Pennsylvania* detonated her aft magazine in an explosion that ripped off her stern.

"Good," he muttered. "Lieutenant Holden. Be so good as to make signal to all units. Reform. Report best available speed. Please order the *West Virginia* to take up station behind the *Pennsylvania*. Any ships that cannot keep to at least twelve knots are to rendezvous with the *Culgoa*."

That took time. Fortunately, thanks to Crenshaw, the Flying Squadron had the time. The Spanish squadron had also reformed, and they slightly outgunned Evans's ships, but that made no matter.

"Lieutenant Holden, signal all ships." He paused. He rubbed the ancient wound on his thigh and remembered charging Fort Fisher.

This will be my last fight, I bet. Let's make it count.

Fighting Bob straightened and nodded fiercely. "Send this: Crenshaw and his crew died to give us this chance. We're going to kick the Spanish out of the Caribbean forever, and it'll be because of that ship, captain, and crew. Gentlemen, fire as you bear and..."

"And what, sir?" asked Holden.

"Remember the *Maine!*"

———

Cast of Characters from Far Better To Dare

All characters in *Far Better to Dare* served on the USS *Maine* at the time of its explosion in Havana Harbor except Seaman Aitken, Midshipman Howell, Ensign Thompson, and Admiral Evans. The first three are fictional sons of men who served on the *Maine* during the explosion. The fourth, Fighting Bob, was one of the U.S. Navy's great admirals of the time.

- Aitken, James, Jr. (son of James Aitken, Boatswain's Mate, First Class, USS *Maine*, 1898)
- Blandin, John (Lieutenant, j.g., USS *Maine*, 1898)
- Boyd, David, Jr. (Naval Cadet, USS *Maine*, 1898)
- Bronson, Amon (Naval Cadet, USS *Maine*, 1898)
- Crenshaw, Arthur (Naval Cadet, USS *Maine*, 1898)
- Evans, Robley "Fighting Bob" (Commander of Great White Fleet, 1908)
- Holden, Jonas (Naval Cadet, USS *Maine*, 1898)
- Howell, Charles, Jr. (son of Charles P. Howell, Chief Engineer, USS *Maine*, 1898)
- McDermott, John (Marine Private, USS *Maine*, 1898)
- Morris, John (Assistant Engineer, USS *Maine*, 1898)
- Nielsen, Sophus (Cockswain, USS *Maine*, 1898)
- Thompson, George, Jr. (son of George Thompson, Landsman, USS *Maine*, 1898)
- Washington, Pope (Naval Cadet, USS *Maine*, 1898)
- Williams James (Gunner's Mate, Third Class, USS *Maine*, 1898)

ABOUT ROB HOWELL

Rob is the publisher of New Mythology Press, creator of the Firehall Sagas, a writer and editor in Luke Gygax's World of Okkorim, a reformed medieval academic, and a retired soda jerk.

Without books, it's unlikely he or his parents would have both survived.

Find him here:

- Website: robhowell.org
- His Blog: robhowell.org/blog.
- Firehall Sagas: firehallsagas.com
- Amazon: amazon.com/-/e/B00X95LBB0
- Twitter: @Rhodri2112
- Rob's Riddles: patreon.com/rhodri2112

A SAFE WARTIME POSTING

Joelle Presby

FALL 1914, GERMAN PORT OF DOULA, KAMERUN, WEST AFRIKA

"A mined harbor! New fortifications! Wonders of German engineering!" The junior lieutenant with his sand-scuffed boots continued like that while an aide tapped my shoulder and beckoned me out of the governor's office to the wide terrace.

A jungle of thick trees and scrub brush I couldn't recognize covered the steep shoreline. But our vantage point, a quarter mile up this foothill of Mount Fako, showed the familiar ocean making a broad harbor for the lonely port city of Doula. It lay undefended, except for the few troops granted by the governor and however many of the local sailors and city dwellers could be convinced to fight on behalf of the foreign colonialists.

My greatest hope was that the young officer under my wing on this war observer assignment got to see nothing at all. Unfortunately, I also spoke no German, so I turned to the man without much hope of conveying my thoughts with any accuracy. The aide scratched a neat brown beard as he regarded me, and I envied him the comfort of his loose cotton civilian clothing.

"That kid," the German said, his English flawless if, well, sounding overly English and not at all American, "is he the cousin or nephew of your President Marshall?"

"Vice President, sir," I corrected immediately. "President Woodrow Wilson is—"

"Yes, of course, of course," the German acknowledged. "Dreadful, just dreadful, the stroke." He shook his head in condolences for a piece of information apparently common knowledge here on the African continent, even though the US papers were not printing it. My superior's letters from home indicated the vice president was praying for Mr. Wilson's full recovery, and he considered it a very poor precedent to assume the presidency himself while the man elected for the position lived.

Mr. Wilson's capability remained a question for physicians back home in the States. They were not sharing their thoughts with a navy chief sent to German West Afrika to shepherd a well-connected young officer in need of a position for his last couple years of service. A position, I was made to understand by superiors, that should bolster a future career in politics without being abruptly terminated by an unfortunate twelve-inch artillery shell.

"Sir, lieutenant junior grade Marshall is the son of the vice president's cousin," I said. Let the German make of that what he would.

The man nodded. "I shall let Governor Ebermaier know."

I suppressed a sigh of resignation.

"Come on, Chief!" Lieutenant Marshall called me back into the governor's office.

Piles of work waited on the governor's desk and his office held few of the luxuries a man in his position could acquire. A bald German manager with a beard too long to be fashionable, responsible for a large colony but without the forces to protect it, I found myself liking him. The governor had also tolerated my superior's excitement at the prospect of war coming here, and I appreciated his patience.

I positioned myself a few steps behind Lieutenant Marshall's shoulder while what seemed to be leave-taking comments were exchanged. A fine oil painting of a gunboat patrolling up the Vuri river with a mixed Afrikan and German crew supervised by the usual white officers hung behind the governor's desk.

My superior, a slight man in his twenties, cleanshaven, and with an incorrigible gleam in his eyes, switched to English for my benefit as he completed his farewell.

"Thank you so much for your time, Governor." He rendered a flawless salute with casual ease, and he added a smooth nod of his head after his hand returned to his side, which somehow gave the standard military courtesy a touch of extra politeness. The governor's mouth twitched up in unexpected appreciation. I credited the Marshall family political training.

I made my own rough salute to the colonial governor and his military aide, whose name I'd never caught, and followed quickly out of the residence.

We passed through a hall with a cleaning staff hard at work. Clerks in the open offices didn't look up, but the crowd in the visitor's hall examined us with open stares.

They were probably trying to guess which of them should be offended at Lieutenant Marshall being granted an audience in advance of their own time, I thought. I did my best to appear inscrutable and discretely encouraged my lieutenant to keep up the brisk pace of a man with appointments and work ahead, instead of what we were: two Americans abroad with little oversight and more than enough time to have waited in that hall until after all of them had been seen.

Outside, we paused to consider our route. The piers of Port Doula and the nearest beaches beckoned again. My superior had marched along them this morning before our appointment. That walk had destroyed the work of the boot boy I'd given a coin to the evening prior to press our uniforms and apply a fine shine to our shoes. I was for a return to our quarters and a change to my second-best uniform before any more exploring caught my officer's interest.

Lieutenant Marshall turned this way and that, examining the buildings around us. Even the colonial government buildings were mostly single story, some brick and plaster, a few painted. Most sat inside a courtyard wall, mirroring the compound style of the older Afrikan buildings in Doula proper. I tapped a finger on the rough brick wall surrounding the governor's compound. Taller than most and with a smooth white plaster, it'd be a challenge for a miscreant to climb, but armed invaders could smash the gate easily enough.

I need to look at the compound around our guest quarters, I thought. There might be a useful spiderweb of alleyways I could use between the walls. Might even be a route all the way to one or another of the smaller piers where I might find a boat seaworthy enough to brave the open bay at least as far as the nearer Spanish islands. I could imagine messy firefighting going house to house, and some extra cover would be helpful if I needed to drag my charge's unconscious form along a retreat route.

The vice president was said to respect Mr. Wilson deeply, of course, but the presidential election of 1916 was only two years away. If the president had recovered sufficiently to run for re-election by then, well and good. If not, my superiors expected me to return a whole and sound young lieutenant to his prominent family in case Mr. Thomas R. Marshall, 28th Vice President of the United States, had an interest in the position of 29th President of the United States.

My orders were clear: I was to ensure a certain young Lieutenant Marshall would be alive and well, so that his family could put him to whatever political purpose most suited that fine ambition.

"Don't let him get himself killed. Don't let him duel. Don't let him eat anything questionable. And by all means, make sure he stays out of gunnery range!" Captain Beach had slapped shut the folder with the printed orders and poked me in the gut with them. "These'll say nice political things about arduous duty abroad and the full faith of the United States Navy and the importance of the young lieutenant's honorable service and on and on. Don't you fall for it. We need more allies in Washington who understand the cost of good strong ships. Keep this kid alive."

I'd replied: "Sir, yes, sir," and here we were.

Doula did boast one larger building. Beyond a flimsy bamboo structure, I considered Port Doula Cathedral, made of solid timber and imported stone, positioned proudly just beyond the governor's mansion. Its steeple stood nice and tall as a quality navigation aid.

I had taken a look at the printed orders themselves, which were clearly a copy of the officer's orders. It was just as flowery as Captain Beach had said. On the final line, a short addendum had been typed in heavy black ink: "Chief Petty Officer Hays assigned to assist."

The large German-built church had enough wood that it could burn, but I doubted the British or French or their Nigerian and Senegalese troops would intentionally raze a holy place.

I suspected no one had told the young officer that he was more valuable in politics than in war and that he was expected to maintain a careful distance from any action. I considered the possibility of dragging him to the sanctuary and sitting on him until any fighting was over.

Priests usually left the doors open back at Saint Mary of Mercy in Pittsburgh, but that might not be the case here.

Lieutenant Marshall interrupted my thoughts by stopping to stare straight up at the narrow bamboo tower. The top swayed in the gentle sea breeze.

"Is this thing a lighthouse?" he asked.

"Um," I temporized.

He circled the structure and found the ladder.

It probably was, but the cement footing around its base seemed insufficient to the task of defending it from wood bores and termites. In daytime, the light above was mercifully out with no chance of it burning down around our ears, but I hoped they paid their caretakers a danger bonus for this swaying terror.

Lieutenant Marshall put his foot on the long ladder and tested it. When the first rung bore his weight, he scampered up as if it were well-maintained rigging and not a wobbling tower of death unlikely to hold anyone heavier than a lamp boy. With regret, I scrambled up after him.

The joins and ties were sturdy and frequent, so I had hopes that the thing would at least hold long enough for us to get back down again. My superior clambered all the way to the lookout platform just below the light and leaned on the rail to take in a view of the wide harbor. I tried not to puff too hard as I joined him.

We could see a half-dozen similar towers on various little points in the nearer part of the estuary to the south and west. The river Vuri snaked northeast into the dark green horizon behind us.

"What did the charts show, do you remember?" Lieutenant Marshall asked. "Twenty some miles of bay from the open ocean to the river mouth here at Doula proper?"

That seemed about right. We couldn't see quite so far, but the height did give a fine view of the nearer inlets weaving in fingerlike from the deeper harbor to shallows filled with crab and shrimp boats.

The continent's coastline turned from east-west here to form a near right angle and head south with the mouth of the Vuri River and its estuary tucked into that continental bend. Generations upon generations had traded here, but the Germans had constructed a pair of new railways into the continental interior, making an already prosperous port into the largest in the region.

Fishing trawlers sailed in with full nets, and the larger vessels carrying the wealth of the colony steamed for open ocean. The narrow points of lush greenery between each inlet had appeared impassible from the water, but from above the distance shrank to something a dedicated landing force could hack through if committed enough and led by savvy guides.

The port defenses didn't look like much to me. Doula proper had a deep enough estuary with dense jungle protecting it from troops landing further south or north and attempting a land assault, but the harbor remained largely clear. I peered again at the ships dotting the waterways.

Steamers puffed in and out of port, most headed just over the horizon to the trade city Malabo on the neutral Spanish island of Fernando Po. Tiny fishing vessels darted this way and that with a carefree navigation that made me doubt the officers in charge of Kamerun's defenses had placed any mines at all.

"Our quarters are down there near the harbor, sir." I pointed. "Not as fine as they could be, but there's another one of these observation posts just beyond there."

"Excellent, Chief!" he said. "I shall have to climb that one for a better view of the sea."

I made a noncommittal noise of acknowledgement. We probably would be climbing it regularly now that I'd pointed it out. More importantly, if the observers at the much more solidly built lighthouse at the Point of Suellaba saw an attacking squadron headed our way, the warning would flash from bamboo tower to bamboo tower right to our doorstep. We might hear of an attack even before the governor did.

My officer studied the nearer inlets once more and snorted.

"Not enough mines." Lieutenant Marshall frowned at the shining bay. "How many steamers do you suppose the governor can use for defense?"

I shrugged. "All of them."

My superior goggled at me, and I only lifted my shoulders again.

"They fly German flags, sir," I explained. "Probably belong to the colony already. Though if the war doesn't come here, might be tough to explain to higher authorities why good seaworthy vessels were commandeered and sunk to constrict a fine commercial harbor."

The lieutenant suppressed a laugh at the idea.

"They haven't got enough mines to protect everything. They'll need to sink a dozen ships at least to narrow the waterway for a proper defense," he said. Lieutenant Marshall paused to consider the port again, turning to look out towards the ocean and then tracing the darker blue of deep channel up to the river mouth with Bonaberi town on the north shore and greater Doula on our side to the south.

Shouting from directly below drew our attention to tiny faces, white and black, looking up at us from the safety of the ground. I took one last look to memorize the waterways as well as I could, and followed my boss down the ladder.

I missed the first of the introductions when I paused to catch my breath halfway down. As soon as my boots touched solid ground, I brushed my uniform off and studied the gold braid to guess the ranks of the two men in front of us.

"This is Major Zimmermann, commandant of the defensive forces here in the Kameruns," said Lieutenant Marshall, identifying the easy one, and I saluted. "Sir," he added, "please meet my chief, Johnny Hays."

The man returned my salute, but hardly glanced at me. "Of course, Lieutenant," he said. "I understand you arrived with just the one staffer, but we can supply you with a few more. Allow me to introduce," the German nodded to the local in an immaculately pressed suit, and his English fumbled as he searched for the right word, "His Excellen—?"

"It's Ntsama Atangana, or Karl, if that's easier." The black man smiled and held out a hand to my boss who reached out and shook it.

"An honor, sir," Lieutenant Marshall said.

"Not at all," Atangana replied. "An honor for me to meet an American prince come all the way to my homeland."

"Um, well, certainly not a prince." My boss blushed.

"Of course," Atangana gave him a nod. "You don't use those terms. My people don't, either. I'm a chief of chiefs, technically. And this continent has plenty of other actual kings and princes, as well. But you are the cousin to the most important man in America."

I opened my mouth to try to explain again Mr. Wilson's continued presidency when my boss stepped firmly on my foot.

The major examined the termite mound near the bamboo lighthouse dubiously and looked up the ladder as if he thought he should climb it himself, but absolutely did not want to.

"Could you see the British cruiser from up there?" the major asked.

My jaw dropped.

"Ah, no, sir," Lieutenant Marshall replied. "There were no military vessels in sight, though it seemed you have a good dozen steamers in port and perhaps some smaller launches you may have equipped as gunboats? Might I suggest deploying a few more mines if you've got them?"

"Excellent!" Atangana agreed.

The major nodded with an expression of resignation. "I've given orders to deploy as many as the workshops can turn out. And," he added, brightening a little bit, "since we have a dignitary of your status with us, the governor has authorized a message by telegraph calling for reinforcements."

"And he's finally allowing our people to fight for their homes," Atangana put in.

"Why would he not?" I forgot myself and actually asked the question out loud. "Um, Your Excellency," I added quickly.

"Karl," Atangana repeated again with another brilliant smile. "Here in the West Afrikas, the kingdoms and the tribes disagree from time to time with trade agreements and taxes for the roads and railways. Not as much within the Kameruns, but for the English or French, and especially for the Belgians, if they bring troops to steal this protectorate from the Kaiser, they'll return to fewer colonies than they thought they had. They may find no workers left on their cocoa plantations and palm oil groves. Maybe they'll find new tribal leaders no longer in accord with past arrangements. Perhaps both."

"There's no profit in an Afrikan campaign." Major Zimmermann shook his head. "We'll need to destroy the telegraph station, of course, but as I've told the governor, I can protect his family and withdraw everyone up the longer rail line towards Ngaundere or march still further north to make a stand at Garua."

I tried to follow the geography in my head, but gave up as Major Zimmermann continued.

"We could have a fine land battle with defensive support from the interior. The locals can harry the troops from the jungle all along the route if the Nigerian conscripts and whatever forces the British can spare choose to follow us inland."

"But the sea!" My lieutenant looked aghast at the German army man. "You must defend the port!"

"We can try, I suppose." The major looked doubtfully towards the harbor. "Or I could get you passage across to Fernando Po."

Yes! I thought. But I could see my boss's face growing red.

"The Spanish are neutral yet," he continued. "And they could see you back to your home country if you feel this conflict exceeds, um—" He fumbled with a way to suggest my boss leave on the eve of a battle while my officer's back stiffened.

"I shall certainly stay, sir!"

"Well, then." Atangana clapped my lieutenant on the shoulder. "Let's see to the defenses. I have runners out everywhere to bring us news. At present, we face only a cruiser, her launches, and a gunboat towed in. Three converted steamers hold some troops, but not so many as to give us trouble if they have to fight through our jungle to reach us. If we hold the harbor, we hold the city."

"We must keep Doula," my lieutenant said.

"Yes," even I had to agree.

————

My boss reveled in a flurry of activity as the cruiser, now identified as H.M.S. *Cumberland*, requested Governor Ebermaier's surrender and was refused.

Most of Major Zimmermann's sixteen hundred soldiers were stationed further in the interior of Kamerun or on the other side of British-held Nigeria in Togoland, but 1st Company, with its artillery and three fine Maschinengewehr 08s and their crews, were in Doula.

I followed behind on the inspection of the machine guns. They didn't seem too great a change from Hiram Maxim's gun, but Major Zimmermann's pride in having the firepower required I keep my thoughts to myself. All three only had the slower Schloss 08 firing assemblies, but with a limited stockpile of the 250-round ammunition belts, I figured it was probably for the best. Major Zimmermann boasted a nearly 3,900-yard range, but a quiet word with the lead gunner confirmed closer to two thousand yards would be better if we hoped the current somewhat out-of-practice gun crew would hit the target.

Atangana listened closely to everything, and when we left, a half-dozen locals arrived with tools.

"We may be able to make use of the spent cartridges to make reloads for the rifles, if not for the machine guns themselves," the Afrikan suggested.

My lieutenant wished loudly for a decent gunboat of our own or the time to find a way to install one of the machine guns on a larger fishing vessel and secure it well enough to allow decent targeting. I inquired after the gunboat in the governor's painting, and was rewarded with a number of stories of previous small battles it had won along the Vuri River. After briefly lifting my hopes, our guides concluded the discussion with the news that *that* gunboat also currently sat upriver in Yabassi undergoing major repairs to the hull.

The major refused my lieutenant's schemes for installing the Maschinengewehr 08s on boats. Instead, we had to make do with finding appropriate placements for the guns along the shoreline and installing discrete floats in the water to act as range markers.

Atangana grumbled when the governor declined to pull 7th and 8th Companies south from Garua and Ngaundere, but he returned with additional strong young men. With my superior's hearty support, he convinced Major Zimmermann to mix his sharpshooters in with the Germans and supply with rifles any local vouched for by Atangana who proved able to hit a target at forty paces.

We sank a full dozen steamers in the port to leave only a narrow, mined approach to Doula. The mine men's wires ran only so long, leaving wet and cold soldiers crouched on the beaches with the detonators, but Lieutenant Marshall ran up and down the beach himself with a spyglass and Atangana ensured the spotters had food and regular relief while we waited for the first wave of attacks.

My officer spent hours with Atangana scheming of ways invaders could be confused, to include constructing portable lighthouses and having teams of porters carry them to and fro on the beach while lit to mislead nighttime attackers.

I appealed to Governor Ebermaier through his aide, Hans, whose name I'd finally gathered. One of the German government steamers was kept back from the harbor blocking effort. She boasted only ten knots and was single screwed, but Zimmermann christened her *Nachtigal* and produced for her one five-centimeter gun and one 3.7-centimeter revolving gun. She couldn't match the British gunboat, the *Dwarf,* a *Bramble*-class vessel equipped with two four-inch guns, four twelve-pounders, and four Maxim guns. And with the *Dwarf*'s twin screws and reported 13.5 knot max speed, she couldn't even outrun her. But Lieutenant Marshall brightened at having at least one armed vessel in what he liked to call "the Bamboo Squadron."

Out in deeper waters, the *Cumberland* began a blockade of Doula and the shipping stopped, leaving the docks oddly quiet for a port city. Nothing much of use could be done with the cocoa filling up the warehouses, but the palm oil delighted both Zimmermann and my lieutenant. They put their heads together, imagining situations where an extra-long burning fire might be of some military benefit.

Hans shook his head and begged Atangana and me to consider that the governor might need to have some resources left to bring in an income for the colony after all the fighting was done. Atangana sent the aide back up to the governor's mansion with encouraging words, but I thought the

Kaiser would be very unreasonable indeed if he begrudged the use of a few warehouses of oil when he'd chosen to give the governor so little in the way of naval defenses.

The first day, the *Dwarf* oversaw a few small skiffs poking at the edges of our defenses and withdrew back to safety at dusk. We left the lighthouses dark that night and watched the waters by moonlight and saw nothing.

Lieutenant Marshall spotted empty British launches on the beach of a nearby inlet when he made his dawn climb. He clambered down and called a warning to an alarmed Major Zimmermann.

A pleased band of locals reported back that the remains of the exhausted and hopelessly lost British cutting out party had been found and had given their parole to some Kamerun tribesmen in exchange for directions back out of the jungle. A compound on the inland side of Doula was converted to hold the prisoners. Hans spoke hopefully of the blockade being broken soon, but even Atangana didn't have the boldness to pretend the capture of a few men from the greater blockading force would do much to save Doula.

For a solid week, British skiffs ground back our mines bit by bit. A few times, the mine could be detonated before the wire was cut or mishandling on the side of the clearing crews bloodied the British, but they had too many lives to spend and there were too few mines in the harbor. And with the powerful *Dwarf* in the shallows, the Kamerun crews couldn't directly attack the mine-clearing boats without being sunk. We'd risked the small boats we had in abundance, but we held *Nachtigal* back.

Atangana, Zimmermann, and my lieutenant considered and rejected a dozen schemes. They attempted the moving of lighthouses, but the *Dwarf* didn't need to continue work at night with our harbor so close to being cleared. And the carrying of even lightweight bamboo in quantity enough to form a full lighthouse required exhausting a dozen men who might be needed to support an armed retreat if the next day proved to be the day Doula fell. So the three gave up on bamboo and turned to palm oil and explosives.

The next night, we lit the lighthouses dimly for our own counterattacks, and several fishing crews gave their lives in desperate struggles with the British mine-clearing boats. Too many wires were cut and the *Cumberland* again sent forward the gunboat *Dwarf* to cover the last of their mine-clearing boats, which made our little skiffs unable to hold their own.

Our machine guns on the shore turned a few invading sailors on overly eager small boats into hamburger, but at nightfall, it became clear that by the following day, the harbor would be all but cleared. It might take the British a few additional days to realize the fact, as Atangana's men had sewed the waterways with plenty of makeshift non-explosive devices to help confuse the mine clearers, but with no response yet to the wireless telegraph and no word by radio, Doula had to assume any reinforcements would arrive too late.

Hans did share encouraging word of tribal uprisings in both French Afrika and British Afrika, but if our attackers knew, they didn't withdraw.

Atangana and Lieutenant Marshall went to Major Zimmermann with a plan to use *Nachtigal* to attack *Dwarf* and afterwards reseed the harbor with more mines improvised by the artillery company. Zimmermann allowed it reluctantly, but held back a core of German troops at the telegraph station and began his plans for evacuating the governor and the other most important officials.

Under cover of dark again, we loaded a barge with explosives and oil barrels and attached poles to the front of a small launch to push it. *Nachtigal* steamed alongside, ready to take on any boat patrols we might encounter on our way to the *Dwarf*'s anchorage. The plan was simple: use the launch to get the barge full of explosives close to the *Dwarf* and detonate them. Then pray we didn't get killed by our own bomb.

The locals nearly mutinied when Atangana attempted to captain the little launch. With great reluctance and palpable anger, he was left on shore and sent a cousin along instead to aid with navigation. The original master of the steamer maintained command of the *Nachtigal*, and additional crew from Zimmermann's 1st Company manned the guns.

From the bleak look on the *Nachtigal* captain's face, I could tell he didn't expect to survive the night, but preferred not to be left behind if his vessel was to be sunk. A respectable choice, but I'd rather he had the stamina to pretend to more confidence. He had crew to think of, after all.

The soft splash of waves against hull did little to calm me. Of course, the lieutenant had to be "at the decisive point," as he'd said. In the launch. Which meant I was also observing this bit of the Great War from a far closer vantage point than I suspect our superiors had intended.

"Sir, my orders preclude—" I'd tried in a fast whispered conversation on the shoreline to keep him off the barge. But Lieutenant Marshall had given me a pitying look.

"Some aunt or uncle of mine tried to order you to keep me safe, did they?" His grin had been infectious. "I take my orders from the Navy, thankfully, and not from them. Don't worry: they like to think they have influence, but it doesn't extend to inside the service." He had given me a one-armed hug, over in a moment, and had climbed aboard.

I would have liked to have had a good crowd of Americans in Port Doula that night to insist on Lieutenant Marshall's importance and to get him put safely ashore with Atangana, but all I'd managed after climbing in after him was to move him to the seat furthest from the barge of explosives. He settled in at the rear of our little pusher boat next to the coxswain.

I crouched at the prow, watching our approach. A trembling young German from the artillery company sat next to me, and the cousin of Atangana's directing all the sailors aboard sat on my other side, grinning like a madman. We pushed the barge of explosives and had one remaining mine with a wire running back to me for detonation.

The white-faced German to my left was supposed to be the one to press that lever, but I snatched it from him at the first sandbar when a small bump of the barge panicked him into reaching for the detonator with us still too close and the *Dwarf* well out of range.

Jutting narrow triangles of peninsula from the south made dark treed shadows in the starry skies. A few boats of Atangana's brave men had made their way along that coastline to flank the *Dwarf*. If we failed, they might make a desperate attempt at a night boarding.

Nachtigal steamed too loud in the soft night some quarter mile ahead. Our little boat had only so much power, and we had the whole weight of the barge ahead to push. I wondered if the *Nachtigal* had already given up and hoped to surrender to the *Dwarf*, but six of the crew on that steamer were Atangana's handpicked sailors, and I doubted the German gunners would support such cowardice, either.

A lookout's cry over the waves ahead of us made me fear we'd been spotted, and the *Dwarf's* guns would soon ensure Lieutenant Marshall never had a political career, when firing instead ranged out towards the south and small bonfires erupted on the coastline.

It wasn't a picket boat and *Nachtigal's* dark shape slid on with no returning fire ahead or to the north.

"The chief of chiefs!" came the too-loud whisper, almost a cheer, quickly shushed. Rather than wait for us to fail, Atangana had staged a diversion for us.

British cries echoed clearly over the water. I made out orders to guard the anchor and directions to fire toward the south.

I cursed. We didn't need an alarmed gunboat with lookouts wary of attackers. Lights from the deck of the *Dwarf* swept this way at that over the water towards the nearer beaches to the south. Worse, our planned course would soon take us between those near shores and the British gunboat, where the bonfires would silhouette us very nicely for the *Dwarf's* gunners.

My lieutenant, smart boy, saw the problem immediately and we slowed, letting the shape of *Nachtigal* slide even further out of protective range. Gradually, ever so gradually, we moved our little vessel about to turn our barge and begin another approach towards *Dwarf*.

This time, we came not from the direction of Doula, where faint flickers of the city light might give us away, not from the nearer little peninsulas where Atangana's men made their desperate attacks, and not even from the far coastline to the north where a prudent British commander might expect another flurry of small craft to venture another attack. We came from behind, from the pitch-black ocean side.

In the clarity of the echoing commands from the *Dwarf*, we could hear the British contempt for what appeared to be pitiful, barely armed boats whose former crews now swam hard for the safety of the shore with bonfires provided to help them find their way.

More gunfire roared as spotters on the *Dwarf* finally noticed *Nachtigal*. The horrible sound of large enemy guns being answered by smaller friendly guns rang out over the waves. The captain of *Nachtigal* turned the steamer to flee, but the *Dwarf's* guns had too great a range. The *Nachtigal* fell silent.

I made an inaudible prayer for the men already in the water, and our barge glided up to the looming shape of the British gunboat. Giving up silence for speed, we reversed our course and surged back with all the power our small craft could muster.

The wire tightened, and at last, I slammed down the detonator.

Fire fountained over the waves, hot against my back and unbearably bright, even with my whole body crouched and turned away. The barge boomed and all sound vanished into the single bellowing *kaboom*.

A heavy wave lapped over the prow of our vessel, and Atangana's cousin with silent open mouth and clear gestures ordered the crew to bail and pressed a bucket into my hands. My lieutenant found me and another bucket as we fought to keep our boat seaworthy long enough to reach a shore.

Fire and roaring still filled the sky. The British gunboat sank with burning oil spreading over the waves. All sound blanketed to nothingness still, but as the brightness dimmed to dull flames, the *Nachtigal* appeared out of the graying night.

The least injured of the sailors pulled us from the damaged launch onto the bloodied deck of the steamer, and Doula's only naval vessel powered for homeport.

We two crews limped up the sandy beach to join with the survivors of Atangana's diversionary attack. The blast from the barge had been seen from our bamboo towers and we were greeted by a triumphant cheering crowd of Germans and locals.

———

By day, we could see *Dwarf's* ruin now joined the dozen sunken steamers helping to guard our harbor. Our own small boats with assistance from the newly eager *Nachtigal* sank the small craft *Cumberland* attempted to send into the shallows.

Hans congratulated us all and encouraged us to come on up to the mansion for a celebratory toast.

The chief of chiefs clapped my lieutenant on the back and asked for the next plan.

With the *Dwarf* sunk and new mining well begun, our port would hold. But *Cumberland* still blockaded the shipping routes, and the spotters now reported that four converted troop transports flying British and French flags waited offshore.

"Four transports, you said?" Major Zimmermann asked with an expression of interest he'd not shown since being ordered to conduct a naval defense.

The local who'd just reported it to Atangana confirmed again and supplied a guess at the total number of troops embarked.

Zimmermann grinned and turned to Atangana. "How would your fighters like to try a proper land campaign?"

I rubbed my ears, convinced that my hearing loss had been more permanent than I'd thought.

"With that many troops waiting uselessly off at sea, the whole of Nigeria is open. We only need get there. And I have inland troops to redeploy if only we can convince Governor Ebermaier that the Kaiser ought to have a larger set of protectorates in the West Afrikas."

"But the cost!" the governor's aide stammered. "The palm oil supplies can be explained, but we still can't ship out our cocoa yet, and we'd lose the whole season's harvest if you took enough men to take and hold the whole of Nigeria!"

"Not to mention the joys of a march through Afrikan jungle," I added, but I kept my voice down and thought only my lieutenant heard me.

"The northern railway goes far enough to reach the grasslands, and it's prairie land all the way west into Nigeria at that latitude," Atangana explained. "But with, of course, enough scorpions, grass vipers, and burning sun to make a man long for a decent bit of rainforest."

Zimmermann shook his finger at the chief of chiefs. "Don't you go backing down now. It's not thousands of Londoners out on those steamers waiting to sack this city."

"Of course, Major. Of course." Atangana made a bow of acknowledgement. "Their forces are mostly hired from my brother chiefs in Senegal and Nigeria, as I believe German mercenaries have also fought in other nation's wars from time to time. But more of their brothers are trying out independence wars. Wait a few more months and you might have Nigeria and even Senegal for the Kaiser by treaty without a war at all."

"Treaties." Major Zimmermann threw up his hands. "Always with you, it's treaties and a new road for that chief and a bridge for this other one. Most of the interior of this territory wasn't fought over at all!"

"It is the more profitable choice," Hans observed.

The German major clamped his mouth shut, but favored the aide with a dark glare that implied the only things he considered more beneath a fighting man's dignity than preemptive peace treaties were the profit motives that drove a bureaucrat to accept them.

Just then, hoots of joy came from the bamboo tower, and separately, a runner came from the wireless station.

"News! News from the Americas!"

My lieutenant and I started bolt upright.

"The South Americas," the junior German messenger added with a nod towards us. "Some weeks ago, our very own Vice-Admiral Graf Maximilian von Spee, who once commanded a gunboat out of this very port, met the British Navy at sea off the coast of Coronel, Chile and defeated a squadron, destroying two cruisers!" He paused in his recitation to add to his superior, "Sir, the British Navy can be bested!"

"Of course they can be bested." Major Zimmermann glared at the man before him with deep affront. "The refitted *Nachtigal* sank the *Dwarf* just this morning, the *Nachtigal* outgunned by eight times, too, I'll thank you to remember!"

And we did it by stealth, with great barrels full of luck and some eighteen dead of the Chief of Chief Karl Atangana's people, not to mention the two dead and six injured on the *Nachtigal*. But I held my tongue and let Major Zimmermann remind the crowd of listening local fighters and German soldiers of our recent victory.

Hans stood up and clapped his hands loudly. "To the Kaiser! To von Spee! To victory!"

Celebration spilled out into the streets and the aide turned to us. "Please, gentlemen, you must come consult with the governor. He may finally have news of the reinforcements."

"Ah, yes," Atangana and Major Zimmermann agreed, but from the expressions, I suspected they were each hoping for a different kind of reinforcement and directly opposite orders on how those forces were to be used.

The men in the governor's waiting hall—who by now I recognized as overseers and grove managers from cocoa and palm plantations, factors from other farms further off, a few of Atangana's junior chiefs, and the men from the railway—all looked as we entered. They not only made no complaint as we brushed past them, disrupting the governor's morning appointments, but first a few and then all stood and clapped for us as we went by.

I ducked my head, but my lieutenant brandished a wide politician's smile and gave them all a big wave of greeting as we passed. Major Zimmermann's spine straightened into stiff march as if he were on a parade field and his cheeks went pink at the praise. Atangana gave a regal nod and exchanged some words of thanks to those of his chiefs present.

But there was little time before Hans hurried us all into Governor Ebermaier's office and closed everyone else firmly out. The man in charge looked to have aged three years in the weeks since the blockade had begun.

He'd not had significant hair on the top of his head to start, but his beard had more gray in it now than I recalled from our last meeting. The lines around his eyes and shadows under them certainly sank deeper.

Major Zimmermann drew himself up and gave the crispest salute I believe I'd ever seen a man give a superior.

"Thank you, Major," the governor said. "Thank you for your excellent defense of the colony. If you would, please sit, all of you."

Noting three chairs besides the one behind the governor's desk, I helped myself to an unobtrusive spot against the back wall, where Hans joined me. Atangana, Zimmermann, and my lieutenant sat with the governor.

"We've had word finally from Togoland," he said, and the despair in his tone made clear than no good news would be coming. "It fell to the combined British and French assault before our blockade here even began."

"We will take it back!" Major Zimmermann stood and pounded a fist over his chest.

Governor Ebermaier rubbed the bare patch of skin on top of his head. "Perhaps." He turned to my lieutenant. "How long can we keep Doula? There's a second armored cruiser out there now, H.M.S. *Challenger*, and a total of four converted steamers packed with mixed French and British troops and of course Nigerian and Senegalese support: porters and fighters both."

"But no more gunboats, Governor? Or at least not of the *Bramble*-class?" Lieutenant Marshall confirmed.

"Not as yet. The Zaians are fighting the French in North Afrika. The Senussi in Egypt are making threats against the British there, but may not yet fight. The Dervish are making attacks on the British in Somaliland with no sign of stopping." The governor shook his head. "But I thought it'd be foolish to bring the war from Europe to this continent at all, and it's now quite clear General Dobell and his French allies disagree."

"Togoland has fallen," Major Zimmermann repeated dully. "Then why did they not land at Victoria and march their forces to Doula with none of this bother with mines and fighting at sea?"

"The rain," Atangana said quietly. "Rainy season makes that route impassible for another two months. A barefoot hunting party with spears could do it. But the mud would swallow whole any artillery pieces they tried to move."

"Just so," the governor agreed.

He pointed a fat finger and circled it around the three men in front of him. "In 1884 at the Berlin Conference," he said, "all these governors swore to one another that on this continent, we would keep the peace with one another even if war broke out at home.

"But even with our neutral observer, and not just any officer, but the very cousin of the American Vice President here." Governor Ebermaier nodded to Lieutenant Marshall and stood, as though the frustration were too much to stay still. He started to pace.

"Even with an American watching," he repeated, "the British and French governors violated their sworn word. The first opportunity! The very first and the promises they made on behalf of their nations are forgotten! They stole Togoland before news could be sent out, but we have not been silent. For weeks now, the message has gone out. The British and French should be ashamed."

He held up his hands. "So be it: we are also reporting by wireless and by radio the location of two armed but small cruisers staying confined to one small bit of ocean. The British Navy is not invincible. A German admiral has sunk two such vessels quite recently, with the loss of only three German lives.

"They have two months to wait here before their land forces have a chance of breaking through. Perhaps they think they can keep up a blockade for that long. I think Germany has a navy, too."

He smiled at Major Zimmermann. "Give me two more months and I'll approve your transfer to command a fighting unit engaged in this Great War back on the continent. Two more months, less, even! And go with my blessing. I strongly suspect that before that time is up, we shall see some German flagged ships come over the horizon and you can return to Berlin in the company of our own officers."

"And you, Lieutenant." Governor Ebermaier saluted my officer, who shot to his feet to return the courtesy, for once surprised. "When you go tell your cousin in Washington what happened here, you shall do it wearing an Iron Cross."

The governor returned to his chair and sat. "That will be all, gentlemen."

We filed out.

I glanced at Atangana. "He didn't promise you anything."

The chief of chiefs raised an eyebrow in response. "I have a country under the protection of a Kaiser who recently unified his own tribes. A ruler who understands small powers combining to be a large power instead of merely being swallowed up in Englishness or Frenchness or," he shuddered, "having to watch the Belgians do to the Kameruns what has been done in the Congo. I have my chiefs and my chiefs have their people. What more could he give me?"

I looked at him and whispered softly enough that I was absolutely certain no one else at all could hear: "Freedom?"

Atangana winked. "When my Beti people are strong enough. Not yet. And not while we're better in this kingdom than out of it. I do like to honor treaties, you may have heard."

He smiled again, and I went looking for my officer convinced that of all the fine politicians I'd met while sheltering my lieutenant, the toughest and most capable was the quiet black man in the pressed German suit still grinning at my back.

I found Lieutenant Marshall outside the governor's compound, with one hand on the bamboo lighthouse and the harbor with the wreck of the gunboat *Dwarf* over his shoulder. A man with photography apparatus scrambled about to set up the shot while a reporter nodded encouragingly and scribbled as fast as his little pencil could move.

"Of course, you must understand I'm only a war observer here," Lieutenant Marshall was saying, "and as such, my role has been quite limited. As I'm sure you're aware, President Wilson greatly values American lives and would not waste our sons' blood in someone else's fight. Germany has sunk some shipping, it's true. But in these last weeks, I personally saw Britain and France, the supposed allies, break a treaty without diplomatic warning. And the German forces held them off, of course.

"It leaves me to wonder: if the American people were one day to enter this war, would we really want to do it on the side that breaks treaties and includes a nation that once burned our capital?"

ABOUT JOELLE PRESBY

Joelle Presby is a veteran U.S. Navy nuclear engineer who grew up in West Africa. She hunts cross genre writing opportunities and has snared gigs for everything from urban fantasy and high fantasy to alternate history and humorous science fiction. She wrote THE DABARE SNAKE LAUNCHER and co-writes in the Multiverse series with David Weber.

Where you can find Joelle Presby:

LinkTree:
https://linktr.ee/joellepresby

Author Website
Joellepresby.com

BEATTY'S FOLLY

Philip Wohlrab

1

26 August 1915
The North Sea

Vice Admiral David Beatty contemplated the sight before him. From the bridge of HMS *Lion,* he could observe three obsolescent American battleships of the *Virginia* class, their distinctive stacked-turret design giving them away. The three ships were steaming forward of the convoy that Beatty was ordered to intercept. As the distance fell below eight thousand yards, Beatty turned away from watching the American ships.

"Signal the commander of the American fleet to turn around at once," Beatty ordered his Signals officer. "Tell them that this will be their only warning before we open fire."

Flags leapt up the lines to either side of HMS *Lion's* forward mast, giving the warning to the American ships. In reply, a series of flags appeared on the forward mast of USS *Virginia* that, to put it succinctly, told the British, "Go to Hell!"

Beatty snorted a chuckle, reading the answering flags before his Signals officer could report what they said. Turning to his Flag Captain, he said, "Well, at least they are a bunch of spirited fellows. Won't do them much good, though; we might be in range of their guns, but they are poor things compared to ours. You may shoot when ready, Captain."

HMS *Lion, Queen Mary, Princess Royal,* and *Tiger,* open fired with their main batteries of 13.5-inch guns. In answer, the USS *Virginia*, *Georgia*, and *New Jersey* replied with their smaller 12-inch guns. The fight was mismatched from the beginning as the four modern British battlecruisers tore through the smaller obsolete American battleships. After repeated hits, the USS *Virginia* capsized and sank abruptly from an explosion in a coal bunker that blew out her port side. She took the Admiral Sims, who was in charge of Convoy G214, with her. *Virginia* was quickly followed by *New Jersey*, which blew up from a hit to her forward magazines.

The USS *Georgia* started to turn away from the fight, but a torpedo from Beatty's accompanying destroyers blew the ship's bow clean off. Her aft guns still firing, the USS *Georgia* sank bow first, the Stars and Stripes fluttering from her foremast. The remainder of the American escort, two old cruisers and ten destroyers, died swiftly under the weight of the Battlecruiser Squadron's superior firepower.

Vice Admiral David Beatty had just handed the US Navy its worst defeat. British cruisers and destroyers raced ahead of his battlecruisers to complete the scattering convoy's destruction. In all that day, the British took 18 prizes, in addition to destroying the three old American battleships and their escorts.

27 August 1915
The Admiralty, London

"Well, that's done it," said First Sea Lord Jackie Fisher. "The Americans are in the war now, officially. But what is it going to mean for us?"

"Well, sir, the American President, that cowboy Teddy Roosevelt, has been in office a long time. He has been a staunch proponent of their naval power, and a firm disciple of the teachings of their theorist Mahan," replied the Deputy Chief of Naval Operations David Keiths.

"Their fleet is respectable, but still a third-rate fleet. I mean, look at the terrible gunnery that was shown by the American escorts," replied Fisher. "Why, they only managed a few hits on *Princess Royal* and *Lion*."

"Yes, sir, but what about the reports of the construction in their yards?" Keiths pressed. "If it is to be believed, they have some very large ships under construction. In light of that, my Lord, I think we need to reactivate the Third Fleet, and bring most of our pre-dreadnought battleships home from the Med."

"I think you may be right, but we cannot split up the Grand Fleet, not with the High Seas Fleet looking for any chance to break out."

"What are we to do about American shipping that wasn't part of their last convoy?" asked the DCSNO.

"Snap it up, of course," Fisher replied. "It isn't like we can anger the Americans any more than we already have. Issue an order service-wide to begin operations against American merchantmen and warships where found."

"Understood, sir. Also..." said Keiths in a worried tone.

"Also what?" snapped Fisher.

"Well, sir, I and the lads in planning are worried about the US naval construction. As I said a few moments ago, they have several bloody great awful brutes under construction," replied Keiths. "Intelligence states that one may have 18-inch guns."

Fisher snorted, but did not interrupt as the DCSNO continued.

"I don't know that that particular monster will be ready anytime soon, but several of their new dreadnoughts mount 15- and 16-inch guns. I don't believe their fire control is up to our standards, but they are going to outrange pretty much everything we have except the *Queen Elizabeth* class."

"I don't believe they can get those 18-inch guns working, at least not anytime soon," replied Fisher in a somewhat animated voice. "As to the rest, think how much trouble we had with the 15-inch guns in development before we got it right. I don't think that will be any easier for the Americans trying to get *two* different gun types into service."

Fisher sat back in his chair after making his point. Still, privately he was extremely worried about US naval construction.

The Americans, while not up to Royal Navy standards, have a lot more yard space then we do, he thought.

Fisher absently scratched his nose as he regarded the framed painting of HMS *Royal Sovereign* hanging on the wall. Battlecruisers had been one of his many ideas to modernize the Royal Navy, and he was quite proud of his new ships.

But will they be a match against the Americans? he mused.

31 AUGUST 1915
THE CAPITOL BUILDING
WASHINGTON D.C.

"Remember the *Virginia*! Remember the *New Jersey*! Remember the *Georgia*! Remember all of our slain sailors," roared President Theodore Roosevelt from the Speaker's Rostrum before a joint session of Congress.

With each cry for remembrance, Roosevelt banged his fist down on the Rostrum, to the thunderous applause of the Congress. These men were furious. Like a previous Congress before them that had had to deal with foreign interference in American policy, they were ready to repay the British for their hostility.

But not just the British, no. Teddy Roosevelt had come to them with a declaration of war against Britain, France, and Russia. France was particularly hated by America for its interference in the US Civil War, interference which had dragged out that internal conflict to 1867. Congress roared its approval; the US was now at war.

President Roosevelt, however, wasn't done with Congress just yet. Newspapers had run with lurid accounts of the short battle, to include fanciful prints of USS *Georgia* going down still fighting, since news had first reached the United States. Teddy Roosevelt was going to use that to his advantage.

Project S-584 had started construction, despite much hemming and hawing by both Congress and the US Navy. It was planned that the super-dreadnought battleship would be the largest in the world, once completed. The target date for completion, however, had continuously slipped as Congress took every opportunity to slow construction on the behemoth. With a fully aroused public at his back, Roosevelt intended to fix *that* particular issue immediately.

"Further, I move that in response to this treachery by Great Britain and France, that Senator Tillman's project S-584 battleship be completed with all due haste and the ship named for the heroic USS *Georgia*! Let her be the spearpoint with which we use to thrust into the treacherous British, and once and for all end their mastery of the sea!"

Congress roared its approval for a second time. Roosevelt had his war, and his battleship.

Retribution may take time, but it will *be certain*, Roosevelt thought grimly. *But first, to Canada.*

2

This isn't a fight, this is a goddamn massacre, thought Lieutenant Commander Fitz Walker. His cool grey eyes watched as the 15-inch shells from the guns of USS *Nevada* straddled the British pre-dreadnought battleship HMS *Mars*. The *Mars* couldn't range on *Nevada* yet, and like the other ships in the British Third Fleet, it was struggling to come to grips with the US Atlantic Fleet. All for naught.

On Walker's fourth salvo, he saw what he was looking for: solid hits to the hull of HMS *Mars*. Gouts of flame and debris marked where three shells from *Nevada's* broadside of ten 15-inch guns had found their mark. Walker ordered a few adjustments to his guns and then...

"Fire for effect!"

On salvos five, six, and seven, taking just five minutes to fire, HMS *Mars* took several more hits. One of the shells plunged through nonexistent topside armor on *Mars* and found the powder magazine under her forward turret. The turret exploded upward with tremendous force, and fire raced the length of HMS *Mars*. No one had time to escape the burning inferno that erupted out of the stricken battleship.

Lt. Commander Walker stepped away from his rangefinder, a grim, satisfied smile playing across his lips for just a minute.

It would have been far better if that were a French warship, what with what they did to America during the US Civil War, but these British bastards will have to do for now, he thought.

Aloud, he said, "A small repayment to the King, gentlemen!"

"Aye, sir, it surely is," answered Chief Petty Officer Harper. The big, burly man's voice still held some of the brogue of his native Ireland. "I had a friend on the old *Georgia*. I hope the Everlasting allows them to see what we are doing here today."

At the mention of the old *Georgia*, Walker glanced over to the new USS *Georgia*, smoke wreathing her from the firing of her great guns. He lifted his fine Zeiss binoculars to his face and peered out in the direction of where USS *Georgia* was firing. Finding his target, he focused the binoculars until the features of what looked like either HMS *Lord Nelson* or HMS *Agamemnon* resolved into some clarity. The ship's upper works were afire from multiple hits from *Georgia*, and one of her masts had collapsed. He could also see that the enemy ship's guns were out of action.

Walker swept the sea to starboard, and all he could see were burning British ships or those settling deeper into the water. The American fleet managed to pin the old and tired vessels of the British Third Fleet up against the coastline of southern Ireland and were now turning them into so much scrap iron and dead men.

"A mess of sailors are drowning or burning today, sir," Chief Harper remarked. The man didn't have the fine binoculars that Walker had, but he cast his gaze to starboard using an old-fashioned telescope to watch the dying British ships. Both men followed the American destroyers steaming past the *Nevada* at high speed. These smaller vessels raced in to make torpedo attacks, delivering the *coup de grace* to the crippled and burning British ships.

Behind USS *Nevada*, 4,000 yards to stern, the USS *Arizona* let loose another broadside, but this time not at enemy warships. The *Arizona*'s guns were targeting suspected British positions on Curracloe Beach, just outside of Wexford, Ireland. It was here that the US commanders had decided to put ashore Lieutenant General George Windle Read's IVth Corps as the spearhead of the invasion of the British Isles. Already, troops from the 29th Infantry Division were boarding boats to begin the assault.

Walker didn't see those boats yet, but he didn't need to see them for this next part. He worked his figures in a notebook, and using his distance finder, he calculated at what angle the guns needed to be to strike shore positions. Orders hadn't been telegraphed from the bridge yet, but he wanted to be prepared for when they were. No one expected the British fleet to be so soundly beaten, so no thought had been given to the entire battleline being used for shore bombardment beforehand. Walker's calculations were rewarded when orders were passed up to his position from the bridge, tasking him with attacking shore positions.

"God bless Teddy's insistence on bigger guns for our warships," Walker said aloud in an almost prayerful tone.

"Aye, aye, Sir," replied Chief Petty Officer Harper.

As the two men were talking, the battleships *South Carolina*, *Delaware*, and *Florida* maneuvered closer in to shore so that their smaller 12-inch guns could join the bombardment. Though Walker and Harper couldn't see it, the men of the British Territorials, 2nd Northumbrian, and 52nd Lowland Division, as well as the Royal Irish Fusiliers, hunkered down into their trenches. Despite the impressive explosions and amount of dirt tossed in the air, the well-constructed fortifications were serving to keep the casualties among the British troops relatively low.

Walker's ears perked up as he heard the distant booms of field guns coming from the Irish shoreline. He was amazed that the sound carried all the way out to him.

Must be an offshore wind, he thought, stepping over to the *Nevada*'s rangefinder. Scanning the shore, Walker could see that one of the firing batteries was within range of his guns.

"Report enemy field guns are within range of our main battery and request permission for us to open fire," he instructed his talker.

"Aye, aye, sir," the talker replied. The young man passed on Walker's request, and then after listening for a minute, he turned to Walker and said, "Sir, permission is granted."

Walker made the calculations necessary for firing and passed them on to the gun directors and fire control stations. Two minutes later, the main gun turrets swung out to train on the distant shore. The *Nevada* class's unique main battery setup had her No. 1 and No. 4 turrets being triple-mounts while her No. 2 and No. 3 wielded two guns in a super firing arrangement. This gave Walker ten of the new 15-inch naval guns with which to target the enemy battery.

Confirming the range and azimuth, he pressed the button to fire the battleship's full broadside. The *Nevada* seemed to leap sideways as the first shells fired. Watching through his powerful rangefinding scope, Walker watched as gouts of earth and flame erupted 800 yards behind the enemy field guns.

Dammit.

In answer to this massive salvo impacting behind them, the British guns went to rapid fire at whatever their target was rather than displacing.

Brave bastards, Walker thought. *They must know they don't have much time left.* The second broadside fell roughly four hundred meters short, and Walker saw guns, horses, and men cut down by fragments. The *Nevada's* third salvo finally hit something important, as a great gout of flame and smoke erupted immediately behind the breastworks housing the guns. The explosion touched off others, and the British guns from this position fell silent. Through his rangefinder, Walker watched as other British gun positions were silenced by fire either from the American battleships, or the cruisers which had moved in close to shore to provide close fire support for American troops landing on the beach.

"God Save Ireland," intoned Chief Harper, "and see the British in Hell!"

18 May 1917
Admiralty House, London

The door to Admiral Jackie Fisher's office flew open, the doorknob splintering the wall paneling behind it. Fisher looked up at the disturbance in time to see the red, florid features of Field Marshal Lord Herbert Kitchener as he strode through the door, a protesting yeoman calling desperately after him.

"WHAT IN THE BLOODY HELL DO WE HAVE A NAVY FOR IF ALL IT'S GOING TO DO IS SIT IN SCAPA FLOW?" roared Kitchener as he stalked menacingly toward Fisher's desk.

"That will be all, Terrence," said Fisher in a mild tone to the yeoman who had come through the door behind Lord Kitchener. The yeoman nodded, his face skeptical at leaving Fisher alone with the furious Kitchener. Fisher pointedly waited until the door fully latched.

"Now, my Lord, if you wouldn't mind having a seat, we can discuss this like civilized men."

For his part, Field Marshal Kitchener wasn't about to be mollified just yet. The news of Third Fleet's defeat had been one thing, but news that Ireland had risen in fresh rebellion was straining him. Adding to this strain was the fresh news that Russia, now under Alexander Kerensky's provisional government rather than the Tsar, was vacillating on whether to continue the war.

"Look here, Fisher: we have got to stop the Americans cold, and right now they control the Irish Sea. What is the Navy going to do about that?" asked Kitchener, still standing over Fisher's desk without having taken a seat.

Jackie Fisher lost his patience then. "By God, man, sit down! I am the First Sea Lord—I will not be shouted at like I were some Midshipman!"

Kitchener harrumphed, but he took his seat.

"Now then, you ask what the Navy is going to do about this," Fisher began, his tone sharp. "Well, what would you have us do more? My fleet is stretched trying to protect the lifeblood of the Empire, protecting our convoys from India, our African Colonies, and South America. Fortunately, it appears that the Americans have relegated their older ships to the Pacific, which means we can get supplies from Australia and New Zealand, but the Japanese have announced that they will not make war against the Americans, and they are apparently in talks to give Formosa back to Germany! It appears they think we are going to lose this war, and with what is going on in France, it certainly makes it appear that way."

Kitchener sat back in his chair as Fisher grew more animated in his explanation. He knew Fisher was right, that the war was going very badly. The loss of Canadian forces in 1916 had hurt and had caused the British Army to effectively cease fighting in the Middle East, as those forces were shifted to the Western Front. The American Army had attacked across Lake Ontario and across Lake Erie, and so far, the only thing that seemed to be holding them at bay had been lack of enough troops to complete their conquest of Canada. Ontario, Winnipeg, and Montreal had fallen, while there was fierce fighting around Vancouver.

"Now, what I could do is send the Grand Fleet after the Americans. God knows we outnumber them in ships almost two to one, while in smaller ships, even more so. But, and this is a very large but, the High Seas Fleet will sail while we are trying to deal with the Americans and I don't know a good way to prevent the Fleet from being caught between two forces that would have an advantage over us in heavy ships if we did so. Worse, with Italy switching sides again, that means the Kaiser could land a couple of his free divisions in the North. Then where would we be?" Fisher rose from his own seat, and as he planted his first firmly on his desktop, he fixed Lord Kitchener with a basilisk gaze. Then a thoughtful expression crossed his face. Sitting back down, he looked back over to Kitchener.

"I apologize. We are both under a great deal of pressure, and I shouldn't have taken it out on you. I think I have an idea that might be worth pursuing."

"Oh, pray tell," Kitchener replied.

"I think we may detach Vice Admiral Beatty's battlecruisers and some of our armoured cruisers. Use their speed to get in among the Americans and disrupt their operations in the Irish Sea. That way, Jellicoe can keep the High Seas Fleet bottled up with a show of force while Beatty deals with the Americans."

21 MAY 1917
IRISH SEA

Captain Robert Ledford, commanding officer of the USS *Nevada*, sat at the head of a long table, around which he had gathered his senior officers. Ledford was a stocky, barrel-chested man with prematurely white hair. Walker had served under Ledford before when he had been a Midshipman on his summer cruise aboard the old battleship USS *Ohio*. Ledford was then the *Ohio's* Gunnery Officer and he had impressed upon Walker the importance of delivering accurate fire. But that was ten years ago, and now Lieutenant Commander Walker served Captain Robert Ledford as *Nevada's* Gunnery Officer.

"Gentlemen, it is now time to reveal to you a secret that has been closely held by the Office of Naval Intelligence for just this time. We have broken the British Naval Code and have been reading their messages for a year now."

A murmur shot around the table at this news, with the various officers looking at each other in some excitement. Ledford continued once everyone quieted down.

"We and German Naval Intelligence have ensured that nothing we have done will alert the British to that feather in our cap. In fact, we and the Germans have known now for about a year that Britain was reading Germany's messages, and it is because of that that the High Seas Fleet has had a couple of major operations blown. The Germans have continued to allow the British to read their messages, to lull them into thinking they have the upper hand."

"So why are they telling us now?" inquired the ship's executive officer.

"The Grand Fleet is splitting up," replied Ledford simply.

The table erupted into buzzing excitement.

"All right, gentlemen, all right, quiet down. I know we are all excited about this prospect. As such, Admiral Knight has devised a trap for the British. They are detaching nine of their battlecruisers and several lighter ships to attack us here in the Irish Sea. In the meantime, the rest of the Grand Fleet plans to sortie to impress upon the Germans that they are in fact still blockaded in Wilhelmshaven."

"Sir, what will be our part of the plan?" piped up Walker, the excitement in his voice clear to the rest of the men around the table.

"I am glad you asked, Mr. Walker. What we are going to do is present the British with what appears to be a juicy target. The battle-scouts *Lexington* and *Concord* are going to range to the north of the squadron, along with a screen of scout cruisers and destroyers. We suspect that the battlecruisers *Courageous* and *Glorious* will be their lead ships, as both are extremely fast. It is our intention that *Lexington* and *Concord* will exchange a few shots, and then using their superior speed, lead the enemy squadrons into a trap consisting of the battleship line, headed by *Georgia*, and then us. We plan to smash as many of their ships as possible, and then we will proceed up the west coast of Scotland, round Scotland, and then try to cut off the rest of the Grand Fleet from returning to Scapa Flow, while the High Seas Fleet comes out to meet them in the North Sea."

The sheer scale of the plan is audacious, thought Walker, *but can we pull it off?*

3

21 May 1917
Rosyth, Scotland

Vice Admiral David Beatty knew trouble was brewing when his adjutant informed him that Sir John Jellicoe, Admiral, Commander-in-Chief Grand Fleet, was coming aboard. Jellicoe had rarely come down to Rosyth from the Grand Fleet's base at Scapa Flow. His doing so now indicated the senior officer had something of great importance he wished to impart to Beatty and didn't trust to communicate via telegraph.

Beatty impatiently took a stroll about the bridge of HMS *Lion* as he awaited the arrival of Jellicoe, vainly trying to contain his excitement at finally being let loose to hunt the Americans. As if summoned by his thoughts, Admiral Jellicoe appeared on the battlecruiser's bridge with his aide...and ominously, with no staff.

"Ah, there you are, Beatty. Say, will you come down on deck with me? I wish to go over some things before you depart."

"Certainly, Sir John," Beatty replied cautiously, gesturing for the Grand Fleet's commander to lead the way. The two men descended the ladder from the bridge and proceeded past the forward gun turrets. Jellicoe led Beatty to a quiet section of the deck and away from listening ears; what he wanted to say was for Beatty's ears alone.

"Look here, I know they have detached you to hunt the Americans, but I don't like it. I have protested the loss of all my battlecruisers to the First Sea Lord, but Fisher has told me to buck up and do my duty. I want to stress on you, David, that we cannot lose your force. Do not become decisively engaged without having a way out. Your ships are fast, your crews well-trained, but let us face facts here: they are sending you against a superior force." Jellicoe's worry was plain on his face.

"Understood, sir, but we have got to break up the American force before they stage further landings. Bad enough that they have landed troops in Ireland, and those rebels sure did rise up awfully fast," replied Beatty, who for the moment was taking everything in stride. Jellicoe's eyes narrowed, but Beatty pressed on.

"The other thing to consider is that with the Irish in full rebellion, Kitchener is worried that the Americans will dash across the Irish Sea and land on the Welsh coast. Our submarines have proved completely ineffective in doing the Americans any real harm, as have our torpedo boats."

Jellicoe grunted at that. He, too, was disappointed at how poorly British submarines had performed. Worse for the Royal Navy, a few German torpedo boats had managed to stage daring raids on the ports located at the mouth of the Thames, and Portsmouth itself.

"Yes, well as I have said, do not allow yourself to be decisively engaged by the Americans. Get in, get your licks in, and get out. I have also decided to send the *Queen Elizabeths* with you."

Mention of that perked Beatty up; his battlecruisers had frequently worked with the super-dreadnoughts of the *Queen Elizabeth* class. "This will stiffen your line and give you some oomph if you need to break away. Also, given the number of large ships, I am hoping that the Americans will decide that they cannot risk losing too many of their ships and turn for home. That is the best case."

"Yes, sir," replied Beatty.

With 15 capital ships to the American's 16, that should certainly give an American commander pause, Beatty mused. *Especially as they know our ships are better.*

"I will be getting underway once the tide favors us, sir, and I will rendezvous with your battleships off Scapa Flow. Has intelligence given us any idea of what the Germans are doing?"

"Apparently, they are sitting still," Jellicoe replied. "Intelligence hasn't picked up on any new signals other than routine traffic to their fleet."

"Well, sir, if that is the case, I think we can be out and back before the

Huns are any the wiser," quipped back Beatty, a boyish grin lighting his face.

26 May 1917, 0900 Hours
North of the Isle of Man, Irish Sea

Lt. Commander Fitz Walker paced his gunnery platform, trying hard to hide his anxiety. The sound of heavy guns sounded in the distance, carrying over the *Nevada*'s normal noises. Even with the auditory reports, the Royal Navy's battleline still wasn't in sight. From the signals being passed back by *Lexington* and *Concord*, they had managed to score a few hits on the enemy before reversing out of range. The two battle-scouts, unique American designs that were as fast as a light cruiser, but carried large guns like a battleship, would pass to the west of the Isle of Man and then into the Manx Sea, an area that was just 37 miles across.

It's going to be an unpleasant surprise when they pass the Isle of Man, Walker mused while baring his teeth. The American battleship line sat just eight miles off the Point of Ayre on the northernmost tip of the Isle of Man, just over thirty miles away from the British fleet's last sighted position. The trap was set and, as Admiral Knight had predicted, Vice Admiral David Beatty was falling into it. Admiral Knight's battleships were going to cross behind Beatty's battlecruisers and pin them between Ireland and the Isle of Man. At the southernmost portion of the Manx Sea, most of the American destroyers and cruisers lay in wait, planning to make torpedo runs once the British battlecruisers tried to escape the trap.

"I can't believe they are doing it, sir. I mean, where the hell are their screens?" asked Chief Gunners Mate Harper. His expression showed true puzzlement.

Like Walker, Harper was raised in a service that viewed the Royal Navy as the gold standard of naval services. Yet, here the Royal Navy was committing to something monumentally stupid.

"Well, Chief Harper, all I can think is this is like the matador and the bull," Walker stated. "Admiral Knight presented Beatty with what he wants to see, and just like the bull charging the cape, Beatty has taken off after the decoy. Still, it isn't one-sided," stated Walker matter-of-factly.

"No, sir, I guess not. Those poor bastards on the *St. Louis*... Those ships don't have much use in this fight."

"You're right, Chief—too old and too slow for this fight, but we needed them to make the British think they were after our scout force."

As the two men conversed in their fighting position, they could feel the sway as the USS *Nevada* picked up speed. She accelerated from a stately five knots to 18 knots, and black smoke poured from her single stack behind her forward superstructure. Ahead of her, the USS *Georgia* did the same, and behind her, the USS *Arizona* and the rest of the battleline increased their speed. Peering to starboard, Walker and Harper could just make out four American battleships moving to plug the North Channel that connected the Irish Sea to the Atlantic. These were the battleships *South Carolina, Michigan, Delaware,* and *North Dakota.* Being the oldest of the dreadnought battleships in Admiral Knight's force, it was decided that they were too slow for the chase of Beatty's battlecruisers and would instead serve as a third blocking force to prevent any from escaping back to the North Atlantic. With them steamed twelve destroyers of the *O'Brien* and *Sampson* classes.

HMS LION
1100 HOURS

Admiral Beatty was in his element.

He stepped out onto the bridge wing to feel the air rushing past his face as HMS *Lion* poured on speed at 28 knots. It was a glorious midmorning with not a cloud in the sky. His mood was only slightly dampened due to the damage that had been done to HMS *Courageous.* The enemy ships had knocked several holes in her thin armor, and she had been forced to reduce speed. Still, Beatty's battlecruisers were pursuing what must be American battle-scouts, given their speed.

Too bad for them their cruisers were not as swift, Beatty thought with a predatory smile. His squadron had drawn first blood that morning, killing a lagging American armoured cruiser. Speed, speed was of the essence, and that is why Beatty had made the decision to leave the *Queen Elizabeth*-class dreadnoughts behind when he spotted these American ships. He had to get them to grips before they could give accurate details of his force.

HMS *Lion* was the third ship back in the line, *Glorious* led the squadron, followed by *Renown,* then *Lion,* and finally the newer *Repulse.* The old battlecruisers *Inflexible* and *Invincible* lagged behind their newer sisters by roughly 3,000 yards, their weary engines gradually losing ground.

Even so, as Beatty watched as his guns fired another salvo at the enemy battle-scouts, the British admiral was confident the older vessels would close up once his force had crippled the two Americans. He didn't think they would really hit, given the speeds and maneuvering that the ships were doing, but rapid course changes were causing the distance to close with the American ships. If he could just get them to 10,000 yards, as doctrine demanded…

"Sir, signal from *Inflexible*! She is under attack!"

"What? "asked Admiral Beatty in astonishment.

The signals officer glanced down at his message form, and then back up at the Vice Admiral. "Sir, *Inflexible* says she is under attack from a strong force of battleships."

Beatty stepped out onto the bridge wing, ready to furiously inquire as to what his staff was talking about, and then he looked for himself. He raised his binoculars just in time to see a forest of shell splashes surround *Inflexible*, their height telling him that the battlecruiser's captain was quite accurate in his report.

"Damn," muttered Beatty, feeling a momentary stab of panic before he regained his composure and sought to save his force.

"Make signal: all ships to fall back on HMS *Inflexible*. Also raise the *Queen Elizabeth* and have Rear Admiral Evan-Thomas get his ships up here as fast as possible. Perhaps we can catch the Americans between us and destroy them."

Beatty was putting on a good face, and everyone on the bridge of HMS *Lion* knew it. Since the Battle of Trafalgar, the axiom that "No captain can do very wrong if he places his ship alongside that of the enemy" had held sway. Turning to engage American battleships with his battlecruisers was a very dangerous proposition.

And can anyone blame us after the Troubridge affair? Beatty thought as he looked at the plot. *Churchill's instructions regarding the court-martial sent a clear message: you will engage the enemy or else.*

As HMS *Lion* completed her nearly 180-degree turn, two things seemed to happen simultaneously. First, HMS *Glorious* staggered in the water from multiple hits. Her aftermost 15-inch gun turret exploded, rendering half her guns out of action. The resultant spall and flooding below the waterline also rendered the battlecruiser a near-cripple, her speed dropping below ten knots.

The second event arrived in the form of a wireless message from HMS *Invincible*. An ashen-faced rating burst onto the bridge and hurried over to the signals officer. That man read the message form and Beatty watched as all the blood drained from the officer's face. Turning to Beatty, the man's mouth worked briefly.

"Out with it!" Beatty snapped.

"Sir, message from *Invincible*: the *Inflexible* has blown up!" the man exclaimed in a disbelieving tone.

Beatty rushed out to the bridge wing and trained his binoculars back to the horizon. What he saw almost made him vomit, as he could just make out the flaming wreckage that was *Inflexible* sinking beneath the sea. Of the Americans, all he could see was dark smudges against the distant horizon, smoke from their engines, and their guns. Splashes were soon being thrown up around HMS *Lion*, and Beatty looked to the stern of the ship to see that the American battle-scouts had turned back and were even now directing fire at his ship and HMS *Glorious*.

They've certainly found their backbone, Beatty thought bitterly. *We'll see how long that lasts when Evan-Thomas gets here.*

Beatty felt anger as he watched the *Glorious* fall further behind. The battlecruiser staggered once again as an American shell found its mark. Her stern was aflame from her aft turret back, and this shell impacted just behind her funnel. A great gout of flame followed by plumes of black smoke showed where the shell had exploded in *Glorious's* engine room. Her speed dropped to nothing, at that point.

"Bloody hell," Beatty swore helplessly. There was nothing to be done for *Glorious* now; Captain Farthing would have to fight with his ship as he saw fit. Beatty could see that more columns of smoke were beginning to show in his rear.

"Damn, what is back there?" he asked aloud.

1130 HOURS

Lt. Commander Fitz Walker peered through his ranging scopes at HMS *Invincible*, the *Nevada's* first target in this battle. USS *Georgia* had engaged HMS *Inflexible*. Much to everyone's surprise, on *Georgia's* seventh salvo from her forward guns, the *Inflexible* had blown up.

Georgia *must have gotten that British battlecruiser's magazines*, Walker thought. *My God, those guns are ship-killers.*

Walker directed his guns to fire a ladder to bracket the enemy warship. What this meant was that each gun turret fired at a point that spaced out every 400 yards, the idea being that one should hit close enough, or on target, to give him the data he needed to hit his targets. As the British closed the range, the *Nevada* turned to present her full broadside to the oncoming British warships. Although this made the battleship a larger target for the British guns, it also allowed Walker the use of his full main broadside and secondaries. The range between the lead British ships and his ship had fallen to 13,000 yards.

Looking up from his rangefinder, Walker could see a blizzard of British shells fall around USS *Georgia*. The lack of explosions told him that the shells failed to penetrate, but had likely splintered on impact.

Probably quite lively on deck, but that beats having something explode in the innards, he thought. *Just ask that Brit crew.* Walker was just glad it appeared that the British were concentrating their fire on *Georgia*. It was a poor tactical decision, as it gave every other USN battleship a chance to fire freely. Behind the *Nevada,* the USS *Arizona* and USS *Pennsylvania* were next in line. They swung out their dozen apiece 16-inch guns and hammered away at HMS *Tiger* and HMS *Queen Mary*.

"Damn, sir, what a sight from up here," opined Harper, his voice betraying his awe. Harper held a portable rangefinder to his face, the smaller device used in case something was to happen to the main rangefinder that Walker currently peered through.

The rangefinders, both fixed and handheld, were odd-looking pieces of equipment. They looked like periscopes laid on their side, with two peering scopes at either end joined to a set of viewing scopes in the center. The stereoscopic view was supposed to help spotters with both the fall of the shot and getting an initial fix on the range. The *Nevada's* various rangefinders, like all US battleships currently in service, were the same Zeiss optics found aboard German warships. These, like the Krupp homogeneous armor, were fruits of the close relationship developed between the US and Germany since the Prussians had helped a war-weary America kick France out of Mexico in 1872.

The cage mast swayed again, and again, each time a volley issued forth from the main guns. But now Walker had the range on *Invincible* and he was moving all his guns to rapid fire. The 5-inch secondaries cracked at a rate below their maximum, Walker having told the gun chiefs to expect a long fight and to conserve ammunition in case the British light forces managed to join the battle. The main turrets, on the other hand, were ripping out a teeth-jarring broadside every two minutes.

It must be hell down there on the guns, Walker thought. A fighting turret was a din of noise in a cauldron choked with dust. Many of the men would suffer permanent hearing damage this day.

Still, as he looked through the spotting scope, he knew things could be far worse. The secondaries scored hit after hit on the *Invincible*, tearing up her upper works. For a moment, he considered what it must be like on the battlecruiser's bridge. No sooner had he finished the thought when he observed a large shell entering into the structure. The ship lost control and staggered out of line for a few long seconds, then started to correct as the auxiliary helm took over.

Well, it looks like we just made a whole bunch of work for the Admiralty, Walker thought.

"Sir, we have trouble coming up," pointed out Harper.

"Which ship do you make her out to be, Chief?"

"Looks like it's either *Indefatigable* or *New Zealand*. She seems to be coming right for us."

"Well, until we deal with *Invincible*, she is the *New Mexico's* problem."

"Aye, sir," replied Harper.

Sure enough, as the two men discussed the new threat, shells from *New Mexico* and *Idaho* splashed around the hull of the sleek-looking British ship. Meanwhile, the *Georgia* had switched targets and was now joining the assault on *Invincible*. The bigger 16-inch shells plunged right through *Invincible's* armor as if it weren't even there. Walker was mildly irritated that *Georgia* was getting in on his kill, but even as he thought this, his irritation vanished. *Invincible* seemed to just come apart when two of *Nevada's* 15-inch shells penetrated her A turret barbette.

Walker watched as the *Invincible's* A turret rocketed into the air on a geyser of smoke and flame, as if it were made of wood and not steel. What followed was the forward tripod mast violently lurching backwards, then shearing off as the explosion spread, lifting the forward superstructure into the air. What had been HMS *Invincible* snapped into two just forward of her second funnel, then turned turtle and sank rapidly.

Walker and Harper were stunned silent for a moment. They had seen the destruction of *Inflexible*, but that ship's death had been mostly obscured by thick smoke clouds. On the other hand, *Invincible* and the poor souls that made up her crew died fully in their sight. The men both simultaneously exhaled, neither realizing that they were holding their breath throughout the vessel's annihilation. Once the shock passed, the men of the fighting top searched for their next target.

To their surprise, HMS *New Zealand*, they could now tell it was her based on slight differences between her and her sister ship HMS *Indefatigable*, had turned away from the US battleline. Walker laid his rangefinder on the ship and looked through it to see that *New Zealand* seemed to have serious damage to her stern.

New Mexico must have jammed her rudders, he thought. *Won't be long for her now.*

1500 HOURS

Vice Admiral David Beatty knew he had screwed up by the numbers. He felt like falling to his knees and praying for divine mercy and raging against the Almighty at the same time, but he could only blame himself for his predicament. His force was being hammered from two sides. Worse, he could now make out American destroyers, their small, sleek silhouettes knifing toward the remainder of his ships like sharks on a bleeding carcass.

Glorious was out of action. To his dismay, the battlecruiser had surrendered when American cruisers had come upon her in the wake of the American battle-scouts. *Invincible*, *Inflexible*, and now *Indefatigable* had exploded under American shell fire. *New Zealand* was out of control after her steering gear had been wrecked by the only hit she had received so far. Remarkably, no one had been killed aboard her when it happened. HMS *Courageous* rolled over on her side, her crew abandoning her; repeated hits had caused her to lay over. In all, six of his thirteen battlecruisers were either sunk or out of action, and he was trapped between two American forces that were both well within range of him.

Beatty was tossed forward into the front bulkhead of the *Lion's* bridge when the ship was tossed about by another large shell hit. The stink of ozone and cordite filled the bridge and had been there since the beginning of the engagement. Now a new smell added itself: that of burning metals, woods, and rubber.

The admiral pulled himself upright and walked out onto the port bridge wing to look over the ship. To his horror, the X turret aft burned furiously, the aft funnel had been shot away, and the aft mast had fallen across his amidships Q turret. Beatty observed sailors working furiously with torches to cut away the damaged mast so that they could get the Q turret back in action. Hoses had also been rigged to fight the numerous fires on deck, though no one was going near the burning X turret. That it hadn't destroyed the ship when it blew up was a miracle in itself.

"Flood the magazines to the Q turret—fires are out of control below decks, and I don't want to lose the ship," ordered a far too calm Captain Wright. His steady voice and controlled demeanor worked to calm other members of the bridge crew on HMS *Lion*. "Give the men time to get out of there and then flood them."

Captain Wright stepped out onto the bridge wing with Vice Admiral Beatty, surveyed the damage, and then brought his binoculars up to glass the distant shoreline for the Isle of Man.

"Sir, two of my main turrets are out, the engine room is a shambles and I have had to reduce our speed to seven knots. Fires are out of control below decks and on our stern. I am going to deliberately beach *Lion* so that she doesn't sink."

"Do what you must, Captain Wright," Beatty stated. Then he quipped, "There appears to be a problem with our ships: they keep blowing up."

As if to punctuate that statement, a series of shells impacted HMS *Lion* in her A turret, originating from the USS *Texas*. The 14-inch armor-piercing shells impacted at an angle just at the base of the A turret, then slanted their way into the barbette and exploded inside the handling room. The blast and hot fragments touched off the stacked bags of cordite that were on their way up into the main turret to be fired in the coming salvoes. British warships had flash-proof hatches in place to prevent an explosion in the handling room from flashing into the magazine, but one of the practices put in place in the battlecruiser fleet by Vice Admiral David Beatty was to jam those doors open to allow for faster passage of powder and shells to the guns.

This came back to bite HMS *Lion*, as the explosions in the handling room flashed back through the turret in a roiling, sailor-immolating conflagration. The fire licked down into the ship's forward 13.5-inch gun magazine, and thermodynamics far outraced mortal attempts to flood the structure. Vice Admiral David Beatty, Captain Jonathan Wright, and the 1,100 men of HMS *Lion* died violently when the flagship became the last battlecruiser to blow up in the Battle of the Irish Sea.

1745 HOURS

The fight wasn't entirely one-sided. USS *Arkansas* was forced to beach herself on the Isle of Man when several hits and near-misses opened great rents in her hull. Despite counterflooding to try to offset the damage, progressive flooding threatened the vessel's engine and fire rooms, so her captain decided to beach her while he still had power. The American battleship came to rest not far from where HMS *New Zealand* had, and the latter's crew decided to strike her colors rather than be hammered to death at close range.

The worst losses for the US Navy, however, were the destruction of USS *South Carolina* and USS *Delaware* at the hands of HMS *Barham*, *Warspite*, and *Valiant*. These three modern *Queen Elizabeth*-class dreadnoughts were the lead ships of the second British force coming south through the North Channel that separated the Irish Sea from the Atlantic. Even though they had been bottled up in the channel, their modern 15-inch guns made a hash of *South Carolina* and *Delaware*. The two American battleships made for the Irish coast, intent on beaching themselves, but sank in relatively shallow water, their cage masts and upper works sticking up from the Irish Sea like grave markers.

But the British Dreadnoughts didn't get off unscathed. HMS *Barham* took three torpedoes from US destroyers, and she turned over on her side. British sailors scrambled up onto her side out of the water when some internal fire found a magazine. HMS *Barham* blew up, taking many of her crew with her. HMS *Warspite* took two torpedoes forward, and taking on water, managed to wreck herself on the Scottish coast, just 6 miles from where she had been torpedoed. HMS *Valiant* managed to turn herself around and, joining the rest of the British dreadnought force, she entered the Firth of Clyde to make for Scapa Flow.

Conspicuously absent from Rosyth was the remainder of the British battlecruisers, trapped with no hope of escape under the USN's heavy guns. They had been caught with no hope of escape. With HMS *Lion*'s destruction, command fell to the battlecruiser HMS *Tiger*'s captain. Realizing the doomed situation, the officer tearfully ordered the remaining ships to deliberately beach themselves on the Isle of Man. He hoped that by doing this, they could later be recovered once the Americans were seen off by Admiral Jellicoe and the rest of the Grand Fleet. Unfortunately for him and the crews of these ships, American Marines were put ashore on the Isle of Man. There, they proceeded to capture the British ships, the crews of which, realizing the futility of the situation, surrendered without firing another shot.

Lt. Commander Walker considered all of this from the comfort of an easy chair in the officers' wardroom aboard USS *Nevada*. That ship, along with the battleships *Georgia, New Mexico, Idaho, Mississippi, Pennsylvania, Wyoming, New York, Texas,* and *Oklahoma*, were even now steaming into the North Sea. With them were the battle-scouts *Lexington,* and *Concord,* and twenty-two destroyers. Admiral Knight had made the decision to leave three battleships and the rest of the cruisers and destroyers to continue to support the four Army divisions ashore in Ireland. In a few hours, the US Navy was going to attack the British Grand Fleet from the north, as the High Seas Fleet hit it from the east in the Skagerak. The British knew this place as Jutland...

3 JUNE 1917
ADMIRALTY HOUSE, LONDON

Admiral of the Fleet John "Jackie" Fisher, 1st Baron Fisher, and First Sea Lord, sat at his desk. His features showed every one of his considerable years. Spread out on the desk before him were his favorite newspapers. Their headlines all spoke of disaster, but even that word was an understatement.

The Grand Fleet had not just been decisively beaten, but its survivors had been forced to inter themselves in Danish ports. Of the twenty-one dreadnoughts that Jellicoe went to sea with, eight had been sunk outright. A further six were so badly damaged that they were scuttled rather than face capture by the Germans and Americans. The rest, cut off from ports in England, had sailed to the Danish coast to inter themselves rather than surrender as they ran out of coal. Admiral Jellicoe had died fighting aboard his flagship, the *Iron Duke*. Fisher's own beloved HMS *Dreadnought*, the revolutionary ship that had redefined warship construction for a generation, now lay at the bottom of the North Sea.

It had been several hours since Admiral Fisher had called for anything, and Yeoman 1st Class Terrence Howard was beginning to get worried.

Getting up from his desk, he walked over to Fisher's door and gently knocked on it. Getting no answer, the Yeoman knocked again, more loudly. Still, there was no answer. Yeoman Howard opened the door to Admiral Fisher's office.

"My Lord," he called out, his accent harkening to the Midlands, "is everything all right?"

Not hearing an answer Howard stepped all the way through into Fisher's office. The sight that met him shocked him to his core. Still sitting behind his desk, Admiral Jackie Fisher's features had taken on the mask of death, his skin grey with lack of perfusion. The shock of Jutland had been too much, and Jackie Fisher's heart had quite literally broken.

ABOUT PHILIP WOHLRAB

Philip Wohlrab has spent time in the United State Coast Guard and has served for more than 18 years in the Virginia Army National Guard. Serving as a medic attached to an infantry company, he earned the title "Doc" the hard way while serving across two tours in Iraq. He came home and continued his education, earning a Master of Public Health degree in 2016. He has written short stories in Mil-SF, Hard SF, fantasy, and alternate history. He currently works as a wargame designer for the United States Marine Corps and has also designed and executed wargames for the USAF, USN, USSF, and the Intelligence Community. He also does game design work for the civilian market. When not crafting new stories or new games he can be found hiking in Appalachia or attending Sci-Fi Cons.

https://www.amazon.com/stores/author/B01HTBZ57A

SKYROCKETS IN FLIGHT

Lee Allred

LATE MARCH 1942
OFF THE COAST OF CEYLON
(MODERN-DAY SRI LANKA)

The brutal tropical sun beat down like trip-hammers as the slender Fleet Air Arm Fairey *Fulmar* droned slowly over the azure roil of the Indian Ocean. The Royal Navy aircraft carrier the fighter had taken off from and its attendant escorts laid seventy miles to the west while, to the east, the isle of Ceylon smudged brown and green upon the horizon.

The two-man *Fulmar* with its anemic Merlin VIII engine had no choice but to drone slowly. A world-beater, it had been designed and built in 1931; drawn up in 1940, the *Fulmar* was about as obsolete as a carrier fighter could be and still stay in the air.

The *Fulmar*'s most visible obsolescence was its two-seater fore-and-aft design their Lordships of the Admiralty insisted on in a carrier fighter. Canvas-and-wire aeroplanes had been two-seaters back when *Sopwith Strutters* first took off from the deck of the *HMS Argus*, and thus they must remained. In the *Fulmar*, the pilot's cockpit was notably separate from the rear-seat observer/radio operator's compartment.

It was that rear seat that had the young sub-lieutenant pilot sweating buckets and sprouting gray hairs by the handful.

Or, rather, who was sitting in it.

Generals and admirals in remote postings are a law unto themselves. Some affect venal accoutrements like corn cob pipes or polished six-shooters worn on the hip. Others merely cultivate eccentric tics.

Vice Admiral Sir James Fownes Somerville had such a tic.

The dour-faced admiral, late of Gibraltar's fabled Force H and hero of the sinking of the *Bismarck* and the crippling of the Vichy French Fleet at Mers El Kebir, liked to play silly beggars in the air. Somerville, who looked more like the bland, stone-faced Whitehall civil servants who told local milk boards why they couldn't have a rise in rates than a fighting admiral, liked to swan about in a crate's backseat manning the radio transmitter set.

Somerville fancied himself a dab hand at tapping out messages on the W/T.

To give him his due, Somerville *was* a dab hand. He had pioneered the use of W/T in aeroplanes in the last war and gone on to shepherd nearly every technical advance in Royal Navy aviation since. No less an authority than Watson-Watt had dubbed Somerville the step-father of naval radar.

But that didn't make it any easier on the poor sub-lieutenant piloting the crate Somerville sat in. Somerville was flying *en route* to the great fleet base in Trincomalee harbor to take command of the Royal Navy's Eastern Fleet. Upon landing, Somerville would be in charge of every British ship, plane, and jolly jack Tar in and around the Indian Ocean. If he pranged this crate with the admiral aboard, they'd crucify him or his corpse.

And even though the Japanese were—for now!—clear on the other side of the Indian Ocean, a lot could go wrong flying in a combat zone coming in over radar-watched territory in a strange plane, even an expected one. There were protocols and procedures for doing so, and the radio airwaves crackled with queries and instructions. Somerville ably fielded the conversations, tapping out (hopefully) satisfactory replies in Morse.

Both pilot and backseat greenhouse canopies were pushed back, allowing air to whistle past, causing more noise than cooling. The sub-lieutenant swung his half-detached oxygen mask over his mouth and worked the intercom switch. "Sir! They'll probably be sending an escort soon to look us over," he half-shouted. "Keep a lookout."

Blast, I just gave the CINC of the whole ruddy fleet an order... the sub-lieutenant thought, bracing himself for an eruption.

"Wilco," the admiral responded, undoubtedly with a twinkle in his eye.

Feeling fortunate for the mild consequences, the sub-lieutenant returned to trying to look in all directions at once, craning his neck up and forward, swiveling it left and right. You could get shot just as dead by your own side as you could by Japanese or Jerries.

Suddenly, two shapes zoomed past them from above. Aircraft hurtling straight down at almost five hundred miles an hour, four times faster than the *Fulmar* wheezed along at. The turbulence rocked the stodgy *Fulmar* like a leaf in a windstorm.

The sub-lieutenant let out a curse that would have mortified his vicar back home, and a voice in back echoed a similar sentiment.

"What the—?" the pilot shouted, both hands on the stick with no time to fuss with oxygen masks and intercoms. He dipped the wing to glance downward and his starboard, only to see those two shapes hurtling back straight upwards at an incredible rate of climb no airplane should have.

The two aircraft leveled off, flanking the *Fulmar*, one on each side.

Now it was Somerville's turn to shout.

"What the blasted devil are those?"

They were aircraft like no other the sub-lieutenant had ever seen.

Twin-ruddered and twin-engined like a *Hudson* or a *Mitchell* bomber, but these babies were pure fightercraft. The twin rudders were six-sided hexagons, not ovals, and the bulbous engine nacelles hung from the bottom of squared-off wings. The fuselage was an elongated teardrop, slender and almost dainty with a rounded canopy at just aft of the plane's bulb of a nose.

But it was the nose of the compact, lightweight plane that made it look like something from the planet Mars.

The wing jutted out in front of that nose!

Only the front six inches of the rounded nose clamped onto the wing's trailing edge, seemingly holding on for dear life like a beagle to a car bumper. It looked like nothing so much as if the airplane had been left in the hot sun and the fuselage had slid backwards off the wing like waxwork in the heat.

Whatever these planes were, they were painted in a grey-blue-and-haze color scheme, quite unlike the sub-lieutenant's *Fulmar* still painted in its brown-green-tan camouflage. The strange aircraft sported a not-quite-right roundel, as well. It was the British roundel of concentric circles of blue, white, and red, but the center inner red dot was missing, leaving just the blue and larger-than-normal blank white.

The sub-lieutenant saw the pilot of the port side airplane from Mars touch fingers to throat mic.

Improbably, an American voice crackled over the radio. "Geez louise, mac! Paint out that red on your wings. Thought it was a Hirohito meatball. Almost shot you down."

The *Fulmar* pilot keyed his intercom.

"I don't know what they're flying, Admiral, but I think they're our escorts."

———

ONE YEAR PRIOR
APRIL 1941
GRUMMAN AIRCRAFT ENGINEERING CORPORATION
BETHPAGE, NEW YORK

The ungainly-looking Grumman *XP-50* fighter plane hadn't even finished rolling to a stop on its tricycle gear before its test pilot slammed back the canopy and yanked his way free of the droop-nosed cockpit, dangling oxygen hoses and parachute straps in his wake. No sooner had his shoes touched tarmac than he'd snatched his flying helmet off his scalp and slammed it to the pavement hard enough to break his goggles, had they been mere glass instead of Perspex.

Jedidiah Grant—Jed to his friends and "that loudmouthed idiot" to his immediate boss—was mad and he wanted the whole world to know it. Particularly that smug Army jackwall that had foisted quote-unquote improvements on the sweetest little craft that ever punched a hole in the sky.

Adrenaline and righteous anger carried him up seven flights of stairs to the control cab on top of the tower.

Sunlight streamed through the ring of glass windows that formed the upper half of the room, forming visible rays as they slanted through thick blue cigarette smoke. Tower radio operators mumbled softly into their R/T sets, shepherding outbound flights of new aircraft leaving the factory. Lucky Strikes and Camels burned forgotten in overflowing ashtrays.

On the other side of the cab, three Army officers clucked sadly at the flight recorder data, ink-needle squiggles scratched on revolving paper discs. Squiggles that confirmed just what Grant had warned would happen beforehand.

A Navy commander stood in the huddle, his face even more disapproving, if that were possible.

"These numbers aren't any better than our original prototype," a Navy commander muttered. "If anything, they're worse." The *XP-50* was the Army redesign of the Navy's *X5F5 Skyrocket* fighter prototype. The Navy had passed on the original *Skyrocket* model, but if the Army was interested in an update, maybe the Navy had better be, too.

"Gentlemen," soothed a Grumman exec named Horton, Vice President in Charge of Buttering Up Buyers or some other nonsense. Horton was one of the new breed of Harvard-bred executives old man Grumman had taken to hiring recently, executives from outside the air industry who didn't know an aileron from an altimeter. "You must understand that there are always teething problems with any new design—"

"I'm not burping a baby here," snapped Colonel Throckmorton. He growled his words around a half-chewed dime-store cigar. "I'm buying an airplane, and you've either got one ready or you don't."

Horton saw Grant tread up the last few stairs and shoved the mess into his lap. "Here's our test pilot now. I'm sure he can explain—"

"I sure can," Grant said, making a bad job of keeping the anger out of his voice. "You jokers added nine hundred pounds of useless changes to the *Skyrocket*, chief of which is pushing the nose forward for that tricycle landing gear. Nine hundred pounds of deadweight and drag when all the original *Skyrocket* needed was the new engine."

The original prototype had used two 800-horsepower Pratt & Whitney R-1535-96. Wright's new R-1820-67/69 Cyclone boasted 400 horses more per engine, and supercharging on top of that.

"Your new engines don't seem to be helping this new plane much." Throckmorton snorted. The Army colonel stopped chomping on his dime-store cigar and spat on the floor.

"Figured I'd give you Grumman folks a whirl, seein's as the Navy thinks so highly of you," he sneered. "Well, they can have you. I'm taking my trade over to Lockheed. They know how to do business over there."

Without another word, he led the rest of the Army contingent down the tower stairs to a waiting staff car.

Horton looked to the lone Navy man, but the commander shook his head. "We already passed once on your *Skyrocket*. Navy's only concern here today was the Army taking up part of your factory output with a new plane when you're already behind on getting our *Wildcat* deliveries out the door."

He descended the stairs, as well.

Horton turned on Grant in a bubbling fury.

"What the devil are you playing at, Grant? That plane will do 420 miles an hour, easy. Today, you didn't push it any faster than 380."

"Oil temperatures. That last-minute cowl modification you insisted on blocks the cooling intake, just like I warned you. If I had pushed that crate any faster, both engines would have blown."

"You might as well have blown up the engines. You certainly blew up the sale!"

Grant tapped a Lucky Strike from a crumpled back and lit up. "Throckmorton was always going to go with the Lockheed job and you know it. He was just tweaking the Navy's nose on our dime."

Jed took a deep drag, then exhaled smoke and a portion of his anger.

"What you should have been doing was getting the Navy to take another look at the original *Skyrocket*. With the new Cyclones installed, the XF5F does twenty-per faster than the Vought *Corsair* they went with and climbs half again faster."

The exec sniffed. "One thing I learned at my time with General Mills: the buyer doesn't want 'old and improved,' he wants 'new and improved.'"

The test pilot stubbed out his half-smoke cigarette.

"Maybe you should have stuck to selling oatmeal, with all that mush in your head."

Red crept up the executive's neck and face till his oversized ears glowed. "If it wasn't so late in the day, I'd march you over to accounting myself."

"Why don't you? Chennault's hiring pilots for his China volunteer group. Double my pay, plus combat bonus and no mush merchants telling me how to fly."

"That's it! When you come in on Monday, don't bother with the hangar. Just march right over to payroll and pick up your check."

———

Harry's Bar and Grill wasn't the fanciest gin joint in town, merely the closest to the Grumman plant. All the Grumman hands hung out there for a drink or three before heading home. At least, the ones hired before all the pinstriped suits showed up.

The décor wasn't fancy, but they kept the floor mopped. Some of the tables and chairs were scratched and dented from previous high-spirited disagreements, and enough tobacco smoke hung in the air to resemble a London fog. Still, the food was cheap, the beers cold, and the bartenders remembered what you drank. If you were a regular, it was usually waiting soon as they saw you walk in.

Grant had plopped himself down at the far end of the bar. He was knocking back his third Old Grandad neat when Gus Taylor sat down beside him.

Gus had been a test pilot, too, until a crack-up grounded him. Old Man Grumman had given him a pity job in sales. The old man took care of his own, or had until the new executives showed up.

Not every place needs new blood, Grant thought.

Gus picked up the highball the bartender had set out. He downed it in one go. Very despondent tonight, Gus was slumped over his empty glass.

"You look like I feel," Grant said.

"You must feel lousy indeed, then," Gus muttered. He accepted another highball and downed that one, too. "Heard that pencil-neck Horton tried firing you and the Old Man read him the riot act."

Grant snorted. "Wish he *had* fired me. That Chennault job's sounding better every day. Naw, what's got my goat is I can't get anybody to even *look* at the *Skyrocket*. Sweetest little plane—aw, forget it."

He set his glass down long enough to light up another Camel.

"Anyway, what about you? What's got you all gloomy? I thought those *F4F Wildcats* sold themselves."

The crippled ex-pilot stared at his drink. "That's just the problem. We're *oversold*. Navy's bought up every F4F we can make and then some."

"Why so blue, then?"

"Because I had a British contingent hit town today. Royal Navy. Want to buy some more *'Martlets'*—that's what they call the *Wildcat*—only I don't have any to sell. You know what the commission on sixty planes adds up to?"

"It's a lousy world, Gus."

"Lousy world, Jed. You got a plane nobody wants and I got a customer nobody wants. They ought to get together," Gus mumbled into his glass.

Grant stared at him. "What'd you say?"

"Just what I said. They oughta get together."

"Hey, Mac!" Grant shouted to the bartender. "Drag that phone over here."

———

The Britisher dug into his steak like he was starving, like he hadn't seen real meat in years.

Given what's been going on in the Atlantic with the U-boats and Europe being occupied, Grant realized, *he probably hasn't.*

A trim man with a sandy mustache, Commander Ian Townsend wore civilian clothes—"mufti," he called it—and limped almost as bad as Gus.

"A little souvenir from my last yachting expedition in the Med," he'd said, brushing it off. "Only temporary."

Townsend's fork speared the last of the steak from his now-empty plate. He made a small, hopeful gesture. "I don't suppose I could—?"

Grant called over the girl serving tables. "Lucy, hon? Burn another cow for the gentleman here. And another round of drinks."

He turned back to Townsend.

"Gus says you want more *Wildcats*. I thought you Brits had your own aviation industry."

The Britisher's eyes grew saucer-sized as he eyed the steak Lucy brought over.

"How much do you know about British naval aviation?" he asked as he sliced up the first bite.

Grant shrugged. "I know you have carriers."

"*The* very first carrier. Most carrier techniques were pioneered first by us," Townsend said, pointing at himself with his fork. The man then stuck the piece of steak on the utensil in his mouth, closed his eyes, and gave a wistful hum.

"We made one big boob, however." By that, Grant took it to mean mistake.

English, my foot. Half the words this guy said were foreign.

"You Yanks kept your naval aviation under your Navy. Ours got rolled into the R.A.F. after the last war, along with land-based army aviation," Townsend continued after swallowing a mouthful and taking a swig of beer. "The land-based wallahs ended up in control, which meant naval aviation—particularly naval aircraft design—got left with the crumbs."

Grant could see the man's face starting to color, even as he took another bite of steak.

"Take our frontline carrier fighter, the Fairey *Fulmar*, for example. Ever hear of an aircraft named the *Battle*?"

Grant shook his head, then stopped.

"No, I have, too. Land-based light bomber, wasn't it? You Brits tried using it at the start of the Battle of France. Whole squadrons got shot down."

Grant sipped his scotch, wincing. "Removed from service, wasn't it?'

"The *Fulmar*," Townsend said, "is the fighter version of the *Battle*."

The test pilot lowered his glass from his lips, not sure if his rising inebriation had affected his hearing.

"Let me get this straight: you made a carrier fighter out of a bomber yanked for being unfit for combat?"

Townsend gave him a wry smile. "At least it's a monoplane. Our torpedo bombers are still biplanes. Our *Swordfish* canvas-and-wire jobs —'Stringbags,' we call them—and its supposed replacement, another biplane called the *Albacore*. At least only the wings are fabric-covered on that one."

"No wonder you want *Wildcats*," Grant said. "Tell me, what's the top speed of this *Fulmar*?"

"*Janes* lists it having a cruising speed of 235," Townsend said reluctantly. Even among friends, military secrets were secrets. "You can guess its top speed from that."

Two-sixty, two-seventy, then. A *Wildcat* was a good sixty m.p.h. faster.

Grant glanced around the nearly empty eating area of Harry's. "How'd you like a Grumman crate that does this?" He surreptitiously held up four fingers. "And has a climb rate of this." Again, he flashed four fingers, this time for four thousand feet per minute, twice that of a *Wildcat/Martlet*.

Townsend actually forgot his steak for a moment. He looked like he'd just been offered the Holy Grail for one skinny dime and two bottle caps. Then he shook his head. "You're having me on. There's no such animal."

Grant smiled. "Come around Hangar D Sunday morning first light, and I'll show it to you."

————

Sunday morning. Dawn stretched out her proverbial rosy fingers as dawn grew into sunrise. Meadowlarks sang in the grassy field surrounding the factory airstrip.

Gus sat on an upturned wooden crate, fretting.

"We could get in a lot of trouble over this, Jed. You're technically fired, and me, I'm not authorized to approve any of this."

"Relax. It's Sunday morning. Nobody's around to complain."

The plant was completely deserted except for Grant, Gus, and a handful of ground staff Grant had slipped a sawbuck each to show up. He took a drag on his ever-present Camel.

"We make the sale, we're heroes," Grant said.

"And if it flops or if something goes wrong—?"

Grant grinned and looked Gus up and down.

"Then Chennault's gonna get himself one crackerjack ground exec along with a new ace pilot. Relax, it's in the bag."

The Britisher arrived in full uniform. He pulled up in a taxi. He got out, shaking his head wonderingly.

"They just waved us right through at the gate."

"It's called peacetime," Grant said. "We're still enjoying it here in the States."

"For now, at least," Townsend said. Grant watched as the British officer scanned the ground, then the sky. The only plane on a tarmac was a nearby *Wildcat* ground crew were prepping for flight. "Where's this wondercraft of yours?"

Grant tossed his smoke and smudged it under his shoe. He motioned to the ground crew who began pushing the hangar doors open.

Inside the gloomy cavern of Hangar D sat two planes, each with twin rudders and twin engines: the tail-dragger *XF5F Skyrocket* carrier fighter and its derivative, the droop-nosed, tricycle-geared Army *XP-50*. The curved nose of the *XP-50* managed to at least sag over the leading edge of the forward-placed wing.

Townsend arched one eyebrow as he looked at the aircraft, then turned back to Grant.

"That thing with the aardvark nose almost looks like a proper plane, but that one—" he pointed at the Navy original, "—that one you forgot to bolt down the wing. The body slid off."

"That's the way it comes."

"Indeed." The Britisher turned to look at the Army plane. "That one's a non-starter. Too tall with that tricycle gear. Never fit in our hangars. The *Illustrious*-class only has a fourteen-foot clearance."

I forgot the British armored their flight decks, Grant thought. The protection had the effect of lowering the height of the hangar deck below.

Townsend had the ground crew fold back the Navy *Skyrocket*'s wings as low as they would hinge, then got out his tape measure. He stood on the wing root and dropped the end to the floor, measuring to the tippy-top of the folded wing.

"Two inches to spare." He measured length and width with the wings folded, checking to see if it'd fit on British elevators. Despite having two engines, the *Skyrocket* was only a foot longer and a foot skinnier with its wings folded than the stubby little *Wildcat* fighter.

"Regular pocket dynamo. Four hundred per, you said?"

Grant grinned. He gestured at the *Wildcat*, all fueled up and ready. "Why don't we compare it to something you know? You're checked out on a *Martlet*, aren't you?"

Townsend nodded. "Still current, if you overlook a leg or two."

"Then why are we standing on the ground for?"

———

Townsend in the *Wildcat* and Grant in the *Skyrocket* made a few mock passes at each other. It was a slaughter.

Grant didn't even try to dogfight or turn with the *Wildcat*. He just zoomed straight up at double the rate Townsend could climb, levelled off, and power-dived past at 500 m.p.h. in mock attack. Before Townsend even knew it, the *Skyrocket* was above him again.

They landed.

Grant helped the Britisher down from the *Wildcat*'s wing. "Okay, now we switch. You take the rocket up for a spin."

They leaned over the cockpit rim of the *Skyrocket* as Grant explained the plane's layout, ran through operating it. "Stall speed is 70. Landing speed just a smidge higher. You'll find the rudder pedals a bit stiff in a stall. Bit of inertia before the ailerons bite. Other than that, stable as a table. The contra-rotating props nix all engine torque usually found in a radial engine plane."

Looking just a tad dubious, Townsend climbed in.

Grant gave out last piece of advice before heading over his *Wildcat*. "Just keep your dives a bit shallow. We know she'll do at least 500 in a power dive, but we've never dared see what she tops out at. The controls start to get mighty stiff at that part."

Gingerly nursing the twin engines, Townsend eased the *Skyrocket* into the air. Grant let him take a few minutes to get the feel of the plane.

Townsend whooped with joy the first time he leapt the plane upwards in a powerful climb. The hackneyed phrase "homesick angel" came to mind. He nosed it over into a dive and darn near past the recovery point before he realized how low he'd zoomed.

But the sheer stability of the plane shocked him. Stable as a table and then some. And yet, surprisingly nimble. The plane's center of gravity seemed to be just in front of where the rounded-off nose attached the wing, in front of the entire fuselage. This had the oddest effect. The plane was stable, yet with a slight push past that inertia Grant had mentioned, the plane would dance left, right, up or down at the slightest twitch of the joystick. Townsend felt like all he had to do was lean left or right in the cockpit and the plane would respond.

And there was one more aerodynamic characteristic.

"Ready for some fun?" Grant's voice crackled over the radio. "Let's try some dogfighting."

A quarter tank later, they landed and Townsend climbed exhaustedly out of the plane. "Where do I sign?" he asked.

———

They found Old Man Grumman sitting on his patio. Despite the warm spring day, he was heavily wrapped in blankets. Out on the manicured lawn, by his express order, lay the croquet equipment just as it was the day he'd suffered a combined stroke-heart attack. The game wasn't forfeited, he'd roar, just delayed.

Grumman's peevish annoyance at being disturbed—"I have VPs for that sort of stuff now!"—vanished as soon as Townsend told him the size of the order he wanted to make, but the Old Man's new smile vanished just as quickly.

"The Navy has every inch of my factory tied up with *Wildcats*. I couldn't build you a tail wheel, let alone an order that size."

When Gus suggested the Brits build them on license, it was Townsend's turn to shake his head. Britain was in the same fix: her aircraft factories and that of Canada's, were strained to the limit, too.

Grant cleared his throat. "There's always the NAF, sir. The Naval Air Factory."

It had to be explained to the Brit that the US Navy had owned its own aircraft plant in Philadelphia since the Kaiser's war. Founded to build batches of specialized planes too small to be economically feasible for commercial plants, these days it mostly fulfilled orders of old, obsolete planes the Navy was contractually obligated to buy but no longer wanted.

Your tax dollars at work, Grant thought, annoyed.

Grumman waved the suggestion away. The NAF was busy building

Brewster SBNs or some other worthless dodo of a plane. It might be years before they were freed up to build *Skyrockets*.

"Not with the kind of pull a British ambassador can bring to bear," Grant replied. A few high-level phone calls later, it was determined that the NAF could set aside current projects and start immediately building the initial thirty-six *Skyrockets* of the Fleet Air Arm's order while arrangements were made in Canada to ramp up for the next sixty to be built on license.

The streets were dark and empty by the time Grant drove Townsend back to his hotel. Getting out, Townsend stopped, then leaned back in. "It just occurred to me that you could have suggested the NAF to build our *Martlets* all along."

"That wouldn't have gotten the *Skyrockets* into production, though. Too sweet a plane to end up unbuilt. What's the beef? You're getting a better plane."

"I'll see you tomorrow at the plant, then."

Grant shook his head.

"Horton fired me and I'm seeing that it sticks. That ought to sink him with the Old Man." He dug in his pocket for his pack of smokes. "Soon as I pick up my severance in the morning, I'm ringing Chennault up on that China group of his. If I'm going to have people shooting my tail surfaces off, I prefer being able to shoot back."

———

MARCH 1942
EASTERN FLEET HEADQUARTERS
TRINCOMALEE, CEYLON

Somerville's backseat arrival caught the outgoing fleet commander by surprise. The welcoming party on the tarmac consisted of a hastily dressed Vice Admiral Sir Tom Phillips, his parked staff car, and the nearest half-dozen aircraft mechanics Phillips could grab, all greasy, sweat-stained, and shirtless.

The airstrip looked just as primitive. The all-weather runways were concrete, at least, but the aprons and taxiways were bare soil, red laterite baked brick-hard in the sun that assuredly turned into a soupy morass in rainy season.

A shirtless bosun in saucer cap and stained white shorts piped the ragged line of mechanics to attention.

Somerville returned an annoyed salute at the sad attempt at military honors. "We can go through all the usual ruffles and flourishes tomorrow," he told Phillips. "My Lords the Admiralty have seen fit to toss me a hot potato, and I'll be tossing some of it at you."

The two men made for the waiting staff car. At five-feet-one, the diminutive Phillips—known as "Tom Thumb" in the Fleet—scarcely reached Somerville's shoulders.

Somerville plucked at his sweat-soaked flightsuit, now zippered open to his navel, and exhaled. "Hot as hinges, and this air's so humid it's gelatinous. I thought the Med was bad."

Phillps smiled ruefully. "Wait till you've sampled the delightful equatorial weather of Port T."

"Yes, and that was another little surprise they dropped on me, wasn't it?"

"I should hope so. The Japanese find out about of Port T, bang goes the war."

Somerville climbed into the waiting car. The seat fabric was scorching. "It might be 'bang goes the war,' anyway. The whole Japanese Imperial Navy is headed for Ceylon."

———

Somerville was just human enough to allow himself the luxury of a cool shower and a fresh uniform before rejoining Phillips in what had been up until this moment Phillips's own office.

An archaic electric ceiling fan did its level best to stir up the sweltering air, succeeding only in rustling loose sheets of paper in Phillip's in-tray. A paperweight held them from fluttering to the floor. Rattan jalousies clattered in their frame.

A rating sat a drinks tray down on the small conference table, then backed out of the room, leaving the two admirals alone. The boy had been the first enlisted rating Somerville had seen on base so far wearing a shirt. The fleet-trained martinet in Somerville wanted to call them out on their state of undress; the practical man in him held his tongue.

A week of this and I might be running around shirtless, also, Somerville thought grimly. *That is, if we're all still alive in a week.*

The new admiral passed on the proffered gin for now and luxuriated in a glass of ice water.

"Tom," he said, after pouring himself a gin, after all. "I'm afraid I'm going to do you right rotten. You deserve a clean start somewhere else, but I'm going to have to ask you to stay on as my deputy. I need you as commander of shore-based defenses. You know the situation here and there's no time to bring a second party up to speed."

Phillips winced. His replacement was effectively asking him to take a demotion in the eyes of the very men he'd been commanding. He nodded reluctantly. "If you think that's best, Admiral."

Somerville held out his hand. "It's always been James before, and we're going to be working much too close for Admiral this and Admiral that."

Phillips took his hand. "James, then."

"Now then, tell me what I've got to stop Nagumo and his carrier fleet."

"Begger all," Phillips replied. He got up from the table and stepped to a map of the Indian Ocean.

If India was an elephant head shape, the teardrop shape of Ceylon was a blob of snot dripping from the elephant's dangling trunk, an island not quite three hundred miles long and just over two at its widest.

"You've got three bases." Phillips slapped the map with a wooden pointer. "Trincomalee here," he slapped the top of the isle's eastern side, "Colombo on the south," he slapped the western bottom of the island, "and seven hundred miles southwest, Port T at the Abbu atoll in the Maldives, a stone's throw south of the equator."

"Port T is top secret and we hope—*hope*—the Japanese don't know about it. It's not finished. No runway yet and they haven't finished building the oil tank farm or the fresh water plant. Lovely sheltered harborage, though. Sixty miles wide." The little admiral gave a lopsided grin. "And a climate that melts steel almost as fast as it rusts it."

The pointer returned to Trincomalee. "Land-based aircraft. You've seen our airstrip here. RAF has a single squadron of *Hurricanes*. No bombers. Some shore-based Fleet Air Arm *Fulmars*."

He slapped the tip on Colombo. "Colombo's civic racetrack has been worked up into a makeshift airstrip. One-and-a-partial squadron of RAF *Hurris*, about the same in naval *Fulmars*, and a squadron of clapped-out *Blenheim* light bombers. Oh, and two *Beaufort* torpedo bombers I wrangled out of Alexandria. The only two effective attack planes ashore."

"Reconnaissance planes?"

"Six *Catalinas* when they run. They operate out of an inshore lake, here." He slapped near Colombo.

"Radar?"

"One station each at Colombo and here. In this climate, they work *some* of the time. Wire terminal corrode as fast as the boffins can clean them."

Phillips continued. "As for ships, I've divided them into Force A, Force B, and of course Force Z." Mention of the last group elicited a pained look on his face. Little wonder, given it was the reason Churchill had personally relieved the little admiral.

"Force A are your fast carriers. Force B are 'Old Ming' capital ships." Royal Navy slang for old, slow, obsolete, worthless drudges. "Force A's currently out in the bay here. Two *Illustrious*-class 30-knot carries, *Indomitable* and *Formidable*. I assume you'll be adding in *Ark Royal* since you've brought her with you. A couple heavy cruisers and five tin cans for escort."

He touched the pointer to the equator. "Force B is down in Port T, rusting away. Four *R-class* battleships that haven't seen drydock since the start of the war. *Ramillies*, *Resolution*, *Revenge*, and *Royal Sovereign*. Builders claimed they'd do 23 knots fresh from the slips. Their hulls are so fouled now, I doubt they'll do twenty. Assorted escort ships usually scattered hither and yon for convoy and anti-sub work."

The pointer rose back up to Trincomalee. "Finally, Force Z. *Prince of Wales* and *Repulse*, not that you'll be allowed to keep them. They've orders for the Med."

"Orders which have been rescinded."

"Winston blowing hot and cold again?" Phillips asked sourly. "The man may rightfully go down in history as the savior of Western Civilization, but on a day-to-day basis, he's a ruddy great nuisance."

Somerville sipped his gin, letting the dull hum of the ceiling fan fill the silence.

Better to let Tom let it all out now rather than when we're in the thick of it, he thought. *Losing his temper in the clutch of combat may do actual harm.*

"Churchill wanted me to steam out of Singapore with Force Z into the middle of the Japanese advance. Without air cover, mind you. In range of *theirs*. Madness."

Phillips set the pointer aside and wearily sat down opposite of his new boss. Somerville poured Phillips a tall gin.

"My orders read I was to exercise 'a kind of vague menace' on the

Japanese commander's mind," Phillips continued. "Steam out and 'vanish among the innumerable islands,' as if I'd be sailing a three-mast schooner in a *Boys' Own* pirate story."

The incoming admiral picked his words carefully. "Winston was always prone to Victorian romanticism regarding anything east of Suez."

"East of the Dardanelles, if you ask me," Phillips shot back, mentioning a subject nobody in their right mind ever brought up around Churchill: Gallipoli.

"'Vague menace,'" Phillps spat again. "It would have been suicide. Worse, it'd have been murder."

But Phillips *hadn't* steamed out with his Force Z. Winston had come down with a galloping influenza and had ended up in hospital. In the interim, First Sea Lord Dudley Pound countermanded the order and sent Phillips and Force packing off to Ceylon out of reach of the approaching Japanese, thereby saving the two priceless ships.

Likely an admiral's life in the process, as well, Somerville thought. *Lancelot Holland doesn't need company in the afterlife's wardroom.*

Phillips held aloft his refilled gin glass.

"Here's to Dudley Pound and the virus I owe my life to."

Somerville kept his face passive as Phillips downed the drink.

"Oh," Phillips said, as if suddenly being reminded of a trifle. "I've also got a couple ships I've no idea what to do with. Light carrier *Hermes*—twelve planes and just about twelve knots. And a decked-over freighter the Lords of the Admiralty are pleased to call an escort carrier. The *Audacity*, or as we're calling her, the *Paucity*. Six planes, fifteen knots. They're down at Colombo getting their boilers cleaned. That's another thing. No real repair facilities. Nearest drydock is East Africa."

Somerville shook a Pall Mall out of a silver cigarette case. He placed the cig in his mouth and lit up. "What," Somerville asked, exhaling blue smoke, "about carrier-borne aircraft?" The fan thinned the tobacco smoke into mere wisps.

"*Albacore* bombers on the fleet carriers. For fighters, I've sent the *Fulmars* ashore and replaced them with those new Grumman *Skyrockets*."

"*Skyrockets*? Is that what those unsightly monstrosities that brought me in were?"

"Don't disparage them, James." Phillips touched a lucifer to his pipe bowl. "Think of them as *Martlets* with a *Spitfire*'s speed and a *Beaufighter*'s range." He puffed on his bulldog pipe. "Speed and range, James. That's the key out here."

He pointed his pipe steam at Somerville. "You're used to the Med. The Med's a lake you can spit across. Out here, you can steam for tens of thousands of miles and never sight land. The Admiralty's blind to it and the Japanese know it in their bones. Speed and range."

Somerville stubbed his cigarette out, then replied, "And I have neither."

———

Trincomalee's officer cub was a stodgy rattan-and-teakwood affair, a relic of pre-war colonial service. Creaking ceiling fans pretended to push air around, doing little but stir up the haze of tobacco smoke.

Along with that haze, an expectant air hung heavy in the base officer's club. The new admiral had sent for all his division officers to gather in the morning and word on the grapevine had it something big was brewing.

Jed Grant pushed his way through the throng and made himself space at the bar. It was easy to follow the uniformed American's progress through the crowd. Not only was he the only Yank, but he was also the only man in long pants instead of shorts. The gold oak leaves of a major and a shoulder patch denoting service in the Flying Tigers graced his khaki US Army Air Force uniform.

Leaning his elbows on the bar top, he caught the bar steward's eye. "Double scotch and a pack of smokes."

"Have to get yer chokers at the NAAFI, sir," the steward said, setting down the drink.

"NAAFI?" Grant asked, perplexed.

"Naval, Army, and Air Force Institute, mate," another officer, a British Army major, chimed in from down the bar.

"Have one of mine," the man crowding in next to Grant said before the American could reply. A hand extended from behind him, holding out a box of Players.

Grant turned, then his eyes eyes opened wide in recognition.

"Ian!" he exclaimed as he pumped the grinning Townsend's hand.

"Heard you were in town," Townsend replied, fitting a Players to his lips. He lit up, then held his lighter for Grant. The two men grabbed their drinks and made for a relatively quiet corner of the club.

The Brit, now a captain and a new one at that, by the look of his shiny new shoulder tabs, gave Grant's uniform the once-over. "Never expected to see *you* in regular service. What happened to your thousand-dollar-a-month mercenary job in China?"

"Seven-fifty a month plus five hundred a kill," Grant corrected, "and Uncle Sam is what happened to it." A sip of scotch, followed by a two-fingered drag on his cigarette. "After Pearl, Uncle nationalized the AVG and slapped us in these glad rags."

He exhaled. "Then Uncle got the bright idea that since I knew so much about *Skyrockets*, I should be the guy teaching limeys how to use 'em. That got me here. What about you? When'd you blow into town?"

"Just arrived on a *Dakota* out of Alexandria. Same deal. Admiral Somerville figured his new Air Ops ought to be somebody familiar with the new fighter."

Grant took another drag on his Players. "I heard old Porgy got the sack." He stubbed out the butt. "Floor sweepings. How do you Brits stand these things?"

"There's a war on," Townsend replied, deadpan.

"Don't I know it. What I wouldn't give for a steak at Harry's," Grant said, shuddering at the culinary indignities he'd suffered since arriving in Ceylon. He bummed another smoke off his friend.

"Is it true what they're saying about your Admiral's meeting tomorrow? Something big afoot?"

Townsend smiled a Cheshire smile.

"You'll find out. The Admiral sent me to fetch you. Seems you made him an unholy believer in the *Skyrocket*, that day you almost shot him down."

Grant laughed.

"He's run me ragged, swapping out the *Ark*'s *Fulmars* with *Rockets*. You weren't joking about your antique planes. The *Rocket*'s the only crate you got here with any speed or range."

"That's exactly what he said."

———

The base cinema doubled as a briefing auditorium. Dozens of bodies packed themselves into the dark, stuffy, sweltering tin Nissen hut. Staff, skippers, squadron leaders, the men who'd have to execute the orders given today. Expectant murmurs and the creak of wooden folding chairs susurrated in the darkened confined, then ceased immediately, knifed off by Admiral Somerville in crisp white shorts and crisp white tunic walking onto the suddenly lit stage.

"Attention!"

Somerville, a long slender pointer in hand, ordered them seated.

"Gentlemen," he said, his council milk board face even dourer than usual. "Admiral Nagumo and the very strike force he used to sink the US Navy at Pearl will shortly be arriving here to do the same to us. A surprise attack on our Eastern Fleet. Five fleet carriers, three hundred aircraft, at least three, possibly four, *Kongo*-class fast battleships, and an unholy host of escorts."

There was a collective gasp as Somerville paused to take a sip of water.

"Nagumo has better ships, better planes, and enough of them to put paid to any existing force foolish enough to go up against him."

Somerville stood poised, one man upon a stage with but a slender reed in his hands. Standing there like Horatio at the bridge.

"We are going to clobber him," he said plainly, a smile creasing his face.

Cheers erupted and feet stomped. Somerville let it simmer down.

"I said surprise attack, didn't I?" Somerville continued once things had dropped to a dull buzz. "Not much of a surprise if we know when and where he's coming. And that is our primary weapon."

At his nod, the black curtain was whipped off the giant mapboard behind him.

"Nagumo will come along the equator, away from shipping routes, and attack from the south of the island," Somerville began, then began moving his pointer over the map as he spoke. "The Japanese will be making a simultaneous airstrike on Colombo and Trincomalee, trying to catch the Eastern Fleet anchored and boilers cold. Simple grammar school math puts his likely launch here, at a place we've designated Point Rabbit."

Somerville slapped the pointer at a spot on the map roughly a hundred miles southeast off the southern tip of Ceylon. "Point Rabbit because we are going to make him *run*."

He took a half-step away from the map and his eyes swept the room.

"Our invincible Japanese friend has an Achilles' Heel: air recce. He hasn't discovered yet the best use of his long-legged bombers is flying off a few for reconnaissance duties."

Somerville glanced over towards the RAF contingent as he said that last part, smiling at the consternation on their faces.

"Instead, he uses short-range float planes from his heavy cruisers. That means he has half the search radius of our *Catalina* flying boats and only a handful of scouts to look for us with. Not only will we spot him before he spots us—he'll be forced to narrow his search arc to about sixty degrees."

A slap of the pointer on the map. "That lets us use the other three hundred degrees to sneak up behind him."

He nodded at his aides, who started passing out ops folders stamped most secret.

"Force A," Somerville said, pointing east and a bit north of the island, "will loiter here out of range and out of his search arc. When our Cats spot Nagumo—" he slid the pointer, "—we'll slip in from behind, pinning him against the island's ground aircraft and our carriers."

He slapped the pointer in his hand. "Colombo, I am told, has an RDF station that occasionally works." He smiled and nodded at Grant. "That's radar to you unlettered Yanks."

Laughter, including from Grant.

"The moment our *radar* detects Nagumo has launched his strike, all land and carrier units will launch a combined strike on his carriers, ignoring any attempts to defend our bases."

There was a low murmur from the gathered group.

"You see, there won't be anything to defend," Somerville continued. "Our planes will be in the air and we're already ordering all civilian vessels out of the harbors. Nothing to bomb but water."

More laughter.

Somerville pointed his stick at Denis Boyd, the rear admiral who commanded Force A. "Denis, you look like you have a question."

"Sir, what about Force B?" The officers of Force B were conspicuous with their absence.

"Force B is making preparations to sortie out of Port T even as we speak. It will join Force A at the loiter point, combining into a single fleet for both protection against surface action as well as bolstering anti-aircraft fire."

"Sir?" Captain Richard Onslow said, hand raised. "You haven't mentioned the *Hermes*."

"You and the *Audacity* are to be designated Force X," Somerville replied. "You will steam due west out of Colombo to a point here well out of Nagumo's range. The moment Nagumo launches, your ships and aloft planes will broadcast fake messages simulating the entire Eastern Fleet. At the very least, this will distract Nagumo. Best case, he'll think Eastern Fleet is off to the west, making our rear attack just that more of a surprise."

He looked out at the assembled men one last time.

"We're taking Nagumo's speed and range advantage out of the equation. With luck and each man doing his part, we'll catch Nagumo with his kimono down around his ankles. Good luck, gentlemen, and godspeed."

And God save us all.

————

Operation Rabbit's wheels began to come off even before the Somerville stepped off stage.

Supply ships reached Port T late, pushing back the replenishment of fuel and fresh water. Force B ended up leaving nearly a day later than planned. They'd still make the loiter point before Nagumo's arrival, but only by the skin of their teeth.

Then the *Hermes*'s props fouled in a submarine net leaving the harbor. Until divers could cut her free, Force X was stuck in harbor.

But the biggest joker in the deck got shuffled in the Japanese.

————

FORCE A
AIRCRAFT CARRIER HMS ARK ROYAL
LOITER POINT NORTHEAST OF CEYLON

Somerville crumpled the latest dispatch from the *Hermes*.

Project further delay of up to twenty-four hours? he thought angrily. *If Hermes doesn't get a move on, she will still be floating in harbor when Nagumo comes calling. At which point, she won't be floating much longer.*

And with total radio silence in effect for Force A, Somerville couldn't even scorch Onslow's tail feather with a reply.

But the useless toy carrier was hardly his biggest worry.

Where is Force B?

Even with their late start, they should have reached Force A by now.

————

FORCE B
BATTLESHIP HMS RESOLUTION

SOUTHEAST OF CEYLON

The battleships of Force B heaved and corkscrewed in the roiling waves and heavy downpour of the sudden tropical squall.

Bad as anything in the North Atlantic, Rear Admiral Algernon Willis thought. Except for the temperature. *That* was still steam-boiler blistering.

Risking a drenching, he stepped out on the wing. Almost dusk, not that visibility could get much worse. He could just make out the *Royal Sovereign* off the port bow through the slashing rain. No sign of the smaller escorts that trailed the big boys in this murk.

Willis would be lucky if there weren't collisions.

Blast the rotten luck!

First, the *Revenge* and her perennial boiler trouble slowing the entire task force to a 13-knot crawl while they affected repairs, and now the sudden appearance of this vest-pocket typhoon.

The storm's one saving grace was that it hid Force B from any lurking Japanese submarines.

He stepped back onto the flag bridge, damp from the spray. According to the plot, they'd soon be crossing Nagumo's projected route. He suddenly had a sickening mental image of stumbling into Nagumo in this muck, but shook free of it. Even with their delay starting, even with their reduced speed, if the intelligence was correct, Force B would be well and gone before Nagumo plied these waters.

Willis looked out into the gloom.

Of course, I hope the intelligence officers are far more accurate than our weather blokes have been.

———

HMS ARK ROYAL

Somerville squinted against the last slanting rays of sunlight. Tropical sunsets were sudden thing, a knife-edge between light and dark. He once again looked down at the flimsy in his hand.

Well, at least Hermes *and her lot are finally out*, he thought angrily. *Almost too late to be of any difference, but just barely under the wire between an immediate relief and a Court of Inquiry when this is all done.* Someone was going to have to be fired, lest a lesson not be learned, but if the intelligence lads were correct, the carriers would still be able to fulfill their decoy role.

Catalina *patrols should be returning just about now*, Somerville mused. Still no sightings of Nagumo. Even with patrol aircraft, the ocean was vast and ships so tiny upon its surface. More concerning than the lack of enemy sightings was the fact Force B still had not arrived.

Blast this radio silence, Somerville thought. His mind briefly turned to Jellicoe at Jutland, where the Royal Navy's strict adherence to radio silence had cost the Grand Fleet an opportunity to end the High Seas Fleet once and for all.

Maybe it's time to launch an Albacore *or two and see what they can find*, he thought. Almost as soon as the musing crossed his mind, logic won out.

Better not risk being spotted and tracked back by our own aircraft, Somerville thought. *If Nagumo has a night to maneuver, he'll kill us all once daylight hits.*

On the other hand, Force B *was* cutting it perilously short. London's firm estimate on Nagumo's arrival time was still, in the end, only an estimate.

There will be the devil to pay if Nagumo is early.

———

BATTLESHIP HMS RESOLUTION

The admiral's flag lieutenant, soaked to the bone, stepped back in from the darkened bridge wing. The storm's strength had been such that night hadn't so much fallen as been dragged down on the force like a great curtain.

"Sir, it looks like this blow is lifting," the young man observed, confirming what Willis could see out the forward bridge window.

Not so much lifting as we're finally parting way with this damned storm, Willis thought, glancing behind him at the flag plot. *Somerville must be ready to kill me, but no point showing up for a battle with half my ships battered to pieces.*

Willis stepped out onto the wing for a better look himself as the last bit of squall cleared. What he saw made him stop, staring openmouthed at the moonlit tableau before him.

My God, he thought. So close that they were easily identified with the naked eye, moonlight glistening off their wet superstructures, were two of the massive *Kongo*-class battleships. On either side of the Japanese battleships cruised their escorts, the entire group in a line abreast cruising formation.

"Oh, bloody hell," his flag lieutenant said, voice quavering.

Then bedlam broke out.

———

HMS HERMES

A cacophony of Morse dots and dashed chattered on the radio, then fell silent.

Captain Richard Onslow, Hermes's master, ripped the radio message from the headphoned yeoman's typewriter. For a fleeting moment, the words made no sense and the world seemed to swirl around him.

Engaged with enemy battleships. Taking heavy damage.

The position given meant Nagumo was early and Somerville's carefully laid mousetrap had *gang aft agley*—ruinously so.

The Old Ming of Force B couldn't stand up to Nagumo's fleet, not by themselves.

Onslow set his jaw, knowing what had to be done, knowing what it cost him and his command.

Force X had barely started its run to Point Decoy. Even at full speed, come the dawn, anyone launching against Colombo would spot them wallowing westward at turtle place. Neither baby carrier would last five minutes in combat. Force X's only chance for survival was to remain silent, not draw attention.

It takes three years to build a ship, he thought, reflecting on Admiral Cunningham's guidance to his commanders before the Crete evacuation. *It would appear that I, too, am about to find out just how many men it costs to follow our Navy's tradition.*

Onslow took a deep breath as he turned away from the radioman, ostensibly to reread the message but in actuality to regain his composure.

"Send this plain language and in the clear," he began, his voice choked. Clearing his throat, Onslow continued. "All carriers under my command moving southeast to help you as rapidly as possible. Hold on. Help on the way. Sign it...Somerville."

Maybe he could draw Nagumo's attention off any wounded survivors of Force B. It was all he could do for them. However, he'd almost certainly turned the Japanese commander's gimlet eye towards him.

"How many hours until dawn?" Onslow asked, looking at the clock.

"Six, sir," came the reply.

"Wake me in four, tell the mess to feed the men at four and a half, and signal *Audacity* we will have all aircraft readied at five," Onslow replied.

———

HMS ARK ROYAL

An ashen-faced Somerville stared at his charts, trying to guess Nagumo's next move. That he'd go after Force X thinking it Somerville's carriers was a given after Onslow's radio communication.

Blast that Onslow and his gallant foolishness! Somerville thought, mildly ashamed that he'd been ready to fire the man just a few short hours before. He turned back to the map.

So where will the blow fall from? he thought.

"Sir, transmission from what's left of Force B," his chief of staff said grimly from the hatch. Seeing Somerville and the rest of the staff look up, the captain continued. "All four of the battleships are lost. Believe they destroyed at least one, if not three *Kongo*-class battleships."

Somerville's eyes narrowed, but then widened as the officer continued.

"Apparently *Resolution* blew one of the big bastards up before going up herself. One more was in flames when Force B disengaged."

"Do you think we should ask what's left to attempt to shadow?" Somerville asked.

The chief of staff looked pained for a moment, then answered truthfully.

"Only if you wish to kill them all, sir," the man replied. "I imagine Nagumo is getting as far away from the remaining cruisers and destroyers as possible, especially if he's exchanged two modernized ships for four *R*-class."

Somerville had to nod at that calculus. Even the Imperial Japanese Navy, currently the most powerful fleet in Asia, could not survive that sort of exchange rate for long.

Somerville turned back to the chart.

Think, man, think, he thought. *What would you do...?*

It struck him like a thunderbolt.

Here, he thought, resting his finger on the map. *West of the island. Away from the* Catalinas *and what's left of Force B, expecting that we'll be focused south where he was and where Force B's survivors will be in the water.*

Somerville tried not to think of the upwards of five thousand British sailors, survivors who had to be ignored for now for the sake of the whole Empire. It was cruel calculus, but nothing could be done for it now.

I need to talk to Tom or this is all going to go sideways, he thought. Reaching for a piece of paper, he quickly scribbled a note.

"Two *Albacores*, both of them to be launched within the hour with this message for Vice Admiral Phillips," Somerville said, trying to do math in his head. He cursed the slow biplanes, but they were the only aircraft that could safely fly and land at night.

Here's to hoping some trigger-happy Army or RAF gunners don't blow them out of the sky.

"Directly to Vice Admiral Phillips," Somerville stressed. "If some staff idiot or duty officer tries to interfere, they are to be informed I will have them shot within the week."

The chief of staff started to crack a smile...until he realized Somerville was not joking.

"We will arc south after the *Albacores* are gone," Somerville said. "We might still surprise Nagumo."

―――――

ROYAL NAVAL AIR STATION COLOMBO RACECOURSE
COLOMBO, CEYLON

"Can't believe Vice Admiral Somerville actually said he'd shoot someone," Grant said, regarding Townsend.

"I'm sure that was exaggerated," the British officer replied, looking at all the activity around them.

The makeshift dirt airstrip was chockablock with aircraft, their camouflaged shapes dully pink in the first sullen rays of sunrise. Somerville's hand-delivered dispatch had ordered Phillips to send Trincomalee's entire air group south to Colombo in the night. Together with Colombo's squadrons, they massed to intercept Nagumo's airstrike.

Fuel bowsers hastily topped off the wing tanks of the Trincomalee planes. Hot engines pinged in dawn's muggy air. Rolls Royce *Merlins and* Yank Wright *Cyclones*. Major Grant's scratch-crewed *Skyrockets* had come south, too.

Can't believe we all managed to make it here with only two prangs, Grant thought, slouching back against his *Skyrocket's* wing. *One hundred ops in China and I've never been more scared in my life.*

The RAF and Fleet Air Arm pilots he'd been training to fly *Skyrockets* —most veterans of the Med campaigns in other aircraft, aces, even— finished forming a horseshoe around his bird.

"I'll go over our orders one last time. Leave the bombers to the *Fulmars* and *Hurricanes* to mop up. *We* go after the *Zeroes*."

The men nodded, some of them ashen-faced at going up against the now near-mythical Japanese *Zero*. Grant smiled. He knew just how they felt, having been there less than a year ago.

"Look, men, I'm living proof *Zeroes* can be beaten," Grant said. "If the Flying Tigers can shoot them down in clapped-out *P-40s*, we'll tear them apart in these babies."

He patted his *Skyrocket* affectionately.

"You know the drill," he said. "No dogfighting. We come up high, dive through them, then climb back up and do it again and again."

He scanned the crowd, making sure to make contact with the former *Hurricane* pilots, especially.

"Zoom and climb, zoom and climb."

Grant's smile grew bigger.

"Aim for the wing tanks," he said. "The bill they pay for being able to turn on a dime is they light better than a Ronson and their pilots have nothing behind them but thoughts and prayers."

There was laughter at that until a downy-cheeked RAF Pilot Officer, one of his few newbies, raised a hand.

"Sir, b-but what if we do find ourself in a d-dogfight?"

"If he's on your tail, break left," Grant answered. "We don't have torque, they do, so it takes him a moment to get around after you. Either dive away or firewall those engines to get your speed up."

Grant looked at the young man to make sure what he was saying registered.

"We got to look at a *Zero* that came down mostly intact," he continued. "Ailerons don't have a lot of force to them, so if you get fast gain, it's like they're trying to drag something through a mud pit. Get away, get back up, then come back down."

The sirens at the end of the runway began to warble. Grant grabbed his helmet, then looked over the group.

"I catch any of you dogfighting, you better hope some Japanese bastard kills you," Grant warned. "If you survive, I'll bust you down to erk, and a non-flying erk, at that. You'll pilot a mop for the rest of the war, understand?"

A yellow flare from the jerry-built tower arced in the lightening sky.

That's the mass scramble signal, Grant thought, grimacing. The flare confirmed that Colombo's temperamental radar had spotted the approaching strike...and it was indeed headed towards Force X.

"Mount up!" he shouted as he turned. To his pleasant surprise, the men were already scrambling for their planes, Simmons at the front of the pack.

A little over an hour later, flying at 20,000 feet over the Indian Ocean, Grant and his companions sighted their prey.

That's...that's a lot of aircraft, Grant thought, looking at the mass of planes resembling the biggest migratory formation he'd ever seen. Swallowing, he made a mental note to buy whomever was handling radar control drinks for the next month. He and his eleven companions were above and behind the Japanese fighters, approaching out of the eastern sun.

Here goes nothing.

Grant waggled his wings and rolled his *Skyrocket* over into a power dive. As per his plan, the group aim focused on the trailing squadron of *Zeroes* cruising a leisurely two hundred miles an hour behind the mass of bombers and attack craft.

They're not expecting us this far out, Grant thought, starting to laugh as he lined up his first target. He had just enough time to fire a burst from his four .50-caliber nose guns before he turned his wings to continue his dive past the target at just short of five hundred miles an hour. There was a momentary impression of a fireball, and then he was busy picking his path back up into the heavens.

Jesus Christ, Grant thought, glancing over his right shoulder. He'd given orders for everyone to choose a target in this first pass before wingmen would resume their duties covering their section leaders. At best, he'd expected four, maybe five of the Japanese fighters to fall to their pass.

There were six *Zeroes* in various forms of disintegration as he brought the F5F back around. The three remaining Japanese fighters from the rear squadron were scattering like frightened quail. To his starboard, the remaining escort fighters were only belatedly starting to turn around to assist their friends, slow and sluggish as they clawed for altitude.

We don't need to bother with the fighters, he realized. *We can...*

The glint of sun on canopy was his only warning that he'd been mistaken about his calculus. Grant would never know how or why the six *Zeroes* had been far, far behind the rest of the formation. All he knew was that the half-dozen fighters were diving on the rear of his formation.

"White Flight, break left!" he shouted, then started to follow his own advice before realizing that would expose his own tail to the Japanese escorts climbing towards him.

White Flight will have to remember what I told them!

"Green Flight, take the fighters to one o'clock!" Grant barked, pulling his nose up instead of turning. "Red, follow me!"

The squadron's middle flight broke towards the fighters at one o'clock, diving towards their clumsy, slowed prey. Adding a quick thousand feet, Grant rolled onto his back to look towards White Flight...and felt his stomach drop at two *Skyrockets* in the midst of the six *Zeroes*. White Two, the section leader's wingman, belatedly remembered his directives, skidding into a dive just as one of the *Zero*s opened up on him. White Four, on the other hand...

"Simmons! Break left," Grant screamed over the radio as he brought his nose down, lining up on the *Zero* that was drawing lead on the turning *Skyrocket*.

Damn kid got himself suckered, Grant thought, firing a desperate burst from long range. His initial burst was wildly off, the Japanese pilot not even flinching as the *Zero*'s nose guns started to flicker. Grant skidded, the *Skyrocket* losing speed as he tried to bring his sights on the deflection shot. The *Zero*'s cannons began spitting at the near-stalling Simmons just as Grant fired again, saw a short spurt of tracers just behind the Japanese fighter...and heard an ominous click.

No ammo, he thought angrily. A low ammunition capacity was the *Skyrocket*'s one weakness, and he cursed helplessly as he watched the Japanese pilot walk 20mm shells across Simmons's left wing, port engine, and then the canopy.

Goddammit, he thought as the *Skyrocket* tumbled out of combat, the motions clearly those of a plane with a dead pilot. It was cold comfort that the Japanese *Zero* exploded a moment later, nailed by Red Three as Grant pulled up. Fighting back impotent rage, Grant suddenly realized that the radio was a cacophony of panicked voices.

"Skipper, I'm out of ammo!"

"Ammo bingo, fuel bingo!"

"Skipper, I've got dry tanks!"

"Rabbit Leader to all conies." The voice of RAF Group Captain Barclay broke through, calm and steady. "Break off and head for base."

There are far too many of those Japanese bombers left, Grant thought, climbing away. Watching their opponents starting to restore their formations, Grant did a fast count while putting his aircraft into quick orbit far above the *Zeroes* trying to reach his altitude.

About half, maybe a little more left, Grant thought grimly. *More than enough to put paid to those poor bastards on* Hermes *and* Audacity. Checking to make sure Red Two had not succumbed to the temptation of attacking the *Zeroes*, he waggled his wings and turned for home, racing to catch up with his formation.

Let's see how bad it was for us, he thought, concerned as he caught up with his squadron. He did a quick head count, then counted again. To his surprise, there were only eight total fighters.

The surviving eight *Skyrockets* and twenty-odd *Fulmars* fought their way clear and headed for Colombo.

They left behind half of the original one hundred and fifty Japanese planes still on course for Force X. They had winnowed the aerial strike force, blunted it, but they hadn't stopped it.

Grant inhaled and looked at his watch.

I just hope that the other Skyrockets *are as bad a surprise for the Japanese CAP as we were for their escorts*, the thought grimly. *Because while we couldn't have stopped this force even if those twenty-four fighters had been with us, it'll all be for naught if they can't keep the* Zeroes *off those biplanes.*

————

HMS ARK ROYAL

Admiral Somerville found himself hunched over the radio in Air Ops, following progress of the world's first carrier-versus-carrier naval battle against an unseen enemy hundreds of miles distant as if it were a cricket broadcast.

It's hard piecing all of this together from a bunch of shouting voices over the R/T and terse, shaky-but-elated after-action reports telegraphed over the W/T by returning survivors, he thought. *But it sure seems like we caught them on the back foot.*

All phases of the battle were starting to peter out as he felt the *Ark Royal's* deck shift as the carrier turned into the wind. While aviators were always prone to overclaiming, it seemed that the *Albacores*, *Swordfish*, and their land-based counterparts had managed to hole the Japanese flagship and two of its companions. Combined with the damage Force B had done, that left one Japanese carrier in fighting condition.

Alas, it appears I have only a handful of aircraft left to throw at them, Somerville thought grimly. *I'm sure men safely away in London will second-guess me not pressing the pursuit more forcefully with* Prince of Wales *and* Repulse *immediately.*

"Bloody horrible show, Townsend," Somerville remarked.

"We were lucky, Admiral," Townsend replied, staring at the grease pencil plots on the vertical plexiglass plotting board. The grease lines showed the staggered attack runs of both carrier and land-based British planes, as well as the bloody toll they'd paid. "Luckier than we ever deserved to be."

Somerville laid a hand on Townsend's shoulder. The uncharacteristically warm gesture only served to show how shaken the admiral was by his near-disastrous success.

"Most of that luck lay in your getting us those new Yank planes," Somerville told Townsend. "Without the *Skyrockets*, with only *Fulmars* to fend off *Zeroes*, we would have been slaughtered."

Townsend nodded. "Thank you, sir," he replied.

"We'll see what tomorrow brings," Somerville continued. "I'm sure the powers-that-be will be angry at me for not turning our remaining heavy ships after the Japanese, but we've saved Ceylon. I'm going to save as many of our men as we can first, get some fighters back aboard, then set off after Nagumo in the morning."

Townsend nodded in agreement with Somerville's planning.

"If the torpedo pilots did as well as they think they did, Nagumo will have to scuttle anything that can't do twenty knots, anyway," Somerville continued. "I want to make sure *Prince of Wales* and *Repulse* have plenty of fuel so Vice Admiral Phillips can chase the so called '*Kido Butai*' to Hades itself if he has to."

Somerville gave a predatory smile.

"As long as we keep *Skyrockets* in flight, there's nothing he'll need to worry about from the air."

———

Author's Acknowledgment

The author is indebted to the following primary sources which proved inordinately useful in recounting the Ceylon Raid. Some liberties were taken with events as recorded.

Jedidiah G. Grant, *Skyrockets at War: the Grumman F5F from Ceylon Raid to Invasion of Kyushu*. Little, Brown. & Harper. New York, 1961.

Admiral Sir Ian Townsend, RN (ret.), KCB. DSO, DSC. *The Fleet that Had to Sink: the Eastern Fleet and the Great Ceylon Raid Victory*. Currier & Iverson. Capetown, 1967.

ABOUT LEE ALLRED

With nearly a hundred professional publication credits, Lee Allred's award-winning short fiction has appeared in *Asimov's Science Fiction Magazine*, anthologies, online magazines, and other venues. His debut novella "For the Strength of the Hills" was named a Sidewise Award for Alternate History finalist.

He's also scripted fan-favorite comic books for DC (*Batman '66, Batman Black and White, BUG! The Adventures of Forager*), Marvel (*Fantastic Four*), IDW (*Dick Tracy*), and Image Comics (*Madman Atomic Comics*).

Lee served three rotations in Iraq as part of Operation Iraqi Freedom for the United States Air Force and retired as a Master Sergeant. He now writes full time.

You can find out more information about Lee and his fiction by visiting his website at leeallred.com.

FIVE METERS FORWARD

A Story of A World Afire

William Alan Webb

1

Note: Times for this battle are problematic, with various sources using different time zones for reference. Those used here are the most commonly referenced times in sources.

ABOARD HIJMS Chōkai, *Five miles east-northeast of Savo Island, Solomon Islands*
0018 Hours, 9 August, 1942

The eight-inch shell could have killed the Admiral...*should* have killed him, and his entire staff. Five meters forward and it would have. Fired from the final United States warship to exchange gunfire with the *Chōkai*, identified as a *New Orleans*-class heavy cruiser, the projectile hit the Operations Room instead of the bridge. In the process, it knocked out 200mm Turret Number One.

But Admiral Mikawa and his staff were not harmed.

To the south, the night sky shimmered with fire beyond the flagship's stern, a roiling wall of smoke and flame marking where at least four Allied cruisers sank into the shark-infested darkness. Mikawa stood on *Chōkai*'s flag bridge with his hands behind his back, eyes fixed on the black waters that rippled orange from the fiery destruction the Japanese task group left in its wake. Nor could Mikawa allow himself to empathize with the Americans, hundreds of whom were even in that moment making the decision between leaving their steel homes for the possibility of being eaten alive or staying on board to die screaming in the flames. In his mind's eye, Mikawa visualized the sea spitting up flotsam and oil, the air rent by the groaning metal of ships breaking up, and one last secondary explosion to thump the air like a closing drumbeat.

No warrior could consider the fate of his enemies until after the battle ended. And Mikawa had not yet made a decision to end the Battle of Savo Island.

"Gunfire ahead to port," someone called out.

Clearing Savo Island on a northerly course, *Chōkai* was not yet out of danger. Eyes trained for night combat turned to the new action. *Furutaka, Tenryū,* and *Yūbari* had broken more sharply to port than the flagship when the first torpedoes were launched. While *Chōkai* and the central formation maintained a more southerly line, those three cruisers pursued a parallel but more northerly track. It was likely they had passed north of Savo Island, then turned back to port, where they had encountered fresh targets. The gunfire now visible over the horizon seemed to be theirs. A signal lamp was used to warn them of *Chōkai's* position while the bombardment continued. Soon enough, it tapered off.

Turning to the assembled staff crammed into the crowded bridge, Mikawa asked for opinions on their next move. Without question, they had won a great victory, perhaps the greatest yet achieved during the war, but was it a complete victory?

"Sir," Vice Admiral Ōnishi Shinzō said, "we are scattered. *Tenryū* has broken formation, and *Kako* is still maneuvering around wreckage. *Yubari* reports rudder trouble. Several ships have taken light damage. Reorganization will take time."

As Mikawa's Chief of Staff, Ōnishi's opinion carried a lot of weight.

"What is the status of your ship, Captain Hayakawa?"

The commander of *Chōkai* answered in a more enthusiastic tone. "*Chōkai* remains ready to fight, Admiral. Repairs to the turret are being made."

"Good."

Ōnishi waited a respectful moment before once again speaking up.

"Admiral, please allow me to remind you that based on radio intelligence of the previous evening, there were enemy aircraft carriers about one hundred fifty kilometers southeast of Guadalcanal," Onishi began. "As a result of our night action, these would be moving toward the island by this time, and to remain in the area by sunrise would mean that we would only meet the fate our carriers had suffered at Midway."

The man paused before continuing.

"By withdrawing immediately, we would probably still be pursued and attacked by the closing enemy carrier force, but by leaving at once, we could get farther to the north before they struck. The enemy carriers might thus be lured within reach of our land-based air forces at Rabaul."

Emulating the Combined Fleet Commander-in-Chief, Admiral Yamamoto, Mikawa only grunted. Turning to his Operations Officer, Captain Ohmae, Mikawa raised an eyebrow.

"And you, Captain?"

"It is difficult to disagree with anything that has been said, Vice Admiral."

"But I sense there is more," Mikawa said rapidly. "Speak plainly, Captain, we have but little time."

"*Hai*. The Army says there are only two thousand Americans on Guadalcanal, that their landing is nothing more than a raid to destroy the airfield. But since I arrived at Rabaul, they have consistently been uncooperative with the Navy, and the quarters assigned to you, the Commander of Eighth Fleet, are more suited for a prison. I have no faith in their assurances, or their estimates."

Ohmae swallowed, looking out into the night towards the burning American cruisers.

"Then I look at the naval power committed to this landing," the man said, gesturing broadly. "So far, we have destroyed *many* cruisers and destroyers, perhaps as many as ten. The enemy has also committed aircraft carriers to this attack...for this to be nothing more than a small diversionary landing of two thousand men. No, such mustering of their strength can only mean they are on Guadalcanal in force, and mean to stay."

Mikawa grunted again.

"You asked for my estimate, Sir. Now you have it."

Nodding, Mikawa had a ready reply. "If we return to sink their transports, we could lose this entire fleet."

"*Hai*. But Vice Admiral, if the Americans *are* here to stay, would such a sacrifice not be justified?"

"It would, Captain. Yes, it would."

No one on the bridge believed the Army could hold Guadalcanal without help. They'd been told, repeatedly, that the Americans were weak, that kicking them off the island would be "trivial." Yet the IJA at Rabaul had refused to commit aircraft, refused to coordinate landing timetables, refused even to share full maps of the coastal objectives. Arrogance masquerading as certainty.

They had all seen the pattern before. And yet...

"Sir," said Ōnishi, "if Captain Ohmae is wrong—"

"Then the sweetness of victory turns into the rotten flavor of defeat."

"*Hai.*"

Mikawa didn't reply at first. Nor was the weight of the moment lost on the Vice Admiral, because only *he* could make the decision to fight on, or retreat to safety in triumph. In the moment, some part of Mikawa's mind understood that his choice could decide the outcome of the war in the Pacific.

Safeguard the Emperor's ships after crushing the enemy, or risk everything for a decisive blow?

He tapped the edge of the plotting table once, twice. Then his eyes drifted across the hand-sketched chart: the cruisers to his rear, the destroyers up ahead, the dark blotch of Guadalcanal off the port beam, and beyond that, Savo Sound and the anchorage known as Lunga Roads.

In other words, the reported transports.

The *real* target.

"Signal from *Aoba*, Admiral," another voice offered. "Admiral Goto requests confirmation...do we withdraw or continue the attack?"

Ōnishi shifted. "We must consider daylight, sir. The American carriers will launch by sunrise. We've already expended at least forty percent of our Type 91 shells. Some destroyers are nearly out of torpedoes. If we delay—"

Mikawa turned to him. "And if we leave the transports untouched? I would rather delay in making the right decision then make the wrong one in haste."

The silence that followed was not uncertainty—it was calculation.

"We have no orders from Combined Fleet," Ōnishi said at last.

"Correct," Mikawa answered. Despite his words, the clock *was* ticking. The words that next came from his mouth seemed to come from somewhere else. "So we follow doctrine. We destroy enemy shipping supporting landings."

Hayakawa stepped forward. "It will be at least two hours to reform into a combat line."

Mikawa walked to the open hatch, staring out into the night. A strong breeze from the south carried the oily tang of burning ships. Somewhere in the darkness, American transports waited. Fat, vulnerable. Likely still unloading fuel, ammunition, and field guns. Maybe even troops. A dozen or more.

No cruisers guarded them now. No destroyer screen. No planes.

And no time.

He stepped back inside. "We are too scattered to reform. If we delay, we miss our chance... I am mindful of Pearl Harbor. A third attack to destroy their oil storage tanks would have been very useful to us..."

Ōnishi exhaled through his nose, but nodded. It was assent. Silent, but assent. The choice had been made.

Mikawa raised a finger and pointed to the signal officer. "Prepare for transmission. Flash light and flag." He spoke with finality:

"All ships: proceed to attack enemy transports at Lunga Roads as able. Independent action authorized."

The surrounding officers exchanged glances, but said nothing. The signalman bowed and repeated the order. Ōnishi was already turning to the helm.

Mikawa stepped to the bridge's railing once more, watching as *Chōkai*'s bow came about. The stars over the sound, sandwiched between the islands of Savo, Guadalcanal, Florida, and Tulagi, flickered behind smoke.

"Let the Army explain tomorrow why I was a fool," Mikawa said, mostly to himself. "I will deliver victory tonight."

ABOARD IJN Y*UNAGI*, *APPROACHING LUNGA ROADS, SAVO SOUND,*
SOLOMON ISLANDS
0105 HOURS, AUGUST 9, 1942

Yunagi's blue-green bioluminescent bow wake split the calm waters of Savo
Sound, like an arrow marking her passage under the low Pacific moon.
Inside her small bridge, Lieutenant Se Okada felt her motion in every
bone and muscle. As the old destroyer sliced through the water, her speed
lowered by months at sea, Se intended to finally use his torpedoes against
enemy vessels. Being part of the screening force meant *Yunagi* was never in
position to use any of her weapons, but with permission for independent
attack, he had no intention of returning to Rabaul with loaded tubes or
full magazines.

To his right lay the black bulk of Guadalcanal, as mountainous as it
was ominous. No features could be discerned, only a shadow blotting out
the stars. The horizon due south was nothing but blackness speckled with
moonlight shimmering off the anchorage.

His bridge was quiet, except for the voice of his exec reading range
estimates. They had orders now: attack the transports at Lunga Roads.
Independent action. No coordination. No reformation.

Good.

Se trusted doctrine more than signals. He'd trained for this, the chaos of night action, torpedo attack in broken formation. The Navy had rehearsed these very scenarios in the Inland Sea years ago. Destroyers like *Yunagi* weren't built for showy duels. They were scalpels. Fast, sharp, and lethal.

Or had been when launched in 1924. Now she was old, slow, poorly armed, and obsolescent. Yet still dangerous.

"Ships bearing starboard one-nine-five, six thousand meters," the lookout called. "Multiple large silhouettes. Speed zero."

Se raised his binoculars.

There they were! The black hulls emerged like ghosts in the starlight. Unloading craft still clung to their sides. He saw faint glints of light, perhaps from portholes or careless deck lamps. Despite the earlier battles, the Americans had no idea they were here.

Perfect.

"Target bearing confirmed," he said. "Prepare to fire starboard tubes. Spread pattern, three degrees spacing."

His torpedo officer bent slightly at the waist. "Set for two meters depth. All tubes loaded and ready."

Unlike most of the other Japanese ships, *Yunagi* did not expend her torpedoes in the earlier battle. Also unlike the heavy cruisers, she did not carry the Type 93 "Long Lance." Pure oxygen, nearly no wake, and more range than anything the Americans had dreamed of. In training, they'd called it the Emperor's divine wind. Instead, she had the older Type 91 torpedoes. But while not as advanced as the Type 93, they remained a deadly killing machine.

"Fire all tubes," Se ordered.

The officer repeated it, then pressed the trigger lever. Torpedoes leaving their tubes resembled porpoises arching through the surf, seemingly as playful as they were slick. The lurch of the launches shuddered through the deck.

One.

Two.

Three.

Four.

Five.

Six.

Unlike the oxygen-fueled Type 93 torpedoes, the Type 91 left a wake, which fairly glowed from the bioluminescence of Savo Sound. Eventually, though, the arrow-like wakes disappeared into the night. Se lowered the binoculars and watched, as if his eyes could follow the invisible paths through the black water. Seconds passed. Then a dull *whump* rolled across the surface, low and heavy.

A second explosion followed, sharper. Then a third, this time with a flash that briefly silhouetted cranes and rigging against the island.

"Three hits," someone said behind him.

Only three hits, out of six. He said nothing. There was no need to confirm. You either struck steel, or you didn't. But he had to wonder how half of his torpedoes could have missed stationary targets...unless they failed to explode.

Se turned to the helm. "Come to course one-five-zero. Open fire with main batteries on the nearest ship."

"Sir, signal from *Yubari*: they're engaging with guns on the east side of the anchorage."

"Good."

Se glanced aft at the fading firelight, then toward the invisible shoreline. The enemy had landed troops today, but those men wouldn't be getting food, water, or ammunition tomorrow.

His only regret was that he couldn't stay to watch them starve.

The destroyer's forward 120mm guns fired their first shells, which glowed red in a long arc toward a nebulous mass of black in the vague shape of a ship. Two flashes along the hull indicated hits; his men had the range with the first salvo! In that moment, all of the grueling hours of training in night combat paid off as *Yunagi's* gunfire ripped into the American fleet.

3

Strains of the battle began to erode Petty Officer First Class Takamura Kenji's energy level, forcing him to concentrate on not showing his increasing fatigue. Gauges inside *Chōkai's* Number Two 200mm turret showed temperatures exceeding 45 °C (113 °F) during their sustained firing, as one Type 91 armor-piercing round after another slid into the cannon. Spent casings added to the stifling atmosphere, as inside the turret, cramped metal walls absorbed heat from each blast, while ventilation struggled to clear cordite smoke and steam.

Crewmen endured the stifling conditions without complaint, their uniforms quickly soaked through with sweat, the air thick with powder residue and machine oil, which created an environment both physically and mentally taxing. Yet, they were trained to not only endure such a challenging environment, but to work through it with precision. The muzzle brake hissed with residual heat after every salvo, and each concussion inside the steel coffin felt like it might stop Takamura's heart, but he kept moving like an automaton.

The hoist thudded, steel on steel, and the turret chief's voice cut through the confined heat.

"Shell down, powder ready!" he called, and the loaders sprang into motion, guiding the next armor-piercing round onto the loading tray as the powder case clanked into position behind it.

"Breech closed, run hot!" came next, as the breechblock slammed shut with a satisfying crash, sealing in the charge and signaling the gun's readiness.

The chief pivoted to the elevation setter. "Elevation ten degrees, train two-five-zero!" he barked, the turret shuddering as motors responded, aligning the twin barrels toward their next target.

"Elevation ten, *hai!*" Takamura said, already cranking.

Then, without hesitation, the chief dropped his hand. "Fire!"

Chōkai's deck vibrated as the next salvo roared from the barrels. Through the gun shield's slit, he caught flashes of orange beyond the smoke: fires licking at a ship's deck, then leaping skyward as secondary explosions ripped its stern away. It was a warship, clear from its silhouette, and thus their use of Type 91 shells. Probably a cruiser.

"New target, bearing two-zero-seven," came the call.

"Switch to Type Zero."

The high explosive shell for thin-skinned ships. *Transports.*

They'd told him in training that enemy warships were sacred targets. "Kill the weapons, kill the men." It was baked into Imperial Japanese Navy doctrine that sinking warships took priority...but others disagreed. "Kill the fuel, kill the food, kill their future."

That night, they did both.

Turret rotation rumbled beneath his boots as the gun team shifted to the new bearing.

Takamura slid to his station, resetting traverse. Another shell loaded. Hands moved in rhythm. The armor-piercing rounds were long, sharp-nosed, and built like a spearhead, designed to punch through steel before detonating deep inside. By contrast, the high-explosive shell bore a blunter profile and a darker fuse band, made to burst on contact and scatter fire and shrapnel across open decks and supply holds.

A crewman slipped, his hand catching the lip of the breech, but despite blood, the man gritted his teeth and reset without a word. They were all beyond pain now.

The fire-control intercom crackled. "Bridge reports direct hit on enemy transport."

The ship names didn't matter; they would be forgotten. The wreckage would not.

Takamura caught a glimpse through the side slat as *Chōkai* passed closer to the anchorage, *much* closer, black water burning with slicks of fire. One ship, already down by the bow, looked as if her crane had melted sideways. In the chaos, he saw a single American in a white t-shirt manning what looked like a .50 cal, firing blindly toward the horizon.

Brave, he thought. *Pointless, but brave.*

The next 200mm shell silenced him forever.

Another salvo. Another fireball. Another scream of rent metal carried across the water.

But Takamura didn't feel remorse. Only reverence.

This was the culmination of everything he'd trained for. He was steel forged in doctrine, and doctrine demanded annihilation.

"Gods do not hesitate," his gunnery instructor once said. "And neither does a turret gunner."

"Shell ready!" someone called.

"Fire!"

The shockwave passed through his chest. Through the heat and the haze, he muttered the words engraved into the lintel of the turret door:

"Duty is eternal. Flesh is temporary."

4

There are moments in life that transcend all previous experiences. No matter how much a warrior might dream of the day he destroyed an enemy, and regardless of how he might picture such a scene in his mind, the reality could not be imagined.

The ocean was on fire, as if the water itself burned.

From *Chōkai's* bridge, Mikawa could see it clearly now. The enemy anchorage stretched in a crescent of flame-streaked water, and across that arc bloomed great orange pillars, red gouts of fire towering into the tropical night. Ships, large, slow, soft-edged silhouettes, were dying one by one. The sea reflected them in crimson shards that flickered, died, and flickered again. Winds from the east rolled smoke over the treetops of Guadalcanal. Yet to the east and south came gun flashes from enemy warships, two of which had visible fires to direct the Japanese gunnery.

"Direct hits from *Kinugasa*, sir," came the report. "Ammunition ship struck, secondary explosions continuing."

Mikawa didn't nod. He merely absorbed the statement. Ammunition cooked off in intervals, each detonation thudding through the air like a drumbeat. One burst was so violent that he saw debris arc a hundred feet into the sky before splashing down like black rain.

Through his night glasses, he counted at least four transports burning outright, two down by the stern, one already listing onto her side. No resistance. No maneuvering. The Americans had been caught unloading, just as expected.

Another explosion rippled over the sea, only this time from the northwest. All heads turned in unison, because the blast came from behind the flagship...one of their ships had been badly hit.

"Message from *Yūbari*, Admiral. Captain Ban reports being struck by a torpedo. The ship has suffered steering damage, with the extent of flooding as yet unknown. He is requesting permission to withdraw independently."

"Granted. Tell Captain Ban to make for Rabaul at best possible speed, but to make for the nearest port should *Yūbari* be too damaged for such a long voyage. No heroism tonight."

The signalman scribbled it down.

Another plume rose from the anchorage. This time not a detonation, but a fuel tank rupture, a long, flickering curtain of fire crawling across the surface like a living thing.

Mikawa shifted his stance, boots creaking faintly against the metal deck plating. His knee ached, a reminder from a fall on a destroyer deck in 1934. He ignored it. He had more pressing calculations to manage.

"Sir," Captain Ōnishi said from beside the plotting table, "we're receiving sporadic signals from *Tenryū* and *Aoba*. They report successful strikes but light damage, one small-caliber return hit."

Mikawa grunted. "The Americans are fighting back."

"Yes, Admiral. But the formations are...dissolving."

"Their formations are destroyed, Captain. *We* have destroyed them."

"*Hai!*"

Through the crowd of ratings and officers, Mikawa navigated back toward the starboard side of the bridge. Below, the crew worked in subdued rhythm. No panic. No celebration. Just steel-minded execution.

This was war done properly, the Imperial Japanese Navy at its best. Not for headlines or theater, but in cold doctrine.

The Army had mocked the Navy's "obsession" with night engagements, but here in the dark, far from the fanfare of Tokyo, the Navy was rewriting the campaign by torchlight. The Army said

Guadalcanal would be taken easily. That the Americans wouldn't hold. That a few days of shelling would clear the jungle.

Mikawa didn't believe a word. The landing had come as a surprise, and Army air had been missing in action since the first report. No reconnaissance flights, no ground-based dive bombers, no help. Just words and delays. As always. Captain Ōnishi called out new orders to shift fire to a shadow passing close in-shore.

Mikawa lowered his binoculars. "How long have we been firing?"

"Twenty-five minutes, Admiral."

He checked his chronometer. 0205 hours. Daylight was coming, and with it, flights of vengeful American aircraft. Their timeline was narrowing. Nighttime belonged to the Japanese, but with dawn that calculus changed.

"How is your ammunition supply?" Mikawa asked.

Ōnishi glanced toward the ordnance ledger clipped to the plotting table. *Chōkai* was down to just under 60 rounds per gun. The other cruisers had roughly the same or less.

Enough for another engagement, perhaps, but not a prolonged fight. And certainly not a daylight battle against aircraft.

"Radio all ships. Continue the attack for another ten minutes," he said. "Then begin breaking contact. Priority to damaged ships, detach them first."

"Understood, sir."

"And prepare for withdrawal on the eastern side of Savo Island. Ships needing the western passage due to damage or position, identify as such to avoid being misidentified as the enemy."

"Aye, Admiral."

Mikawa turned back toward the anchorage one last time before stepping away. Below the waves, a transport exploded in a white-hot blossom, as if the sea itself were peeling open.

Have we struck a blow the enemy will be unable to recover from? Mikawa pondered. *Perhaps, but at what cost remains to be seen.* Regardless of the eventual cost, they had also sent a message. After Midway, the Americans thought they could fight the Japanese Navy on equal terms. The Americans had come to Guadalcanal thinking they could take and hold a foothold without consequence. The Army had shrugged, but the Navy had answered.

And tonight, *he* had written that answer in flames.

5

Yunagi's radar shack was dark. Not because of malfunction; the structure's intended purpose simply didn't exist, as the IJN did not have nearly enough sets to spare for the old destroyer. Instead, Lieutenant Commander Se relied on eyes, searchlights, and the superb binoculars and night optical devices manufactured by Nippon Kogaku.

Time was running out to finish striking blows at the enemy. Admiral Mikawa's order to withdraw left no room for doubt, and anyway, *Yunagi's* magazines were nearly empty. All of her torpedoes were also gone.

"Visual contact: new silhouette, bearing zero-seven-five. Larger hull, higher freeboard. Possibly a troop ship," his executive officer reported.

She appears to be down by the stern, Se thought, nodding.

"Range?"

"Estimate twenty-two hundred meters. Speed zero."

Not the best firing angle as the ship steered out of Savo Sound, a target nonetheless.

"Helm, make for the eastern passage around Savo Island. Speed twenty knots. Target that troop ship."

"Hai!"

"Fire at will."

There was virtually no trajectory to the 120mm shells that screamed from the gun tubes. Red streaks sped through the night to impact against the American steel in blasts of yellow and orange. Then came a blast, a jagged white tear followed by a concussive boom. The ship staggered in place like a man hit in the gut.

Se stared through his binoculars as fire licked skyward from the stricken ship. Dark dots illuminated against the intense heat might have been men jumping overboard.

"The arrogant Americans dared to oppose the Emperor's navy, and we have answered with the spirit of Bushido," he said, addressing those nearby. "Swift, absolute, and without mercy."

Now hopefully we have enough ammunition to get home, Se thought grimly.

———

Roughly 8,000 yards away, the *Chokai*'s gunners were similarly conducting final touches to the IJN's victory.

Panting from heat, exhaustion, and the adrenaline-soaked excitement of being in a major gun battle at sea, Petty Officer First Class Takamura wiped his face with his sleeve. Not that it helped. Sweat poured down the inside of his collar. His hands ached from gripping, loading, bracing. The smell of burnt lubricant and detonated powder clogged every breath.

"Magazines are near empty. Two more salvos, then cease fire," the turret chief shouted.

The next round slammed home. The deck rocked slightly beneath Takamura as *Chōkai* once again changed course to port. Other vibrations shook the ship. Takamura didn't know if it was a distant torpedo detonation, or secondary explosions from some dying ship, and it didn't matter.

They were almost done.

He took a moment to peer through the slit as the inferno beyond. The sky itself was turning a muted gray with approaching dawn. Not full light yet, but enough to strip away some of the shadows.

He saw one American transport, lower in the water than before, bow aground. Men were on the deck trying to free a davit with ropes. He could make out their helmets, even a pair of hands waving.

Too late.

A final salvo fired. The shells crossed above the men's heads and struck the hull just behind them. The detonation tore the stern wide open.

He felt nothing.

Not anger. Not elation. Just...rightness.

———

Information came in bursts through radio static. From what Lieutenant Commander Se understood, there were casualties on both sides. The Americans had fought back, especially the warships, but now as they headed away from Guadalcanal, the seas were still. The echoes of destruction rolled behind them.

"What is our damage status?" the Captain said.

"Minor flooding in boiler room one. Number three gun crew suffered multiple casualties, a near miss. There is splinter damage along the waterline near the forward magazine, but temporary repairs should hold until we reach Rabaul."

"Good, good, that is very good. Any reports of damage to other ships?"

The signals officer replied: "*Tenryū* has rudder damage. *Yubari* is badly hit, making 12 knots. *Chōkai, Kinugasa* and *Kako* all report moderate damage from shell fire."

"Have the men stand at battle stations. We can expect air attack shortly after dawn. Have them fed as possible at their stations."

Their attack was over. Just the hiss of fuel burning and the dull thunder of exploding ammunition to remind the Japanese of the death left in their wake. But with the cessation of their incursion, the impetus shifted to the Americans and their deadly bombers.

He gave one last order: "Best speed through the channel east of Savo Island."

———

They weren't firing anymore. Orders had come down: cease fire.

Takamura leaned back against the bulkhead, arms limp. His face and arms were streaked with carbon, like black war paint. His hearing was a ringing haze.

"Secure the guns."

Along with the others who locked down various gears and pulleys,

Takamura reached over and closed the breech, as if tucking the huge cannon under a blanket for the night.

In the viewport slit, the fires of Lunga still burned. Black smoke curled into the early light, drifting like banners from a victory parade no one would see.

He didn't smile. He didn't blink.

This wasn't pride.

This was duty fulfilled.

6

The fires were well behind them now and partly hidden by the bulk of Savo Island to port. Only a faint orange glow lingered on the horizon, smeared across the rising mist like the embers of a battlefield pyre. Mikawa stood with his cap tucked under one arm, staring into that glow as if it might rise again.

It did not.

The fleet was underway but loose. The formation that had left Kavieng as a tight blade of steel had unraveled into a staggered line of tired predators, spread across twenty kilometers of water. The urgency now shifted from sinking enemy ships to regaining a tight-knit formation to repel the air attacks that surely were coming soon.

Captain Ōnishi stepped onto the flag bridge with a clipboard tucked under his elbow and a streak of oil on his sleeve. He saluted crisply, then relaxed his shoulders.

"Damage reports coming in, sir."

Mikawa turned slightly and nodded.

"*Tenryū* suffered steering damage, and her rudder is jammed five degrees to port. Captain Sano estimates his speed to be no more than ten to twelve knots. He is able to steer the ship using his engines. She's maintaining for now, but any sudden maneuvering will be difficult."

Mikawa's face remained unreadable.

"Keep her close to *Aoba*. She'll need cover if she falls behind."

"Yes, sir. *Yubari* reports a major hull breach aft to starboard from a single torpedo hit and shrapnel. Her aft deck is awash, but pumps are handling it. Engines are intact."

"I am pleasantly surprised that she is still afloat. Casualties?"

"*Tenryū* reports five dead, thirteen wounded. *Yubari*, thirty-three dead, many injured. All other ships report varying degrees of damage, from light to moderate, but none report speed or steering compromised."

"Noted."

Ōnishi hesitated.

"There is one other item, sir."

Mikawa raised an eyebrow.

"*Kako* is well north of Savo Island, and broke radio silence to issue a brief contact report. Directional fix suggests it went northward."

"Did she intercept an enemy transmission?"

"Apparently so. It is mostly likely a submarine..."

Mikawa waved a hand.

"If they didn't know where we were before, they know now."

He turned and walked slowly to the open bridge wing. The sea stretched wide and empty, the stars overhead paling with the coming dawn.

Behind him, Lunga Roads burned. The American landing force had been gutted, if not outright smashed. Transports sunk, supply lines severed. No reinforcements. No fuel. No food. Only embers and ash.

A decisive blow. Now, with dawn, would come the cost.

And yet, he could already hear the whispers that would come from Rabaul. The Army would claim the Navy had risked the fleet needlessly. That the victory was theirs by default. That the transports were unarmed, the Marines would have fallen anyway.

He exhaled through his nose.

"They'll say we were reckless," Mikawa said.

"Sir?"

"The Army. They will say I took an unnecessary risk. And we have yet to endure the full force of the enemy's wrath."

Ōnishi stood beside him. "They weren't there, sir."

"No," Mikawa said, "but they'll write the reports."

"Forgive me, Admiral, but you answer to Combined Fleet, not the Army. To hell with their reports."

Mikawa paused a moment longer, then straightened.

"Signal all ships: proceed to Rabaul. No delays. Inform *Yubari* and *Tenryū* that if they must fall behind, they are to rendezvous with the submarine tender at Mussau."

"Yes, Admiral."

"Send to Combined Fleet: *'Enemy transport group destroyed. Objective achieved. Fleet withdrawing. Losses light. Enemy air attack expected during daylight.'*"

Ōnishi nodded and turned to pass the order.

Mikawa remained still as the wind picked up over the rail, dry and cool and clean.

This would not be the end. Not of Guadalcanal. Not of the war. But tonight, he had done what duty demanded, and what doctrine had prepared him for.

He whispered it aloud, just once:

"Thank you."

———

No. 2 Turret, IJN Chōkai
En Route to Rabaul
0345 Hours
9 August

The turret was cooler now, quieter. Heat still hung in the air like a sleeping beast, but less, and the vibrations of firing had ceased. Takamura sat with his back against the shell hoist, one knee up, breathing through his mouth to steady his heart's beating. His right hand was wrapped in a stained cloth, a minor burn. His ears still rung, all sounds seeming muffled.

They'd gone silent nearly an hour ago. Cease fire, turret lock, magazine sealed. No need for gunnery now. Only speed.

The deck beneath him shivered with the churn of *Chōkai's* engines. At full bell, she was racing north-northwest with the others, scattered and worn, but alive.

A last look back allowed a final glance at the orange glow on the far horizon. Fading, distant, but unmistakable.

Takamura didn't feel pride, exactly. That wasn't the right word. There was satisfaction, yes. A kind of fullness in the chest that came from doing one's job completely. From fulfilling the unspoken promise between ship and sailor: that when the order came, you would not fail.

He'd seen the Americans. Not just the ships. The men.

The one with the machine gun. The others trying to launch lifeboats. They'd fought, even as their ships died under them. They hadn't begged. They hadn't broken.

He respected that.

But it changed nothing. If anything, it made victory all the more satisfying.

Takamura adjusted his seating slightly, easing the ache in his shoulder. No one else in the turret moved. Some of them slept upright. Others just sat like he did, thinking, or not thinking at all.

He whispered aloud to no one in particular:

"We are steel. We did what steel was made to do."

Outside, *Chōkai* steamed on, her wake foaming like an arrow pointing to a target for the American airplanes that were surely on the way.

* * *

7

It was the moment just before the sun first crested the eastern horion, although Santa Isabel Island blocked direct sight of the new day's dawn. Although still dark overhead and to the west, a thin ash blue covered the eastern sky. It gave the sea an oddly sterile look, like gunmetal washed clean.

Se leaned on the bridge rail, staring aft. Arms crossed, he imagined American bombers lifting off from the decks of their carriers. If the enemy aircraft carriers were southwest of Guadalacana, as expected, those planes should be overhead within an hour.

The fires of Savo Sound were long gone now. Lunga Point had vanished behind the curvature, the glow of the burning anchorage swallowed by cloud and distance. Now came *their* time to burn.

His helmsman stood silent at the wheel. All unnecessary conversation had ceased two hours ago. The crew had settled into the tempo of retreat, alert but quiet.

A petty officer handed him a folded sheet.

"Final torpedo inventory: 0 rounds. Main guns: 32.7% ammunition remaining. Fuel status: minimal."

"Is our fuel sufficient to make Rabaul?"

"Hai!"

"If we come under air attack, we will have to maneuver at speed. Inform me if your fuel situation grows critical."

The younger man nodded, once.

The Japanese formation had closed up again, not as tight as the previous day, but no longer a ragged mob. If enemy planes attacked, they could at least put up a fight now. *Tenryū* rode low to port, followed by *Aoba,* her bow down, her wake listing oddly from the jammed rudder. She would make it. Probably.

Se turned back forward.

Mikawa's flagship was barely visible through the morning haze, gray on gray, running fast and straight. No signals. No lights. Just the silhouette of purpose.

The salt air had rarely tasted so good, or felt so fresh.

It had been a good operation. Messy, disordered, decisive.

He closed his eyes for just a moment, listening to the wind. A rating handed him a cup of *mugi-cha*, the roasted barley coffee substitute forced upon the Japanese by wartime shortages. As did the crew, Captain Se ate his breakfast of rice, salted bonito, and miso soup at his battle station, the bridge. As he slurped the last of the soup, *Yunagi's* Executive Officer joined him.

"The ship is ready to repel air attack, Captain."

"We are low on fuel. Be aware in case we use too much avoiding bombs."

"Hai! Sir, last night's battle...it will surely go down as one of the greatest victories in our history!"

"Mmm..."

"You disagree?"

"No, you are surely correct. Yet the Americans will rebuild, of course. That is their way. We must therefore continue to smash them. They will remember this defeat and will come for revenge. It will our duty to continue defeating them, until they finally realize they cannot win this war. But be assured, they *will* remember the Battle of Savo Sound."

"If they learn so slowly, they will surely die in great numbers."

Once more, Se grunted. He *wanted* to share the younger officer's optimism, the assuredness of the superiority of the Japanese Navy...

"Put on extra lookouts," he said, changing the subject. "Pay particular attention to the southwestern and southeastern skies."

"*Hai*, Captain."

Yunagi churned forward, clean wake vanishing behind her, as the sky lightened to the color of blood.

———

Rabaul Naval Headquarters
1938 hours
9 August

If the Army had been cold toward the Navy *before* the Battle of Savo Island, it was outright hostile in the aftermath. Sitting in the quiet of his headquarters office, Vice Admiral Mikawa expected nothing else.

A single fan creaked overhead, pushing around air too thick to cool. Mikawa sat at a battered wooden desk, stripped to his white shirt, collar open, an untouched cup of *mugi-cha* cooling near his elbow. Behind him, the window was wide open, letting in the sound of distant truck engines and barking dogs. Tropical heat never slept in Rabaul.

Eighth Fleet Chief of Staff Vice Admiral Ōnishi Shinzō entered without knocking.

"The reply from Combined Fleet has arrived, Admiral," he said.

Mikawa didn't look up. "Let's hear it."

Ōnishi read from the folded slip of paper in his hand:

"*To Vice Admiral Gunichi Mikawa, Commander Eighth Fleet. Mission accomplished with skill and distinction. Losses minimal. Aggressive action appreciated. Report results as soon as known. Continue operations as necessary. Congratulations. Yamamoto.*"

A pause.

"That's all," Ōnishi added.

Mikawa nodded once.

"No questions. No follow-up. No mention of the Army. The Commander-in-Chief wrote that himself, it is his style."

Mikawa leaned back in the chair, letting the fan's air wash over his face. His shoulders ached. His uniform still smelled of gunpowder from *Chōkai's* upper deck. He hadn't changed since returning to shore.

"Any word from the Army?" he asked. "*Civil* word, I mean."

Ōnishi hesitated.

"They have requested a transport timetable for reinforcements. They claim to have only just now been made aware the anchorage had been attacked. They assumed your fleet had withdrawn immediately after the cruiser engagement."

Mikawa laughed once, a short, dry exhale with no smile behind it.

"They assumed wrong."

"Yes, sir."

The Admiral reached for the *mugi-cha*, but didn't drink. He just held the cup for a moment, watching steam curl into the air like one last thread of smoke from Lunga.

"Draft a reply to Combined Fleet," he said.

"Yes, sir."

He paused, then spoke quietly:

"Enemy shipping destroyed. Landing force disrupted. Army requests that Navy transport reinforcements to Guadalcanal. Banzai! Mikawa."

Ōnishi didn't write it down. He only nodded.

Outside, more trucks rumbled, more dogs barked, and the jungle, while far to the south, iron and steel lined the bottom of Savo Sound.

The End

ABOUT WILLIAM ALAN WEBB

William Alan Webb grew up devouring history books, often wondering what might have happened had things gotten just a little bit different... this led him to major in History and Creative Writing at the University of Memphis. World War Two has always been Webb's primary area of study. In addition to being published in *World War Two* magazine, Webb is the author of the three books in the *Killing Hitler's Reich* non-fiction series. His Alternate History series *The Last Brigade* has sold more than 100,000 copies, while future series include the World War Two epic *A World Afire*, and the Roman series *The Unbroken Lion*. Webb lives in West Tennessee with his wife and five dogs.

At his website: www.thelastbrigade.com
On Patreon: https://www.patreon.com/c/WilliamAlanWebb
On facebook: https://www.facebook.com/keepyouupallnightbooks

NAKED

Kacey Ezell

Author's Note: This story is based on true events, and an actual photograph taken by renowned Navy photographer Horace Bristol. You can find the photograph and the photographer's account here: https://rarehistoricalphotos.com/naked-gunner-rescue-rabaul-1944/ The author begs Lieutenant Commander Bristol's pardon, and hopes he enjoys her reimagining of the story in her own universe.

The heat was the worst. Or maybe it was the humidity. Either way, Lydia felt the air surround her like hands over her mouth and nose, smothering her in the scorching wetness that was January in the South Pacific. She'd grown up in Southern California, and though the winters were balmy, they were nothing like this. She sighed at her reflection and started braiding her brown hair back close to her skull. It was already starting to frizz out beyond recognition.

"Lydia." her uncle's voice hit her seconds before the man himself leaned in her open doorway, making her gasp and turn in that direction. His normally handsome, slightly weathered face was ghostly pale under his tan, and a fine sheen of sweat broke out along his hairline. Sure, it was warm, but this was excessive.

"Uncle Horatio!" she said, tying off her hair and heading over to him. Careful not to invade his privacy, she extended her senses to pick up the edge of his outer mind. Achy, swirling misery greeted her, making her pull her power quickly back within her own barriers. "You look awful. What happened?"

"I don't know," he said. "I woke up in the middle of the night with aches and fever. I feel like death. I... I don't think I can make today's flight."

"Oh no," Lydia gasped softly, her fingertips coming to her lips. The flight was the whole reason they'd made the trip out this far. Horatio was better known as Lieutenant Commander Horatio Driscoll, Naval Aviation Photographic Unit. But to Lydia, he'd always been her mother's younger brother, Uncle Horatio.

When he'd shipped off to the South Pacific to take pictures for the Navy, Lydia had accompanied him as his darkroom assistant. That was the polite way to put it. It was more accurate to say she'd *run away*, but that didn't sound as romantic and official. Not that it mattered to her; she'd just wanted out of Whittier, and away from the stifling life and attentions of people who'd known her—and her power—since she was a little girl.

Uncle Horatio hadn't exactly been pleased, at first, but he was sympathetic to her plight, and managed to pull some strings to allow her to stay with him, reasoning that at least this way, he could assure the family that she was safe.

Of course, then he took her to the South Pacific, where conditions were anything *but* safe, but they had agreed not to tell the family about that part.

And truth be told, it wasn't that bad. Uncle Horatio got her set up with a darkroom at Henderson Field, and while he was gone on assignment, she processed and developed the negatives that he and the other photographers brought in. Then, after work, she'd meet up with some of the nurses from the hospital and have dinner. It was hard work, but a lot of fun.

But Uncle Horatio didn't look like he was having much fun at the moment.

"Are you going over to the hospital?" she asked.

"I will, but... I need you to take this flight today. Styver said that he really needed some shots of a PBY crew in action."

"Me—?" Lydia squeaked, her voice cracking in surprise.

"Yes, you'll be great. I've already cleared it with the squadron CO. You're a fantastic photographer, Lydia. You have that knack of catching people's emotions right on their faces. That's exactly what Styver wants. Help me out, will ya?"

Lydia drew in a deep breath and nodded, despite her shaking hands.

"Of course," she said. "Of course, Uncle. You brought me here—I owe you. Of course I'll help you out. But you have to promise me you'll go see the medics."

"I promise. Now here, I brought you my camera and bag. You need to be on the flightline in an hour..."

———

Forty-five minutes later, Lydia's hands were still shaking.

"You the photographer?"

She looked up to meet the light blue eyes of the young sailor who'd shouted the words over the roar of aircraft engines. Something leapt inside her mind at the sight of his handsome, open face, but she locked it down hard and forced herself to focus.

"Y-yes. Lydia Driscoll."

"Good to meet you," he said with an easy grin. He shifted his lanky frame and stuck out a hand. Lydia hastily tried to switch the camera to her other hand and dropped it to bang awkwardly against her stomach on the strap. She felt her cheeks heating up as she took his offered grip. "I'm Aviation Ordnanceman Second Class Eric Warner."

"Nice to meet you, too," she mumbled. Or tried to mumble. The engines were still turning not too far away, so she had to shout to make herself heard.

"This way," he shouted back, giving her hand a quick squeeze before dropping it. Then he turned and beckoned for her to follow as he walked down between a line of parked aircraft toward the one that had been making so much noise.

She walked closely behind him, careful to keep well clear of the wings, even though the PBY's turning props were high above her head. She climbed into the aircraft after him, and when he pointed at a headset, she pulled it on over her ears. He did the same.

"Can you hear me okay? Give me a thumbs up if you can," he instructed. She copied his gesture, then looked around for a place to not be in the way. Warner stepped into the PBY's starboard "blister," a dome-shaped window that allowed for maximum visibility on that side of the aircraft. There was a blister on the port side, too, and a serious-faced man fussed with the waist gun on that side.

"You can sit there, on those ammo cans," Warner said, pointing to a spot forward of both blisters on the port side. Then he nudged the port gunner with his elbow. "Seth here doesn't say much, but he's a good man. If you have any questions, you can speak by holding down this button here. Just press your lips right up to the boom mic on the headset. Perfect. Say hi to the photographer, Seth."

"Hi to the photographer, Seth," Seth said without looking up. Lydia startled herself with a laugh. But because she didn't push the button, the sound was lost in the pulsing drone of the PBY's props.

"All right, that's enough chatter back there," someone said through the headset. "Are we all secured?"

"Aye, sir," Warner replied, giving Lydia one last thumb's up and stepping in to his own blister.

"Right, let's go." The noise from the props got louder and slightly higher in pitch, and Lydia could feel an ache beginning just behind her ears. The PBY lurched forward, which was backward from Lydia's perspective, and began to taxi. She suddenly remembered her job and lifted Uncle Horatio's camera to snap off a few shots of the men working with their weapons, and leaning out into their blisters to look around the aircraft.

Before too long, the PBY wheeled about in what felt like a ninety-degree turn, and the prop noise ratcheted up even higher. The aircraft frame felt like it was shuddering as the sound built all around her, until finally it leapt forward with so much force that Lydia nearly tumbled off her ammo can. She had to reach out to steady herself on the nearby bulkhead.

Both men stood with legs splayed, braced in their blisters as that same voice said "rotation" in her headset. Then the PBY pitched up, making Lydia glad she'd found her handhold, and began to climb into the sky.

Even with the protective headset, the noise was punishing. Lydia could barely hear as the men spoke about important, flight-related things. She tried to make out the words, but they just disappeared into the background drone of the engines and props, and the rush of air around them.

The PBY banked to starboard, and Lydia caught a glimpse of the airfield through Warner's blister. She got her camera up just in time to take the shot, and then lowered it as she realized that it would probably be censored, anyway.

Warner turned and said something to her, but she couldn't make out his words. He pointed to his position, as if offering to swap places with her so she could get a good view, but she shook her head in the negative. It probably wouldn't do to have him off his weapon for that long. Plus, she could tell he was busy looking around and speaking often into the boom mic that rested against his lips. She took a few shots of him, and then sat down morosely on her ammo can, wondering how on earth Uncle Horatio managed to do this when he couldn't communicate with his subjects. If only she could *hear* them...

A thought occurred to her so suddenly that she nearly dropped the camera. Her mouth went suddenly very dry, and her hands began to tremble once again, but the sheer audacity of it made her wonder. She *had* to get some good shots; otherwise, Uncle Horatio could very well face disciplinary action. After the way he'd played fast and loose with the regs to allow her to accompany him, she knew he couldn't afford a black mark. And now he needed her help.

Lydia took a deep breath and let the tiniest bit of slack in the bonds of will she'd wrapped around her own mind. She pictured a heavy steel door, like the ones meant to contain fires aboard a ship. Then she allowed the door to crack open an infinitesimal amount, just enough to let her power start to trickle forth. She would brush against Warner's outer mind, just enough to get a sense of how he felt, and what he meant.

I hope it's enough, she thought.

The starboard gunner turned to face her with surprise in his eyes, and threw his barriers wide open, welcoming her in to all his delicious maleness. Lydia's power leapt forth with joyful acceptance, and without meaning to do so, she found herself locked in a psychic net with the young ordnanceman.

You're psychic? Eric asked, his mind tone incredulous. *Why didn't you say?*

Why would I? she asked back, too amazed at this turn of events to prevaricate. *People hurt witches, or at least lock us up.*

Don't call yourself that! Eric said, with surprising ferocity. His wide eyes narrowed in a frown, and he turned back to his blister to look outside. *That's a horrible thing to say!*

Everyone else says it, she said. *It's just a word.*

Not to me, he said. *My mother's psychic.*

Ah, so she taught you how to link?

Yeah, he said. *But she never felt as strong as you. She kept her power hidden, though. It always made me sad. She said it wasn't safe to let everyone know, so I guess you're right. I just never thought...she always linked with us kids. It was useful when we'd be out running around in the mountains.*

Oh? Lydia asked, happy to change the subject. *Where are you from?*

Northern California, he said, and his lips curved in a tiny smile as he craned his head to look aft around his weapon. *Little town called Auburn.*

Then he keyed his button and spoke into his mic: "Friendlies, seven o'clock," he said. "Looks like a flight of Corsairs."

"Roger," came the pilot's voice from up front, and unlike before, the words were clear and distinct through Lydia's headphones.

Wow, she said. *This is so much better! I can actually hear what's going on. It must be because I'm hearing through your ears, too.*

Yeah, same for me, Eric said. *This is cool. We could link Seth in, too...*

I'd rather not, she said quickly. *I don't want... I mean, you seem trustworthy, but...*

Oh, he said, and she could feel sadness seeping through their link. *It's not just hypothetical, then? Someone really did hurt you?*

Well, not exactly, she said. For just a moment, she wondered how on Earth she had gotten to this point. She'd only met Eric a few minutes ago, and now here she was ready to share the deepest secrets of her soul with him. Was that the bond? Her grandmother had warned her that it could be a seductive thing, especially when linked with a man who was not a member of her blood.

Well, what, then, exactly? Unless you don't want to say, he added, as he turned his head away from her to continue doing his job. She had to give it to him: he was super professional, even while holding a conversation with her.

There's a boy back home. A man, really, I guess, but I've known him since he was a boy. He's always kinda had a thing for me, and I've tried to be kind... Lydia thought, then trailed off in her mind.

But you're not interested in him, Eric filled in.

Not that way, no. He's got a cruel streak that I don't appreciate, Lydia thought. She shuddered as she pushed away a memory.

Anyway, awhile back, he actually proposed. He'd done it before, but I always put him off, saying I'm too young, and so on, Lydia continued. She clasped her hands between her knees, the camera lying on her legs.

Well, this time he came to me and said that it was high time we got married, and if I didn't say yes, he'd turn me in to the law for using my psychic powers to convince people to do bad things, Lydia started again after a few moments. She turned to look out the blister past Eric, her stomach flip-flopping.

When I asked what evidence he proposed to show, he said he would...well. He'd hurt some people, some people who'd been mean to me when we were young, and that he'd say I had coerced him to do it.

Eric was silent for a long time. Lydia watched the back of his blond head as he turned this way and that, scanning both sky and ocean for enemies.

You were right the first time, he said after a long moment. *He's not a man at all.*

I guess you're right, she said. *Anyway, that's part of why I'm leery of letting people know about my talent. My hometown mostly knows, and it hasn't turned out well.*

Another flight of *Corsairs* flashed past in a climb.

Is that why you're out here? Eric asked after several long moments scanning to make sure the fighters weren't after a threat.

Pretty much. I followed my Uncle Horatio, and he pulled strings to let me stay when I told him what awaited me back home.

Eric paused and scanned towards something distant. Lydia heard some rapid radio chatter, but was unable to follow what was being said.

Sounds like a good man, Eric said, smiling over at her.

He is. The best, Lydia said.

What I'd like to know—

Lydia never found out what Eric wanted to know, because their pilot's voice crackled over the intercom system in their headsets.

"Change of plans, boys. Just got a call. Downed *Corsair* not more than ten minutes' flight from here, in Rabaul Harbor."

"Rabaul Harbor?" Seth asked, his voice ratcheting up in pitch. "That's sticking our head into the lion's den, isn't it?"

"Yep, Jap harbor guns shot down one of our pilots," the pilot replied. "He got a call off, so he's still alive for the moment. We're not going to leave him to die or be captured."

"Hell, no, we won't, sir," Seth said, racking his weapon. Without realizing that she meant to do so, Lydia lifted the camera to her face and snapped off a shot of his steely-eyed, determined expression.

Okay then, a rescue mission, Eric thought to her as he prepped his own weapon. *You just hang tight, Lydia—this won't take but a minute.*

Lydia felt the tension rise, not needing a psychic link to know that what they were about to do was apparently much more dangerous than a normal mission.

Can I photograph you guys? Lydia asked. *I mean, I won't get in your way, right?*

Of course. Just stay there in your seat and hold on, Eric thought. Lydia could feel the tinge of false bravado in his thoughts. *The pilots may have to do some fancy flying to avoid getting shot down like the guy we're going to rescue.*

Unbeknownst to the distracted gunner, Lydia could feel Eric's half-hysterical, dark humor. If a *Corsair* couldn't dodge the harbor guns at Rabaul, how was the slower, bulkier PBY supposed to do it?

Lydia didn't have an answer, so she said nothing as they banked it up to make a sharp turn to the left and headed toward the mouth of hell itself.

———

"Dropping down over the water! Gonna get low to try and keep clear of those damn harbor guns!" the pilot said into his microphone up front. Lydia closed her eyes and held on to the bulkhead with one hand and her uncle's precious camera with the other as both blister gunners fired long, rattling blasts from their guns. The aircraft banked hard to the right, then back down to the left in a maneuver that made her feel like her stomach was about to fly out of her mouth.

"Can you guys see anything back there?" another voice, that of the copilot, said. His tone carried a shrill edge of anxiety. "It's hard to make anything out up here. There's so much smoke, I can't see where there might be any wreckage or anything!"

"Kinda busy, sir," Seth grunted as he turned his gun and continued firing. "Damn enemy fighters are like flies on roadkill out here!"

Eric didn't say anything, he just focused grimly and continued firing as the Japanese fighters swung down and spat searing lines of fire toward the PBY. A trickle of frustrated despair ran through his mind.

I don't know if we're going to find this guy, he thought in response to the pilot's question. *The smoke is too thick, and I can't take my eyes off these damned fighters for a second!*

Hang on, Lydia said as a thought appeared with crystal clarity in her mind. *Maybe I can help...*

What—?

His thought cut off as Lydia withdrew from their link. What she was about to try would take all of her attention, and even then, her power might not be enough. But she had to try.

She took a deep breath, closed her eyes, and consciously dropped her barriers. She reached out with her mind, stretching her awareness as far as she could. Eric's psyche pulled at her, but she flinched away from the siren call of his mental landscape and kept searching.

Beside her, she tasted the hint of Seth's fear and fatalism as they tangled in his outer mind. He kept scanning and firing.

Forward, the two pilots, men she hadn't even met, mere voices in her headset, hung on with grim determination as they fought to keep the PBY flying low and fast through the smoke that clung close to the water's surface.

Then out, further forward, sweeping for any sign of anything...

There!

Terror clawed at her throat as choking water the temperature of blood swamped her mouth and nose. Her eyes fought to see, but all was black agony and flashes of light that had nothing to do with the external world. Pain wreathed every tortured breath as panic gripped her...

"I found him!" Lydia shouted out loud as she ripped her mind back to her body. She didn't key the mic, but Eric was looking at her and saw her lips move. He turned his upper body in her direction, and she quickly reached out to reestablish the link between the two of them.

Where? Eric asked, urgency throbbing through their connection.

Up ahead, and off to the right—starboard, a little. He's in a lot of pain and blinded.

"Sir, possible sighting ahead to starboard," Eric said over the intercom. "Looks like that's the source of some of this smoke. Could be the wreckage. Can we get closer?"

"Roger." The pilot's voice came back emotionless and focused. The PBY banked to the right, and Lydia could see the dark, greasy wisps of smoke starting to stream past Eric's blister.

Here, Lydia invited, opening her mental channel to the gunner wider. *I bet I can find him again. I'm going to warn you...he's in pretty bad shape.*

I'll handle it, Eric said.

All right, Lydia said. She took a firmer grip on his mental landscape and then reached out again. Not so far this time...

There! The beacon of agony and fear called to her, and once again, she felt the searing impact of the wounded, dying man's mind.

Somehow, Eric held it together, even though his knees buckled as pain and terror flowed down the conduit from her mind to his.

"Got 'im, sir!" the gunner transmitted into the mic. "11 o'clock low, four hundred meters!"

"Contact," the pilot said. "Slight left turn, on the approach. I'll get us as close as I can, let's hope he can swim through the wreckage to us."

Swim? Lydia's mental gasp rocketed out from her mind to Eric's. *Eric, there's no way! He can't even see!*

"Sir, he looks like he's in pretty bad shape from here," Eric said, "I think I'm going to have to go in after him."

"You think you can get to him in time? And not let him pull you under? Or he could be dead already!"

"I've been a lifeguard since I was fifteen, sir," Eric said. "I'll knock him out if I have to, but I can see he's alive. It don't sit right to leave a man behind, sir. Not without giving it a try."

"Damn straight, Warner. All right, go for it."

With that, Lydia felt a *bump*, which struck her as strange. They were landing the aircraft on the water, shouldn't it be more of a splashing sensation? The noise from the props changed again as the pilots maneuvered the now-watercraft through the debris from the wreck.

You may want to avert your eyes, Eric thought to her as he stepped away from his weapon and hung his headset on its hook. He began unbuckling his pants and toed out of his boots. His shirt came off over his head, leaving the long, lean muscles of his back bare, and then he shucked off his pants and kicked them over against the bulkhead.

Before Lydia could do more than blush, he took a few running steps and dove out the rear door. She surged to her feet and followed, bracing herself in the door as her eyes and mind followed him, watching to be sure he surfaced again.

"Starboard's out!" Seth yelled into his mic, even as he continued firing at the circling Japanese fighters.

"I have him in sight!" Lydia said, keying her mic for the first time. "Uh... it's the photographer. I can see the starboard gunner, he's approaching the downed pilot... He's calling out to him. The pilot looks really badly hurt...burns on his face and his eyes... Starboard has him—"

"Shit! That harbor gun just fired! Brace!" The copilot's voice cut through Lydia's commentary just in time for her to hang on tight while the PBY bucked skyward as a shell exploded in the water on the other side of the plane.

Get down, under the water! Lydia had the presence of mind to scream at Eric. *The harbor guns are firing at us!*

She felt Eric wrap his arms around the wounded man and duck under the water. Once submerged, the gunner used his powerful legs to drive them through the water toward the shadow that indicated the PBY's position.

The barely alive pilot struggled in Eric's arms, but the gunner used all of his considerable upper body strength to haul the slighter man in toward his chest and keep moving. They surfaced, and Lydia felt Eric drag in a breath of air. His legs burned with fatigue, and the PBY still seemed so far away...

No! You're so close! Lydia shouted, leaning precariously out the door. *I can see you! You're less than a hundred yards away. Don't give up, Eric! Just keep swimming towards me.*

He's heavy, Eric sent back, and Lydia gasped as the exhaustion seared through her.

I know, but you can do it! You're going to save him! Just keep coming towards me! You can do that.

Happy...to...for...you...

The words didn't register at first.

Eric Warner! Are you...flirting with me?

A...little...

Lydia squared her shoulders and leaned further out, conscious that the turbulent air from the props and the spray had already plastered her blouse to her skin. She wasn't indecent yet, but she wasn't far from it. Her mother would snap at her to cover up, but if acting like a hussy saved two lives...

I think you should take me out on a date, she thought to the gunner fighting to drag the now-limp pilot toward the PBY. *Somewhere nice and fancy. I have a red dress I'll wear for the occasion. You like red, don't you?*

I...do...now... Eric thought in a mixture of amazement and, Lydia realized, a touch of lust followed by a massive rush of embarrassment.

Fifty yards! Come on, Eric, you gotta earn that date!

"Photographer!" the pilot's voice pierced her attention as the PBY heaved up and then down again in the turbulent, explosive-ridden water. "Sorry, I didn't get your name! How's our gunner doing?"

"H-he's close, sir," Lydia stuttered into the mic. She'd been so focused on Eric and his struggle that she'd totally forgotten about the other men on the aircraft. "He's about twenty-five yards away and gaining every second."

"Port, get back there and help her. Those harbor guns aren't letting up, but the fighters are breaking off for the moment. They're going to circle back around to try and strafe us, I'll bet. We really need to get out of here!"

"Excuse me, miss," Seth said then, tapping her on the shoulder. "Better move back now. I'll have to pull him in and get back on my gun quickly."

"Oh, right!" Lydia said, and stepped back. Eric's weary protest reared up in her mind as she disappeared from his sight.

I'm right here! she thought to him. *Seth's going to pull you both in. The pilots said that the fighters are circling around and the harbor guns are still firing, but you're so close...*

"Got him!" Seth shouted into the mic. Sure enough, Lydia watched as he hauled in the limp figure of a man with terrible burns on his face. The port gunner put the man down on his side, and the wounded pilot coughed and spat, then dragged in a great, wheezing gasp of air.

Seth turned back to the door, just in time to grasp his friend's hand and heave his body backwards as the PBY bucked from another explosion. Eric landed half-in, half-out of the aircraft. He grabbed the bulkhead with both hands and pulled himself forward on his belly until he could scramble up to his knees, and then his feet.

Without bothering to pause for his clothing or boots, he lurched toward his blister, shoved his headset on his wet head and began firing his weapon at the returning Japanese fighters. The light from the punishing South Pacific sun gleamed in the water droplets on his back, shoulders and buttocks, and without even thinking about it, Lydia grabbed her uncle's camera and took the shot.

The PBY rocked again, and Lydia gradually became aware of Seth screaming, "We're in! We're in!" over the intercom as he fired his weapon in tandem with Eric's. She let the camera drop to her chest and dove for the wounded pilot, who was struggling to get to his hands and feet. The moment she touched his skin, his pain and fear came roaring into her mind. She may have screamed out loud, but it was lost in the sound of the PBY's engines as the pilots poured on the power and began hurtling through the choppy water toward the relative safety of the sky.

You're safe! You're safe aboard a US Navy PBY! she shouted into the man's mind. *You're going to be okay! We're taking you to the hospital!*

The man turned his ruined face toward her, made a motion that looked like it was supposed to be a blink, and then promptly slumped back to the deck unconscious, severing the link. Lydia sighed in relief as his agony ceased abrading her mind. She levered her body over from where she'd landed on her knees to sit leaning back against the bulkhead as the PBY pitched up into the sky.

He's still breathing, she sent to Eric as she tipped her head back and let her eyes close. She felt as if she'd been run over by a jeep...or a convoy of jeeps. She'd never used that much power in her life, and it showed. Her stomach gurgled loudly, and a stab of hunger reminded her that she'd need to eat a lot, soon, unless she wanted to follow the unfortunate pilot into unconsciousness.

Good, Eric said, still firing. He didn't say anything else, and Lydia didn't press it. But since he didn't cut the connection between them, neither did she. She could still hear the men of the crew talking over the intercom in her headset, but she said nothing and just let them work to keep her and their other new passenger safe and get them home.

After awhile, when the sharp *ka-chunk* of the waist guns fell silent, Eric reached out to her again.

Lydia? Are you sleeping?

No, she said, lifting her head and smiling at him. He wore his trousers and boots once more, though his chest remained bare. *Just trying to stay quiet and out of the way.*

How's he doing? Eric asked.

He's alive, seems to be breathing all right, Lydia thought after a moment's assessment. *That's all I know. It's probably better for him to be unconscious right now. I can't imagine how much he must hurt.*

You don't have to imagine, Eric pointed out.

No, Lydia said, giving him a tired half-grin that she knew didn't reach her eyes. *It's just an expression.*

Thank you, Eric said. *For helping me, before. I wasn't sure I could make it. I'm a strong swimmer, but that...*

I never doubted you, Lydia said.

Well, thanks, he said again. *That was the toughest swim I've ever done. And, you know...if you didn't mean it...about the date...*

Eric Warner, Lydia shot back, putting as much sass as she could summon in her mental tone. *If you think you're backing out of our date now, you've got another thing coming, Buster!*

His mental laughter rolled through their connection and wrapped around the contours of her mind like some deliciously silky, furred fabric.

So you want to go, then? On a date? With me?

Didn't I just say that? she asked, archly. *Of course I do. Though normally I'm a "no shirt, no shoes, no service" kind of girl.*

Yeah, Eric said, his smile twisting ruefully. *I ripped it when I took it off in such a hurry. I'm sorry about all of that. I hope I didn't embarrass you.*

Never apologize for what you did today, she said, her tone firm. *You saved a man's life. I may be an unmarried woman, but I hope I've got enough good sense not to let my delicacies get in the way of that! You were breathtaking.*

He turned his face toward her, and the light from his blister lit up his irises until they seemed to glow blue.

I couldn't have done any of that without you.

I bet you're wrong, she said.

I bet I'm not, Eric said wearily. Lydia smiled internally and let the discussion go.

You don't think your uncle will mind me taking you out, do you? Eric thought after a few minutes. *I mean, he is an officer, and I'm just a lowly enlisted man.*

After what you did today, you're a hero. You could marry *me and he'd be proud to know you.*

Is that so? Interesting... Eric said, then smiled.

What? Lydia asked, raising an eyebrow.

Nothing.

———

"These are good," Uncle Horatio said, pulling one of the newly developed photographs out of the solution. "You captured the intensity on their faces as they're firing. Did you get any of the pilots up front?"

"Ah, no," Lydia said, blushing a bit. Not that he could likely tell, here in the red-lit darkroom. "I got a bit distracted when the rescue call came in, and then they were shooting at us and..."

"Yes, I heard! What a wild ride. Do me a favor and don't tell your mother I sent you out on a combat rescue mission, please. She'd flay me alive." Uncle Horatio moved with quick assurance to hang the photograph on the line, where it would dry.

"Let's see what else you've got..." he said as he turned back to the developing bath. He trailed off, though, and picked up a pair of tongs to pull one of the other prints closer. "Oh, Lydia..."

"Careful, Uncle," Lydia said, "You don't want to bend too close and splash solution on you."

"Who is this?" he asked, as if he hadn't even heard her warning.

"Eric," she said, knowing very well which photograph he'd found. "Aviation Ordnanceman Second Class Eric Warner. He's the one who performed the rescue."

"Why is he naked?"

"Well," Lydia said. "He'd just pulled the downed pilot out of the water, but the enemy fighters and the harbor guns were hammering us, so there wasn't really time for the niceties. He just got back on his weapon so we could get out of there."

Uncle Horatio lifted the print from its bath and held it up, angling it to see better.

"This is a winner, right here," he said. "This is perfect."

"Really, Uncle?" Lydia asked with a grimace. "I'm a little embarrassed that I took it. It's hardly proper—"

"Lydia, this is a war. There's nothing proper about it. But this photograph perfectly captures the spirit of the American fighting man. He does whatever it takes, you see. Just like your young man here. Whatever it takes to save his brothers-in-arms, whatever it takes to get his crew home alive. Whatever it takes to complete his mission...whatever it takes to win this damned war. Come hell or high water, he's going to do his job, naked, if he has to, and he's going to succeed."

Uncle Horatio turned toward her, his face lost in shadow.

"And *you* caught that, Lydia. That perfect moment. Damn fine work, my girl. *Damn* fine."

"Uncle," Lydia said, panic creeping into her voice. "You can't credit me! I'm not even really supposed to be here, and I absolutely wasn't supposed to be on that mission."

A long moment of silence stretched between them

"No..." he said slowly. "I suppose you're right. But damn it, it's wrong that you don't get the credit for this beautiful photograph."

"I don't want it," she said. She could hear the high, squeaky fear in her voice. "It was your mission. You would have taken the same shot, had you been there. It's your photograph, Uncle, please. I can't... People can't know I was there!"

"All right," he said, reaching out and patting her shoulder softly. "All right, Lydia, it's all right. I'll say it was me, if that's really what you want."

"It is, Uncle. I swear to you, it is. And keep Eric anonymous, too. That way, it will be harder for anyone to trace the photograph back to the flight I was on. Not that I think anyone will care, but..." she trailed off, uncertain what to say.

"Lydia," Uncle Horatio asked, his voice sharpening. "Why is this so important to you? Why are you afraid people will know you were on that plane?"

She swallowed hard and took a deep breath before answering.

"I used my abilities, Uncle. My psychic powers. It was the only way we could find the survivor in the smoke and chaos. Only Eric knows, but if word got out..."

"Ah," her uncle said. "I see. And you trust this young gunner?"

"I do," she said, swallowing hard again and forcing her voice to remain firm. "I trust him with my life."

"It sounds like you already have, if he knows about your abilities."

"His mother was psychic, Uncle. He...we linked up, during the flight. His mind was..."

"What was it, Lydia?" Uncle Horatio prompted, with something like a smile in his tone when she fell silent.

"Delicious," she said, and felt her cheeks heat up.

"I can nearly see you blushing from here," Uncle Horatio teased as he turned back to hang the provocative photograph on the line. "You'd better cool it before you ruin these negatives with all that light coming from your cheeks!"

That surprised her into a laugh. "Uncle!"

"Well, no wonder the photograph is so gorgeous," he went on. "You're half in love with the model!"

"More than half," she muttered. Uncle Horatio's hands went still.

"Ah," he said. "So it's like that?"

"It might be," she admitted. "We're supposed to go out on Friday."

"Go out?"

"Well, go for a walk," she said, "See the morale flick together. Nothing scandalous."

"No more nude photography?"

"Uncle! Of course not."

Uncle Horatio laughed, and then stepped toward her and wrapped his arms around her in a hug. She clung to him, grateful as always for his unwavering love and support.

"Well, I hope he's worthy of you, my girl," her uncle murmured into her hair. "He's certainly brave, if your photo is any indication."

"*Your* photo," she said, "And yes, he's brave, and kind, and I do think he's worthy."

"Good," Uncle Horatio said. "Bring him by on Friday before your date. I'd like to shake his hand."

ABOUT KACEY EZELL

Kacey Ezell writes emotionally charged adventure fantasy and science fiction. She is a three-time Dragon Award Finalist for Best Alternate History and won the 2018 Year's Best Military and Adventure Science Fiction Readers' Choice Award. She has written multiple bestselling novels published with Chris Kennedy Publishing, Baen Books, and Blackstone Publishing. Additionally, she is a retired helicopter pilot with 3000+ hours in the UH-1N Huey, Mi-171, and EC130 helicopters. She is married with two daughters. You can join her fan community and get free stories at https://kaceyezell.net/the-dragons-horde/

Get Magelight here, or at your favorite bookseller! https://www.baen.com/magelight.html

- Join The Dragon's Horde: https://kaceyezell.net/the-dragons-horde/
- Follow Me On BookBub: https://www.bookbub.com/profile/kacey-ezell
- Check Out My Website: www.kaceyezell.net
- Come Hang Out On Youtube: https://www.youtube.com/c/KaceyEzellWriterLife
- Follow Me On Facebook: https://www.facebook.com/AuthorKaceyEzell
- Follow Me On Instagram: https://www.instagram.com/kaceyezell/
- Follow Me On X: https://x.com/KaceyEzell1
- Follow Me on TikTok: @kacey.ezell

CORSAIRS AND TENZANS

Philip S. Bolger-Cortez

EARLY MORNING, JANUARY 5, 1944
200 MILES OFF THE COAST OF ITALIAN SOMALILAND

"Why are we even out here?" Leutnant Heinrich Metzger griped as he flew his Fw200 C-4 Maritime Patrol aircraft.

"Because it's our job," Leutnant Schmidt deadpanned in response. Schmidt was keeping his eyes on the aircraft's radar.

"Well, obviously," continued Metzger. "I mean, why are we flying out here in what's probably a typhoon? Why does command think the Americans and Japanese are going to come this way? If I were the head of their alliance, I wouldn't."

Of course you wouldn't, thought Schmidt. *You'd order all troops to stay safe and warm and dry and then still find a way to complain about it.* Schmidt did not remember a time his fellow pilot was not constantly complaining—about the heat, about being reflagged from a bomber squadron to a patrol squadron, about being based in Africa, about missing out on the action, about having to fly combat missions, or any number of other paradoxical nonsense. If it wasn't lies, it was exaggeration—Metzger's "Typhoon" was a mild storm, at best, one the Fw200 would easily be able to handle.

"They did beat the Dutch," said Schmidt.

"Oh wow, big military power there, the fascist Netherlands," Metzger said, rolling his eyes. "This Oahu Pact, they declared war, what, eight months ago? We've been at war since '39. We've taken the Polish, the French, the British, and will soon have the Soviets. Why would they even want to fight us, the world's premier military power?"

"Did you forget about the sub contact last night? Several Italian ships took damage."

"The Italians always whine," said Metzger. "I doubt their ships are anywhere near as damaged as they say. I had to work with them in North Africa, you know."

Maybe that's who you picked up all this complaining from, Schmidt thought.

"And that's the thing about submarines," Metzger said. "It could've been a rogue Briton, or one of their commonwealth lackeys. It isn't like they come up to surface and announce who they are and why they're shooting at you."

Schmidt didn't have time to respond, as his cathode ray screen began showing a surface contact. Schmidt looked again and made sure he had the right readout.

"Metzger, pay attention," he said. "Radar's got something. Looks like... dead on from us. Distance is 30 miles or so."

The two pilots looked at each other. Metzger's eyes were wide.

"Oahu Pact?" Metzger asked.

Schmidt nodded.

"Well, let's not dawdle," said Metzger. "For all we know, we're right over their AA and they just haven't seen us yet. Break off, we'll alert command."

ADMIRAL'S WARDROOM, IJN MUSASHI

"I trust you've enjoyed your stay, commander?" Admiral Yamamoto Isoroku asked.

"Yes, sir," replied Commander Bailey.

"A bit different from US vessels, I assume?"

"Definitely different from the subs I'm used to," said the Commander, grinning. "Less cramped, and the food's better."

Admiral Yamamoto smiled slightly at that.

The admiral was wearing his blue high-collar uniform, gold on the collar and braids on the sleeves. He had abstained from wearing his medals, choosing function over form. His leather gloves, the admiral's only concession to wet weather gear, sat next to his plate—he'd taken them off to eat—next to his hat. Though he normally ate in private in his quarters, he craved a bit of companionship, so he'd come to the wardroom.

"Did you ever think you'd serve on a Japanese ship?" Admiral Yamamoto asked.

"No, sir," said Bailey, shaking his head. "Truth be told, we expected we'd fight you."

Admiral Yamamoto chuckled slightly. "When your president and our emperor signed the Oahu Pact, I was quite surprised. I, too, had envisioned our nations on a crash course in the Pacific. I am glad we chose warmer relations instead."

The wardroom was deserted, save for the American liaison, who had been onboard the ship less than a week. The two had shared a brief breakfast. Commander Seth A. Bailey was a hulking Texan with the kind of confident can-do attitude Yamamoto found common among American career officers. The admiral imagined the big man must've been quite uncomfortable onboard the tight quarters of a submarine. Bailey wore tan fatigues with USN markings, most of which Yamamoto recognized.

Bailey nodded. "Likewise, sir. Especially with Europe under the Swastika, we need to stick together."

Yamamoto did not want to tell the US officer how much the destruction of the British Monarchy had perturbed the Imperial Navy. The Nazis had made it clear, despite their nominal affinity for monarchs in places like Spain and Italy, that they would dismantle any rival power structure given time. The American did not need to know about the insecurities of Japan, Yamamoto decided.

"Sir," Bailey spoke up. "I don't mean to be rude, but could I clarify, make sure I know what assets we've got? Last time I did anything with surface ships was nearly a decade ago."

"Of course," said Admiral Yamamoto, hiding his slight concern that the big Texan had not retained the information. "We have one battleship division, consisting of this ship, the *Musashi*, and its sister, the *Yamamoto*. We have the remnants of your battleship division, the USS *Alabama*, since the USS *Maryland* was crippled by the Dutch."

"Well, at least the carriers are fresh," Bailey said with a wince. "I am familiar with our task force, but I am not familiar with yours."

"We, like you, have cruisers with our carriers," Yamamoto said.

He does not need to know we lack the oil to bring the Kongo*-class with us all the way out here*, Yamamoto thought. That had been the subject of much contentious debate within the IJN's staff.

"The *Soryu* is about the equivalent of our *Yorktown?*"

Yamamoto smiled thinly. "More or less."

"For obvious reasons, I get the destroyers," Bailey said, and Yamamoto favored the submarine officer with a smile.

"RearAdmiral Truog was not as happy that I insisted on a heavy escort for the carrier task forces," Yamamoto replied.

Bailey rolled his eyes, then realized what he'd done.

"Sorry, sir, surface commanders always want more destroyers," Bailey said. "They don't understand how happy we submariners are when they strip the screen around the capital ships. Do you have six destroyers to a screen like us?"

"Not usually," Yamamoto answered. "Ours run flotillas of four."

He really does not understand surface combat that well, Yamamoto thought, surprised. Bailey had only arrived on the ship with the recent change of command, so it was probably unreasonable to expect him to have a perfect grasp of the situation.

The man is also quite young for a commander. The Americans seemed to promote their officers far more rapidly than the IJN.

"What do we think the Germans have, sir?" Bailey asked. "Intelligence seemed confused when they briefed me."

That is something common for both of us, Admiral Yamamoto thought as he considered the question. The man wished he had a better answer, but intelligence was unclear on what, precisely, was coming, besides a combined force of German and Italian ships.

"We can expect them to also have a sizable battleship presence," Yamamoto replied. "Thankfully, neither of our opponents invested heavily in carriers, but we are close enough to their African colonial holdings that they may have shore-based aircraft that come after us."

Bailey nodded again.

The admiral was one of the only Oahu Pact leaders to have seen heavy combat—he cut his teeth at the battle of Tsushima Straits, fighting the Russians. It cost him two fingers on his left hand. He had a role quelling the rebellions in the 1930s, as well—it was Yamamoto who ran down the naval cadets who had attempted to assassinate the Prime Minister, and Yamamoto who testified at the 1936 Army Treason Trials. Some of the Americans had seen action in the Great War, as had some of the Japanese officers, but none of them had been part of a fleet action before. Yamamoto, in many ways, was the only logical commander of the joint force.

Before Yamamoto and Bailey could continue their conversation, a junior officer burst through the wardroom hatch. Clad in wet weather gear and soaked from the ongoing rain, the officer nearly blurted out a report.

"Sir," he said. "Ensign Takeda reporting with a message from the Officer of the Watch. The American destroyer pickets report contact. Enemy patrol aircraft, followed by heavy gunfire. It's their main force, as we feared."

"We do not fear, Ensign," said Yamamoto, neatly folding his napkin next to his plate. "We expect. Then we react. Has the destroyer screen fixed an enemy?"

"Not yet, sir" the watch officer said. "They've reported several targets and reported taking fire, but the storm is causing trouble getting a good fix. They're attempting to develop a better picture before breaking contact."

Yamamoto nodded. One of his favorite things about working with the Americans was their commanders' tendency to take the initiative. Yamamoto glanced out the wardroom's porthole, and grimaced.

"Still raining? I assume the carrier aircraft are grounded?" said Yamamoto.

"Yes, sir," said the officer. "Carrier Division 1 reports the rain is still too heavy to scramble aircraft. The Americans also report no flight operations."

This posed a problem. The aircraft were the big strength of the Oahu Pact fleet. The '41 Pearl Harbor War Games had proven their utility, but they would be useless under such a cloud of rain.

"You said the destroyers had radar fixes. Do they know what of?" asked Yamamoto.

"Initial report is unclear," said the action officer. At that moment, a sailor ran up and interjected. The sailor hurriedly passed a paper into the officer's hands. The officer read it, and his eyes went wide.

"Sir, Admiral Oshima of the Carrier Division reports his destroyers are in contact with the enemy, as well," the officer said. "They've identified several large radar contacts, and are taking heavy plunging fire."

Yamamoto grimaced. If the Germans had used the storm to move up heavy guns, it would be difficult to counter.

"A formidable enemy," said Yamamoto. "We cannot let this aggression go unanswered. Instruct the battleships to prepare for combat. Get us into a position to support either the Japanese screen to the North or the

American to the South. Whichever is taking heavier fire, the battleships will move to support."

"Yes, sir!" the messenger said, and as he hustled to the bridge, the alarm bells began clanging. In the great turrets of the *Musashi*, the gun crew began the arduous process of loading the heavy Type 94 naval guns. On the deck, crewmen donned helmets and manned AA guns as petty officers shouted excitedly while the rain poured down on the deck. In sickbay, the doctors prepared to receive casualties, the smell of antiseptic and rubbing alcohol clogging the air, while damage control teams closed watertight doors in preparation for combat. The engines set to flank, and the mighty battleship was on its way towards the fight.

The first contacts had been reported by the forward destroyer screen, almost 25 miles west of the *Yamato*, *Musashi*, and *Alabama*. The Imperial Japanese Navy's twin battleships, the *Yamato* and *Musashi*, steamed towards their adjusted position, supported by the USS *Alabama*. The battleship line formed as they headed towards combat.

On the *Musashi*'s flag bridge, Yamamoto listened as his various task groups reported in. As the ships passed within 15 miles of the destroyer screens, Yamamoto heard reports from the carrier groups—still no aircraft in the sky. The American battleship, the *Alabama*, was relaying contact reports from American destroyers. Unfortunately, the reports were only general, as the heavy weather was preventing the radar returns from delivering targetable data. Soon after, the *Yamato* and *Musashi*'s systems picked up the same contacts.

They are far closer than we thought, Yamamoto thought. *Five miles from the destroyers is far too close.*

Looking out across the roiling sea, the clouds showing perhaps just a sign of breaking, he viewed the *Yamato* and the *Alabama* moving on line. On the horizon, he saw little through the haze of rain.

Well, at least there won't be a long, tedious run in, he thought. All around, officers buzzed and barked orders as the ship sailed towards its destination.

"Sir," reported a signals officer. "The *New Orleans* reports the loss of three friendly destroyers to surface gunfire, originating somewhere in the Northwest. The USS *Clark* remains in contact. Rear Admiral Truog is calling again, asking for more support."

"Tell him the battleships are on their way," said Yamamoto. "He must hold for roughly an hour."

———

In actuality, Admiral Yamamoto's estimate was slightly optimistic. Playing a game of deadly tag in the gloom, Admiral Truog managed to drag the Axis battleships back towards the Oahu Pact force in exchange for most of his destroyers. The *Yamato*, *Musashi*, and *Alabama*'s arrival came as an unpleasant surprise to the Axis light forces harrying their Pact counterparts, with a *Hipper*-class heavy cruiser dying spectacularly under the American battleships' guns. Yamamoto's counterpart, Vice Admiral Erich Bey, temporarily turned his force away to give his Italian contingent time to catch up. Contrary to the *Condor* crew's scuttlebutt, the Italians' *Littorio* had been the only vessel damaged by the British submarine's torpedo spread. Although slowed to just under twenty-two knots, the vessel maintained the ability to use her main battery.

Thus, it was shortly after 1100 that the *Bismarck*, *Tirpitz*, *Littorio*, *Roma*, and *Vittorio Veneto* hove south to engage the *Musashi*, *Yamato*, and *Alabama*. With the skies clearing, both sides scrambled to launch from their carriers.

USS *YORKTOWN*
READY ROOM

The cramped room was full of aircrew and pilots as Lieutenant Commander Nathan "Skip" Leibowitz shuffled in. Without pausing, he headed to his specific seat next to the rest of his flight—Lieutenant Hall, Lieutenant Mallek, and Ensign Broward.

At the front of the room, Commander Hart, the squadron commander of VF-42, stood in front of a chalkboard.

"Good morning, men," he said. "You may have heard the scuttlebutt— we've found the Jerries."

A quick murmur rose, but stopped almost as quickly—the appetite to hear more overrode the wish to talk about it.

"Our destroyers are in contact. We've already lost a few, and the main force is engaging as we speak. Not sure how many of theirs we got, but Intel says the krauts used the storm to move close. The enemy feels confident. That's their mistake."

Hart drew a few icons on the blackboard, in quick succession.

"We've drawn the short straw," he continued. "We'll be escorting in a flight of our pals from Japan—an outfit our liaisons have designated 'Naginata Squadron.'"

"Nagi-whatsit?" asked Ensign Broward, a big burly pilot that Leibowitz knew to be a perpetual groaner. Broward was one of those guys who only worked well when he was miserable.

"It's a type of Japanese spear," Leibowitz offered in his Minnesotan lilt. "Now why don't we all keep ourselves quiet while the commander finishes the brief, okay?"

Leibowitz privately wondered why the squadron would have such an unusual name. From his encounters with the Japanese, they tended to use unnamed, numbered squadrons. His curiosity was not enough to interrupt the commander's briefing.

Hart nodded in appreciation, and continued speaking.

"Naginata Squadron is the Fleet Main Air Effort," Hart continued. "Their mission is to sink the battleship *Bismarck*, the enemy's flagship."

Hart motioned to a functionary, who rushed up with a blown-up photograph of the battleship. Leibowitz's breath caught in his throat—the *Bismarck* was truly a monstrous ship. He saw some of the men in the room look wary.

"Lot of anti-air on that," came a rumbling from Leibowitz's right. There was a certain value in quantity of lead you could sling skyward, and the *Bismarck*'s builders had understood that.

"We don't want to get close," said Hart. "Just get the torpedo bombers into position. We'll be the third wave of attacks against this beast."

"Third wave, sir?" asked Broward. Hart nodded.

"The USS *Lexington*'s got first dibs—fast-flying dive bombers. Think of them as a jab. We're the uppercut."

The usually grim Broward grinned at that.

"Now," Hart said. "The Jerries aren't going to just give us that shot. They'll be sending planes up after our pals from the Orient. That's where we come in."

A series of flash cards were passed around among the pilots. Before he even received his, Leibowitz knew what they were going to be—*Zeewolfes*, plus some Italian planes that Leibowitz privately doubted would even work. The flash cards confirmed that.

"These aircraft are being flown by men with a lot more combat experience than we've got," cautioned Hart. "But they're still cherries when it comes to carrier operations. Those *Zeewolfes*, the ones on the cards you're seeing, those are brand new kraut planes, based on their successful model that beat the Russians. Besides them, be on the lookout for anything coming from the shore. We know the Italians have airbases in their African holdings. Intel isn't sure if they coordinated with the German fleet, but I'd rather be safe than sorry."

Leibowitz flipped through the cards. He didn't see anything surprising. He tucked them into his leather jacket.

"Are there any questions?" asked Commander Hart.

A hand shot up beside him, and Leibowitz fought the urge to fix its owner with a hard glare. Lieutenant Hall was an upstart kid out of Philadelphia. Guy was a track star, and the stereotypical fighter jock. Leibowitz had his own thoughts on the young pilot's attitude, but kept those to himself unless his wingman screwed up.

"Yes, sir, I've got one. What do we get for shooting down the most krauts?"

You might want to be a little more concerned with doing your job and keeping my tail clear, Leibowitz thought, this time letting his glare sweep over his wingman. Hall shrank back down in his chair.

Commander Hart grinned, noting both the rebuke and that it had been received.

"A pat on the back, maybe a handshake," Hart said. The various pilots murmured to themselves. Hart asked if there were any other questions, but there weren't.

"Pilots, man your planes," the intercom crackled. "I say again: pilots, man your planes."

"Well, there's our casting call," Hart said.

USS NEW ORLEANS

Goddammit, Rear Admiral Jacob Truog swore, watching as the U.S.S. *Winslow* split in half from an Italian 15-inch shell. *Any time that Japanese admiral wants to close with the heavy ships, I'd appreciate it.*

The *New Orleans'* guns cracked away at a target. Truog forced himself to ignore reports on the heavy cruiser's effectiveness. The vessel had lost her radar to a salvo from the big German brute that had been annihilated by the *Alabama*, so odds were she was missing much more than she was hitting.

"Sir!" an officer interjected. "The *Yorktown* reports that she is launching aircraft."

About damn time, Truog thought.

There was the sound of ripping canvas, followed by the high singing of steel fragments going past the flag bridge's open hatches. Screams and calls for corpsman told Truog that the splinters had found some casualties.

"Well make sure they know where we are," Truog said sarcastically. "I guess we can leave out the part about us maybe not being here much longer if those flyboys don't hurry up."

————

Leibowitz nervously touched the Star of David that held around his neck. In his ears, he could hear squadron radio chatter, and the back and forth with the *Yorktown*'s tower. Leibowitz was anxious. He was hot in his flight leathers—the equatorial heat made wearing such a pain, but he knew he'd need the warmth when he was up above the clouds. He'd been sweating since before he'd sat down in the cockpit, and the slimy feel of his helmet and the strap of his goggles made him all the more anxious to get into the air.

His plane sat on the deck, along with Hall's. The gull-winged *Corsair* was painted in typical naval camouflage—blue top, white bottom, with the American roundels prominently displayed so he wouldn't get misidentified and shot down by a friendly in a fight. The 2,000-horsepower radial engine thrummed along happily, waiting to propel Leibowitz through the sky. Leibowitz checked his instrument panels for the fiftieth time, then shook his head.

Nervous as a bride on her wedding night, Leibowitz thought, briefly glancing at his wife's picture taped to the top of the instrument panel. Leibowitz hadn't been in combat, but they'd scuffled often enough with the Australians who had fought the Germans in North Africa. After each mock combat, the groups of pilots had sat down to discuss what the Americans had right and wrong.

"You have to be more aware," one of the Aussies, a double ace, had said. "It's not just awareness of the enemy, but of yourself. You must know what's working, what's not, and how much fuel you've got—be a damn shame to win a dogfight and go down in the drink because you weren't paying attention to your fuel levels."

A dead pilot from a crash is just as dead as one torn apart by 20mm cannon, Leibowitz thought. Leibowitz also, when he was feeling particularly anxious, thought about how awful it would be to stranded in the deep ocean, treading water and hoping none of the local marine life was feeling too hungry.

Something the controller said broke Leibowitz out of his reverie. He never heard what the island had directed, but saw that the sailor at the end of the flight deck was motioning with his paddles. Pulling into position, Leibowitz watched as the man signaled for Hall to take off.

Well, here goes, he thought as Hall's *Corsair* taxied forward. The dark blue fighter sailed off the *Yorktown*'s bow, dipping just a bit as it cleared the edge of the flight deck before clawing into a climbing turn.

The flight control officer motioned again. Leibowitz taxied forward, and hit the throttle. His stomach lurched as his *Corsair* cleared the carrier. As the storm broke, the cloud ceiling receded.

"Blue Two, Blue One," Leibowitz said into his radio. "Let's get up to angels three and head to the RV."

"Roger," Hall acknowledged. The two planes began the process of climbing. The *Corsair* was Leibowitz's third aircraft, after a trainer, and a stint in the *Buffalo*. Of the planes Leibowitz had flown, the *Corsair* was easily his favorite. The gull-winged fighter was a beast, and didn't do well going slow...but if you could crank it up to speed, you could dive, or turn, with the best of them. He flew up through the breaking clouds, Hall slipping back into position. Turning, he took a heading for the rendezvous as the rest of the flight caught up.

Let's go find our friends, he thought.

AERIAL RENDEZVOUS POINT ABLE

Lieutenant Yoshida Ichiro was happy to be in the air. In the cockpit of his B6N *Tenzan* Torpedo Bomber, he felt like he was the instrument of the heavens, here to dole out justice. Well, technically, it would be Ensign Fujiwara Shinji, his weapons operator, or possibly Petty Officer Matsui, the tailgunner, doling out justice, but it was Yoshida's responsibility to fly the plane to the right position.

His two crewmen were young. They'd both been cycled in after the skirmish off Haiphong with the French that had precipitated the current conflict. Yoshida didn't yet know the other two crewmen very well, but they'd come recommended. The officer had written his wife, Reiko, saying that being responsible for such young men had reminded him of his own daughter, Megumi. Reiko's response had icily noted that it was good he was getting practice as a father, given that he'd had so few opportunities to do so in the past year.

It wasn't that Yoshida was old—he had not yet hit his thirtieth birthday—but after seven years in the Imperial Japanese Navy, including peacekeeping tours in the Philippines and Manchukuo, he had become aware of some of the truths of the military that junior men do not realize. Yoshida had seen no combat as a *Tenzan* pilot yet, but to him, it was merely a new platform for the same kind of job, a new window into war. He did not share the young men's lust for glory and battle.

Still, he was required to do his duty to the Emperor, and to his nation.

The B6N *Tenzan* was the IJN's newest torpedo bomber model, fielded right before the declaration of war against Axis Europe. Yoshida's plane was painted teal on the fuselage and white on the undersides. The only exceptions to the subdued colors of the plane were the distinctive Rising Sun emblem of Japan. The plane was also painted with the squadron markings for the 44th Attack Squadron, or Sento Hikokai 44, known onboard the *Hiryu* as Naginata Squadron.

Orbiting at the RV point, he saw the American *Corsair* fighters that were to be their escorts. Yoshida did not understand command's decision to have the Americans escort his flight—the *Zeroes* onboard the *Hiryu* should've been enough, but Yoshida had heard good things about the *Corsair*.

The gull wings make them easy to pick out, he thought. *In any case, it is always better to have escorts than not. Plus, if I must coordinate with them, I know my English is good enough.*

"Think the gaijin are up to the task?" asked Fujiwara. "I've heard they're nothing but cowboys that don't even train for their tasks."

"Nonsense," said Yoshida. "Have some respect. I've trained with the Americans. They're every bit as capable as us."

"Yeah," opined Petty Officer Matsui. "Yoshida-*san* was at the '41 Pearl Harbor wargames. He'd know."

Fujiwara stayed quiet, harboring whatever prejudices he held in silence. That was fine by Yoshida. He needed the young gunner to hit his targets. What he thought about foreign affairs was none of Yoshida's business.

"What did you fly in '41, sir?" asked Fujiwara. "Still bombers, right?"

"I flew the Aichi *E13*," said Yoshida as he checked his instruments. "Off the back of the *Yamato*."

"You flew with the admiral?" asked Matsui, surprise in his voice.

"No," said Yoshida. "The admiral was still using the *Nagato* as his flagship at the time. I was the spotter for the *Yamato*."

"Well," said Fujiwara. "Much better to be on a torpedo bomber, sir. We'll be the ones to sink the big ships!"

The voice of the Yoshida's flight leader broke over the radio, informing Yoshida to get in formation. Yoshida assumed a wing side position alongside another *Tenzan*, two American *Corsairs* leading them in.

As they crossed the sea, just above the fading storm clouds, Yoshida thought about purpose.

THE SKIES ABOVE THE INDIAN OCEAN

"Red One, Blue One," said Leibowitz on squadron communications. "Got about three hours of fuel left. We've just passed Waypoint Charlie."

"Red One acknowledges," replied Hart. "No enemy contacts yet. Everyone, keep your eyes peeled."

Hall was flying maybe 500 feet to Leibowitz's port side. Broward and Mallek were off to Leibowitz's starboard. Behind him, Leibowitz could see the four Japanese *Tenzans* they were escorting, though not well—the torpedo bombers were keeping their distance, and preparing for their own strike. If intel was right, they'd be over their targets soon enough.

Suddenly, tracers arced down from above, passing nearly right in front of Leibowitz.

"Tally ho! Enemy fighters!" he barked, pulling up abruptly to scan for his assailant. He didn't have to look long—a *Zeewolf* screamed down in front of him. It was only due to sheer fortune, or the opposing pilot's mistake, that Leibowitz lived. The German's wingman followed right behind him, having inexplicably not fired.

"Fighters, one o'clock high!" Broward called into the flight radio channel. Leibowitz turned to look at what his subordinate had seen and felt the blood drain from his face. Four *Zeewolf* were diving, opening fire as they came. Instinctively, Leibowitz kicked his rudder, but still felt two thumps as shells hit his fuselage.

Broward never had a chance. The *Corsair* was perforated by 20mm rounds, one going right through the top of the cockpit. At this distance, at this speed, Leibowitz couldn't say for sure whether or not he saw the blood spatter.

Shit, shit, shit, he thought. The first flight of *Zeewolfes* had made the mistake of breaking off their dive to try and turn in after the *Tenzans*.

"Blue Four is down," Hall reported over the radio. "I'm in pursuit."

"Get your ass back into position, Blue Two!" Leibowitz barked, reefing his stick over to dive towards the enemy fighters. The *Corsair* rattled with the gs, and he felt his vision darken as he brought the big fighter around just on the edge of a stall.

The German flight leader realized his error just as he was about to fire at the Japanese torpedo planes. Unfortunately, it was far too late for him to do anything, as Leibowitz squeezed his trigger. The six .50-caliber streams ripped the *Zeewolfe*'s starboard wing off, the structure nearly flying back to hit Leibowitz as he hurtled by.

"Splash one!" Hall called out as his flight leader pulled up. Looking back, Leibowitz saw his wingman had ignored his orders and gone after his own *Zeewolfe*. Even as the German fighter fell away in flames, Leibowitz saw two more flights of Germans joining the fight.

The next sixty seconds were total chaos, as the second wave of *Zeewolfes* split their attentions between the escorting *Corsairs* and vulnerable *Tenzans*. Realizing they had the single flight of *Corsairs* temporarily outnumbered, the Germans struck and moved away. The tactic worked briefly, as the *Tenzans* were vulnerable targets. Two of the Japanese craft tumbled from the sky, their wings shorn by German cannon. The remainder, including Yoshida's, conducted evasive maneuvers as they attempted to make room for the American pilots to intercept.

It was at that point that the rest of VF-42 arrived, Commander Hart having made the decision to abandon the *Yorktown*'s dive bombers in order to help his Blue Flight. Striking two of the Germans in the bounce, the tables were quickly turned as three *Zeewolfes* spun down into the Indian Ocean.

Leibowitz felt sweat pouring down his spine as he reached the top of his Immelman turn. Spotting a *Zeewolf* closing in on a *Tenzan*, he traded altitude for speed to bring himself down on the German's port side. Just as with Leibowitz's last victim, the *Zeewolf* was focused on the *Tenzan* in front of him, its tail gunner firing ineffectively back at the closing German.

Boy, is this bastard in for a surprise, Leibowitz thought angrily. He pulled the trigger on his joystick, and six fifty-caliber machineguns barked at once, spitting streams of tracers. The three-second burst arced behind his target, and Leibowitz skidded desperately to add more lead. Belatedly realizing his danger, the German panicked and broke to port, greatly easing Leibowitz's gunnery problem. Nearly stalled, the German's vulnerable underbelly rolled towards Leibowitz at barely one hundred yards. The subsequent burst slammed up through the unarmored belly.

I must've caught something good, Leibowitz thought in a mixture of jubilation and horror as the the *Zeewolf* lit up like a torch. He arced back around to give the enemy plane another burst, then stopped as he watched the enemy pilot pull the canopy back.

I'm not a damn Nazi, he thought, thinking to reports of the Germans' actions over Great Britain. As he passed the doomed pilot, he saw that his opponent was wreathed in flames as he jumped.

"More bogeys coming in!"

"Let's cover our friends, gents!" Hart's voice crackled over the squadron radio. "Get them some space!"

How many carriers do the Krauts have out here? Leibowitz briefly wondered. He saw a *Zeewolf* nail a Tenzan with a deflection shot, then die himself as two separate *Corsairs* shot the German to pieces. The VF-42 pilots had to break to avoid one another, and the dead German's wingman turned to follow one of them. Seeing that his own wingman had gone missing again, Leibowitz chased the *Zeewolf*. He was too late: the German's cannon fire setting his prey ablaze.

Goddammit, Leibowitz raged. The Nazi waited an extra moment too long, perhaps hoping to shoot at the *Corsair*'s pilot. Leibowitz dipped in right behind the German, and put enough .50 caliber rounds downrange to end the enemy pilot's victory streak. Unlike his latest victim, he did not remain, immediately breaking away from the burning *Zeewolf* to clear his own tail. Suddenly, the skies around him were clear.

"Blue Flight, status report," Leibowitz barked.

"Blue Three damaged, I splashed one."

"Blue Two, joined up with Gold Three."

"Red One, Blue One, my flight's scattered all over the place," Leibowitz said. "We're rejoining up on our charges."

There was silence.

"Anyone hear from Red Flight?" Leibowitz asked.

"This is Red Four," came a shaky, familiar voice. "Red One collided with Red Two. Red Three was shot down."

Oh shit, Leibowitz thought. He had just become a squadron commander.

"Bandits, three o'clock!"

Sure enough, there was another wave. Leibowitz banked right, and the *Corsair* turned hard, rumbling as it did, the g force sinking Leibowitz into his seat. He flew head on into the enemy formation. To his right, he saw Hall moving in.

Those must be different Germans, he thought. The airframes didn't look like *Zeewolfes*, being more slender, but they still looked threatening to the *Tenzan* flight. He lined up on the leader as the two groups slashed into one another, firing a burst then breaking left. He heard Hall give a victory woop as he pulled up, then turned around to see that Blue Two had come in and finished what he started. The enemy aircraft, despite being more slender, seemed much more clumsy and fragile than the *Zeewolfes*.

"Blue leader, this is Naginata leader," an accented voice said over his radio. "We have eyes on the enemy main force. We are engaging."

"Roger," acknowledged Leibowitz, his arms shaking from fatigue. "We'll keep the top covered. Let's make some space for 'em, boys!"

THE BRIDGE OF THE IJN *MUSASHI*

Admiral Yamamoto was concerned, even as his face remained impassive as the *Musashi* shrugged off another Italian battleship shell. Rear Admiral Truog was doing what he could with his remaining vessels, but the Axis light forces were starting to have enough of an advantage that a second torpedo attack was certainly in the offing. The first had heavily damaged the USS *Alabama*, even as that vessel had seen off the *Roma* with a salvo of plunging fire. The *Yamato*, while still technically floating, had been forced to flood her main magazines.

If I had a choice, I would send her out of the line, Yamamoto thought grimly. *But she is absorbing fire, and her secondaries are part of the reason the Axis are being very careful before they commit another torpedo attack.* Even more importantly than the two destroyers she had destroyed, the *Yamato*'s guns had crippled the *Littorio* and gravely injured the *Vittorio Veneto*. The Italian vessels had clearly not been designed to fight at long distance, their decks lacking the ability to stand up to plunging fire. As Yamamoto listened, the initial air strikes were swarming the damaged ships.

"Admiral," the action officer said. "Fleet air main effort reports contact with the *Bismarck* battle group."

It is about time, Yamamoto thought. As if on cue, the Germans' next salvo thudded into the flagship. *Their* shells were fully functional and effective, if not as deadly as their designers had likely hoped at this range.

"Excellent," said Yamamoto. "Direct all aircraft to engage."

Lieutenant Yoshida piloted his B6N closer to the target. Behind him, his bombardier excitedly called out the targets they were overflying.

"That's a Z-class destroyer! And a *Hipper*-class Cruiser! We've found the enemy main force!"

Matsui radioed the initial sighting as Yoshida accelerated. He kept it steady, trying to ignore the bullet holes in his starboard wing. The engine was sounding a little funny, too; perhaps a machine gun round had nicked it, but his instruments were showing nothing out of the ordinary, so Yoshida kept his mind on the task at hand.

"Excellent," said Yoshida. "Let's keep an eye out for the *Bismarck*. Soon as we see her, we're dropping."

He looked again at the reference picture on his dashboard before looking back up. Through the broken clouds, punctuated by plumes of fire and smoke, Yoshida saw it. His heart raced. The mighty battleship had been damaged by an earlier attack by American dive bombers—its rear turrets appeared to be inoperable, with one smoking, badly. The radar mast was shorn off, as were a number of communications antennae. Yoshida knew he was here to deliver the killing blow. Just to be sure, he checked the profile against his target card, before looking back to make sure he was still flying on target.

"That's the *Bismarck*," he said, as Matsui notified the squadron.

The six remaining B6Ns dropped low and level, over the water. As they did, they invited fire from the *Bismarck*'s escorts. The beast's screen opened up with everything they had, tracers snaking out towards Yoshida and his comrades. One of the rounds slammed hard into Yoshida's windscreen, startling him with the impact. The rush of slipstream through the cracks made an eerie whistling sound as Yoshida leveled off.

Now comes the hard part, Yoshida thought. Off to starboard, one of his wingmen suddenly splashed into the water as flak blew out the B6N's engine. Far above, he saw the American *Corsairs* stop a sudden rush from enemy fighters.

Not was many of them as there were when we started, Yoshida thought. He stayed level, no longer worried about the threat from above, then checked his airspeed. Muttering, he dropped a few knots to get back within range and then fought to keep his aircraft at optimal height. He had not come this far to have his weapon hit too fast or at the wrong angle and thus fail to arm or go off-course.

Look at the size of that thing, Yoshida thought, looking at the smoking, burning German battleship. He kept the *Tenzan* steady, the run seeming like an eternity even as his mental countdown told him it was less than ten seconds. The entire world seemed to move in slow motions, each piece of it spiraling at once—the German and Italian ships shooting anti-air, the other *Tenzans* off to his left and right, the breeze coming through the cracked cockpit windshield with more than a hint of an oil and smoke smell. It was terrifying—Yoshida knew he was vulnerable at this height and speed. It was also, in an odd way, quite serene with the falling water from splashes and spray.

From behind, Fujiwara gleefully announced release. The torpedo dropped from the B6N, and the aircraft lurched upwards as the weighty munition headed towards the surface. The torpedo hit water as Yoshida sped up and then rapidly pulled up, evading the latest round of flak and machinegun bullets from the nearby ships. The other *Tenzans* dropped their torpedoes in the water and then peeled out of the free-fire zone.

The five Type 91 torpedoes sped through the water, towards the *Bismarck*'s port side. Aboard the *Bismarck*, her captain realized that he would not be able to avoid the five weapons from Yoshida's drop and the seven coming in from starboard. In a last-minute effort, the man rang for all flank and turned towards the seven weapons, hoping to outrun the five from port.

The maneuver may have worked, had the *Bismarck* not been damaged. Two torpedoes missed entirely through the luck of the draw. One hit, through sheer chaotic fortune, a German Z-class destroyer, dooming the escort craft to be sunk. All seven of the torpedoes from starboard were successfully dodged.

Unfortunately, the *Bismarck*'s evasive maneuvers weren't quite enough to get the warship out of trouble. The first torpedo hit, right on the ship's stern, the explosion blossoming directly beneath the painted swastika. The blast flooded the battleship's steerage compartment, and a nearby damage control crew was torn to shreds by fragments of the ship.

The next torpedo hit the ship's port side, exploding against the battleship's belt. The damage wasn't enough to penetrate into the vessel's vitals, but killed several of her crew and weakened her plating.

Yoshida's torpedo also struck the port side of the *Bismarck*, but the pilot wasn't sure how much damage had been done. Aboard the *Bismarck*, the damage control teams began their work. As Yoshida gained altitude, he saw, dispiritingly, the *Bismarck*'s two bow turrets open fire again. He'd failed.

Yoshida saw the rest of his flight align. His flight leader ordered the formation to return to base.

Yoshida shook with the energy of fear and disappointment. He did not come this far to fail. He would not just surrender now.

He broke formation, ignoring his squadmates' complaints on the radio, taking his *Tenzan* on a dive.

"Lieutenant!" shouted Fujiwara. "What are we doing?"

"Finishing this," growled Yoshida.

Visions raced through his head—his *Tenzan* crashing into the bridge of the *Bismarck*, the explosion killing the German admirals and staff members. A hero's funeral at home. The Nazis in full retreat. The smiles of his ancestors.

But as he turned to align his aircraft for the final approach, more visions passed through Yoshida's head—Reiko and Megumi crying over a flag-draped coffin, a jingoistic speech offering them no comfort. His parents unable to live peacefully without his care. His town decrying him as just another selfish samurai man, a relic from before modern times. His plane crashing into the side of the *Bismarck* and doing no more damage than a fly crashing into a mountainside.

Yoshida righted himself, ignoring the increasingly frightened demands of Fujiwara.

As he brought the plane up, narrowly escaping the enemy anti-aircraft fire, he saw something—his torpedo had done more damage than he thought. The *Bismarck* was moving, but slowly, and locked in a circle!

As he flew off, he radioed into his squadron leader the updated battle damage assessment, and hoped it would get to the right people in time.

USS *New Orleans*

The enemy gunfire had let up. It hadn't stopped, but Rear Admiral Truog had some room to breathe. Overhead, Pact and Axis fighters dueled in sprawling furballs as dive bombers broke cloud coverage to attack enemy ships. The air was filled with the smell of smoke, cordite, and oil, tainted just a little bit with what Truog recognized as the unmistakable stench of death.

The *New Orleans'* AA defenses rattled off as an Italian dive bomber poked its way through the air coverage. Truog thought about trying to man one of the AA guns himself, but made the wiser choice to take cover against a nearby bulkhead. The 20mm shells shredded the enemy aircraft, and a sailor whooped as the enemy plane caught fire, impacting the water in front of the ship.

Damage control had gotten the A turret working again, and the *New Orleans* was firing as much as it could, but Truog knew the screen was all but destroyed. He had started with two destroyer divisions—eight in total. The *Clark* was all he had left, and the *Clark* was sinking.

IJN MUSASHI
THE FLAG BRIDGE

The *Musashi* wasn't quite dead, but the big battleship was roughed up. Admiral Yamamoto was bleeding from his head, blood obscuring his vision, smoke clogging his lungs as the smell of gunpowder, oil, and death strangled his nostrils. The ship's captain was considering ordering abandoning ship.

We must hold on, Yamamoto thought. With the *Yamato* now immobilized and the *Alabama* sinking, the *Musashi* was the only heavy unit left. With Admiral Nimitz roughly four hundred miles away on the rapidly closing *Ranger*, sacrificing the command and control of the *Musashi* would doom the ships that accompanied her.

Still, I may not have much command and control left as is, he thought. His chief of staff was dead, torn in half by fragments of the *Musashi*'s heavy armor. Many of his staff had joined the man in death or were being dragged to the nearest makeshift sick bay. Commander Bailey, the American liaison, was helping drag wounded off the bridge.

Too many guns, he thought. *We were foolish to think the Musashi and Yamato were the equal of any two of their vessels.* Even without penetrating the *Musashi*'s hide, the German and Italian vessels had done grievous damage

"Sir!" a signals officer said. "The gunnery officer reports the *Bismarck* is circling, crippled!"

"The *Bismarck*? How?" asked the *Musashi*'s captain.

"Torpedo bombers, sir," the signals officer said. "They managed to hit her stern!"

"Likely damage to the steerage compartment," remarked Yamamoto. He strode to the speaking tube down to the navigational bridge "Captain, let us finish this!"

The *Musashi*'s captain acknowledged, the *Musashi* coming about to turn her broadside to the German battleship. Even as the secondaries began to engage the Axis destroyers that reacted to the maneuver by initiating a torpedo run, the gunnery officer laid his director onto the circling German. The *Musashi*'s three heavy turrets matched, as the gunnery officer took two long minutes to make sure that he had the *Bismarck*'s pattern down. All three barrels tracked in their path, then in beautiful unison, all nine guns fired.

The shock caused the battleship to leap in the water, nearly knocking Yamamoto off his feet. Closing his eyes against the concussion, after several breaths he opened them and raised his binoculars.

In his cockpit, Yoshida prayed, while above him, Leibowitz scanned the skies for any lingering Germans.

Aboard the *Bismarck*, Vice Admiral Bey watched the smoke waft back from the Japanese battleship and knew what the sound of ripping canvas meant. Even as the men around him crouched, the German admiral remained defiantly upright. He had watched the massive Japanese battleship guns destroy his Italian counterparts and maul the *Tirpitz*. Now, with a crippled flagship under his feet, Bey was well aware that his fate could be sealed.

It was not a perfect salvo. The majority of it was long, the last shell in the pattern hitting the *Bismarck*'s heavily armored deck amidships.

. . .

Yoshida could not see what was happening to the enemy ship, but from behind him, his two crewmen cheered.

"The *Musashi* has the range!" he heard Matsui shout.

"Not quite," Fujiwara replied. "But I am sending the correction!"

Onboard the *Musashi*, the heavy guns were busy being reloaded. With some damage to the hoists and reduced power, it was an arduous process. After two of the longest minutes of her crew's life, the triple turrets roared again. Unknown to the *Musashi*'s gunnery officer, the hit had slowed the *Bismarck*'s circling speed, and the nine shells landed in a close pattern just forward of the German battleship's bow.

The process repeated once more, then again, each successive salvo resulting in another couple of hits. Even as *Musashi* evaded the German destroyers' final torpedoes, her guns fired for a fourth time.

For years afterwards, historians would debate exactly what had killed the *Bismarck*. Was it the torpedoes? Was it unexploded ordnance from the dive bombers? Or was it the naval gunnery from the *Musashi*? They'd all take credit, but the truth was the *Bismarck* would've survived, were it not for all three. Four of the *Musashi*'s rounds impacted, although only the first hit was necessary. The shell punched deep into the vessel's forward magazines before exploding, its hot fragments doing the rest. In a series of volcanic blasts, the vessel's forward section disappeared in a ball of flame.

———

The *Bismarck*'s demise coincided with the arrival of the second wave of strike aircraft from the Oahu Pact's carriers. With their German counterpart's fighters either decimated or in the process of refueling, the second wave wrought havoc upon the former Axis screening vessels. The overall Axis commander, Admiral Erich Lutjens, ordered a general retreat from the carrier *Graf Zeppelin*.

As the *Ranger* task force, including the Japanese carriers *Akagi* and *Kaga*, reached maximum range, the weather continued to favor the Oahu Pact's pursuit. For the pilots who had been forced to abandon their aircraft in the early afternoon, *PBY Catalinas* and *H6K Flying Boats* rounded up the survivors. By nightfall, the attack aircraft had managed to finish the retreating Italian battleships, with only the threat of land-based airpower and the need to try and save the damaged *Yamato* and *Musashi* that prevented Admiral Nimitz from conducting a general pursuit. Even without it, the Axis fleet had lost all five battleships it began the day with.

IJN *Musashi*
The Flag Bridge
Three weeks later

"Well, I wish we were meeting under better circumstances, Admiral Yamamoto, but it is good to finally make your acquaintance," Admiral Chester Nimitz said, extending his hand.

Admiral Yamamoto gingerly accepted the American's gesture. While his wounds were far from major, it still hurt to move rapidly.

"Welcome to Singapore," Yamamoto said, gesturing for the man to sit down.

How odd the world is, Yamamoto thought. *Here I sit with an American admiral in a former British base preparing to discuss what comes next.*

"Thank you, Admiral," Nimitz replied. He nodded at Commander Bailey. "I trust our liaison has worked out well?"

Yamamoto smiled.

"I believe you have seen the citation I wrote for him?" Admiral Yamamoto replied. He enjoyed the look of surprise that flitted across Bailey's face.

"Yes, I have," Nimitz said. "I think Commander Bailey will be joining one of the *Corsair* pilots on my flagship for a presentation in the coming weeks."

Bailey was completely agog at that statement. Lieutenant Commander Leibowitz was already famous through the Oahu Pact for his actions during the Battle of the Horn and immediately following. The war's first ace after downing a couple of *Condors*, it was an open secret that Leibowitz would be getting a Navy Cross, if not the Medal of Honor.

"Very good," Yamamoto replied. "However, you did not come here to discuss presentations."

"No, I did not," Nimitz said, his face going grim. "With the heavy losses, I understand your government has asked for a temporary pause to offensive operations?"

"Yes," Yamamoto said, his tone neutral. The loss of the *Yamato* had shaken the Navy Staff. Taken under tow, several of the battleship's transverse bulkheads had suddenly buckled under the strain of an Indian

Ocean gale. Thankfully, only a skeleton crew had gone down with her, but it was still a most unpleasant coda to the Battle of the Horn.

"There are those in Washington who wonder if your reluctance is a sign of continued mistrust towards our nation," Nimitz said diplomatically. "Given the reports of the Italian Navy's mutiny, followed by the Germans seizing their ships as well as those of Britain and France, it would appear that now was a perfect time to strike *somewhere*."

"I understand," Admiral Yamamoto replied. "But as you are well aware, our nations have spent much of the last two decades preparing to fight one another. That we lost one of our two largest vessels and had the other one crippled has led to some of the more unsavory members of our government to claim a conspiracy."

Nimitz nodded. "You and your men fought well," he stated simply. "Well enough that ol' Adolph has apparently put a couple of his senior admirals up against the wall."

Yamamoto raised an eyebrow at that.

"While that worked for the Royal Navy once, I think he will find that less than helpful in the long term," Yamamoto replied. "It could be argued that I should have retreated rather than stay and fight once I realized the Italians were not nearly as damaged as we believed."

"I would have done the same in your shoes if I had two vessels like this one," Nimitz stated. "I do, however, have nine battleships and five carriers. Please impart onto your government that I would truly love to have several more I could count on."

Yamamoto nodded, standing. Nimitz followed suit.

"I will fervently do so," he stated. "With the hopes that this is not the last time we will work together, Chester."

ABOUT PHILIP S. BOLGER-CORTEZ

Philip S. Bolger-Cortez is an American author of urban fantasy, alternative history, and post-apocalyptic fiction. In 2019, he released The Devil's Gunman, a novel about an unemployed hitman in the fantasy underworld, set in a Minneapolis where myths are alive just out of sight.

Philip has also written numerous short stories, including two set in an alternate universe where Japan became a liberal parliamentary monarchy instead of a militarist dictatorship, and then allied with the United States.

Philip lives in Montgomery, Alabama, with his wife Victoria, and two dogs, Robert the Bruce and Francois Guizot.

ATLANTIC FLASH

William Stroock

"0530 hours, Admiral," said the steward.

"Thank you, Freddy," Admiral Readington replied.

Freddy put the tray of tea on the table in front of the couch. A second steward hung a pair of cleaned and pressed khakis on a hook by the door.

The stewards left Admiral Readington alone in his flag stateroom.

Readington sat up in his bunk. He wearily rubbed his face and reached for the teacup. He sipped and nodded. Freddy had made the tea exactly as Readington preferred, with a pinch of sugar. Freddy was a new man, transferred to USS *Lexington* just before she set sail from Brooklyn Navy Yard the week before. On his first morning aboard, Freddy had prepared Readington's tea wrong. The chief of the mess gave Freddy a tongue-lashing.

"Don't you think a man like Admiral Readington deserves to get his morning tea made right and proper?" the chief had thundered.

He hasn't screwed it up since, Readington thought. Not sure what kind of man that makes me, though.

Readington finished the tea and stood. He went to the head and relieved himself and looked in the mirror. His classmates nicknamed him "Red" his first year at Annapolis, and Red had been his callsign flying a *Grumman F2F* biplane off of USS *Saratoga* in the mid-30s. Now sailors called him "Red" because of a bomb blast which had snapped USS *Bunker Hill* in half at Kodiak Island and permanently singed the left side of his face. The blast took Readington's left eye, too. He'd worn an eyepatch ever since.

Readington shaved and put on the cleaned and pressed set of khakis and his eyepatch. He pulled on a dark blue wool sweater. He'd bought the sweater during his time at the United States Embassy in London as a naval attaché to that sonofabitch Joe Kennedy. The sweater had kept Readington warm throughout the Pacific War.

"Freddy!" Readington called.

Freddy came back into the flag stateroom.

"See that my things are packed up and sent over to the captain's quarters."

"Right away, Admiral."

Readington was turning over his stateroom to the VIP expected to arrive late in the day and moving into Captain Ritter's stateroom. Readington wondered who Ritter was displacing.

Readington stepped out of his stateroom and started down the corridor. Sailors saluted and stood aside as Readington passed. He heard the whispers behind him: "There goes Red," or "One Eye," or "He was at the Aleutians and the Bering Sea and..."

A Marine guard waited at the CIC. He saluted and opened the hatch. Readington walked into the CIC. The flag liaison officer, Captain Ritter, assigned to mind Readington, was sitting on the bench by the hatchway. Lt. Commander Dudley saw Readington and walked over to him, a folder tucked under his arm. He handed Readington his morning folder and saluted.

Readington casually saluted back. "Thanks, Dud," he said. Over the last week, he'd taken a liking to the young, enthusiastic naval officer.

Commander Polaski, *Lexington*'s XO, was actually running the CIC and leaning against a desk by the teletype on the right side of the CIC. He held a cup of coffee in one hand as he read a report. Polaski had flown *Wildcats* off *Enterprise* during the Aleutians and the Kuriles campaign. He turned down other commands after being *Lexington*'s XO for two years.

"Why skipper a destroyer now when I can skipper the *Lexington* later if I'm patient?" Polaski had explained to Readington when they'd met the week before.

Readington walked over to the surface plot. It showed Task Force 15 deployed in three crescents facing Point India at the entrance to the English Channel. The Destroyer USS *Hullett* was closest to Point India, Task Force 15's tripwire in case trouble came out of the Channel. The surface plot showed a contact a hundred seventy-five miles east of Point India.

"What's that in the Channel?" Readington asked.

"A large radar contact. We don't have eyes on her yet," replied the surface plot officer. Readington looked askance at the lieutenant. He seemed young, like he was probably in school during the Aleutian Campaign.

Readington pointed to the contacts directly northeast of the Task Force, off the Cornwall coast. "And those?"

"Civilian boat traffic. So far, they're hugging the coast."

"Good."

"And there's one German destroyer at zero-nine-five, 19 nautical miles south of our southernmost picket."

Readington nodded. "Shadowing the task force? Not acting aggressively?"

"Not at all."

"They've been shadowing us since forty-five," Readington said.

The *Kriegsmarine* had gotten more aggressive each year as their surface fleet expanded with several large cruisers and even a few carriers in the shipyards to supplement the battleships.

"Air contacts, Dud?" Readington asked.

"Mostly over Gatwick, Heathrow and the Cornwall aerodromes. Just after the sun came up, one of our fighter CAPs intercepted and turned back a civilian aircraft."

Readington nodded. He walked over to the hotseat in the center of the CIC. Dudley had made sure another cup of tea was waiting for him. Readington sipped and nodded in satisfaction while he looked through the various dispatches.

"The top dispatch seemed most urgent, Admiral," said Dudley.

Readington opened the folder and held the brief up to his good eye, which was already going bad. "Soon I will need a monocle," he'd joked to his wife back in Florida. "*Bismarck* last spotted off Bremen. *Tirpitz* still at the mouth of the Humber."

"Yes, Admiral," said Dudley. "It seems there are some British holdouts on the south bank of the river. The BBC was broadcasting about the Brave Boys of Barton and Beverly... Also, Significant British forces remain north of the landing area around York. The Germans have been bombing the city."

Readington read on, "*Frederick* was south of the Humber off Anglesey." He looked at Dudley. "Was? She moved?"

"Aye, aye, Admiral."

"Where to?"

"We don't know yet."

"How unlike Jerry," Readington said. He'd picked up the British affectation during his time in London.

"And the *Graf Spee* still running sea trials in the Kattegat. The Danes do get along with the Germans now, don't they?" Readington said, though he couldn't blame them. With France gone and the *Wehrmacht* in Moscow, what choice did the Danes have? "How do we know this?"

"German radio broadcast the sea trial last night."

"Okay."

Bismarck was thought to be as unsinkable as *Yamato* had been and world renowned. In America, toymakers sold *Bismarck* model kits. Readington's own son had one, to his dismay.

Readington came to the next brief.

"Land estimate this morning, Admiral," said Dudley.

"Peterborough?" He said. "The *Wehrmacht* has reached Peterborough?'

"Aye, Admiral. This intel comes right from the embassy. They were monitoring local comms all night."

Readington turned over the brief. On the back was a map with enemy positions marked. A great black blob encompassed the Humber River landing areas. From there, black arrows pointed north and west, with a great arrow stabbing south.

Dudley said, "Peterborough is 70 miles north of London. From there, the *Wehrmacht* can threaten Northampton or Cambridge. Or maybe dart east to Norwich."

Readington raised an eyebrow at the Lt. Commander. "Did you join the army, Dud?"

Dudley laughed. "No, Admiral. But I have read Liddell-Hart."

Clever of the Germans to land in the Midlands, Readington admitted. Both Whitehall and the Pentagon assumed the Nazis would attack across the channel from Calais or perhaps Normandy. For months, the *Wehrmacht* had built up a massive army around Caen, or so the British thought. But that army was a phantom. The real invasion had come from Norway, preceded by a devastating atomic attack that destroyed Manchester, Birmingham, and the Royal Navy's home fleet at Scapa Flow.

Since arriving at Point India, *Lexington*'s intel section had been monitoring German English radio broadcasts of the invasion. The broadcasts were made by men speaking in the Trans-Atlantic accent used by many Hollywood stars. Americans were the target audience. German news readers bragged about their use of their Atomic "Super Weapons" and their Space Age jets. On the hour, special correspondents reported from the *Wehrmacht* landing zones on the Humber and with "Rommel's Flying Column," said to be "dashing south on the road to London and victory." According to the British, those German troops were wearing alien-like rubber suits and gas masks to shield them from the effects of Heisenberg's Bomb.

After the Atomic attacks on the Midlands and the German landings at the Humber, the British Army had all but collapsed. The Pentagon thought the British could hold out for 30 days. After what he'd seen since the task force arrived at Point India, Readington wasn't so sure. He pondered the map showing black arrows stabbing down into the heart of England toward London.

"They won't last 30 hours."

"I'm sorry, Admiral?" Dudley asked.

"The British Army. I don't think they'll last 30 hours."

"Really, Admiral."

Readington didn't answer. He recalled the way the US Army collapsed after the Japanese landed on Oahu's north shore in December of 1941. General Yamashita pushed his two divisions relentlessly south through Oahu's central valley against shocked and badly outgunned American troops. Three days after the Japanese landing, Mayor Petrie declared Honolulu an open city. General Short, holed up in the Makaha Valley on the western side of Oahu with what was left of the 24th and 25th Infantry Divisions, surrendered in January of the new year.

The Germans had landed four divisions around the mouth of the Humber River, dropped two airborne divisions behind the coast, and quickly reinforced them the next day.

"What's happening in the North Sea?" Readington asked.

"I'm afraid *Kriegsmarine* ferry operations across the North Sea are proceeding unabated now, Admiral."

"Not hard when the British don't have anything left, unfortunately," Readington observed grimly. "Even if the last gasp was a 'good show,' as the Brits used to say."

The last British destroyer squadron had mounted a "Charge of the Light Brigade"-style attack against the Germans in the North Sea the previous morning. All ships were lost, but they did take several barges and the *Seydlitz* with them. Readington had been there when the Imperial Japanese Navy launched a similarly suicidal attack against Halsey's 4th Fleet off Hokkaido in 1943.

I suspect historians will consider both charges a similarly hopeless waste of men and ships that changed nothing.

Readington moved on to other dispatches.

"Wallace Administration's diplomatic efforts continue…" he read. "Hell of a lot of good that's done anyone this last month…" He didn't trust Secretary of State Joe Kennedy one bit.

Readington sipped his tea and shook his head.

After that long war in the Pacific, Washington rattles its saber and is ignored.

He put a hand to the left side of his face.

Victory was worth it, though, Readington joked to himself.

He read the weather report.

Overcast, but no rain forecast. Light swells. That will help operations.

"That was the last one?"

"Yes, Admiral."

"Time to go see for myself, Dud," Readington said.

"Aye, aye, Admiral," said Commander Dudley.

He finished his tea.

Admiral Readington walked out onto the wing overlooking the flight deck. Several *F9F Panthers* were parked below with crews making them ready for takeoff. He felt a gust of wind and was grateful for his English wool sweater. Readington inhaled deeply, taking in the salty, breezy air. The sea was gray-green but smooth. The sky above was overcast, with clouds at ten thousand feet. The weather fit Admiral Readington's mood.

A sailor stood watch in sock hat and peacoat.

"Admiral, sir," he said.

"What do we have this morning…?" he asked.

"Seaman Fangio, Admiral." The sailor turned on his Geiger counter and held it up. "Not a peep from Miss Geiger, Admiral."

The bomb blast sites were more than 300 miles from Task Force 15. Given prevailing winds across the Atlantic, there was no worry about fallout. The Geiger counters were unnecessary, Readington knew, having been an observer at the Bikini Atoll tests. But the ranking member of the Senate Armed Services committee had made a fuss about radiation in an interview with Walter Winchell, demanding to know what President Wallace was doing to "protect our boys from Oppenheimer's infernal invention." In response, the Navy Department equipped each ship with a Geiger Counter.

"Miss Geiger?" Readington asked.

"I sat next to a girl named Geiger in school. A nice Jewish girl. I felt bad for her. We all did."

Readington shuddered at the thought of what the Nazis had done to the Jews.

"Last year," Fangio added

"Last year?"

"Aye, aye, Admiral. I enlisted in the Navy right after I saw that movie about the Marines defending Midway to the last," he said.

Readington put his binoculars to his good eye and panned across the fleet. A line of destroyers formed a crescent facing northeast. Behind that was a second line of light cruisers and amphibious landing ships. Behind these was a trio of jeep carriers. All jeep carriers laid down during the Pacific War, but completed and launched after the war's end. Their decks were packed with helicopters.

Readington panned north. He just barely made out the Cornwall coast. Even then, boats were gathering at Penzance, Newlyn and other small ports in Mounts Bay. A pair of US Navy destroyers picketed the bay, with orders to prevent the boats from leaving and making for Task Force 15.

He panned northwest to the Islands of Scilly. The previous morning, a Marine landing force seized the largest of the islands, St. Mary's. Local authorities turned the island over to the marines without resistance or objection. "There's hardly a government left in London, anyway," said the mayor of Hugh Town. "All we hear comes over the Beeb, Prime Minister Halifax telling us to fight on...." A transport carrying a battalion of Seabees docked at Hugh Town soon after, and by the afternoon, they were busily expanding the island's small airstrip so it could accommodate American C-47 transports. With the landing, Operation Atlantic Wind was officially underway.

Below Readington, an *F9F Panther* roared down the flight deck and catapulted into the air. A second *Panther* followed. Readington still hadn't gotten used to the roar of jet turbines. He closed his eyes for a moment and thought about standing on the wing of his first command, the escort carrier USS *Dover*. He recalled the Bering Sea squall beating *Dover's* deck full of Marine *Corsairs* as she turned into the wind to launch against incoming *Zeros*.

Readington watched the two *Panthers* bank east and pass over USS

Aleutian. She was the USN's newest aircraft carrier. Laid down in 1945, *Aleutian* was longer and wider than the mighty *Essex* carriers which had fought in the great battles of the north Pacific. She carried a larger carrier air wing and boasted an angled deck, as well. Three more of her class were in various stages of development, with the USS *Robert A Taft* conducting sea trials out of Norfolk.

The sun rose above the horizon, lightening the dank North Atlantic clouds.

At 0630 hours, the first flight of three *Chickasaw* helicopters took off from USS *Kodiak*.

"There go General Campbell's Marines," Readington said.

In a triangle formation, the *Chickasaw* helicopters flew over Cornwall and then banked east toward London. A second flight of *Chickasaws* took off from USS *Dutch Harbor*. These carried a platoon of MPs. Another *Chickesaw* trio took off from USS *Kuluk Bay*. This group carried a score of administrative and medical personnel to help process rescue applicants. These were the lead elements of Grosvenor Force.

"Admiral, look," Fangio said. "One, two, three, four...four of them." He pointed to a line of aircraft in the western sky.

Readington put his binoculars to his good eye. "Ah, the first flight of C-47s."

Four squadrons of C-47s were positioned at Aldergrove airport outside of Belfast. An army battalion was there, as well, to deter the Republic from making any moves north. With the current crisis, Dublin was rife with talk of "reunification." Washington had warned Eamon De Valera against any action and dispatched several companies of military police to patrol the border. Their commander, a Colonel Hamilton, had briefed Readington on the Irish.

"Cold climate and colder people," Hamilton had said. "It ain't like patrolling the streets of Tokyo."

I just hope they aren't dumb enough to complicate things, Readington thought.

Readington panned his binoculars from east to west one last time. More helicopters rose from the jeep carriers.

"Gatwick Force," Readington said.

"It's a hell of a fleet, isn't it, sir?" Fangio said.

"The largest task force we've assembled since the Pacific War," Readington replied.

"I was in school."

"I was there," Readington said. "Right here, actually." He pointed to the deck. "We saw the whole fleet at the surrender in Tokyo Bay. Off the port bow, a half-dozen battleships in line...like they were blazing away at the Japanese line at the battle of the Sea of Okhotsk..."

The young sailor whistled.

"We'll never see the like again," Readington said wistfully. He looked out at the sea again and exhaled. "I've seen enough."

Readington nodded to the sailor.

Time to check in with Captain Ritter, he thought. Ritter was one of Readington's men, having been *Lexington*'s CAG during the Kurile Islands Campaign.

"Admiral on the bridge."

"At ease," Readington said.

Readington took a moment to look around the bridge from which he had skippered the *Lexington* throughout 1943.

"Good to have you on the bridge, Admiral," said Captain Ritter. "I've had my stateroom prepared for your things."

"That's good of you, Glenn. How's she riding today?" Readington asked.

"Well, Admiral," he said. "The seas should get smoother in the afternoon."

"All the better for the jeep carrier helicopter ops."

"Aye, aye, Admiral."

"*Panthers* coming onto the deck, I saw."

"And another pair after these," Ritter said. "We're ready to arm the *Banshee* squadron below, if need be."

"Between *Lexington* and *Aleutian*, we're packing a hell of a punch," said Readington. If the Germans did make trouble for Task Force 15, Readington would move *Lexington* forward into battle first.

"If it comes to that, I'll fight her for you, Admiral. Like you did at Tsugaru Strait."

For a moment, Readington recalled that awful morning as wave after wave of Kamikazes out of Honshu struck the 5th Fleet. The Japanese had hit the screening light cruisers particularly hard. Every few minutes, a new explosion mushroomed into the sky west of *Lexington*, signaling the death of another US Navy ship. Later, Kamikazes attacked the pair of minesweepers sent to rescue survivors.

"Let's hope it *doesn't* come to that," Readington said. "Now, what's the plan for the VIP's arrival? Who's leading the delegation?"

"Commander Polaski."

"You won't lead the delegation yourself?" Readington asked.

"My duties will keep me on the bridge," Ritter said sarcastically.

Readington smiled. He wouldn't be part of the delegation, either.

"Polaski is mad at me after I kicked him out of his quarters," Ritter quipped. "This ought to keep him happy. Besides, I don't want to be down there on the deck greeting that..."

"Careful now," Readington said, though he agreed with Ritter.

Readington had been in the embassy at Grosvenor Square when word came over the radio that Prime Minister Halifax had secured a ceasefire with Hitler. "We have reached an agreement and there will be no invasion of Britain," Halifax declared. Most of the embassy staff was relieved. Not Readington, who was seemingly the only man in the room who understood just how difficult a cross-channel attack would have been for the Germans. That sonofabitch Joe Kennedy had actually clapped his hands and cheered. "Get Washington on the phone," Kennedy had gleefully told his assistant.

Readington shook his head and muttered, "That...man is now the Secretary of State."

"Sorry, Admiral?"

"Nothing," Readington said.

The intercom buzzed.

"Yes..." said the ensign manning the station. "Right away. Excuse me, Admiral. Commander Dudley says you're needed in the CIC."

"All right, thank you. Captain Ridder," Readington nodded.

Readington returned to the CIC.

Commander Dudley was waiting. So was another cup of tea at the hotseat.

"Radio report from *Blue Gill*," Dudley said.

No ship or aircraft were supposed to travel east of Point India, according to Washington's orders—but those orders had said nothing about submarines. So Readington had sent USS *Blue Gill* into the English Channel. She was skippered by one Commander Ted Taylor, who came recommended by Admiral Collins, Commander ComSubLant, an Annapolis classmate of Readington's.

Definitely have the right man at the right place there, Readington thought. Collins had recounted how Taylor had skippered an S-Boat off Hilo after the Japanese took it, raising havoc with the IJN. Taylor had then commanded a bunch of war patrols after, to include one that had earned him a Navy Cross in the Bering Sea, then his second one off Hokkaido.

Somehow, I don't think Collins was joking when he said Taylor had cursed out some stuffed shirt at BuPers when they tried to give him a desk job. Glad he didn't need a steady hand in the Channel.

The previous day, Taylor had reported that the Channel was clear of German surface forces but suspected one of the new Type VIIX class U-Boats was in the area.

"Thanks, Dud." Readington took the message and read it.

"Multiple sonar contacts middle of Channel...approaching to get eyes on contacts, will update."

Readington gave the message back to Dudley. "What could that be?" he wondered aloud.

Dudley said, "The Germans could just want to show the flag."

"At Hokkaido, we thought the subs had spotted a few cruisers," Readington replied. "It turned out they were the lead ships of the *Musashi* and *Yamato* battlegroups."

Dudley winced at that statement.

"I remember watching the night light up from the four *Iowa*-class trying to stop those two monsters and their friends," Readington said. "*New Jersey*, *Iowa*, the second *New York*, and *Wisconsin* all hurling volley after volley of 16-inch shells at the approaching Japanese battleships."

Stopped them from getting to Nemuro Bay, Readington thought. *But only at a helluva cost.*

Commander Polaski interrupted Readington's reminiscence.

"Sir, the BBC is about to deliver its seven-thirty update."

"Put it on," Readington said.

The BBC update began with the typical chime and radio introduction, as if the nation hadn't suffered a nuclear attack and been invaded. After the introduction, a great disembodied voice from London spoke.

"Whitehall advises all persons in and around London to remain indoors. The home secretary further stated that aiding the enemy in any way is a criminal offense... Downing Street insists British forces are assembling to defend capitol...."

"We'll see about that," Readington said.

The BBC newsreader went on. "The number of casualties suffered in the atomic attacks in the north is now estimated by the Home Office to be in the hundreds of thousands...."

"Jesus," Dudley said.

Readington remained stone-faced. The United States had done far worse in firebombing Japan. He'd seen the burned-out remains of Tokyo days after Curtis LeMay's sustained weeklong attack in June of '44. "LeMay's Deadly Days," the Air Corps had nicknamed his Tokyo firebombing campaign.

At least we haven't nuked a city, Readington thought.

"When asked, neither Number 10 nor the palace commented on the Royal Families' whereabouts but insisted they remained in the United Kingdom."

I know where they're heading, Readington thought.

"In America, President Wallace stated the United States will not become militarily involved in the conflict but stands ready to assist in any other way it can."

Dudley said, "Admiral, General Campell on the TBS."

General Campell commanded ground operations from the USS *Chiniak Bay*. He'd led a battalion in the Kodiak Campaign and later a regiment at the Adak Landings. He commanded the 3rd Marine Division during the Hokkaido invasion and fought them into Sapporo.

Readington took the receiver from Dudley.

"What do you got this morning, Camp?"

"Mornin', Red," General Campbell began with his usual cheery twang. "Gatwick Force is down and the perimeter is secure. The airport is ours. Authorities are cooperating and British troops are maintaining a perimeter as promised in talks last night."

"Okay," Readington said.

"Grosvenor Force is also down. I'm afraid the situation is more chaotic. Word has gotten out that the Germans are approaching London. People have taken to the streets. A crowd is forming around the embassy."

The American Embassy in London was a thorny problem. It was located in MacDonald House at Grosvenor Square. The evacuation plan called for the Marines to seize Grosvenor Square across the street from MacDonald House and use it as a helicopter landing pad.

"And there's a problem with the helicopter landing area in Grosvenor Square. The pilots said it's tight and they want the Marines to cut down some of the trees."

"So tell them to go ahead."

"Well, sure, Red. They're digging up some axes."

"Why didn't anybody think of bringing axes?"

"Young officers, I suppose," Campbell joked "The Marines could use C-4 to down the trees and then pull them right off the green."

"Do they have rope?"

General Campbell laughed. "We'll make sure to send some rope."

"Well, worse comes to worse, I suppose the Marines can roll the trees out of the park."

"If it comes to that, Red."

"What about the local authorities?"

"So far, the Bobbies are maintaining order around the embassy, but they're not happy about the park situation at all, I'm told."

"Well, you've got to keep the embassy clear and a corridor open."

"I understand, Red. I'm going to send in another platoon of Marines. They're on deck now."

"Go ahead," Readington said. "And keep me updated. Out."

Readington gave the TBS receiver back to Dudley and looked at his watch. "Troops on the ground before 0800 hours," he said. "On schedule. Inform Washington."

"Right away."

"Admiral, new contacts," Polaski said.

As he spoke, the plotter was making a pair of red dots on the surface plot. "Spotted by the southern aerial picket. Two destroyers, at zero-eight-one bearing three-seven-five."

Readington pondered the status board for a moment.

Now why would two destroyers suddenly pop up like that?

"Where do you think those destroyers came from, Dud?"

"Almost certainly out of Brest," Polaski interjected.

"Yep," said Dudley.

"Almost certainly," Readington agreed.

"They're probably just keeping an eye on us," Dudley said. "We did the same when the *Bismarck* and her battlegroup transited the Denmark Strait last year."

"Yes," Readington said.

In 1941, one of President Taft's first acts in office was to quarantine the Norwegian Sea and declare no German ships would be allowed to sail past the so-called Iceland Line running from Greenland to Iceland to Scotland. In 1949, after President Wallace took office, the *Kriegsmarine* crossed the Iceland Line, anyway. The Wallace Administration took no action, arguing that the *Kriegsmarine* was no match for the United States Navy. The

Canadians were furious. Britain was dismayed. The Germans were encouraged.

"They'll be challenging us in the Atlantic soon," said Dudley.

Readington agreed.

Why else would Germany have spent the last several years expanding the French occupied ports at Brest, Saint Nazaire, and La Rochelle?

"They've got big plans," Readington agreed, then turned to Polaski. "Do these destroyers have air cover?"

Polaski looked at the radar control officer, who shook his head.

"No."

"Okay. Find out what's on deck and tell Captain Ritter to scramble a pair of *Panthers* and buzz the destroyers."

"Provocative, Admiral," Dudley said. "We wouldn't like it if *ME 292s* overflew the task force."

"It's a friendly visit. Make sure the pilots wag their wings," Readington said only half-jokingly. "Besides, we are the United States Navy. Let's remind Jerry of that."

Readington got up and paced the CIC, looking at the radar and sonar plots.

"Admiral, the first choppers have lifted off from Gatwick. General Campell has dispatched a second wave of choppers," Dudley reported.

While Readington waited, the first wave of choppers returned. These carried most American embassy personnel and their dependents. Ambassador Taylor remained, though, and would not come out till the last minute, along with the VIP.

Readington heard the first of two *Panthers* roar down *Lexington*'s flight deck.

From his desk, Commander Polaski said, "Admiral, the BBC reports that the Germans are driving quickly south and are approaching RAF Stansted. About twenty miles from London."

The second *Panther* roared down the flight deck.

"Yes, Admiral, it seems British are evacuating RAF Stansted. They still have secure aerodromes in Cornwall."

Those aerodromes could be a problem. What if RAF aircraft tried to rendezvous with the task force? Readington had suggested seizing the bases in Cornwall. But Washington didn't want the diplomatic headache, and General Campbell was reluctant to scatter his Marines across Cornwall. Certainly not when Readington couldn't guarantee air superiority.

Readington walked over to the aerial plot and folded his arms. "What's the *Luftwaffe's* status?"

"Several Combat Air Patrols over the French coast, now," said the plotter.

"What about the British?"

"Uh...aircraft out of bases in Cornwall had been heading north and northeast. To protect London."

"Had been?" Readington asked.

"We haven't detected any launches in about an hour, Admiral," Polaski stated. "A few aircraft had returned."

"Meteors?"

"Yes, several flights of them," Polaski confirmed.

"What do you all make of it?"

"*Meteors* did well against *Me-262*s," Dudley answered. "But the new *Me-292s* clearly outclass them. To say nothing of *Hawkers, Hurricanes* and *Spitfires*. Those are all outdated equipment."

"So are our *Corsairs* and *Hellcats*," Readington noted.

Hellcats and *Corsairs* had made mincemeat of Japanese aircraft over the Aleutians and the North Pacific. During the Battle of the Kuriles, Navy aircraft had shot down incoming Japanese *Zeros* and *Zekes* by the dozen.

Readington folded his arms. "How do you think our *Panthers* and *Banshees* would do against the new *292s*?"

"Uhhhh...." Dudley said, clearly reluctant to answer.

Readington laughed and said, "Carry on, son."

Most fliers thought that the *ME-292* was superior to anything currently in the American inventory. They'd bettered the British *Meteor* over the skies of Britain. American jet aircraft had yet to be combat tested. Readington knew *Lexington's* and *Aleutian's* CAG, another one of his men from the Aleutians campaign, had elaborate plans for engaging flights of *ME-292s*. Readington's orders from Washington were to avoid contact at all costs.

The technician monitoring the BBC called Polaski over from his desk. He nodded and turned to Readington and said, "Admiral, the BBC has announced that the Prime Minister is about to make an address. Ten minutes, they say."

Readington nodded. "This must be it," he said.

"Given the latest assessment, I'd say so," said Dudley.

"If all goes according to plan, the PM will be boarding a chopper at

Grosvenor Square soon," Readington said. "Polaski, you better get ready to greet him, Commander."

"Right away," Polaski replied nervously.

"Dudley can run the CIC."

"Aye, aye, Admiral."

Polaski saluted and left the CIC.

"The CIC is yours, Lt. Commander," Readington said.

Dudley sat at what had been Polaski's desk. "Thank you, Admiral," Dudley beamed.

Readington returned to the hotseat. While he waited, he listened to reports of choppers coming and going from the task force to London, Scilly and Gatwick. Past 0900, the plot recorded *Bismarck* entering the English Channel from the North Sea. *Probably just trying to make a show of force,* Readington thought. *Tirpitz* was reported to have entered the Channel, as well.

"Now that's interesting why?" Readington asked. "Why...?"

Dudley said, "New message from *Blue Gill*."

Readington took the message and read. "*Graf Spee* spotted in the Channel?"

Dudley shrugged.

"Just off the Isle of Wight...speed fifteen knots bearing southeast."

Readington walked over to the surface plot. "What the hell are they doing there?" He pondered the plot for a few moments and considered his orders. He couldn't send ships or aircraft into the English Channel, but he had carte blanche over British airspace. "I don't like this at all. Tell Captain Ritter to send a bird over the Humber to make sure *Graf Spee* is still there."

"Aye, aye, Admiral."

Dudley picked up the intercom and relayed the order. A few minutes later, a *Banshee* roared down *Lexington's* flight deck.

"Sir, the PM is coming on now."

"Put it on the radio," Readington said.

The BBC chimed and then a perfectly posh voice said, "Ladies and gentlemen, the prime minister."

In a few sentences, Prime Minister Halifax announced the Germans would enter London soon, and the British government could go on longer carry on. He would be resigning and leaving the country immediately.

"My god," someone said.

Someone else whistled.

Silence fell over the CIC for several moments until Readington said, "Raise General Campbell."

"Aye, aye, Admiral."

Here we go, Readington thought.

Dudley nodded to Readington. "On the TBS, Admiral."

Readington picked up the TBS. "Hello, Camp."

"We're good to go, Red," Campbell said. "Two birds are on standby at Grosvenor Square. Two platoons of marines are guarding the location. A platoon of MPs stands ready to make its way to Number 10, if needed."

"You have reinforcements, if necessary?"

"Sure do, Red. I have a company of Marines and the choppers to deliver them."

"Very well. Inform me when they're up."

"Will do, Red."

Readington hung up.

"I'm heading out to the wing," he said. "Notify me if anything important comes over the comm."

Readington walked out to the wing. Now past 1000 hours, the sun was higher and the sky had turned from gray to white. The air was a bit warmer, but still cool and salty. A different sailor stood watch with the Geiger Counter now. When he saw the admiral, he straightened up and saluted. This one was older, in his mid-30s, to Readington's eye.

"Petty Officer George, Admiral."

"At ease, sailor," Readington said.

"The Geiger Counter is negative, Admiral."

"Thank you, George."

"If you don't mind my saying so, sir, it's good to see you again."

"Oh?"

"I was aboard *Lexington* when we finished off the Japanese carriers, sir," the petty officer said. "We really gave it to the Japanese navy."

"We sure did."

"Hell of a victory, Admiral."

"It sure was," Readington said as he thought back to that evening with waves of dive bombers descending upon the remains of the Japanese carrier fleet. "Well, it sure as hell is different circumstances now, isn't it?"

"Aye, aye, Admiral."

Readington breathed in the cool salt air again and felt the wind against his face.

The intercom buzzed.

Readington hit the comm switch. "This is Readington."

Dudley spoke. "Admiral, this is the CIC. General Campell informs you that the prime minister is up and on his way. ETA 33 minutes."

"Okay."

Readington turned back to the sea.

To the north, he saw a pair of dots a few miles apart, flying northwest toward Aldergrove Airport outside of Belfast. Readington watched them for a moment.

George said, "I've been watching those things for a while, Admiral, a regular aerial convoy to Aldergrove."

Readington nodded.

Americans were on those C-47s, and Londoners who had worked for the bevy of American agencies that President Wallace had sent to Britian to help prop up the Halifax Ministry. Thousands of them.

I don't need to see this, Readington thought. He went back to the CIC.

"New contacts, Admiral," Dudley said

The surface plot showed ten contacts now out of Brest.

"Looks like a squadron of destroyers and a few light cruisers," Dudley said. "And we're seeing increased air activity over Brest. It looks like the Germans are scrambling a lot of aircraft."

Readington looked at the aerial plot.

The aerial plotter was marking the progress of the PM's chopper with little bowler hats. A line of bowler hats started in London and stretched west over Cornwall. Just then, the plotter was drawing a bowler hat above Lands End. He'd also marked the progress of *C-47s* in the air corridor with a line of handdrawn airplanes between Belfast and London.

I can't launch more Panthers *while waiting to receive the PM*, Readington thought.

"Tell *Lexington* to get more fighters in the air."

Dudley delivered the order via the TBS.

"The PM will arrive in a few minutes, Admiral,' Dudley said.

Readington sighed. "I'm heading back to the wing."

He wanted to see Halifax's arrival.

Petty Officer George was still there. He saw the admiral and pointed north to a speck in the sky.

"There she is, Admiral."

"I see."

The *Chickasaw* grew larger till she was over *Lexington*. Captain Ritter had cleared the flight deck for the chopper's arrival. The flight crew stood to the side, watching as the chipper landed.

A party consisting of Commander Polaski and a few sailors and half-dozen Marines acting as an honor guard stood by the landing pad. The small party held their hats to their head as the chopper approached. The *Chickasaw* landed on the flight deck. A sailor trotted over and opened the door. Out stepped a couple of men in suits who looked at Commander Polaski and shook hands. There followed the prime minister. Commander Polaski saluted and spoke and motioned for the PM to follow him inside *Lexington*'s command island.

Readington watched the now former prime minister walk across the flight deck. Halifax was tall and skinny, his face thin and elongated and pale. He wore a blue overcoat which he hadn't buttoned, revealing a suit jacket and vest. Atop his head was a bowler hat. Readington wondered how he kept the hat atop his head in the wind. Halifax looked straight ahead as Commander Polaski led him to the hatchway. He stepped into the hatchway and disappeared inside *Lexington's* island.

I will have to meet the man soon, Readington thought, dreading the encounter. *What does one say to a leader who just lost his country?*

The intercom buzzed.

"This is Readington."

"This is the CIC," Dudley said. "Admiral, you are needed here."

"On my way."

When Readington got to the CIC, Dudley began.

"Three problems, sir. First, lots of aircraft taking off from RAF and civilian strips in southern England and heading our way. It seems lots of boats are departing the coast, too."

"Okay," Readington nodded.

Was kind of expecting that, unfortunately, he thought.

Dudley pointed to the aerial plot.

"Second, many more contacts over western France. It seems the Germans are launching a lot of aircraft. *ME-262s, ME-292s.*"

Readington made a face and nodded. "Then we better scramble more aircraft."

"Third, new message from *Blue Gill.*"

Dudley handed Readington the message.

"Four, repeat four German capital ships in the channel and steaming southwest toward Point India, 20 knots."

"The *Graf Spee, Tirpitz, Frederick* and *Bismarck.*"

"Damn it," Dudley said. "I told Washington we should have a battleship division in Task Force 15. What about those German surface contacts out of Brest?"

"Still just over the horizon."

"But in a position to move in and coordinate with those big bastards in the Channel."

"Aye, Admiral."

Readington looked at the plot. Most worryingly, the four great German battleships were approaching the task force in line at 20 knots. To the south, the collection of German cruisers and destroyers was steaming north, at ten knots and thirty nautical miles south of the task force's southernmost picket.

"I have seen this movie," Readington, said thinking back to the various engagements he had fought against the Japanese.

He walked over to the aerial plot.

"Many contacts over Brest," the plotting officer said. "Dozens, Admiral."

Readington folded his arms and considered the aerial plot.

It sure looks like the Germans are gathering their strength for an attack, Readington thought. *Looks like isn't certain, though.*

"Tell Captain Ridder to start launching the *Banshees*."

Dudley went over to comms, picked up the phone and raised the bridge.

"This is the CIC. Scramble," he said.

Readington listened as the carrier's engine power increased. A few minutes later, he could feel the vessel turning into the wind. Dudley grabbed the intercom when it buzzed, nodded, and confirmed the report's receipt.

"*Banshees* will be heading up in two minutes, sir," he said solemnly.

"The *Kriegsmarine* flotilla is still coming our way."

"How far?"

"Twenty-three nautical miles and closing."

Damn, Readington cursed to himself.

The first *Banshee* roared down *Lexington*'s flight deck.

"Maybe they're just linking up with that group out of Brest?" Dudley suggested.

"Could be," Readington said. "And having a large battlegroup at Brest while we are at Point India would give us something to think about while showing the flag."

A second *Banshee* roared down the flight deck.

Readington wondered if they could even sink *Kriegsmarine* battleships from the air. *Yamato* and *Musashi* had taken a hell of a drubbing from the battleship line at Hokkaido. Sustained barrages from *New Jersey* and *Iowa* had rendered *Yamato* inoperable, but destroyers still had to go in and launch a torpedo salvo before *Yamato* sank.

"Admiral, USS *Hullett* reports they've spotted the *Kriegsmarine* flotilla," Dudley reported. "Visual contact. Bearing three-two-oh, speed twenty knots."

"Raise Jerry," Readington said. "And ask them what the hell they are doing?"

"Aye, aye, Admiral."

"And inform Washington."

"Aye, aye."

The radio officer began the call. "Hello, *Kriegsmarine*, this is USS *Lexington*... Hello, *Kriegsmarine*."

Silence greeted the radio call.

"*Kriegsmarine*, this is USS *Lexington*."

"Admiral," Dudley said. "German aerial contacts above Brest are headed this way. We are vectoring CAPs to intercept."

Readington held up a finger. "Meet but not engage," he cautioned.

"Aye, aye, Admiral."

We're outgunned, Readington thought. *If I have to retreat...*

Dudley said, "Admiral, we can't raise *Hullett*."

Readington held out his hands. "You can't raise *Hullett*... Have the Germans already engaged?" Readington pondered the surface plot, with two black arrows heading right for the task force.

We've no choice, he concluded. *Looks like the Germans are calling our bluff.*

Another *Banshee* roared down the flight deck.

"Dud, send an order to the task force, come about to..." He looked at the surface plot again. "Three-ten-zero, 20 knots."

"Aye, aye, Admiral."

Let's get the hell out of here, he thought.

Yet another *Banshee* roared down the flight deck.

"New message," Dudley said. "From USS *Atlanta*..." She was the farthest light cruiser on the eastern screen. "They report seeing a flash of light."

Readington pursed his lips.

It couldn't be, he thought.

He stood up.

"Dud, I'm going to the wing. Time to see for myself."

Readington got to the wing just as a *Banshee* catapulted into the air. Petty Officer George was gazing at the eastern horizon and didn't notice Readington's arrival. Readington could see why: a dim but persistent orange fire was on the eastern horizon. Readington thought he knew what it was; he'd seen them before, during the Bikini Atoll tests.

"Jesus," Readington said.

"Oh, sorry, Admiral," George said.

'Quite all right."

Readington saw several ships coming about, showing their profile to *Lexington*. Like *Lexington,* to starboard, *Aleutian* still steamed into the wind, launching *Banshees.*

George squinted and then put his own binoculars to his eyes. "Admiral, I think I see ships on the distant horizon."

Readington looked. "I think you're right."

A stiff wind came in from the east. Both men heard a crackling sound.

"Admiral," George said. 'The Geiger Counter..."

The Geiger Couter needle bounced from the center to left. Then Readington heard several loud *booms*. He looked up to see a blinding flash of white light...

ABOUT WILLIAM STROOCK

William Stroock is the author of more than 20 novels and two history books. He is a former teacher and adjunct professor of history. Will has published dozens of military history articles with magazines in North America and Europe including *Strategy & Tactics, History Magazine, Military Heritage, Civil War Quarterly, Medieval Warfare, Ancient Warfare, Military History Matters* and many others. Will lives in northern New Jersey with his wife and three daughters.

Will blogs at Stroock's Books (they rhyme) and Substack. His novels are available at Amazon.

DECISION OVER CAM RANH

Justin Watson

1

The *Marceau's* steel prow crested another white-capped wave. The destroyer was pitched about the volatile sea as if it were a simple skiff rather than a mighty, albeit compact, warship. Standing on the bridge, peering out the glass into the storm-wracked night, Commodore Louis Lefebvre's stomach plummeted with the nose of the ship as it smashed back into the ocean on the other side of the breaker. He gritted his teeth against a wave of nausea. Already, most of the new men, and even many of his experienced sailors, had started emptying the contents of their stomachs into whatever receptacle they could find.

Lefebvre knew, as any experienced sea captain would, that there were times when God's wrath turned the ocean into a death trap of salt and abyssal depths. All of man's genius in creating the steel titans that battled upon the waves left them still subordinate to nature's *Fury*. Normally, he would've sailed around the storm, or even put into port to avoid it—but his mission was too vital, and so they risked the typhoon. They hadn't a day to waste on their way to Cam Ranh Bay.

The possibility that God might, indeed, want his mission to fail gnawed at Lefebvre's mind. France was a client state of Germany, there was no denying it. Louis had no illusions that the Greater Reich was just or benign. France now operated under the countenance of Hitler. France's foreign policy was subject to the approval of his minsters, French soldiers bore German arms, their every move forced into alignment with

Germany's goals. Lefebvre tried to console himself that he was doing his duty to his country, and surely the Lord could not hold that against him. If France lost its colonial possessions in Southeast Asia, and especially the rubber imports from Vietnam, they would be looking at either economic collapse or even deeper dependence on German largesse.

The war in Indochina had gone their way for several months. His comrades in the French Army were mere kilometers from Haiphong. If they could take the deep water port there, they would cut the sea lane by which America had supplied the Viet Minh. To do that, the Army needed the cargo aboard his charges. Louis and his sailors guarded five merchantmen loaded fat with ammunition, diesel fuel, and spare parts. Their treasure would sustain the German self-propelled assault guns and tanks that comprised the armored fist of the Vichy French Mobile Groups.

While Indochina was unsuited to the sweeping, mechanized envelopments that Germany had used against Poland in 1939, and Lefebvre's homeland in 1940, smaller combined arms actions had still proven devastatingly effective, even in Indochina's restrictive terrain.

French superiority in armored fighting vehicles was one of their key advantages—but keeping those armored fighting vehicles running required France to maintain a supply line of epic proportions.

The Tsarina and the Shah defied any French attempt at aerial or overland resupply. The damned Americans had hired their former enemies, Japanese submarine captains, to harry France's seaborne resupply efforts—with an unfortunate degree of success.

The ships under his charge for this mission held the life's blood of a final push on Haiphong. It was the largest and best guarded convoy to date. In addition to the *Marceau*, six other destroyers, all German cast-offs of the 1936B class, vied against the vicious tides alongside the five cargo vessels, steaming desperately for Cam Ranh Bay. According to their own newspapers, though they had issued no declaration of war, the Americans were preparing to send the Viet Minh their own tanks and more artillery, along with "advisors" to halt "Nazi aggression."

Louis Lefebvre was no Nazi—he was merely a patriot with a hard duty. The Army *had* to take Haiphong before the Americans could reinforce their Viet Minh puppets. If the Americans made good on their promise, France would lose first Indochina, then her other colonies. Without them, she might remain under Germany's boot heel forever. He collaborated today so that his children might someday know liberty.

At least, that's what he told himself as he drifted off to sleep each night, senses and conscience dulled by several drams of brandy.

"Commodore, signal from merchant *Mackerel*," the sailor manning the radio spoke up. "They're saying they're taking on too much water—they're requesting we make for the edge of the storm."

Lefebvre cursed fluently under his breath and lurched across the pitching deck to stand next the radioman.

"Get a status report from the other merchies and escorts," he ordered.

Louis listened as each of the merchantmen and his own subordinate captains checked in. Though the naval officers hid their trepidation more carefully, it was clear to him that all his captains, civilian and military alike, feared capsizing in the dreadful storm.

Frustration knotted in Louis's chest and he had to resist the urge to slam an impotent fist into a bulkhead. The supplies were no less lost if the storm claimed a ship than if a mercenary submarine sank them. And he might be able to do something about the submarines.

"Signal all ships to alter course heading, bearing two-seven-zero; make for the edge of the storm."

Praying he'd made the right decision—praying that God had forsaken neither him nor France, Louis led his flock to calmer waters.

2

Benny awoke as gravity shifted and he was pulled to the side, out of the serviceable position he'd fallen asleep in, head leaning against the aircraft's porthole window. Several months of combat missions had taken a massive toll, and exhaustion was just a way of life now. More days than not, Benny was pulling high-gee maneuvers to survive against French-piloted German jets.

Robin Olds, his massive, mustachioed friend and fellow fighter pilot, sat next to Benny. Robin nudged Benny and nodded out the window.

The C-47 banked wide over Subic Bay, giving them a good view of the American naval presence in the Philippines. The flat-topped hulls of two American aircraft carriers formed the centerpieces of the task force. Benny also counted three battleships, four cruisers and a passel of destroyer escorts and tenders. It was a truly impressive force. For a moment, he fantasized at what this force could do to the French fleet streaming supplies into Indochina.

But of course they wouldn't. Just as France had avoided directly engaging any American flagged vessels traveling to and from Haiphong, the United States wouldn't risk a direct, overt naval engagement with French forces by American forces.

Since the start, the war had been an intricate dance. France and her master, Germany, attempted to reconquer Vietnam without provoking America into open war, while America tried to stop them without appearing to be the instigators. There were more than ten thousand Americans fighting on the ground and in the air over Indochina, but they were all "volunteers," or "observers," or "advisors."

Benny understood the logic. America was still weary from the Great Pacific War. The Nazis were deeply unpopular in America, but the average citizen wanted to get on with their lives, enjoy the peace and prosperity they'd damn-well earned. The men who'd shot and blasted and bayoneted their way across a hundred jungle islands had no appetite for another general war.

To Benny's way of thinking, the current balance of power in the Pacific was so favorable to the United States that the smart play would've been to strike decisively so that the French and Germans were presented with a *fait accompli*. The entire French Navy was no match for this one carrier battlegroup, and by the time the Germans could sail a force of sufficient size to challenge the mighty American Pacific Fleet, the issue in Vietnam would likely be decided.

Robin exchanged a knowing glance with Benny. Benny knew Robin Olds very well, and knew the aggressive fighter had probably been thinking the same thing as Benny—if only America would take the gloves off, a lot of their friends would still be alive.

"I wonder what the hell we're even doing here," Olds shouted over the clamor of the C-47's massive engines. They started their descent.

Benny shook his head, an angry scowl on his face. He and Robin were two of *twenty-four* pilots aboard the C-47 pulled from the 4th American Volunteer Group. That represented a quarter of the total American pilot strength. That the shadowy powers behind this operation had deemed to pull two dozen pilots off the line even as the French continued to gain ground in Thang Hoa seemed like insanity to Benny. The air over the front was still very much contested.

Benny's scowl of fury faded, and his eyes clouded over with worry and fear. A woman he cared deeply for was still back in the heat of everything, flying tank-busting missions in her rocket-armed helicopters while he was wasting time in the Philippines, a thousand miles from the fighting.

Old leaned closer to be heard without shouting.

"Don't worry, buddy. Margot's as good as they come; she'll be all right."

Benny nodded and managed a faint smile as the C-47's wheels hit the airstrip, but then his expression hardened again as it taxied to a spot right in front of a line of waiting jeeps.

"I tell you, Robin, whoever called this meeting better damn well have a good reason. Super secret spy agency or not, if this is some fact-finding conference, I'm going to reach down their throat and rip their guts out myself."

The jeeps drove them to a two-story white stucco building. As soon as the small convoy rolled to a stop, two US Army NCOs in khaki tropical uniforms ushered Benny, Robin, and the other pilots through the front doors and upstairs into a large conference room. A jolt of surprise ran up Benny's spine as he recognized that there were already six men awaiting them in the conference room—six Oriental men dressed in the dark blue uniforms of the Imperial Japanese Navy.

"What the hell are Nips doing here?" Olds muttered, but the man's mutter *carried*. And judging from the dark looks on several of the Japanese officers' faces, at least some of them spoke English.

"They're here for the same reason you are, Mr. Olds."

A short pale man with thinning gray hair and thick horn-rimmed glasses perched on a beak of a nose strode through the door opposite the one they'd just entered. He wore khaki pants and a white short-sleeved button-down shirt. The unassuming accountant persona had cracks, though. On closer examination, Benny noted a degree of wiry musculature in the man's arms and shoulders incongruent with a desk jockey, as was the confident glint in his gray eyes behind his glasses.

"They're here to help stop the Nazis from taking over the world," the short man said, smiling wryly. "And of course to get paid well for doing so. Previous unpleasantries between our two great nations are secondary to the current mission. Am I clear?"

"Clear as crystal," Olds said. "And just who the hell are you?"

"You can call me 'Mr. Feldman' or 'sir.' I'm in charge of this operation."

"By whose authority, sir?" Benny spoke up for the first time since entering the room. He kept his tone fractionally less belligerent than Robin's.

Feldman smiled, an indulgent expression.

"That's not the way this works, Mr. Jakes," Feldman said. "Let's put it this way: if I say so, you're on a slow boat back to the States with your last paycheck and those two last kill bonuses you're due."

Benny kept his features impassive, though he seethed inwardly. "No need to make threats, *Mister* Feldman," he said through tight lips.

"It's not a threat, it's an offer," Feldman said, then he looked past

Benny at Olds and the other pilots. "This is going to be an extremely difficult and dangerous mission and anyone who wants out can cash out now. Casualties are likely to be high, but if we don't succeed, the war is almost certainly lost."

"All right, Feldman," Olds said. "What's the mission, and what does the Japanese Navy have to do with it?"

Feldman regarded Olds with flat gray eyes for several tense seconds. Despite being nearly a foot taller and likely sixty pounds heavier than the little gray man, it was Olds who bent.

"Excuse me," he said between gritted teeth. "What is our mission, *sir?* And what role do our new Nipponese friends have in it?"

Feldman gestured to one of the Japs, a short, cadaverously thin man with hard black eyes and black-and-gray stubble on his face.

"Commodore Tanaka commands the submarine squadron that has been strangling French resupply efforts," Feldman said. "Were it not for the efforts of these men, we calculate that the French would've been able to field forty-two percent more tanks, thirty-seven percent more artillery, and twenty percent more aircraft in all categories, as well as trebling their available diesel and ammunition stores."

Well, Lord knew Benny had seen more Me503s than he needed to see in a lifetime. If Feldman wasn't just pulling numbers out of his ass, then Benny was grateful the Frogs didn't have a fifth again as many fighters.

"I commend Commodore Tanaka and his men for their fine work." Olds gave a small, stiff bow to the thin Jap, who returned it with an equally stiff gesture. "How can we help? None of the airfields we still hold in Vietnam are within range of the shipping lanes the Frogs are using."

Feldman smiled.

"That's correct, Mr. Olds. Which is why the Free Vietnamese Air Force is going to take delivery of their next two squadrons directly from the flight deck of the U.S.S. *Hornet.*"

———

Tanaka Masayoshi listened intently as Komatsu, his executive officer, voiced a running translation of Mr. Feldman's conversation with the Americans for those of the captains who, like Masayoshi, didn't speak English. Masayoshi had met the American spy several times; he had received his crew's combat bonuses as well his personal supply of Nat Sherman cigarettes from Feldman. It gave him a bit of grim pleasure that he was, apparently, better connected with the man behind America's war in Indochina than these arrogant American pilots.

As Feldman talked and Komatsu translated, Masayoshi let his gaze drift over the faces of the American pilots. The big one with the stupid mustache didn't like working with Japanese. Fair enough: America and Americans could all go to hell, as far as Masayoshi was concerned.

Only decorum kept him from staring openly at the black man. He'd never seen one before. The United States had deployed several thousand blacks in the Great Pacific War, of course, but Masayoshi hadn't been fighting on land, nor were any of the Negro regiments assigned occupation duties in his home prefecture. Imperial Japanese propaganda had depicted American Negroes as savage, ape-like, and servile, even more brutish than their barbaric white masters.

Masayoshi had long since learned that his country's propagandists had as much taste for truth as he did for their bullshit, but he was still surprised to see an American Negro in a pilot's uniform. The man's frank, piercing eyes and alert expression seemed to indicate a keen intellect, and his bearing was, if anything, much more reserved and professional than his big, boisterous comrade's.

The remainder of the pilots looked much as any round-eye looked to him. Larger than necessary, bulkier than necessary, and obnoxiously loud, even when they were silent, just by their *presence*. Some of them, perhaps, had even dropped bombs on his homeland or strafed the desperate civilians forced by Tojo into futile resistance against the American invaders. Images of the charred rubble of his hometown distracted Masayoshi from Komatsu's narration for a moment, but with an angry frown, he returned his attention the matter at hand.

————

Benny had dealt with Japanese often enough to note the oddly open look of rage that passed briefly over the senior Jap's face. Feldman had said his name was Tanaka. For a moment, Benny idly worried if "Feldman" would bother assigning *nom de guerre* to Japanese mercenaries.

Not that it mattered what the man's name was—what mattered was if they could trust this thin, vicious-looking Nip and his fellow captains. Benny had been stationed in occupied Japan post-invasion for several years. He'd seen the crushing poverty and knew that the pay these men were getting would likely allow them to live like kings in comparison to most of their countrymen, but would that be enough to assure their loyalty and willingness to stick it out in a hairy situation?

And the mission, from everything Feldman was telling them, was going to be hairy, to say the least.

"There are five cargo ships in the next French convoy, escorted by six destroyers, all old German models from World War II, but crewed by the French and modified with surface and air search radar, as well as the ability to fling depth charges in all four directions. If we send the subs up against them alone, they'll get to cut to pieces.

"As Mr. Olds already pointed out, there are no friendly airstrips that could support a strike on the convoy," Feldman said. "That's why the *Hornet* and her escorts will sail to a point just outside the range of the enemy's guns and launch your two squadrons. The *Skyraiders* will engage the convoy's escort destroyers, clearing the way for the submariners to sink the cargo vessels. The *Sabers*, or I suppose I should use proper Navy nomenclature, the *Furies* will engage the fighters the French will scramble from Cam Ranh so the A-4s can make it out of there."

"First, how is that not a direct act of war?" Benny asked. "And second, only a third of us have any carrier experience. Nesmith—"

Benny turned to one of the other AVG flyers, one who'd come from the Navy rather than the Air Force.

"How long would it take you to bootleg carrier-qualify us Air Force types?" Benny asked.

Nesmith looked thoughtful for a moment. "For you? A few weeks. For Olds? Maybe a year. I don't have sufficient crayons to explain how tailhooks and arresting cables work to a West Pointer."

Olds laughed. "Fuck off, Brad," he said amiably.

"Does it change the equation if you only have to teach them how to take off, Mr. Nesmith, not how to land on a carrier?" Feldman said, cutting off the banter.

"Yes, sir," Nesmith said. "That's definitely the easier part of the process —but where exactly are we landing after we kick the tiger in the nuts? You don't pay me enough for a kamikaze mission—no offense." Nesmith nodded to the Japanese.

To Benny's surprise, once his aide translated it for the senior Japanese sub skipper, the rail thin man actually smiled, slightly, and rattled something off in reply. Benny didn't speak much Japanese, but he caught the dry humor in Tanaka's tone. Feldman must've spoken Japanese, because he laughed along with the Japanese submariners.

"Translation?" Olds asked.

"Essentially, he said, 'Us either, white boy,'" Feldman provided.

A moment of general laughter suffused the room before Feldman continued.

"You'll be landing at Hainan Island," Feldman said. "The old Flying Tigers' airbase, appropriately enough. We've arranged for tankers to meet you at two points along your flight path to get you in. The Chinese government will allow you to rest, refuel, and rearm before you have to fly to Hanoi."

The man smiled.

"The fact that you are *not* coming back to the *Hornet* after your attack is our fig leaf. Once you take delivery of the warplanes and ordinance on behalf of the Free Vietnamese government, the US government can't be held responsible for what you do with them."

Benny frowned. "And if the French naval commander doesn't see it that way?" he asked.

"Well, we rather hope you'll have sunk his ships and killed him so his opinion will be immaterial," Feldman said. "But even if you utterly fail, an attack by six 1930s-era destroyers on the *Hornet* carrier battlegroup would be suicide, as well as the *causus belli* we'd need to intervene directly in Indochina."

"Trying to start a war, Mr. Feldman?" Benny asked, sharply.

"The war is already started—I'm trying to win it. Or do you think the Greater Reich controlling everything from the Hindu Kush to the South China Sea is in America's best interest?"

"It's not quite a kamikaze mission," Olds admitted. "But it relies on a lot going right. This is a Hail Mary at best, Mr. Feldman."

"While I did not play football at our dear Hudson Highland Home, Mr. Olds," Feldman said. "I do believe a Hail Mary is exactly the play you call when you're behind with seconds left in the game and the end zone is a long ways away."

"You're a West Pointer?" Benny didn't bother to hide the incredulity in his question.

Feldman reached into his pocket and pulled out a class ring, holding it up for them to see.

"Class of '17," he said. "I commanded an infantry company in World War I and a battalion of paratroopers in the Great Pacific War, before I was tapped for...other duties. I tell you this because you need to know that I'm here for the same reasons you're here. None of you are mercenaries;

not really. This was a chance to fight for your country and you took it same as I did. This is how we ensure the Nazis don't encircle us in the Pacific the way they have in Europe."

"The extra pay *is* nice," Nesmith said.

"You'd do this on your Lieutenant's pay, Nesmith, don't bullshit me," Feldman said. "The only question now is if we take our ball and go home because it got too rough, or do we dig and do what it takes to win this fucking thing?"

As he spoke, Feldman opened a drawer under the massive map table and pulled out a thick stack of typewritten documents. He threw the ream on the table with a thud that knocked over many of the flags denoting the various air and naval assets in his plan.

"That's what they've got in those cargo ships," Feldman said. "It's not just fuel, parts, and ammunition for what they've already got—they're getting a full combat engineer regiment with mechanized earth-movers and bridge-layers and a full battalion of the new German self-propelled air defense guns."

Benny inhaled sharply. That German short-range ADA would wreak havoc on the helicopters—Margot was already risking her life every day."

If the French got those guns—

Tanka spoke up again. Feldman clearly understood what he said, but waited for the junior Japanese officer to translate for the benefit of the other Americans.

"Captain Tanaka would like to remind you, Mr. Feldman, that we *are ronin*—that is to say, mercenaries, and this mission involves substantially more risk than what was agreed upon in initial negotiations," the young man said. "While we have no great love of the French or the Germans, our commitment to aiding your foreign policy is, I'm sure you understand, more limited."

Benny had never heard *What's in it for me?* phrased so inefficiently before.

"Of course," Mr. Feldman. "That is why, in addition to doubling all your salaries and kill bonuses, the United States will increase economic and agricultural aid to Japan in all categories by fifty percent, effective January 1st. Additionally, in the event of Vietnamese victory, the Vietnames government has pledged to sell all rice exports to Japan at minus fifteen percent what it charges any other customer."

Tanaka's face was an impenetrable mask again. He spoke in rapid-fire Japanese as soon as Feldman's words were translated.

"We already have congressional approval," Feldman said, not waiting for the translation this time. "The appropriate bill is past committee in both houses and will win on the floor—provided you do as asked. Our politicians can't sell the public on another open war right now, but neither party wants the Nazis to win in Southeast Asia."

Tanaka said something in an extremely sharp voice that his junior did *not* translate. Feldman responded in Japanese, his voice glacially calm. Tanaka was silent for a moment, and then he bowed from his waist. Feldman returned the gesture.

"Excellent," Feldman said, returning to English. "We have one week until launch, gentlemen. Let's make the most of it."

One Week Later, aboard the Marceau

Since they'd cleared the typhoon, the weather had been kind to Louis Lefebvre's command, nor had they been troubled by enemy submarines. He'd almost believed the voyage might conclude without a complication.

More the fool, I.

"Commodore, the American carrier and her escorts have turned into us, range to target, twenty kilometers and closing."

The surface-search radar operator's voice was calm, but strained. Understandably—they were no match for an American carrier group. His second-in-command, Lieutenant Commander Henri Allard, walked across the command center to stand next to his squadron commander.

"What are they playing at?" Allard asked in a low voice. "Surely the Americans aren't going to attack us."

Lefebvre shook his head.

"They're almost certainly playing games with us, but just in case…man battle stations."

Aboard Hornet

WHAMMMMM.

Benny was slammed back into his cockpit seat as the hydraulic catapult flung his FJ-*Fury* off the flight deck and into the clear blue sky. He immediately pulled easily back on the stick and eased into the racetrack pattern to clear the flight path for the next launch. Once he'd climbed enough to establish vertical and lateral separation from the launch, he pulled into a racetrack pattern to watch the rest of the squadron launch, and then the *Skyraider*s.

Twenty-four birds, all into the air—it was nothing short of a miracle. One week to train and plan. The red-yellow-and-blue tricolor that had replaced the stars and stripes on his vertical stabilizer was still a little runny.

Olds's voice sounded in his headphones.

"Tiger One-One, this is Tiger Two-One," Olds said, calling for Nesmith, who'd been appointed to lead the *Skyraider* squadron since he had the most recent prop-plane experience flying *Thunderbolt*s on close air support missions. "Tiger Two Flight Airborne."

"So are we, Tiger Two," Nesmith's voice came back. "Let's go see how well Frogs swim."

MARCEAU

"Sir, I have twenty-four airborne tracks diverging off the American carrier headed straight for us." It was the air-search radar operator who spoke up now. "Twelve are too fast to be prop-planes, but we can't make out their specific signature yet."

Lefebvre shared a worried look with Allard.

"More posturing?" Allard asked.

"Perhaps," Lefebvre murmured.

Why only twenty-four aircraft? Each of those carriers could disgorge three times that number.

"A smaller force to provoke a reaction?" he mused aloud. "We fire on this force and they send the rest of their planes to destroy us?"

"Should I tell the gunners to hold fire?" Allard asked.

Lefebvre gave himself a moment to consider. If those planes were equipped with anti-ship weaponry, two squadrons were more than enough to wreak havoc on his convoy. But if they were bluffing and he fired, provoking them, that American Carrier Group would shred his entire command in a matter of minutes. Though it was against his nature, caution seemed the order of the day.

"Yes, send to all ships: continue to track but do not engage without orders."

. . .

I-201 Submarine "Funayarei"

At periscope depth, Tanaka Masayoshi had no trouble hearing the roar of the American jet engines overhead, followed by the lower rumble of the propeller-driven bombers trailing them. At least privately, Masayoshi admitted to no small relief they weren't hunting him. He'd spent too many years on the receiving end of American anti-submarine aircraft's depth charges.

"They should be within range of the French anti-aircraft guns by now," Feldman mused from behind him. "I wonder why they haven't opened up yet."

Masayoshi had been surprised when his secretive American handler had appeared on the gangway. When he'd pressed the little American for a reason, he'd simply smiled enigmatically.

"Perhaps I'm simply bored and wish to be where the action is," Feldman said. "And perhaps I wanted you to understand that this mission is important enough that I would share the risk with you."

"I respect your courage," Masayoshi said. "However, the only assurance I require from you is my men's pay and the aid package your politicians promised my homeland. You can assure neither should this go poorly and you were to be killed."

Feldman's enigmatic smile remained.

"While I may be the architect of this operation, I am not indispensable. The aid package is already passed, the President signed it this morning, and your men's pay will be waiting for them in Haiphong."

Feldman paused for a moment, head cocked as if trying to listen through the hull.

"The French still haven't opened fire," he said, meditatively. "That seems foolish."

"They likely think this move a provocation on your part," Komatsu volunteered. "They expect you are sending American planes as bait to draw their fire so you may engage the convoy with your entire fleet. They're trying to, what is the phrase, 'call your bluff?'"

Masayoshi agreed with his subordinate's assessment.

"Let's hope they don't realize until it's too late," he said. "With the destroyers gone, our part will be a little more than a glorified live-fire exercise. Apologies, Feldman-*san*, if that is insufficient excitement for you."

Feldman gave low chuckle. "I imagine I shall console myself somehow."

MARCEAU

"Sir, we're having trouble tracking the prop-driven squadron from surface clutter," the radar operator said. "The jets are at approximately ten thousand feet and orbiting in a slow racetrack pattern around us."

If the Americans were trying to rattle him, it was working. Perhaps it was best to open fire and then run for Cam Ranh. The airfield there was already scrambling fighters—

"Report from lookout," one of the deck officers shouted. "One of the jets got close enough to see their markings: they were blue-yellow-red tricolors, not US Markings."

"*Merde!* All batteries, open fire, weapons free! If it flies, it dies!"

TIGER-TWO-TWO

Benny banked right again, keeping his wing tilted so as to be able to keep an eye on the action below. Even with drop tanks on each wing, the navalised *F-86* was more responsive and maneuverable than the *P-80*. Despite the crazy-ass mission he was on, Benny was glad to be back in the cockpit of a *Saber* again, even if it was the squids' version of it.

Below, Nesmith and his *Skyraider*s had descended to damn near wavetop level, close enough their props were creating trails of sea spray behind them. Given the thermals coming off the South China Sea, those boys must have been having one hell of a ride. When Olds had pressed Nesmith about how accurately they could shoot, given the low-level turbulence, Nesmith had grinned.

"Well, you see, even small warships are a lot bigger than tanks and have far fewer things to hide behind. Besides, better that than come in high and give their triple-A time to turn us into Swiss cheese."

Nesmith was proven at least partially correct when the French destroyers below suddenly came to life with orange-and-black flashes of machine gun and cannon fire. Clearly, they had been emplaced to protect against dive-bombers, though their angle of fire was poor, indeed, to address the sea-skimming bombers approaching them.

"All right, Tiger-Two, one pass, one short burst." Olds's voice came over the radio. "Remember the *Skyraiders* will sink the ships—we're just fucking with their aim. We're going to need our ammo for the *Messerschmidts*."

Benny and his wingman banked around into position, Benny in lead, his wing with about a kilometer of trail. Benny dove first on their prey, the lead French destroyer. He lined up his gun sight as best he could and walked six streams of glowing .50-caliber tracer rounds over the deck toward one of the ship's AAA emplacements. He was past the target and climbing back to altitude too fast to assess how effective his attack had been.

He resumed his racetrack pattern, joined by his wingman a few seconds later. Benny dipped his wing just in time to see Nesmith's squadron pouring their rockets into the French warships with devastating effect.

Nicknamed the Holy Moses by the pilots who'd first fired them toward the end of the Great Pacific War, the *Skyraiders* were each carrying a dozen of the armor-penetrating variant. The screech of their rockets was audible even over the roar of own jet engine, and the streams of incandescent white-hot wrath unleashed upon the destroyer-escorts was like something from a science fiction pulp—or perhaps from the Book of Revelation.

MARECEAU

His entire command, save his own flagship, had been rendered combat ineffective in a matter of minutes. With no squadron to coordinate, Lefebvre made his way up the narrow steel stairs to the bridge. He found a cacophony of incoming damage reports and snarled commands. The destroyers at the tail of the convoy had been hit first, but soon it would be *Marceau's* turn.

"Right full rudder, turn into the attack," Allard screamed at the helm. "Do not give them our profile!"

Lefebvre braced himself against a bulkhead as the destroyer pitched and cornered like a speedboat. Two of the propeller-driven American bombers were bearing down on them, head-to-head like some kind of modern joust, their mounts piston-driven raptors, his a steel-clad killer whale.

The planes were visibly bouncing from the turbulent air for a moment, and then their wings flashed with fire. Lefebvre's heart thundered as the rockets streaked toward his flagship. Allard had made the right call: the vast majority of the unguided projectiles splashed harmlessly into the water.

But three hit the foredeck, thirty meters from the bridge. A dozen men were instantly incinerated in the explosion and steel sheered off the deck, flying in all directions. Lefebvre instinctively threw himself to the deck a split-second before shards of steel shattered the bridge's window into thousands of pieces.

As quickly as it began, the attack was over. Gasping for air, Lefebvre pushed himself to his feet, slicing open his left hand on shattered glass in the process. Ignoring the wound, he looked around, frantic to assess the catastrophe.

Henri Allard lay dead in the center of the room, brown eyes fixed and staring at the ceiling as blood welled from a jagged piece of glass embedded in his throat. Out the shattered window, a massive black-and-white hull loomed large. They were on a collision course with one of the merchants.

"Helm, full left rudder!" he screamed, but a quick glance showed Lefebvre that the man at the helm was missing a quadrant of skull.

Lefebvre staggered across the distance and yanked the dead man from the helm station and pulled the controls until the *Marceau's* prow was pointed at the cargo ship's wake. They missed the big ship's fantail by a matter of meters.

Lefebvre snapped his fingers at one of the seaman who looked more or less intact.

"Ducault, take the helm. Keep us steady for now."

"Aye, sir," the young seaman acknowledged shakily, taking the blood-slick wheel in his hands.

Lefebvre picked up the ship's intercom and demanded a damage report. Slowly, his department heads checked in. They'd taken no damage to their engine or screws, their forward five-inch guns were inoperable, but their torpedoes and depth charge racks were still fully effective. Counts of dead and wounded were still underway.

As he'd feared, all five of the other destroyers were damaged beyond their ability to fight, though two might be able to limp into Cam Ranh.

Despite the bodies littering her bridge, it was clear that *Marceau* had gotten off the lightest in blood and battle damage—all because his now-dead friend had made the right call in the final seconds of his life.

The airbase at Cam Ranh had scrambled two fighter squadrons to avenge his losses on the American aircraft now fleeing north. Unfortunately, with most of the newer *Me 503s* deployed further north to counteract the American mercenary flyers, it was the older *Me 262s* that were left to guard Cam Ranh Bay—Lefebvre was no aviator, so he merely had to hope that quantity would overcome the American qualitative edge with their newer jets.

As a damage crew began to clear the deck of bodies, steel frag and broken glass, Lefebvre began to wonder how he was going to fit the survivors from the rapidly sinking destroyers onto the *Marceau*. Then something occurred to him that impacted like a physical blow to his gut.

The cargo ships were untouched by the air strike, though. Why would they target the warships? It was the merchants whose cargo might win the way. Realization dawned, and Lefebvre cursed his own foolishness.

"Helm, come about one-eight-zero degrees and assume flank speed," he snapped.

Tiger Two-Two

"Nice work, Tiger-One. Now get the hell out of here, we'll see you in Hainan." Olds sounded nearly jubilant. "Tiger-Two, let's treat 'em rough."

Benny grinned behind his oxygen mask as he led his flight up to forty-thousand feet. Once they were level, he and his men ditched their drop tanks. Making a gun-run weighed down was one thing; air-combat maneuvering with the extra weight, even against inferior jets, was another.

Two minutes later, they spotted their prey—a dozen *262s* in loose formation at one-o'clock low. The *262's* service ceiling was no match for theirs.

Surprise, assholes!

"Tiger Two-Two flight, follow me," Benny said, and he pushed his stick forward and applied right rudder to get a side angle of attack. He activated his radar-guided gun sight and allowed a moment for the glowing red reticle to adjust based on the range data the system gathered.

The *262s* tried to scatter, but Benny and his mates were upon them. Benny raked two of the German-designed, French-painted jets with .50-

caliber rounds in a matter of seconds, sending them spiraling into the sea. His wingman accounted for two more before they extended, pushed their throttle and left the confused flock of *262s* winding around trying to engage them.

Just in time for Olds, with the other six *Furies*, to slice through from the opposite direction. As Benny looped back around for a second pass, he saw they were almost equal in number after the winnowing. He grinned wolfishly.

To the Frenchman's credit, none of them tried to run and many acquitted themselves well in the ensuing furball, but the *Fury* was faster, more maneuverable, and its improved avionics made it even more lethal.

Benny pulled hard on the stick, pushing his gunsight out in front of the last *262* as it tried to trade altitude for enough speed to run, and depressed the firing button. His tracers intersected with another stream of glowing red rounds, right into the Frenchman's fuselage.

"Ha, gotta share that one, Tiger Two-Two," Olds said as his *Fury* crossed low and left across Benny's windshield.

"Thanks for cleaning up my leftovers, Two-One," Benny responded. "Anybody got anything else?"

"I'm clean and no joy," Olds said. "Anyone else."

A chorus of negatives responded from the rest of the squadron.

"Tiger Elements, this is *Hornet*," a much fainter voice crackled over their radio. "We have six more launches from Cam Ranh airbase. Cross section indicates twin-engine turbo prop."

Twin-engine propeller-driven planes...German anti-sub birds? Easy meat without fighter escort, but there was no way they had the fuel. Benny checked his fuel gauge—they were just at "bingo." If they were going to make it to the first rendezvous point for in-flight refueling, they were all going to have to fly smart and think light thoughts.

The *Me 206s* were downed, and Nesmith and his bombers had too good a lead on anything sortieing from the mainland now. It was time to *di di mau*, as their Vietnamese allies said.

"Two-One, this is Two-Two," Benny said on the squadron frequency. "Brother, we are running low on gas."

"Copy, Two-Two," Olds said, his voice now dejected. "Tiger Two Elements, proceed to ARP One and watch your fuel gauges."

FUNAYAREI

Their hull reverberated around them from the aftershocks of their torpedoes as they detonated against the hull of the trailing French merchant carrier. Staring through the periscope, Masayoshi grunted approvingly as the fat container vessel began to list, at first subtlely, then violently, to port. The new gashes in her hull admitted a deluge of seawater into the vessel.

Even more gratifying—sixty seconds later a series of smaller explosions ripped through the vessel's superstructure. The fires must have ignited fuel or ammunition stored aboard the vessel, just about the same time one of *Funayarei's* pack-mates engaged the next merchant in line with similar effect.

The billowing black smoke from burning vessels was actually making both target identification and navigation a challenge.

"Signal to squadron," Masayoshi called down from the tower. "Three-One-Two, and Three-One-Three engage Merchant Three; Three-One-Four and Five, Merchant Two. We're going to swing east and then run to catch the lead merchant."

"Aye, Captain," Komatsu acknowledged, his voice bright with the thrill of battle.

"Helm—right half rudder bearing forty-five degrees," Masayoshi said, trying to steer them out of the black billowing clouds so they could see the lead merchant to chase her down.

But just as they cleared the smoke, another explosion rippled through the water—and Masayoshi knew it wasn't one of their torpedoes.

"Sonar, what was that?"

"Depth charges, Captain," the operator said. "And I've got screws on the surface that are too fast for the merchants. Bearing two-niner-zero, range one-five hundred yards."

Masayoshi swung the periscope in the indicated direction and dialed in the magnification. Damn, there it was: though trailing black smoke and bearing obvious battle damage, one of the French destroyers was clearly maneuvering under power, and flinging depth charges off every quarter as it cut through the water.

Marceau

Lefebvre swore fluently as explosions wracked the starboard hull of the third merchantman in his convoy.

"Signal the container ships to run for the bay. Helm trail the last two merchies, but keep us erratic," Lefebvre commanded. "There are at least four submarines in the area. Sonar, keep feeding targeting data to the depth charge crew."

The young lieutenant who had taken over the communications station looked forlorn.

"We're not dead yet, Lieutenant," Lefebvre said. "Our anti-sub aircraft are fifteen minutes out. We've just got to keep them busy until then."

Three more waterproofed bombs flew from their launchers into the water, sending up geysers of foaming white as they detonated fathoms under the service.

FUNAYAREI

"Sir, we just lost contact with Three-One-Four," Komatsu reported.

"Pickups consistent with hull breach on that last depth charge," the sonar operator reported.

"Helm, come about, bring us in behind his screws," Masayoshi said. "Weapons, get me a firing solution on the French destroyer."

"Captain Tanaka, your mission is those merchant vessels," Feldman said, mildly.

Masayoshi glared at the man, who was short for an American, so they were eye to eye.

"And I will kill them both, as soon as I've disposed of the French destroyer that's murdering my men."

"Captain, six air contacts," the surface-search radar operator reported. "Propeller-driven, not jets."

"The anti-submarine squadron out of Cam Ranh," Feldman muttered. "Damn."

"Signal all ships, go deep and evade," Masayoshi said. "I'm afraid you're going to have to be happy with eighty-percent success, Mr. Feldman."

Feldman looked unhappy, but the man was clearly neither suicidal nor stupid.

"Of course, Captain," he said. "You and your crew did all that could be reasonably asked of you."

3

HAINAN ISLAND
TWENTY-FOUR HOURS LATER

There were still pictures of the original Flying Tigers on the wall in the Officer's Club at Hainan Airbase. Those pilots, under a madman named Claire Chennault, had downed hundreds of Japanese planes. While how large their strategic contribution to the Chinese theater was a matter of debate, their courage was unquestionable, and they *had* shaped the American imagination for the wider war to come.

Benny wondered if he and Robin and the rest were doing the same. He was aware that they were getting a lot of press coverage. That Brit photojournalist, Murrow, had submitted several more pieces to *Life* after that first one. A letter from his father informed him that one of the studios was seeking to contact him concerning a movie script based on his life. It was going to be led by an up-and-coming young Negro actor named Sydney Potter, or something like that.

The propaganda push was mighty, and they'd just committed the largest provocation of the war in sinking eight French-flagged vessels with a strike launched from the deck of an American aircraft carrier. Had he just helped plunge America into another war?

An unexpected storm front had kept them on the ground in Hainan a day longer, so Benny, Olds and Nesmith were sitting at a table in the corner, drinking Old Crow with far less ice in it than prudence dictated. Their mood might have been less somber if the results of the mission had been less mixed.

"All the fucking Nips had to do was sink five fat fucking cargo ships," Nesmith said aloud. "How hard is that?"

"Hard with a destroyer and six anti-sub planes bearing down on you," Benny said levelly. He shared Nesmith's frustration in spades, but he couldn't fault a man for not committing suicide.

"I should've engaged them," Olds said, flinging his glass of cheap whiskey back and slamming the empty on the table.

"Oh, drop it, Robin," Benny said. "We'd all've been in the drink."

They kept drinking in silence for several minutes until the door to the bar swung open, allowing a blast of rain and cold air in. A short, slight shadow stepped through. As it advanced into the barroom, it coalesced into a man, dressed now in a gray suit, attaché case in hand, horn-rimmed glasses gleaming in the dim bar light—Feldman. He looked around for a moment, then catching sight of Benny, Olds, and Nesmith, he walked straight up to their table.

"Good evening, gentlemen," he said, politely.

"Evening, *Mister* Feldman," Olds said. He poured a finger of whiskey into his glass, slid it across the table to Feldman and signaled the waitress to bring him another glass. "Have a drink."

"Thank you kindly, Mr. Olds." Feldman sat down, threw back the whiskey without a grimace, then poured a heavy slug for each of them once the waitress deposited more glasses.

"As it turns out," he said. "I have good news. The convoy bearing the bulk of the equipment for the Free Vietnames 1st Armored Regiment set sail from San Francisco Bay this morning."

Benny felt the iron band of worry that had been constraining his chest loosened just a little.

"It's about fucking time," Olds said, slamming his Old Crow back.

"Thank you, Mr. Feldman," he said.

"Just thought you boys should know, it wasn't for nothing," Feldman replied. "Now, is drinking the most rotgut horsepiss imaginable some kind of pilot thing, or can I interest you in something a little smoother?"

Feldman retrieved a bottle of Old Forrester from his attaché case and set it on the table.

Benny and his friends grinned.

"Hell, Mr. Feldman, I knew I liked you," Olds said.

Their glasses filled with *much* better whiskey now—Feldman held his up.

"Absent companions."

CAM RANH BAY

Louis Lefebvre watched the two surviving cargo ships, crawling with coolies drawn from across France's colonial possessions, unloaded unto Cam Ranh's piers. Tracked and wheeled vehicles screeched down gangplanks that looked entirely too narrow for the purpose, and into assembly areas for transport north, to the front.

His own ship was done for the duration of the war, and it was unlikely another command would be forthcoming. The admiralty had decided to paint him as the hero of the day, foiling American treachery with daring and skill, his lone ship against the New Colossus.

He knew better. He knew his hesitation to fire had allowed the American bombers to close to optimal firing distance unmolested. He knew that *Marceau* only survived because poor dead Henri Allard had made exactly the right call with only seconds to do so.

The French and German governments were making a lot of noise about the attack, but thus far neither had done anything to widen the war effort. France's fleet had just lost ten percent of its effective warships in one day. While Hitler encouraged his subordinate states to fiddle with their overseas empires, Lefebvre seriously doubted he would commit German warships to the Pacific at this point.

So the soldiers would have to win the war with what they had. The battalion of mobile air defense guns had made it, as had enough fuel, ammunition and spare parts to revitalize two armored mobile groups. It might be enough, it might not. It seemed God was allowing this one to be decided on the battlefield.

Further down the docks, a white hulled ship painted with a red cross was docked. Sailors, not coolies, maneuvered a long train of caskets up onto that vessel. The merchantmen and sailors who'd died under his command.

The war was still in question, but Lefebvre doubted very much if there was much question left about the disposition of his soul.

ABOUT JUSTIN WATSON

Justin Watson was the last member admitted to West Point's Class of 2005, though, thankfully, he didn't graduate in the same slot. Justin commissioned into the Field Artillery and spent his career with line Field Artillery and Infantry units, deploying twice to Iraq and once to Afghanistan. Justin was medically retired from the Army in 2015.

Justin settled in Houston with his wife Michele and their four kids where he doubled down on his lifelong writing aspirations.

He is the author, with Kacey Ezell and Tom Kratman, of the Romanov Rescue and its upcoming sequel 1919: The Romanov Rising.

You can see his work at www.justinwatsonbooks.com.

DREAMS OF GDAŃSK

Eric G. Swedin

When should a man obey orders? I write this so that my grandchildren and people in the rest of the world will know why I did what I did. As a naval officer, I was ordered to do something so horrible that later we found we couldn't tell people that we had served our country with honor and distinction. We found it more prudent to lie and say that we were not even in uniform during the Fire.

My story began on October 24, 1962, a Wednesday. It was night. It was my third tour as part of the Gold Crew on the *Patrick Henry*. We were the second boat of a new type of submarine, where our torpedo tubes were a relic of a different age, because our goal was to hide and then emerge to fire our sixteen *Polaris* ballistic missiles. Each missile was tipped with a miniaturized hydrogen bomb as a warhead, possessing over forty times the explosive power of either of the atomic bombs dropped on Japan.

We left our anchorage near the submarine tender *Proteus* during the dark in order to avoid detection by any communist observers on the shores of Holy Loch or other parts of Scotland. I know that people may scoff at the idea of communists hiding among the Scots, but hundreds of anti-nuclear protestors had descended on this remote loch just last year when it was announced that an older World War II submarine base had welcomed the new ballistic missile submarines from the United States. We still ran across the occasional protestor or their encampments when we went ashore. I'm all for free speech and all those rights, but these protestors seemed clueless about the evil of the communists.

They also didn't seem to understand the role that our boat played in the larger drama. Our job was to deter the Soviets from attacking the United States or NATO with nuclear weapons. It's simple to say that, but the ideas behind the policy were complex. Nuclear weapons had changed the rules of war, or at least, we thought they had changed the rules of war. The job of our submarine was not destruction, but the threat of destruction, a promise to the Soviets that if they attacked America, that America could almost certainly strike back just as hard. Mutual assured destruction was a promise that paradoxically maintained a more stable world.

I was proud to be part of that promise. I was proud of my profession, I was proud of the *Patrick Henry*, I was proud of our dedicated crew, and I was proud of our role in controlling the nuclear genie.

The crew were my brother sailors, but also my children, since I was the executive officer and responsible for discipline. It was a good boat; discipline was not an issue. Other than the captain, whose name is a matter of public record, I will not name any of the other sailors on our boat. They deserve anonymity.

During the night, we stayed on the surface, passing through Wemyss Bay and Kilchattan Bay, then out into the Firth of Clyde. This body of water was deep enough for us to submerge before dawn. Setting our depth to one hundred feet, we passed the Isle of Arran, turned west to enter the North Channel of the Irish Sea, passing between the peninsula of Kintyre and Ireland, not quite thirteen miles apart. The open North Atlantic beckoned.

We cruised at a leisurely fifteen knots, atomic power fueling our way, descending to a depth of two hundred and fifty feet. Our navigation was dead reckoning, which tended to be more accurate underwater because we were unaffected by the winds and waves, and currents could be compensated for in our calculations. Compared to older submarines, we had unlimited power; we even used it to make potable water and air for our submarine. Just last year, our own boat had spent over sixty-six days underwater on her first deterrent patrol.

A day out, we came to periscope depth, and the captain stood on the raised platform in the control room and took a peek. We slowed to only a couple of knots—enough to maintain headway—in order to prevent the periscope from leaving a wake. It was nighttime, making it harder for anyone to see us, and we found the waves were at least a dozen feet high. It was a heavy sea. The sky was overcast and the moon was absent; it would have only been a faint sliver, anyway; the new moon was a day away. We could have slipped up our aerials, but the waves crashing over the aerials would interfere with reception, so the captain decided we would try the next night.

———

We passed seaward of the Outer Hebrides Islands and reached the wide gap between the Faroe Islands and the Shetland Islands by the next night. We closed to periscope depth, found the area clear, and pushed our telescoping aerials up above the surface.

It was the evening of October 26. The radio room was busy. One aerial checked for any radar pulses. If we detected them, we would immediately submerge and evade, fearing that the Soviets may have developed a new form of airborne radar that could detect a submarine's periscope and aerials. Very unlikely, but we were paid to be paranoid and remain hidden.

Another aerial tuned to pick up the latest orders from USLANTCOM (United States Naval Atlantic Command). Still another aerial picked up signals from the Loran C network of transmitters to give us an accurate navigation fix. A fourth aerial picked up commercial networks, like BBC, Voice of America, or anything on the shortwave.

One of the radiomen swore. I was at the hatch between the radio room and the control room, watching the four radiomen at work, and my first instinct was to encourage more professional decorum. He pulled off his earphones and offered them to me. "You've got to hear this, sir."

I put on the earphones. It was the voice of JFK, our president, speaking somberly, and I still remember the words: "Even the fruits of victory would be ashes in our mouth--but neither will we shrink from that risk at any time it must be faced." The announcer then interrupted what was obviously a recording. His voice was British, so I assumed that this was BBC. "So, as you can see, the Americans are very serious about Cuba and the missiles."

A teletype machine hummed with clicking printer arms, giving us the latest orders from Atlantic Command, which were continuously being transmitted on a frequency reserved for the missile subs. We only listened, we did not transmit, because that might give our position away. Protocol was to monitor the airwaves for ten minutes, then retract the aerials and return to our skulking under the water. We followed the rules.

Our orders from Atlantic Command were to continue performing our current missions. No further information on the "current crisis" was available. Listening for just a few minutes to BBC and Voice of America made it apparent that the Soviets had smuggled troops and weapons, including nuclear-tipped ballistic missiles, into the communist-controlled island of Cuba.

It wasn't until the next day that we learned that the president had imposed a "quarantine" on the island to prevent more weapons from arriving, since apparently some of the actual ballistic missiles were still at sea on Soviet freighters. They were obvious in aerial photographs because the missiles were in oblong canvas-covered containers on the decks since they were too big to fit in the ship holds.

An announcer on BBC helpfully explained that this naval blockade was not being called a blockade, because international treaties defined a blockade as an act of war. JFK was tiptoeing around going to war.

You've heard the daily sequence of the crisis from other people, how the crisis just kept escalating. We learned about it from our orders, which gave us less information than you would except, and mostly from listening to BBC and Voice of America. Our normal practice was to come near to the surface only every two or three days to pick up radio signals, but the captain changed that maneuver to every day. I took it upon myself to type up a daily summary of what we knew to be passed around to each member of the crew to read. I wanted to prevent rumors and confusion from happening, where stories change in subtle and not-so-subtle ways as they are passed along.

On October 27, we picked up a signal from Atlantic Command ordering all units to DEFCON-3. This didn't really mean anything to us because we effectively were always at that alert state while at sea—we were ready for war with no advance notice. The captain and I talked about this. The defense condition system was only six or seven years old.

The captain said, "I assume that this is just our government posturing, showing to the Soviets that we are serious. Trying to increase deterrence." I agreed with him on this.

The next day, we heard that Khrushchev had rejected American demands on the previous day. We were tempted to stay near the surface longer, to pick up more than mere snippets of transmissions, but our primary job was to remain hidden. We had reached our patrol area, a large box in the Norwegian Sea off the northern Norwegian town of Bodø. The Lofoten archipelago and a smattering of other islands were in the area. We stayed away from land, cruising at a depth of three hundred feet and peeking up every day. The Arctic Circle was not far away and formed the southern boundary of our patrol area. Our missiles could hit Moscow or Kiev from our patrol area, as well as much of the northwest Soviet Union, East Germany, anywhere in Poland, and parts of Czechoslovakia.

The next day was quiet on new developments in the crisis. Then, on October 30, our nation launched massive airstrikes on Cuba. Not nuclear, but conventional bombing. This was sobering: the crisis hadn't felt completely real, mostly diplomats talking and bold statements to the press, but now bombs were falling and people were dying. We assumed that Cuban and Soviet soldiers had been killed. It's much harder to stop a shooting war.

Even more disturbing was that we picked up a repeating message on an Air Force Strategic Air Command circuit that SAC forces were to go to DEFCON-2. Similar orders did not come from Atlantic Command. The SAC orders were sent in the clear, which is one reason that we could understand them, and I recalled from one of my briefings before joining this boat that SAC transmitted their DEFCON orders in the clear to make sure that everyone received them. It was common for different units to be at different condition levels, but it made sense that we should be at the same level as the Air Force.

There was a more serious consequence, which was that when we reached DEFCON-2, we were authorized to break open our target list. The captain and I discussed this in his cabin. We decided to wait a day and see if the Navy followed the example of the Air Force.

Every day after the crisis started, the captain and I had a private conversation in his cabin. This was not something we planned, but it quickly became a habit and we noticed its absence if we hadn't talked. We both held a powerful responsibility, as represented by the key that we each carried on a string around our necks, and we talked about a lot of things, but never about that responsibility. It was the topic that we talked around.

I admired our captain, Commander Roger F. McNeil, a graduate of Annapolis, two years younger than me. I always found him competent and smart. He also had a nice collection of history books that he shared with anyone who wanted to read them. I enjoyed reading many of them. This was my second patrol with the captain, and I noticed that the book collection was completely different this time.

It was easier to talk about books than what was happening at the time. History had the wonderful virtue of being fixed; what happened was what had happened, while the present made us nervous. We didn't know how it would turn out. One day, I forget which day during that patrol, we were talking about the Civil War. My own family had arrived long afterwards and had no role in that horrible bloodletting, but his family had been in the thick of it.

He confessed that he was the direct descendent of a Civil War general, Brevet Major General John McNeil, the "Butcher of Palmyra." His ancestor had sanctioned the execution of ten Confederate prisoners of war in Palmyra, Missouri, during the war in reprisal for the disappearance of a Union sympathizer. The killings were pure revenge, no trials, and the men were chosen randomly. The reputation of his forefather laid heavy on his shoulders, though the captain told me that he refused to be considered a pariah for what his great-grandfather had done. I told him that we can't be responsible for who our parents were, but we could be responsible for who we became. This revelation of his family's past was deeply personal to him, and to me, a bond that bound us.

As for myself, I had made myself a Navy man through and through. As a child, I was entranced by the ships I saw outside the windows of our apartment in Baltimore. Ever since I joined when I was seventeen, I had devoted my life to the Navy. I had entered as a raw recruit, and left for a while after I mustered out in 1947 in order to go to college on the G.I. bill and became an engineer. I returned to the service during the Korean War. It took a couple of tries, but I finally transferred into the nuclear program. Like everyone who sought to be a nuclear engineer, I was personally interviewed by Rear Admiral Rickover, the engineer of engineers who ran the nuclear Navy with a tight focus on safety and competence. I joined an elite priesthood.

The goal of our priesthood had been to harness nuclear reactors and make them small enough and safe enough to power ships and submarines. We had succeeded. Only later did the idea that we should also carry nuclear weapons become another goal for us. Rocket technology had advanced quickly, and the Navy wanted to be part of the mutual assured destruction solution.

One problem was that our missiles lacked precise accuracy. Test firings demonstrated a circular error probability of 5,900 feet for the *Polaris* missile. That was over a mile. The CEP meant that the warhead would explode, about a mile up in the air, within 5,900 feet of the aim point, fifty percent of the time. That is why we had such a powerful warhead, to make sure that we destroyed our target, even if we missed by several miles. The fireball itself would be 5,700 feet in diameter. That number makes our CEP number not as disappointing.

We discussed the details, like processing the targeting instructions. The reason we needed our target information was we had to program our missiles just before launch to take into account our current location. Because our current location was always moving, we had to regularly recalculate the instructions for the missile. Fortunately, we didn't do this with pencil and paper, since we had a specialized simple analog computer that did the job for us. Our weapons officer and navigation officer still spot-checked the output of the computer with hand calculations, just to be sure.

Halloween came. I knew my sailors had brought aboard masks and treats, but by unspoken agreement, any celebration was cancelled. The bombing of Cuba continued. Our DEFCON level was unaltered, but we decided to open the target list. There were standing orders to always be followed, but there was also a degree of discretion so long as the captain and I agreed. The Navy did not want a sole officer to be completely in control when it came to anything to do with nuclear weapons.

We went into the control room, over to a row of electronic switches and other controls and stood before a metal box on the bulkhead that had two padlocks sealing it. We each thumbed the tumblers to match the separate codes we had memorized. He opened his padlock, then I followed. There were several envelopes inside. Each contained a different target list. We had not received orders to use an alternate list, so I removed the primary envelope.

As the XO, I was the one expected to sit down with the target list. It was sixteen rows, with two numbers on each row. Latitude and longitude of each target. Our *Polaris* missiles only had a range of about 1,200 miles, which meant firing our missiles over Norway, Sweden, and Finland to reach the Soviet Union and other nations controlled by the communists. I was familiar enough with what was in range that my eyes were immediately drawn to numbers that were outside of the Soviet Union.

I wanted to be sure, so I went to the navigation room and pulled out a chart. We had targets all over, but the most disturbing were the two targets in East Germany: one just outside of East Berlin, the other at Rostock, the largest coastal city in East Germany, and main base of the small East German Navy.

In Poland, three locations were targeted: somewhere next to Warsaw, a major Soviet troop garrison at Borne-Sulinowo, and Gdańsk, a shipbuilding city on the coast of the Baltic Sea. I had heard that these targets were really military bases, industrial centers, or ports, legitimate targets like those, which I supposed was true. But all those targets were often also near large cities, and the size of our bombs would also affect the cities. Our nuclear weapons were city killers.

I stopped for a moment, so stunned that it was difficult for me to notice the sailors around me. In my own mind, I was confessing about what I rarely mentioned to anyone else. I was a Pole, or rather, I had been born a Pole.

I was from Gdańsk, having been born there in 1925. I have no memory of Poland, because my parents immigrated to the United States when I was just a toddler. America had severely restricted immigration from Eastern European countries by then, but my father was able to claim Swedish citizenship because his own father was from Sweden and slip his small family into the promised land. I was christened Piotr Kowalski, but by the time I was old enough to learn my last name, my dad had heard too many Polack jokes and had shortened our last name to Kowal. He also started to call me Peter, though my mom still called me Piotr; I think that most people just thought that it was her thick accent, but I knew she was using the Polish version of my name.

Most of my closer family members in Poland died during the war. Either at the hands of the Nazis or the Soviets later, we didn't know, just that they were now gone. I didn't know anyone personally who still lived in Gdańsk, yet it still represented my ancestral home.

The other targets were all in the Soviet Union and even included Moscow. I understood the rationale: weapons from a single source, such as our boat, should be sent against a variety of targets. There were four other boats like ours that would also scatter their weapons widely. We were only part of the arsenal.

The Air Force had almost fifteen hundred bombers bringing nuclear bombs, and thirteen hundred air tankers so that they could make repeated bombing runs. The Air Force also had some two hundred missiles with intercontinental range and over one hundred Thor and Jupiter missiles in Britain, Italy, and Turkey, all created for the sole purpose of delivering a nuclear warhead. The master plan guaranteed that all targets would be hit by multiple sources of weapons: efficient, destructive, and complete.

I had heard that the Air Force jockeys, who were called missileers, had no idea what their missiles were aimed at. They didn't need to know because their origin point was already known and wasn't going to move. Frankly, I would want to know. Or I had *thought* I would want to know.

Actually knowing was horrible.

———

Being a submariner wasn't for everyone. Spending long amounts of time closely confined with other men in a metal tube underwater could erode a man's sense of will and sense of tolerance. My first submarine back in 1945 was the *Dentuda*, a *Balao*-class boat. We only went on one war patrol. Our captain was Commander John S. McCain, Jr., the son of the illustrious admiral. Pickings were slim by that late in the war and we only sank a pair of patrol boats and damaged a freighter. Even so, I had seen war or rather had experienced the excitement of firing our torpedoes at the enemy.

The *Dentuda* was cramped, with our crew of eighty living on two decks. The upper deck was where we really lived—slept, ate, worked, used the head—with the lower deck, the hold, being mostly full of batteries, machinery, and supplies. The *Patrick Henry* was big, four times the displacement of my first boat, and we carried thirty-two more men and were spread across three decks. Even with the sixteen missiles taking up so much space, we still had a lot more room on our boat than in the past. Even though the nuclear reactor and its shielding also took up space, it was really nothing compared to the space taken up by fuel tanks and battery banks on the *Dentuda*.

You knew a man was starting to crumble when his sense of humor left him. Only in retrospect did I realize that my own sense of humor had abandoned me. The days that followed the start of the Cuban Missile Crisis increasingly felt claustrophobic to me. I kept all of these feelings inside myself. I performed my duties, I listened to the radio transmissions, and typed up the daily summaries of the crisis happening outside of our little world. In my mind, I worried about Gdańsk. Hadn't Poland suffered enough? Why should more Poles die because the Soviets had coerced their nation into communism and being allies?

I remembered the tiny photo album that my mother still treasured, small square black-and-white photos, many taken with a Kodak Brownie box camera that she had been given as a young teenager. Part of the charm for her was that the camera had been made in America. For her, America was the promised land of prosperity and movies, a paradise very different from Gdańsk, which struggled to recover from the First World War. The misery of the Great Depression had arrived in Poland before it arrived elsewhere. That is why my parents had fled.

The pictures showed family members, small houses in the country, or apartments in the city. The pictures showed a city full of life. She took other pictures of ships, cranes, and smoking factories because they interested her. My father had trained as an engineer and they were drawn together by their fascination with machines and technology. That is something I inherited from them.

———

Fantasies of how to stop the crisis unfolding above us and not ever having to launch our missiles fluttered around the edge of my consciousness. I actively suppressed those tempting thoughts. That way led to frustration, a feeling of impotence, and ultimately madness. Even so, one night I awoke from a dream—a nightmare, from a certain point of view—where I had refused to fulfill my responsibility as XO.

If the time came to launch the missiles, the captain and I were each required to simultaneously use our keys on the launch computer. A single person could not reach both keys and turn them at the same time. This made more sense in an Air Force missile bunker, where only two missileers stood on duty at a time. On our boat, other sailors could stand in our place and turn the keys with their own fingers, but the strict rules of the ship required that the captain and XO both agree to launch the missiles. The Navy did not want a sole officer to have that responsibility. This was contrary to how we behaved in every other aspect of naval life and naval warfare, where commanders made decisions and officers and sailors obeyed to implement those decisions. The Navy feared that a sole officer could act as a madman and order the crew to launch and complete his delusion.

I imagined myself in my dream saving Gdańsk from destruction by putting my key into the lock and then bending the soft metal of the key and breaking it off. The keyhole would be jammed with the remains of the key and the launch computer could not be used and the missiles would remain in their tubes. Was I actually strong enough to break a metal key? I had no idea, but in dream logic, I was strong enough. I saved Gdańsk.

I remembered the dream because it had just reached its narrative climax with the broken key when I awoke. The feeling of exhilaration that the dream provoked immediately crashed into confused shame as I realized that I had disobeyed orders. I wish I could say that I then carefully analyzed my feelings and sorted out the moral implications of my dream. I did not. I am a man who is not inclined to obsess over my emotions. I put the dream away and returned to my duties.

———

The Soviets and their Warsaw Pact allies started to shell West Berlin in retaliation for the bombing of Cuba. The city was undefendable, being an enclave deep inside East Germany. We had troops there, as did the British and French, but the troops were to act as a tripwire, not to put up a serious defense. We anxiously waited for the world to explode into World War III, hoping both sides would hold back their nuclear weapons.

Three days after Halloween, the Americans invaded Cuba with Marines and Army troops. The Air Force and Navy had pounded the island for four full days. I am sure that our generals and admirals thought that the Cubans and Soviets would be easily brushed aside, since we now had command of the air. The Soviets shocked us by hitting our invasion ships with tactical nuclear weapons hidden on the island. Our generals and admirals had not imagined that the Soviets would deploy tactical nuclear weapons with their own troops on Cuba and give them permission to use them. Over thirty-seven thousand American soldiers, sailors, Marines, and airmen died.

———

I knew what a nuclear explosion actually looked like. I was still assigned to the *Dentuda* when less than a year after the end of the war against Japan, we took our submarine to Bikini Atoll in the southern Pacific. The Navy had assembled an impressive fleet of ships, some ready to be scraped, others taken as war booty, and still others, active ships or boats in our Navy. They wanted to see what effect an atomic bomb would have on ships at sea.

We left the *Dentuda* at the target area and were among the tens of thousands of sailors, scientists, engineers, and gawkers on ships far enough away to be safe. On the morning of the Able test, we watched a Fat Man implosion-type atom bomb explode, about 23 kilotons, fifty percent more powerful than the bomb dropped on Nagasaki. We all had dark goggles to protect our eyes. We removed the goggles after the flash and watched the mushroom cloud rise into the sky. The bomber had missed its target by almost half a mile. We were ten miles away, and when the sound of the blast reached us, it was not an impressive boom, but more of a sigh. In its own way, that muted sound felt more appropriate.

The initial neutron and gamma radiation burst would have killed any crew aboard the target ships. We went aboard the ships and our boat afterwards, Geiger counters in hand, finding that the radiation levels were not too bad. The bomb may have missed its target, but it was an air burst five hundred feet up, so the fallout radiation effects were minimized.

Our boat was used in the Baker test three weeks later, where the tethered bomb exploded underwater. There was no flash and the sea rose up in a massive bubble. That was impressive. There was no mushroom cloud. Radioactive fallout was trapped in the water that showered down on the ships and left them severely contaminated. Our boat was underwater, without its crew, and stationed like a goat far enough away that the damage was minimal. We decontaminated what little residual radiation there was and sailed home to Pearl Harbor.

————

For more than a day, the crew of the *Patrick Henry* held our collective breath along with the rest of the world. Then America plastered Cuba with nuclear weapons, just to make sure that the Soviets didn't have any other surprises hiding on that island. That was November 5. Only much later did we learn that there was a hidden surprise, a *Beagle* light bomber, concealed on a plantation. Its crew, cut off from higher command, flew to New Orleans and destroyed an American city on the next day. They had a military purpose, to destroy the infantry division located there that was prepared to invade Cuba in a second attempted invasion.

We learned about the loss of New Orleans from a Voice of America broadcast in the early morning hours of November 7, a Wednesday. Naval Command ordered all ships and units to go to DEFCON-1. Everyone on the boat walked around with long faces, clearly in shock. I walked through the crew quarters and no one was asleep. Most sailors lingered near their action stations, even if they weren't on duty, waiting for the next act in their lives.

We moved to our preselected position fifty miles from the small island of Rost, Norway, at 67° 57' 34" North, 10° 33' 30" East (67.959444° N, 10.558333° E.). The numbers are still imprinted in my mind. All our targeting calculations were run and checked again using this location.

The captain decided we would peek up on the surface again just before dawn. We moved up and found new orders from Atlantic Command. I remember the blunt words.

USA UNDER ATTACK. EXECUTE TARGET LIST ALPHA IMMEDIATELY. AUTHORIZATION CODE: UY33 VXPO F343 JJI1

We checked the authorization code: it matched. The launch coordinates had already been placed in the *Polaris* missiles. I asked the navigation officer to verify our position via Loran C. He confirmed that we were where we expected to be.

The captain and I approached the console where we were more than eight feet apart, far enough to require two people. We placed our keys in the locks. I was so nervous, drowning in a moral panic, that my fingers shook, and if I hadn't wrapped the string around my palm, I would have surely dropped the key.

"Ready," the captain said. "Three...two...one."

I turned the key and was astonished to see the red bubble light above my keyhole turn on, rather than the green bubble light next to it. We had failed to authorize. I turned to the captain with an exclamation that died on my lips. The captain stood there with a pair of pliers in his hand. He had broken off his key in its keyhole.

"I'm sorry, Peter," he said in a calm voice. "I can't do it. I will not be a butcher. One is enough."

A moral choice had been made. Now it was my turn. I looked back at the bridge crew. Everyone stared at us and the silence, though momentary, felt oppressive.

My duty was clear. I reached for the squawk box and keyed it. "Master-at-arms to the control room."

One of the chief petty officers, normally responsible for all the electrical systems on our boat, also served as our master-at-arms. The chief came bustling up from the engine room, a substantial distance because he had to rush through the missile farm that separated us. He came into the control room and looked at us in confusion.

"Chief, arrest the captain, confine him to his quarters," I said.

The chief turned his gaze to the captain. The captain, to his credit as a man and to his training, nodded. "Do it, Chief. Lieutenant Commander Kowal is in command now."

The chief followed the captain out of the control room, and I called for a machinist's mate to bring a pair of needle-nose pliers. The mate appeared and I told him to figure out how to turn the broken key. He grasped the remains of the key inside the lock and we turned the keys together. The moment of the captain's decision had been dramatic but easily bypassed.

Afterwards, I realized that it would have been so much more effective for him to have hidden the key somewhere or to have completely destroyed it. I am sure he knew that, but he chose to go for the drama. I don't condemn him for that. I think he needed to make a choice that was public and bold, not a choice that was more private and hidden.

This was my dream—my nightmare—except it was ass-backwards. The captain's decision had clarified my own course of action. I had dedicated my life to the Navy. I could not disobey. Oddly enough, though he disobeyed, the captain made no attempt to maintain his authority. He still remained disciplined in his own way and honored his oath.

We slowed to a single knot of headway at a depth of one hundred and twenty-five feet. I ordered the launch of all missiles. The hatches opened and water flowed into the narrow spaces around the missiles. The first missile was expelled by a blast of air, pushing it to the surface, where the solid-fuel rocket engine ignited to fly away. It was a high-tech version of a bottle rocket, almost thirty tall, four and a half feet thick, over fourteen tons of power. The pair of helmsmen rotated their wheels, adjusting the orientation of our hydroplanes to adjust to the loss of so much weight.

Twenty seconds later, the second missile launched. The crew adjusted the submarine so that we would not porpoise into the open air. We worked our way through the sixteen missiles and less than five minutes later, the *Patrick Henry* had completed our purpose. We were empty of destruction.

I heard men crying. I couldn't see who they might be because my own eyes were so blurry.

———

We didn't try to return to Holy Loch. We returned directly to the United States and were ordered by Atlantic Command to Hampton Roads. No one celebrated our return. The city was happy to have us dockside because the damaged power grid was unreliable and we sat in dock and provided substantial and reliable power for them. We learned that our nation had been hit by about thirty warheads and thirty million of our fellow citizens were dead within the first two months. There were still one hundred fifty million of us left.

The Soviet Union had been erased from the planet. Two-thirds of all the Soviets and their subject peoples in Eastern Europe were dead after five years. Western Europe had been shattered by nuclear weapons carried by shorter-range missiles and shorter-range aircraft. Half of them were dead within a year and the continent suffered from the collapse of industry, fallout patterns, and breakdown of agriculture.

The United States was protected by its oceans and the Soviet lacked many longer-range ballistic missiles or many longer-range bombers that could cross those oceans. By a quirky coincidence, the Soviets had not been planning for an immediate nuclear war and almost all of their submarines with nuclear weapons aboard were in harbors, not out at sea and hiding like we were.

———

The Fire came and our sixteen *Polaris* missiles were part of that fire. How many people died as a result of the nuclear warheads from the *Patrick Henry*? Thousands? Certainly. Tens of thousands? I am sure, since there was little warning for the people on the ground to run and hide. Hundreds of thousands? Probably. Half of our targets were bases inside or near cities. Millions? Maybe. Does the exact number really matter when the number gets that large?

Am I a war criminal? Am I guilty because I feel guilty? I certainly do feel guilty. Should I feel guilty as an individual or feel guilty because my nation decided to create, expand, and then use the awful destructive power of nuclear physics? Was it a failure of imagination? No, we knew what nuclear war could do. We knew what we had built. We just convinced ourselves it was only for deterrence and would never actually be used.

We lied to ourselves.

AFTERWORD

An account emerged over fifty years after the Cuban Missile Crisis in which the 873rd Tactical Missile Squadron in Okinawa received launch orders during the crisis in October 1962. Their protocol was to program their TM-76B *Mace* cruise missiles with their targets and directly launch, because the orders system was thought to be flawless. These missiles reportedly carried one megaton nuclear warheads. One launch officer, Captain William Bassett, was disturbed by the irregularity of the order and broke protocol to telephone his superior officer, who immediately ordered the whole squadron to stand down.

The Air Force completely denied that such an event had ever happened. That denial may be true; it may not be true. There may be a kernel of truth to this account, because based on the range of the cruise missiles and the nature of the SIOP-63 plan, the targets for the unit were probably either in North Korea or China. Neither country was involved in the Cuban Missile Crisis. The Single Integrated Operational Plan was a plan to most efficiently use all American nuclear weapons to destroy the Soviet Union and all its allies. Early versions were very inflexible. An automated message implementing the part of the SIOP for cruise missiles on Okinawa would have targeted other communist countries. We are very fortunate that the officers in this unit did not act like cogs in a machine, but used their free will and intellect to question orders that made no sense within the context of the ongoing crisis.

Mazel tov for humanity.

Bibliography

Aaron Tovish, "The Okinawa Missiles of October," *Bulletin of the Atomic Scientists* (October 25, 2015) - https://thebulletin.org/2015/10/the-okinawa-missiles-of-October/

Jon Mitchell, "The Cuban Missile Crisis: The View from Okinawa," *History News Network* (July 21, 2012) - https://www.historynewsnetwork.org/article/the-cuban-missile-crisis-the-view-from-okinawa

Author's Note

This story has been set in the world created by my book, *When Angels Wept: A What-If History of the Cuban Missile Crisis* (Potomac Books, 2010).

Eric G. Swedin
August 2025

ABOUT ERIC G. SWEDIN

Eric G. Swedin is a professor of history at Weber State University. His doctorate is in the history of science and technology. His publications include numerous articles, seven history books, four science fiction novels, and a historical mystery novel. His *When Angels Wept: A What-If History of the Cuban Missile Crisis* won the 2010 Sidewise Award for Best Long-Form Alternate History. The short story in this volume, "Foolish Games," is set in the same timeline.

Eric lives with his family in a house built in 1881.

His website is http://www.swedin.org/.

MR FORD'S CATS

James Young

DEDICATION

For Doug Dandridge.
I wish you were able to give me a new story for this anthology.

1

STORMS, DINOSAURS, AND HOUNDS

SKULL THREE
1700 LOCAL
POINT NEMESIS
18 APRIL 1975

"Skull Leader, call the ball..."

It'd probably be a lot easier him to call the ball if some idiot hadn't decided to take your battle group through the outskirts of a typhoon, Lieutenant Commander Damon "Rigger" Peters thought uncharitably.

Rain was pounding the canopy of his F-14B *Tomcat* at increasingly shorter intervals, making visibility a problem as their fighter made its own final turn into the landing pattern. Up front, he could hear Lieutenant Johnny "Spinster" Craig, his pilot, grunting as he fought the sudden gusts of wind buffeting the massive, twin-engine fighter. Damon glanced worriedly out at the outstretched wings, looking at their destination, the U.S.S. *America*. The supercarrier was the centerpiece for Task Force 77, an ad hoc carrier battle group (CVBG) formed by Seventh Fleet in response to what news reports were calling the "Third Vietnam Crisis."

"Skull Leader has the ball..."

Even if we somehow survived the impact, Damon thought out the window at the plane guard destroyer plowing through waves to try and keep pace with the *America, there's no way the* Dahlgren's *pulling us out of that water in time*.

"I don't know who those assholes think they're hiding from in this slop," Johnny seethed as he rolled the wings level.

"Skull Three, say again last transmission," *America*'s LSO called over the radio.

Jesus Christ, Spinster, Damon thought, shaking his head as he began monitoring the *Tomcat*'s sink rate and airspeed. *At least once a week you fuck up that damn intercom and radio switchology.*

Spinster was a "mustang," i.e. a former enlisted sailor who had transitioned to officer ranks. He was the deadly trifecta of blunt, outspoken, and acerbic, something that had *not* helped his career. Indeed, Spinster was so sharp-tongued that the former F-8 pilot had allegedly driven his last RIO, a young ensign on their first cruise, to jump off the stern of the *Enterprise* two months before.

I think the "Dear John" letter complete with Polaroids of the young lady in a state of undress with his former best friend had more to do with it than Johnny riding the young lad, Damon thought, *but it certainly didn't help. Would've ended most careers, but when you've got six MiGs to your credit, allowances get made.*

"On speed, 650 feet per minute," Damon intoned, keeping his eyes fixed on the instruments. "Watch that sink rate."

"Damn downdrafts are getting a bit insane," Spinster snapped, the *Tomcat* bucking as if to prove his point.

"Hate to do this in a *Spectre*," Damon replied, referring to the McDonnell Douglas fighter that had preceded the *Tomcat* in the fleet.

"I wouldn't know," Spinster responded through gritted teeth, giving a slight bit of rudder to counteract a gust from their port side. "Not used to having company in the damn cockpit during times like this, either."

"Speed's a little high, let's bring it back down," Damon replied calmly, ignoring Spinster's not-so-subtle directive to shut up. "Sink rate is 620."

Thank God this isn't an A, Damon thought, fighting to keep his growing apprehension down. *He's handling the throttles like a damn teenager learning to drive a stick.*

The original *Tomcat*, like the twenty-four in *America*'s VF-1 "Wolfpack" and VF-2 "Bounty Hunters," was powered by a pair of TF-30 jet engines. The TF-30 took to sudden throttle manipulations about as well as feral cats took to being bathed by small children. Sooner or later, fighting the throttles like Spinster was ended up in one or both engines deciding to opt out of functioning. At higher altitudes, that meant the *Tomcat* usually opted out of controlled flight. At lower altitudes, it meant the two men inside opted out of life.

Spinster audibly sighed at Damon's commentary.

Okay, why in the hell are we still sinking when he's got so much throttle involved?

Damon's answer came a moment later from the F-14 bobbing up like a cork as the downdraft pushing on them suddenly ceased. He had the sensation of rising up in his seat before Spinster managed to make a correction.

"Skull Three, call the ball," *America*'s landing signal officer said.

"I have the ball," Spinster snarled.

The optical landing system, a.k.a. "the ball," was a lighted array located on the supercarrier's stern. With Spinster lined up on the angled deck, the array provided a visual reference on the *Tomcat*'s height and alignment while simultaneously relaying signals from the landing signal officer (LSO). Damon fought the urge to look at the array, knowing that Spinster was already growing agitated with his guidance from the backseat.

With our fuel state and this weather getting worse, Damon thought, *we've got maybe two stabs at this.* It spoke volumes that *America*'s air group was not currently conducting any operations, with the carrier's forward bow conspicuously full of chained down fighters and strike aircraft. *Technically,* the carrier could launch in all weather. Only an idiot or, in this case, *idiots* would have tried to land in this weather.

"You're a little high, Skull Three," the LSO corrected.

"Airspeed's good, sink rate's good," Damon stated, drawing another annoyed grunt from Spinster. "We should be hitting the burble in about ten seconds..."

Damon was glad to hear the *Tomcat*'s twin engines advance for a brief two count, then drop back. The "burble" was the disturbance caused by a carrier's island as a jet came in for a landing. Having flown off *America*'s half-sister *Kitty Hawk* in the *Spectre*, Damon was well aware of the difference between the burble from the carrier in front of them versus that of *Enterprise*'s truly massive superstructure.

Shouldn't be as much of a... Oh shit!

Damon slammed upwards in the seat restraints once again as another downdraft and the burble both hit at once. For a terrified moment, it felt as if the *Tomcat* was going to keep going down for a flat landing in the Pacific.

"Pull up, Skull Three! Pull up!" the LSO all but screamed into the radio.

"Everyone's a goddamn critic," Spinster snapped, his voice far too calm for the situation at hand.

Damon fought the urge to look at the altimeter as the *Tomcat*'s broad wings did their job. Almost as if he'd planned it that way, Spinster eased them back into the appropriate slot position about a half-mile astern of *America*. Even as the rain intensified and the carrier's stern seemed to go through a particular violent upward swing, the *Tomcat* settled into the final four hundred yards of landing. With just a slight final flare, the big fighter slammed down onto the deck, pitching both men forward into their restraints as the arrestor hook caught the number two wire.

Jesus, thank you, Damon thought, reflexively reaching up towards the cross that was around his neck. He took a moment to gather himself as the flight deck crew, fighting against the wind blowing across *America*'s deck, began directing their fighter towards the deck edge elevator.

"Skull Three, need you to stay in the aircraft until we get you struck below," his headset crackled. "Captain's orders—we've already nearly lost some flight deck crew."

Maybe creeping along with a typhoon wasn't the best idea, then? Damon thought, exhaling, then starting his post-landing tasks.

Need some time to calm down, he thought as he safed his ejection seat while Spinster assisted the flight deck in moving them across the pitching deck. Feeling the *Tomcat* shifting, he skipped the step of safing his ejection seat.

If this bitch starts to roll off the deck, I want a snowball's chance in hell of getting out, he thought. Then he glanced at the roiling waves.

Suicide's a sin, but I'd probably just be better off shooting myself.

As he turned off his oxygen, then his radio, Damon considered how to approach the problem sitting in front of him. Were Spinster a normal lieutenant, i.e. a junior officer having just starting his second sea tour and convinced he knew everything, he'd have simply had what one of his former superiors called "a good ol' fashion church burning."

No point in yelling and screaming at him, Damon thought as their *Tomcat* lowered down towards the hangar deck. *If I'm so concerned that I need to yell and scream at someone who has been in the Navy almost as long as I have, it's just time to fire him and be done with it.*

Well aware that silence was often a RIO's best weapon, Damon continued his checklist as the big *Tomcat* was stowed on the elevator. The big fighter rocked in the wind as Spinster swept its wings back to the full stowage position, the aircraft acting as if it wanted to lift up like a giant frisbee. Cognitively, Damon knew that the odds of that happening were slim. Even in its current state with almost eighty percent of their fuel burned off, the F-14 was far too heavy for anything short of a tornado to simply pick up and toss. As the flight deck crew brought the big fighter into the hangar, Damon finally safed his seat, then began to unbuckle as Spinster raised the canopy.

It has to be a hellish day on the tin cans, Damon thought, feeling the massive supercarrier gently rolling as the ground crew swarmed around the F-14. *You'd hardly know we were in bad weather here, though.*

Even as the storm raged on outside, the hangar deck was humming with activity. Looking forward, Damon saw *America*'s striking arm of A-7 *Corsair*s and A-6 *Intruders* being prepped for offensive operations that would ensue the following dawn. Turning aft, Damon noted that the efficient deck crews were parking the other three VF-84 "Jolly Rogers" *Tomcats* in front of the VF-1 and VF-2 F-14As. Purple-shirted deck crew stood by with hoses ready to drain the fighters' wing tanks, and Damon once more considered the sheer insanity of having launched six hundred miles away from *Enterprise* with nothing more than their cannon rounds and a single *Sidewinder* apiece.

Sure, all the intel pukes think that the Russians are sitting this one out despite Brezhnev's bellicose speeches to the contrary, Damon thought. *But man, if we'd arrived overhead about the same time as some of those new* Backfire *bombers, we'd have just been spectators.*

"Sir, CAG wants to speak with you and your pilot immediately," a sailor stated from his left, startling Damon. He turned to see a senior petty officer, the man's face sympathetic as he passed the news. Damon shook his head, accepting a hand up and out of his seat. The petty officer looked surprised as Damon stood to his full height.

No, I did not slouch during my physical, please stop implying that with your look, Damon thought as the noncom climbed back down the boarding ladder so Damon could get out of the fighter. He'd started as Navy's defensive end his final two years and, as Army's right *and* left tackle could attest, with his size came no small degree of quickness. It was always startling to people the first time they saw him climb out of an aircraft, even one as large as the *Tomcat*.

Spinster climbed down from the fighter beside him, and the few passing stares increased. The pilot's call derived both from his perpetual bachelorhood and his small, slight stature. Barely within the minimums for Naval Aviation in the first place, how Spinster had been able to manhandle first the *Fury*, then the *Crusader*, and now the *Tomcat* was a scientific anomaly. Having seen the man lift weights, Damon was quite certain there was some secret government lab involved, but that was a discussion for another day.

"Walk with me, Lieutenant," Damon said, setting off for the carrier's bow.

"Uh, sir, didn't the chief..." Spinster started, looking worriedly back to where the other VF-84 officers were starting to move towards the gallery deck.

"I don't have a hearing problem, even with this wind," Damon replied firmly, leaving Spinster no option but to hustle to catch up with him. Damon let the pilot stew for the entire length of the hangar deck, his stride and the extra weight of their gear making it less than a leisurely stroll for Spinster.

"In a little over a month, I will go past twenty years of service in this man's navy," Damon started. "I believe you passed twenty-two years last week, correct?"

"Yes, sir," Spinster replied.

"So as two grown-ass men, I think we can both acknowledge that bullshit with the radio and the general disrespect you've shown me over the last two weeks since we've been assigned to one another is a conscious choice," Damon stated flatly.

Spinster started to speak, but Damon cut him off before even a full syllable came out.

"Which means you're either confused as to how the *Tomcat* works or got entirely too comfortable bullying a damn nugget in the two months since you both came aboard the Big E."

Spinster's face began to color as Damon continued.

"Well, I have some bad news for you, Spinster: that shit stops immediately. I'm sorry we didn't have any air-to-air Aggressor hops to figure our teamwork out. It's unfortunate that you haven't really had a chance to get to know me since they sent you over from the Aces."

Damon stopped and looked his smaller companion dead in the face.

"But I'll be damned if you're going to fucking kill me when I plan on retiring in six months," he concluded. "So if you *ever* do something like that shit when we landed today, I will end your goddamn career. Do we understand one another?"

"Yes sir," Spinster replied quietly.

"I don't care if you have to do chair drills, I don't care if you have to tattoo the damn switch layout on the back of your hand like we're in the county jail," Damon went on after they dodged around a parked deck tug. "But you will figure out the damn switches between the intercom and the radio."

"Yes, sir."

"Now get your ass to the Wolfpack ready room," Damon concluded. "Once I'm done having the CAG take a bite out of my and Keg's ass, I'll come by to quiz you on the NOTAM."

That he was being treated like a brand-new ensign was not lost on Spinster. To his credit, the man came to attention and nodded as they finished their half-circuit of *America*'s flight deck. Passing through a hatch, Damon began the climb to the CAG's day cabin. Once more, he drew looks as he moved past officers descending the ladders as he turned sideways to let them past. There were a couple of greetings and nods as he passed folks who knew him from previous duty assignments once they got past their surprise. He knocked on the closed hatch, then waited.

"Enter!"

Damon opened the hatch, took one look at the tableau before him, and inwardly steeled himself for an ass-chewing. VF-84's squadron leader, Commander Tommy "Keg" Hanson, stood at attention in front of a solid steel desk that had obviously seen better days. Behind the furniture sat a short, balding man wearing a captain's silver eagle and looking down at paperwork on his desk.

Captain John "Nightmare" Connor, how wonderful to see you again, Damon thought resignedly. *Why, it seems just yesterday you were having them haul that same desk out of the* Columbia's *burnt-out ready room.*

"Close it behind you and get in here, Lieutenant Commander," Connor said quietly without looking up. "I see that you apparently forgot your way around a *Kitty Hawk*-class carrier since we last saw each other."

Sometimes the best thing to say is absolutely nothing, Damon thought, focusing on the bulkhead behind Connor. The former military assistant to one Senator Carl Vinson, Connor was not known for his racial tolerance on the best days. Damon had known that his little detour around the hangar deck would likely piss the man off, but quite frankly could care less.

"It is customary to apologize when one wastes a senior's time, Lieutenant Commander," Connor said, his voice rising as he looked up from the desk. "Or do they just do things different where you're from on *Enterprise?*"

"I'm certain that there were safety reasons for Lieutenant Commander

Peters' transit, sir," Keg said, his own Southern drawl thick. "With all due respect, given our long flight and the need to prepare for operations, you can bring your concerns up with Vice Admiral Stockdale when the Big E joins us tomorrow evening."

Connor's face began to resemble that of a ripe tomato.

"What did you say, you sonofabitch?" he asked.

"I said that I'm done playing fucking stupid parlor games when I just flew four goddamn hours around a typhoon, sir," Keg replied. "Call my mother a name again and I'll take my chances with a captain's mast."

Connor stood up behind the desk, his face well and truly the color of a ripe tomato. Damon thought the man was going to come around the desk for a brief moment.

Keg has never made an idle threat since I've known him, Damon thought worriedly. VF-84's commander may have looked like a dandy, but he'd been captain of the Naval Academy's boxing team Damon's sophomore year. More importantly, he'd been Vice Admiral Stockdale's personal aide up until one year before. While arguably none of that mattered, unlike Connor's connections, Keg's were literally eighteen hours away and would become the senior commander at Point Yankee once he arrived.

I much prefer being in the damn cockpit, Damon thought, watching as Connor's nostrils flared with the man's obvious rage. *We could be dealing with dozens of communists tomorrow and these two are having a dick-measuring contest.*

There was a knock on the hatch. Connor continued to stare hard at Keg, the squadron leader staring right back in the silence.

"This conversation isn't over," Connor seethed. "Enter!"

"Sorry to interrupt, boss," a familiar voice said from behind Damon, "but Rear Admiral Lang is on his way down. We just got a high priority FRAGO from CINCPACFLT. He wants you, Keg, Fangs, myself, and Rigger to be present."

Well, well, well, this day just keeps getting better and better, Damon thought, feeling a combination of relief and apprehension. At first, he'd believed Lang was coming down to personally rip Spinster's head off and shit down his neck. But it appeared something else was afoot, as rear admirals seldom, if ever, left flag country.

I'd say it's weird he's doing it without America's *captain*, Damon thought, bracing himself as the carrier seemed to go through a particularly deep swell, *but I think this storm might have something to do with that.*

"At ease, gentlemen," Connor snapped, staring daggers in Damon's direction.

I'm just going to let you stew there, friend, Dagger thought, and turned towards the hatch. A smile crossed his face as he regarded the tall, lanky commander standing there, a VF-2 "Bounty Hunters" patch prominent on his flight suit.

"Long time, no see, Rigger," Commander Harold "Warlock" O'Kane said, extending his hand.

"Yes, sir, it certainly has," Damon replied, shaking hands with his former RIO instructor as Keg and Connor both looked on in surprise.

"Rigger and I were both at Nixon's Inauguration," Warlock explained to Keg. "I was Nixon's aide...then Agnew's aide...and then they switched me out two weeks after Ford took the oath like it was *my* fault we'd gone through three presidents."

Damon gave a polite smile as Keg and Connor laughed in shock.

The year with three presidents...and a nuke, Damon thought, thinking back to 1973. *And a funeral, but no one remembers "some Negro schoolteacher from Detroit."*

"I was sorry to hear about Jennifer," Warlock continued, his tone somber as he proved Damon's mental musings wrong. "How are the twins?"

Damon smiled.

"Despite my best efforts, still at Air Force," Damon replied. "Todd..."

"I'm glad you guys are experiencing old home week," Connor interrupted angrily. "But if there's about to be a rear admiral here in five minutes, someone better give me more information than..."

"Attention on deck!" a lieutenant shouted from outside in the passageway.

Ope, looks like you just might get to be surprised like the rest of us peons, jackass, Damon thought.

Rear Admiral Michael "Hangman" Lang was a short, stocky man with thinning gray hair. He clutched a flimsy in his hand and an unlit cheroot in his mouth. Like Connor, Lang was a former attack aviator. Unlike almost everyone else present, he'd been in the Mediterranean-based Sixth Fleet most of his career.

Playing cat-and-mouse with the Commies while trapped in a fishbowl might explain stunts like steaming through the outskirts of a typhoon to keep the damn Soviets from tracking us, Damon thought, bracing himself once more.

"At ease, gentlemen," Lang said, waving his hand. "Captain Connor, we're going to need to secure your hatch so everyone can talk freely."

"Aye aye, sir," Connor replied, then gestured for a chief petty officer standing at the end of the hallway.

"The rest of you, follow me," Lang said, not waiting for Connor to conclude whatever orders he was about to give the petty officer.

"Close the hatch," Lang ordered his aide, drawing a momentary shocked look from Damon and his companions. The aide closed the hatch, then assumed a position by it waiting for Captain Connor to knock.

"Some jackass in Washington overruled CINCPACFLT," Lang said without preamble. "It would appear that there is an unwillingness to, and I quote, 'risk the *Tomcat* and its advanced systems being captured by Communist forces.'"

What the fuck? Damon thought. His shock was reflected in everyone else's faces.

"Why we made sure to have the *America*," Lang said, then turned and pointed at Keg and Damon, "as well as your four birds rush here at high speed if we're too scared to use our newest fighter is beyond me. However, my opinion does not matter, and we're going to have to figure out a way to use the F-4s off *Midway* and *Oriskany*'s F-8. That's a bit of an issue, to say the least."

Spectres *are no match for that new MiG-23 the damn Soviets gifted the North Vietnamese*, Damon thought. Crusaders *would get eaten alive*.

Lang slapped the flimsy down on Connor's desk just as the CAG reentered the room.

"I need you fine gentlemen to read this order, then come up with a plan," Lang said. "You've got four hours; otherwise, we have to scrub the strike until we can get the *Constellation* up here."

Speaking of ships you don't want to be around in a storm, Damon thought grimly. *Connie the Can Opener leads the pack.*

"In addition, the idiots at Pearl added a new wrinkle to the plan," Lang continued. "It would appear that some dinosaurs will be aiding in our reprisal operations against the North Vietnamese."

U.S.S. MISSOURI
POINT DAISY
1845 LOCAL
OFF THE COAST OF SOUTH VIETNAM

The firing gong's buzz reminded Captain Nathan White to close one eye before the sextuplet of 16-inch guns of the U.S.S. *Missouri*'s No. 1 and No. 2 turrets ruined his night vision. With a flash and roar, the long, narrow rifles flung glowing shells off into the darkness towards the coast of South Vietnam. A few hundred yards ahead of the *Missouri*, the U.S.S. *New Jersey* sent her own full broadside of nine 16-inch shells a couple of heartbeats later. Both ships lay at anchor, the better to take navigational fixes that ensured their gunfire would arrive where it was supposed to.

With that, Operation Pulling Guard begins, White thought to himself, *and another bunch of Communist tankers learns what happens when you take a coastal highway with the United States Navy involved.*

Ten miles inland, two regiments of North Vietnamese armor had been moving up to affect a breakthrough of South Vietnamese lines north of Quang Tri. The People's Democratic Republic of Vietnam, for reasons unclear to the United States, had opted to make a third attempt to reunify their nation under the Pham Van Dong government in Hanoi. The People's Republic of China and, to a moderate extent, the Soviet Union had provided multiple forms of assistance. The Ford Administration, in response, had provided a clear, succinct warning on what would happen if North Vietnam violated the South's sovereignty. Now the Navy was putting words into action.

I just hope we're not about to chew up a bunch of empty fields and jungle, White thought. *If intel was right, we're about to be a very unpleasant shock for some North Vietnamese tank crews.*

"Holy shit, look at the cruisers," someone muttered on the *Missouri*'s darkened bridge. Turning to his left, Captain White gazed off the *Missouri*'s port quarter as barrage after barrage of 8-inch shells left the guns of the U.S.S. *Des Moines* and U.S.S. *Salem*. The two heavy cruisers were roughly 3,000 yards away, their broadsides lighting their outlines like mistimed strobe lights. The relays of shells were mesmerizing, forming an almost steady arc of glowing light off towards their distant targets. On the horizon, flashes began to erupt as first the battleships', then the cruisers' salvoes began to land. *Missouri*'s guns fired once more, followed again by the *New Jersey*'s in the darkness.

"I don't know what they're targeting, sir," the officer of the deck, Lieutenant Jenkins, declared, "but it's probably about to be dead."

White laughed at that.

"I was a young ensign on the *Des Moines* when the Norks tried to force the issue at Pusan," White said. "Captain Donahue made sure that all of the wardroom got to go ashore and see what we'd done over the next couple of days."

White's mirth remained on his face as he thought about the sight of burnt-out and broken North Korea T-34s.

"When you see a tank tossed a hundred yards like it was a bathroom toy, you don't forget it," he continued. "Those were 8-inch shells."

Missouri's main battery boomed again.

"The tanks are probably heavier," White chuckled, "but so are those shells."

The Army had always claimed that they would have managed to blunt the North Korean offensive before it actually reached Pusan's docks. White had his doubts, but the two atomic bombs that had turned Pyongyang into the world's largest open-air crematorium made the whole discussion academic.

Twenty years on and it seems the song remains the same, though, he thought, considering what his orders were once the bombardment completed. *Commies attack us, we strike back, nothing gets decided.*

"Has Commander Downes reported the status of the *Regulus* missiles yet?" White asked Jenkins, looking at the clock.

"No, sir," Jenkins replied, then paused as *Missouri* fired again. "There was a problem with some of the magazine feeds again."

White raised an eyebrow.

Why is this the first I'm hearing of it? he thought. Jenkins must have caught his expression.

"The XO indicated that he believed the delay would be less than fifteen minutes," Jenkins stated. "His understanding of your directions prior to opening fire was to only disturb you for a major interruption, i.e. something that would affect launch operations tomorrow morning."

I hate it when my officers actually listen to me, White thought, nodding at Jenkins's report. *Almost as much as I hate the abominations the Navy saw fit to perform on this ship.*

Like the *New Jersey* in front of her, the *Missouri* had begun life as an *Iowa*-class battleship. Unlike her three sisters, *Missouri* had not escaped unscathed during the final amphibious operations against Japan. Six land-based *Okha*-bombs and a suicide boat had made a right mess of her aft portion, so much so that the Navy had considered scrapping her. Instead, they had used portions of the unfinished but cancelled U.S.S. *Kentucky* to make her whole, then turned her into a test bed. That had lasted right up until the Soviets had detonated the first hydrogen bomb, followed shortly by launching a satellite that orbited the globe twice.

At that point, in their wisdom, the Bureau of Ships had decided to finally settle on making the *Missouri* a combination cruise missile launcher with an extensive anti-aircraft battery. Rather than going with a relatively simple path, BuShips had come up with the brilliant idea of serving two very different types of missiles from the same magazine machinery. Meaning, of course, that some sort of Rube Goldberg arrangement had to be employed, meaning the battleship had experienced nothing but trouble since she'd been assigned to a fleet whose supply line originated in San Diego.

Little hot work here on the gun line, then we head north, White thought, glancing at the clock once again. *I think the North Vietnamese are going to be rather surprised to see us.*

A runner came onto the bridge, out of breath. The petty officer held a closed envelope with borders that seemed almost pale in the light of *Missouri*'s battle lamps.

Oh shit, White thought, waving Jenkins off as he headed to meet the sailor at the bridge's entrance. He would likely need a white light to read the document, anyway, and the TOP SECRET stenciled on its front meant it was unlikely to be frivolous news.

Last time I received one of those envelopes, White thought, *it was to inform all commands that the Israelis had popped Alexandria and Damascus, the Soviets had gone to DEFCON 1, and it was looking like we all were about to get practical courses in nuclear delivery.*

"Sir, flash traffic from Pearl," the comms petty officer huffed out, handing White the envelope. He took the document with a nod. "Flag confirms that Vice Admiral McCampbell has the message, as well, and will be providing no additional orders at this time."

That's odd, White thought. *Flash traffic that doesn't create a change in orders arguably shouldn't be flash traffic.*

"Lieutenant Jenkins, inform the XO he has the con," White called across the bridge, drawing an affirmative before he continued. "I'm going to the conning tower to read the traffic."

White glanced at the comms NCO's nametag out of the corner of his eye as he turned.

"Chief Powers, follow me."

It was a short trip to the *Missouri*'s conning tower. Captain White quickly waved everyone back to their duties as he entered the structure, finding a corner away from prying eyes as he opened the envelope.

FLASH FLASH FLASH

1. NATIONAL INTELLIGENCE ASSETS HAVE DETERMINED THE PRESENCE OF OSA-CLASS MISSILE BOATS AND POSSIBLE FIXED-WING ANTISHIPPING PLATFORMS NEAR HAIPHONG.
2. COMMANDER U.S.S. MISSOURI IS DIRECTED TO REMOVE ALL NUCLEAR WARHEADS DURING RESUPPLY OPERATIONS PROCEEDING OPERATION HAMMERHEAD.
3. INTELLIGENCE CONFIRMS PRESENCE OF ADDITIONAL MIG-23 FLOGGER REGIMENT VICINITY OF HANOI. REGIMENT IS BELIEVED TO BE MANNED BY SOVIET "VOLUNTEERS."
4. ADDITIONAL REGIMENT OF BADGER BOMBERS REPORTED BY SATELLITE AT KAMENNY RUCHEY. COMMANDER TF 77 WILL TAKE PRECAUTIONARY MEASURES TO MEET THIS THREAT.
5. TF 77 REQUEST TO ALLOW F-14 DEPLOYMENT WITHIN 50 NM OF THE COAST PROVIDED THERE IS EA-6 SUPPORT IS APPROVED.
6. COMMANDER TF 77'S REQUEST FOR CVS TO CLOSE WITHIN 150 NM OF HANOI IS DENIED. CINCPACFLT WILL RECONSIDER REQUEST ONCE E=MC2 HAS ARRIVED ON STATION.
7. COMMUNIST BLOC WARSHIP OR INTELLIGENCE VESSELS SIGHTED WITHIN 100 MILES OF TASK FORCE 77 OR TG 64.2 MAY BE ENGAGED WITHOUT WARNING AFTER 0645 LOCAL TIME. DEMONSTRATIONS OF INTENT MAY BE CONDUCTED IN VESSELS' VICINITY AT COMMANDER, TF 77 AND TG 64.2

FLASH TRAFFIC END

. . .

Well, tell me you're concerned about ol' "Show Me Bullseye" living up to her reputation again without telling me, White thought, annoyed. In addition to her *Regulus III*, the *Missouri* carried two twin launchers for *Terrier* and *Talos* missiles. In addition, the battleship had been the test bed for the Mark 45 5-inch gun, with ten of the guns located on either side of her superstructure.

She's not invincible, but a few damn missile boats shouldn't be a problem.

A talker interrupted his musings, reminding him that he had a gunnery problem to run.

"Captain, spotters are reporting the target is in flames and that we may cease fire at our leisure."

"Thank you," White replied with a nod. "Tell guns shoot the shells in the tube, then cease fire."

Missouri's master then turned to Chief Powers.

"Chief, take this message to the XO," he stated. "Tell him I want to meet in CIC along with Beans and Guns at 2030 after we conclude launch operations."

"Aye aye, Captain," Chief Powers replied, his breathing almost back to normal.

"No need to run the message all the way to Battle Two," White said with a smirk. "I don't feel like explaining why you fell down a ladder to the Surgeon."

"Yes, sir," Powers replied with an answering smirk, then departed out the hatch to carry out his task.

"Sir, signal from flag," the talker stated again. "Godspeed and happy hunting."

Missouri's firing gong sounded before White could reply, and he paused to let the main battery clear its barrels.

Now the real work begins, White thought. *Here's to hoping this old lady's engines are in as good of shape as the dockyard workers claimed.*

"Reply as follows: Thank you, will give Mr. Van Dong your regards."

White's comment brought a round of laughter around the conning tower.

"Gentlemen, that man is going to wish he'd just let ol' Uncle Ho have the whole country back in '53," White said, pitching his voice to carry across the compartment. "Tonight, we're about to show North Vietnam and the rest of the commies that America has a new stick."

White paused as the conning tower became bedlam, with its occupant breaking into shouts and cries of agreement. White gestured to bring the noise down, then motioned for the ship's intercom.

Here goes nothing, he thought, taking the 1MC. *Always dangerous to speak to the crew without notes.*

"Men of the *Missouri*, this is your captain speaking," White stated. "First, congratulations on introducing the North Vietnamese Army to the power of naval bombardment."

He paused, hearing the cheers from adjacent compartments.

"Second, as you all should have heard from your division heads, this ship is about to conduct operations in the finest surface warfare traditions," White continued. "John Paul Jones asked for a swift ship, and we're about to demonstrate to the good citizens of Haiphong just how fast this old lady can dance."

This time, the cheers were long and raucous.

"Sir, *Des Moines* is heading our way," the runner shouted over the din.

"Thank you," White said, glancing at his watch.

Ten minutes until launch, he thought, keying the microphone again.

"Men, do your job," he continued, "and history will talk about our bombardment in the same breath as the great raids by Decatur, Cushing, and Halsey. The age of the gun ain't dead, and we're going to keep reminding people of that all week long. May God have mercy on our enemies, because we'll show them none."

If I didn't know better, I'd swear the deck is shaking this time, White thought, passing the microphone back to its original owner.

"I'm going back to the bridge," he informed the conning tower's senior officer, shouting to be heard over the crew's repeated chant of "Show Me! Show Me!" echoing across the ship. With a smile, he turned and shouted across the conning tower as he left.

"Ten minutes until launch, if anyone needs to hit the head."

White stepped back out into the companionway, chased out by raucous laughter and comments about old men's bladders. He arrived back on the bridge just as *Missouri*'s turrets were circling back into the train position, the guns lowering back to their usual angle.

Still a little hot, looks like.

"Sir, XO reports that the ammunition feed has been restored and that he will inform you of what is wrong with it at the 2030 meeting," Lieutenant Jenkins reported as White walked to his chair.

"Understood," White replied. "Have the destroyers checked in?"

"Yes, sir," Jenkins replied. "The *King* and *Waddell* are conducting one last ASW sweep of the rendezvous point. *Maddox* and *Turner Joy* have detached from the screen and will be joining us once the *Des Moines* has passed astern."

White nodded at the report. The *John King* and *Waddell* were the *Missouri*'s anti-aircraft escorts, but also destroyers first and foremost. Although the odds of a hostile submarine this close to the coast of South Vietnam were about the same as an alien UFO doing a drive-by, the USN had learned the hard way about Communist pigboats being where they weren't supposed to.

Still think that sub putting tin fish into the Columbia *off Hainan should have led to Beijing getting an unscheduled sunrise,* White thought. *Would have neatly solved that problem before LBJ ended up having his heart attack. Guess we'll find out if President Ford is more decisive.*

"All hands, all hands, stand by for missile launch."

The call over the 1MC brought White out of his reverie. Taking a deep breath, he glanced up at the clock on the bridge's forward bulkhead.

"Hope the boys down in the magazine double-checked they put the right bangers on the missiles," Jenkins muttered nervously. White shook his head at that thought.

That's why the Regulus warheads with their own pockets of sunshine are painted black, son.

"I'm reasonably sure the XO checked them himself," White replied. "I don't think anyone is going to start World War III here tonight."

"Yes, sir," Jenkins replied sheepishly.

Although Brezhnev's saber-rattling is going to make this an interesting next couple of days, White mused, keeping his expression neutral. The Soviet Union's leader had stated outright he would deploy nuclear weapons against any American or Western nation that employed weapons of mass destruction against any member of the "fraternity of nations." Just who was in that fraternity or what weapons of mass destruction entailed had been left open to interpretation after Damascus.

Can't help but feel that this is a test to see how far we're willing to go in a post-Damascus world, White thought. *Thankfully, Uncle Ho might be dead, but his generals still know what they're doing.*

"All hands, all hands, launch in two minutes," the 1MC sounded. "Man your missile launch stations."

Here we go, White thought, fighting the urge to walk out onto the bridge wing. The *Missouri*'s lookouts came shuffling into the larger structure, closing the watertight hatch to the outside. White listened as the runners received reports that all external hatches were "buttoned up" aboard the battleship, nodding to himself when the final reports came in.

"Launch in sixty seconds," the intercom sounded again. The *Missouri*'s bridge became almost silent, only the low hum of machinery and wind gusts rattling the battleship's windows.

"Ten...nine...eight...seven...six...five...four...three..."

As the countdown reached its end, White heard the muffled roar of the *Regulus II*'s engine spooling up. The sound reached a crescendo as the missile shot off the angled launch ramp on the *Missouri*'s stern, its engine bright as it accelerated down the ship's length and upwards into the night. A moment later, the starboard launcher followed suit. The two bright dots quickly receded into the night as both missiles accelerated to their supersonic attack speed.

"Launch in eighty seconds," the 1MC crackled again. In his mind's eye, White could see the automated missile machinery going through its complex dance to ready the next bird on the rack. On time, the next pair of *Regulus II*s shot off the ramp, moving slightly faster to catch their first two brethren.

Here's to hoping all the programming works like it's supposed to, White thought. *The best eggheads in the land trying to make sure all those things arrive over Hanoi right in the middle of Van Dong's scheduled speech to the Politburo.*

THE UGLY FISH
NORTHERN HANOI (2 MILES SOUTH OF PHUC YEN)
1910 LOCAL

"Golden Lion!"

The shout in badly accented Russian made Lieutenant Colonel Misha Sorokin pause midstep as he entered the small, smoke-filled dining room. The pause was only momentary, as stopping led to him being nearly trampled by his much larger and clumsier companion.

I should know better than to get between Alexei and food, Misha thought, waving off his subordinate's apology. Like Misha, Alexei was a child of the Great Patriotic War. Unlike Misha, who had been fortunate enough to be relocating to Moscow from his native Smolensk when the Germans came, Alexei had been in Leningrad. A fact that explained both his ability to eat *anything* without consequence.

A stomach once severely starved of food does not release it so easily, Misha thought, making a face as a pungent aroma wafted from The Ugly Fish's kitchen. *On the other hand, some of us would murder for some simple borscht right now after the sustained assault my intestines have suffered the last three weeks.*

"Lieutenant Colonel Sorokin!" the voice called again, this time accompanied by a furious motion from the far-left corner. The restaurant's din got slightly lower as individuals turned to stare at Misha or the small, slight man trying to gain his attention.

Well, there's someone I was not expecting to ever see again, Misha thought, eyes narrowing as the man stood on a pair of prosthetic legs. *Usually, people who get cut out of a cockpit with a pair of tourniquets don't make it very long.*

Clearly, Quan Ngo, former MiG-21 pilot, was either too stubborn or too stupid to die. Given how he'd come to lose his legs, Misha was betting on the former. He noted that his interlocutor wore the uniform of a North Vietnamese Air Force (NVAF) colonel. Just as he was about to reply, another individual entered from the colonel's left.

"Attention! Attention!" the North Vietnamese Army political officer bellowed, causing the room to fall silent. "The Rightful Leader's address is scheduled to commence in five minutes!"

"The People's favor on the Rightful Leader!" the Vietnamese present shouted in return.

"The Leader's favor on our people!" the political officer replied, then took a seat.

"I am not going to sit with that man, sir," Alexei rumbled from behind him. The taciturn bombardier was holding a bowl of something that immediately made Misha's stomach turn.

Whatever concoction that is, Misha thought, *I, too, do not want it at the table with me.*

"Alexei!" a feminine voice called from the other side of the restaurant. Turning his head like a Kodiak that had just scented prey, Alexei squinted, then nodded and raised a hand. The woman wearing an East German Air Force uniform waved back happily, drawing giggles from her two Vietnamese and slightly older Caucasian woman in plain clothes at the table.

"Go, friend, save yourself," Misha said mockingly in German. "Make happy future people's warriors with her for the good of the people everywhere."

"No need to be cranky because you are chained at the hand," Alexei rumbled back in the same language. "Besides, your vomiting all over the table would just ensure both of us slept alone tonight. Helga is a wonderful woman."

I assure you that my chains are silken and quite comfortable, friend, Misha thought, thinking of his dear Katarina. *I do hope she's enjoying herself in Kiev.* With a final shake of his head, Misha stepped back towards Ngo's table.

"I see your bombardier still has a touch with the ladies," Ngo observed wryly, drawing a chuckle from his two companions. "At least no one at that table is going to get you arrested by the local authorities."

Misha glanced at the table next to them that had now sprouted a second political officer out of nowhere. The two men were supposedly holding a conversation, but Misha was well aware that both were actually straining to hear what was about to be discussed at his impromptu gathering.

Not quite as paranoid as the North Koreans, Misha thought, *but not even on the same continent as "trusting."* He was less sure than Ngo that no one was going to end up arrested due to Alexei's cavorting.

"Gentlemen, this is Lieutenant Colonel Misha Sorokin," Ngo said, speaking slowly.

"Greetings, gentlemen," Misha said, regarding the two other Vietnamese officers, one an older lieutenant colonel and the other a young captain. He noted both wore pilot's wings, one with a gold outline around the North Vietnamese national insignia, indicating he'd seen aerial combat.

His face looks familiar, Misha thought.

"I wasn't aware your country had provided any IL-28 support," Ngo said, switching back to Russian.

"For the chance to kill capitalist running dogs?" Misha scoffed in rapid-fire Vietnamese. "After Damascus, our country would send aid to Lucifer if he wasn't merely an oppressive creation."

"I think Comrade Brezhnev greatly underestimates the capitalists' willingness to kill the Third World in large quantities," the lieutenant colonel said bitterly. "I do hope for your sake and ours that he is ready to, as they say, trade Leningrad for Hanoi."

Misha kept his face passive, even as he saw the two nearby political officers pause mid-conversation. Both men started to turn their heads towards Misha's table before realizing that would clearly violate their cover.

You are either incredibly well-connected or stunningly stupid, Misha thought, reaching for a cigarette to cover up his silence. *To question state policy* with two political officers in earshot *is like punching a shark while bleeding arterially: Even if the fish is not hungry, it might just bite you out of principle.*

"Lieutenant Colonel Sorokin, I don't think you've met Lieutenant Colonel Bay," Ngo said, his face clearly showing his displeasure at the junior officer's impertinence. "Or, I should say, *Colonel* Bay as of midnight tonight."

Sorokin searched his mental rolodex, then realized why Bay looked familiar.

"Ah, the 'Hainan Hatchet,'" he said with a grin, drawing a sour look from Bay.

"If I ever meet the French reporter that gave me that nickname, I'm going to strangle them with my bare hands," Bay snapped.

"Her," Sorokin corrected, "and as you heard when I walked in, she has a way of giving men nicknames that sell well."

Ms. Friang also knows combat both theoretically and from practical experience, Sorokin thought. He'd met the woman in the aftermath of what history called the "Ten Day War" in late 1968.

Sorokin took a long drag of his cigarette.

"In any case, I would think the three regiments of our newest fighter, submarines, tanks, and the surface-to-air missiles would be enough to convince you of Comrade Brezhnev's wisdom, generosity, and commitment."

Bay scoffed.

"Your 'newest fighter' handles like the suitcase that it is nicknamed after," the Vietnamese lieutenant colonel spat, lighting his own cigarette. "You should have the engineer hanged, saved at the last moment, then shot again."

The political officers were not even feigning having their own conversation now.

Comrade, it is never *a good day to get a commissar's attention,* he thought grimly. *If the rumors are true and the "Yankee air pirates" will be coming soon, you cannot shoot down enemy fighters from a jail cell.*

Sorokin took a long pull from his cigarette, then started drinking from the glass of water that had appeared next to him. He looked up to thank the waitress, but noticed she was already standing by the political officers, ostensibly taking their order. A revolver of some sort was conspicuously tied around her waist.

Oh yes, the responsibility of every citizen to be armed lest the need to shoot at American aircraft arises, Sorokin thought. *It would be amusing if they hadn't shot down at least several aircraft during Second Hainan. Of which most were American.*

"You have to excuse Comrade Bay," Ngo said, his tone stern. "He still yearns for his MiG-17."

Sorokin coughed on his drink.

"Are you suicidal?" he asked once he could talk. "Why don't you just ask for a Antonov biplane while you're at it?"

His comment drew a snicker from the captain, who immediately shrank from Bay's subsequent glare.

"You are here in that twin engine monstrosity, yet you mock the MiG-17?" Bay asked, his voice barely above a whisper.

"Yes, my bomber is old," Sorokin replied, choosing his words carefully. He paused, then smiled. "But at least we have acknowledged reality and gotten rid of the tail gunner."

Sure, we did not replace that saved weight with anything useful, he thought angrily. *Like electronic countermeasures, chaff, or flares. I am sure those three extra knots will help me outrun a missile this week.*

Bay's opportunity to respond was cut off by the opening strains of the North Vietnamese national anthem. Sorokin quickly scuttled to his feet, assisting Ngo as the other man nearly stumbled. Every Vietnamese in the room began singing at the top of their lungs. Sorokin drew shocked looks as he joined in after "Fatherland," his baritone joined by Alexei's.

Works every time, he thought, seeing the looks of appreciation. *Anywhere you're going, learn the damn national anthem.* He and his bombardier had practiced the song often during the training period for their current mission, especially the long overwater navigational flights off Vladivostok.

Hopefully we will not have to...wait, what is that?

The sound that had triggered his curiosity was drowned by a handful of sonic booms. The broadcast anthem ended abruptly just before anti-aircraft guns began to open fire in the distance, followed belatedly by air raid sirens. First one boom, then a second, then four more in quick succession rattled the restaurant's windows.

"Everyone outside!" Ngo bellowed. "Pilots to Phuc Yen, immediately! Controllers to the bus!"

Sorokin stepped to the side as Vietnamese began heading for the exits like there was a grease fire. Speaking of the kitchen, he saw Alexei leading the women he'd been accompanying towards the establishment's rear, past the still-burning stoves.

"Aren't you coming?" Ngo asked, wisely trying to avoid the bustle.

Sorokin gave a grim smile.

"I fly a bomber," he replied. "Me taking off just means I'd complicate *your* job."

Ngo's face was a war of emotions that finally settled on a grim smile of acceptance.

"I notice you never did tell us why you are here," he said finally.

Sorokin exhaled heavily.

"I suspect, given the Americans' criminal activity, you will find out soon enough," Sorokin replied.

2

TREES, SUITCASES, AND CURTAIN RAISERS

U.S.S. AMERICA
0430 LOCAL
SHERMAN STATION (200 MILES EAST OF HAIPHONG)
19 APRIL 1975

The buzzing of his alarm clock brought Damon back to consciousness.

What the...oh, wait, he thought, his brain reminding him that he was now aboard a different carrier.

"You know, Rigger, I never realized how annoying your alarm clock was," Keg muttered. "No wonder you bring that damn thing everywhere you go."

"For a small piece of Singapore crap, it has a sound you aren't sleeping through," Damon replied, yawning. There was a hard thump as some sort of aircraft slammed down on *America*'s deck. The carrier wasn't quite bedlam, but it was clear that the vessel was sailing into harm's way in a couple of hours.

There was a knock on the hatch.

"Gentlemen, CAG has directed me to make sure you are awake," a voice called.

"Yeah, we're up," Keg replied, turning on their borrowed stateroom's light. They'd apparently displaced some poor bastard in the medical staff, but it had been a necessary evil.

"Sir, Captain Connor directed that I was to lay eyes on both of you," the officer replied sheepishly.

Of course he did, Damon thought, swinging his legs out from the bottom bunk. He strode to the hatch and opened it, Keg swinging down from the top bunk behind him. Opening the hatch to find a short ensign who didn't look a day over eighteen, Damon gave the officer a big grin.

"Give my regards to CAG," he said with a nod, then closed the hatch.

"Jesus, Rigger," Keg said, shaking his head.

"What?" Damon asked, innocently.

"That poor kid looked like he'd seen Sasquatch, that's what," Keg said, gesturing from the deck to the overhead at his larger companion. "Not to mention, you *know* Connor's going to go apeshit after that stunt you pulled last night."

"The man's not cleared for the Tree," Damon replied. "He screwed up when he asked 'What is Combat Tree?' and had a dumbfounded look on his damn face."

Keg raised an eyebrow as Damon began getting his gear together.

"Rear Admiral Lang's aide and his intel officer weren't cleared for it, either," Damon continued. "Are you saying I should have let them stay?"

"They're not leading a strike today, Rigger!" Keg replied.

"Dropping bombs on a fuel facility shouldn't require knowing a damn thing about splashing MiGs," Damon replied.

Combat Tree was the whole reason that Flight 300 had made their harrowing journey the day before. In the aftermath of the Second Hainan incident and Israel's War of Attrition, some eggheads working at Wright-Patterson had figured out the key to Communist air defense systems. In order for the air defense network to work at optimum efficiency, the Soviets had developed transponders that worked with their air defense radars. This both facilitated the controllers' jobs and had the added benefit of keeping trigger-happy SAM operators from blasting their own MiGs out of the sky.

I personally would have just figured out a way to make all of our transponders radiate a friendly return once in hostile territory, Damon thought. *But I guess that would have meant we'd have to worry about our own fratricide.*

"You can't deny that you felt a bit of pleasure when Lang reminded that asshole technically our flight was detailed to *his* command, not Connor's air wing," Keg pressed. "What is the deal with you two?"

Damon paused, putting toothpaste on his brush.

"You mean, other than he's a racist asshole who repeatedly and publicly expressed his belief 'my kind' doesn't belong anywhere other than the galley serving food or shining shoes?" Damon spat bitterly, drawing a surprised sound from Keg. "Well, for one, we can start with my callsign."

"Wait, what?" Keg asked, his eyes narrowing.

Oh, guess I don't tell that story all that often anymore, Damon thought. *Too much water under the bridge and most of the people involved are very, very dead.*

"When I got to VF-74, the squadron commander was Jack Stennis, ol' Connor's best friend," Damon started slowly. "The two of them had apparently met in flight school and were best friends."

Keg winced at the name.

"Oh no," he said. "I think I've heard stories about Stennis."

"Whatever stories you heard were probably the sanitized versions," Damon replied.

"You're going to break that damn toothbrush," Keg noted, nodding. "Either that or I'm going to have to explain how you stabbed it through the side of your mouth here in a second."

Damon looked down and realized he was indeed gripping the toothbrush like it was a prison shank.

"We don't have to cover this now if you don't want," Keg said quietly. "Connor's an asshole and that's good enough for me if it is for you."

"No, Keg, I think I should probably tell you the whole thing," Damon said after a moment's consideration. "In any case, I'd just gotten back from the RIO radar course for the *Spectre*. The Bedevilers had just got the Bravo model and thus had a horrific maintenance rate for their -72 radars."

Damon paused, taking a deep breath.

"There I was, recently promoted to jay-gee," Damon continued, voice thick. "Thinking here was an opportunity to show those two jackasses that maybe the electrical engineering degree and getting selected to do an internship with Westinghouse right out of the Academy happened for a reason."

Keg, having started brushing his own teeth, spat out a mouthful of toothpaste.

"Huh. You know that's not in your file?" he said, giving Damon a suspicious look.

"Oh, you mean having a first cousin who just happened to work in BuPers has its perks?" Damon asked bitterly. "I think you'll see why it came off my records in a second."

"Go on," Keg replied around his own toothbrush, then spat out the mouthful of paste.

"It took me three weeks," Damon said flatly, "but I figured out what the maintenance problem was just in time for the *Columbia* to start heading east for the First Hainan Crisis. Had to go the long way around thanks to the continued festivities between the Israelis and Egyptians, that was fun."

"Worst nine goddamn years in the Navy," Keg agreed, shaking his head as he turned off the water to the head. "Almost makes me wish the Israelis had nuked Cairo while they were at it."

What's a couple million more dead people between friends? Damon thought, once more going to full Sphinx as he opened his shaving kit.

"Anyway, north of Diego Garcia, passing the *Ark Royal*," Damon said. "Each squadron gets to select three officers to go and pass pleasantries while we do impromptu screen exercises."

For all the good those did when it all hit the fan.

"Which means you really got to go get a chance to drink," Keg said, laughing. "Officially drink, that is."

Damon gave a slight smile at the allusion to "medicinal liquor" from the flight surgeon.

"Thing is, Connor can't handle his liquor," Damon replied. "Bastard's a lightweight, despite being a 'crew cut bell end,' to quote *Ark Royal*'s captain at a later date."

"Easy," Keg cautioned, his voice stern. "I think he's an asshole, too, but you can't be calling a CAG a dickhead in front of your squadron commander."

"Don't ever forget who is who..." Damon thought, keeping his face passive as he nodded. His father's advice before he'd gone off to the Naval Academy had seldom failed him, and it looked like VF-84's commander was just one more cautionary tale.

Keg continued to look at him for a second, then broke out in a laugh.

"No, fuck that asshole," Keg snapped, turning back to the mirror to finish shaving. "I'm just messing with you."

Damon gave a heavy exhale, shaking his head at his superior.

Fine, not everyone is bad.

"Anyway, you were talking about going aboard the *Ark Royal*," Keg said. "Which, she's a wonderful ship, I did some cross-decking with her back in '70. You know they call the F-110 the *Phantom*?"

"Brits always seem to give our planes weird names," Damon said as he started shaving.

"*Phantom* is a better name, anyway," Keg opined.

"So we're talking shop and Connor is getting sauced," Damon resumed. "The Brit squadron leader mentions they're having similar radar problems to ours."

He paused and took a deep breath.

"Connor, without missing a beat, says, 'We can just send over our nigger to do some rigging...'" Damon said flatly.

Keg came to a dead stop.

"He said what?"

"I'd rather not repeat it, if you don't mind," Damon said simply, then resumed shaving. "You can imagine that went over about as well as if Connor had asked the *Ark Royal*'s captain if he could borrow the man's daughter next time he was in London."

"How in the fuck was Connor not relieved?!" Keg asked, his eyes wide, face pale.

"Funny things happen when your battle group admiral is from Mississippi," Damon replied with a shrug. "To be clear, Captain Fell did file a formal complaint, put together a write-up for me to get an award, and raised so much Cain that Connor got restricted to his stateroom until Second Hainan cooked off."

Damon looked at the bulkhead clock.

"Which, of course, enraged Commander Stennis," he said, wiping his face and starting to put his uniform on.

"And that's how you got your callsign Rigger," Keg said, shaking his head. "Oh, boy."

"Yep," Damon said, his voice mockingly chipper. "Happened right around Indonesia when the *Ark Royal* took a left to go to Singapore because the Brits had second thoughts about the sanctity of international waters when the Chinese moved a division across from Hong Kong."

"Amazing how your allies don't want to potentially lose a colony over an intelligence ship," Keg noted. "Can't say I blame them, though."

"I don't blame them at all," Damon noted. "Just like I don't blame ol' Scooter Ford for asking for another pilot once I was no longer 'Ursa.'"

"I'm assuming because calling you 'Bear' might have led to some confusion?"

"Exactly," Damon said with a smile. "I got reassigned with Hector Jimenez, and us 'fellows with a permanent tan' got stuck on night CAP while the rest of the squadron went off to find glory."

Damon laughed bitterly.

"Of course, that meant we had a front-row seat when *Columbia* caught her two fish," Damon said. "I didn't think she was going to make with how badly she was burning."

Just glad that racist asshole Stennis got to linger on for a few days after getting roasted across half his body, Damon thought. *Shame about the morphine getting triaged.*

The churlish thoughts were only there for a second before Damon pushed them away, his stomach nauseous with shame. He reached up and touched the cross around his neck.

Forgive me, Lord, wrath is a sin.

"You know, every time you have a questionable or impure thought, you grab that cross," Keg observed, drawing a laugh from Damon. "It's a little eerie having a pious man as one of the best RIOs I've ever met."

"When half of your squadron gets roasted like pork loins and you miss it because you're burning holes in the sky, it kind of reconnects you with your faith."

Damon paused.

"That it also allowed Mongo and me to become the ranking aces of that incident before we got mysteriously rotated out when the *Columbia* got towed out of danger," Damon said.

"That's right, they made you both come home to prep for the Board of Inquiry," Keg said, then his eyes narrowed. "Although I meant to ask, how did he get that callsign? Never got a chance to ask him before...well, you know."

Yeah, I do know, Damon thought sadly. *Crying shame about their F-14 departing.*

"You a fan of comics?" Damon asked.

"Not really," Keg said.

"Stennis was a huge fan of Flash Gordon," Damon said. "Once commented that Hector had a head 'the size of a planet.' Mongo is the planet in Flash Gordon."

"It's a miracle you didn't kill that man," Keg muttered. "At least, before the Chinese did."

Damon looked at the clock again.

"If we're planning on getting anything to eat," he noted, "we better get moving."

Keg nodded, then took one last look around the cabin.

"I'm going to be so much happier when we're back on the Big E," he said.

"You and me both," Damon replied. "Let's go splash some MiGs."

. . .

Phuc Yen Airfield
0535 Local

Misha was surprisingly upbeat for a man who almost certainly was witnessing his final sunrise. The same, however, could not be said of the men bustling all around him.

I'd probably be more upset if it was my *Party Headquarters that was hit by two cruise missiles last night*, he thought, watching as North Vietnamese ground crew hustled and bustled all around the MiG-23 *Floggers* that were beginning to taxi into takeoff positions. *Or had at least twenty American carrier bombers mine my largest port.*

That last bit was balanced out by three, possibly five of the American bombers being shot down. Quite familiar with lesser nations' tendency to overclaim, Misha had been skeptical until he'd had a chance to talk with the Soviet air attaché earlier that morning.

If Comrade Popov is certain he saw three planes going down in flames last night, I'm inclined to believe him, Misha thought. *Although looking at the North Vietnamese revetments, I'm not sure how many of those might have been friendly aircraft.*

Misha counted four of the *Floggers* missing. As the aircraft was a notorious fuel hog and the interceptors had apparently chased the American aircraft out to sea, it was entirely possible they'd landed at another North Vietnamese Air Force field. But that the missing aircraft were all from a separate flight made Misha doubt everything was benign.

"I am surprised to see you here, Comrade Sorokin," an angry familiar voice spat. "Given Comrade Brezhnev's speech an hour ago, I thought all of you cowards would be 'observing' conflict from locations nowhere near a possible target."

I so love being the only Russian in a ten-mile radius when Party leadership makes a policy decision, Misha thought, turning around. Despite the speaker's angst, he pointedly did *not* drop his hand towards the Makarov in his shoulder holster.

Doesn't sound murderous, Makarov thought, regarding Colonel Bay. *Just deeply disappointed and sad.*

The fighter ace was glowering in his flight suit, looking like he hadn't slept at all.

"I'm told Comrade Mao has also decided that having just fixed Hainan, the Dragon does not wish to repair it once more," Misha observed with a shrug. "More capitalists for us, it would seem."

"Us?" Bay asked, his face looking confused.

Misha gestured towards the eight hardened aircraft shelters roughly a quarter-mile away. Large structures, the finest that Yugoslavia could provide, each was large enough to hold three IL-28s if arranged just so.

"I did not bring forty-eight of the People's finest light bomber crews all the way from the Arctic to hide out while the Americans oppressed you," Misha replied with a shrug.

He did a last check for political officers. Seeing none, and reasonably certain Bay was also a dead man walking, he continued.

"Comrade Brezhnev sent us, a bunch of multinational fighters, here because we are expendable."

"But he stated this morning that his forces will observe the one-hundred-mile exclusion zone the American president has declared around their task forces," Bay replied. He looked no less baffled. "If Russian bombers…"

"If Russian bombers in the People's Volunteer Group livery attack an American carrier and manage to set one afire," Misha replied, "it will be a great embarrassment for the United States Navy. So much so the Americans may cease strikes upon your country."

Bay looked skeptical as Misha continued.

"After all, as you pointed out, the IL-28 is obsolete! How could an obsolete, ancient, and decrepit bomber manage to pierce the vaunted 'circle of steel' the Americans have kept going on about with their new missiles?"

"You are insane," Bay snapped. "How do you expect to get anywhere close to American carriers?"

Misha laughed in a way that conveyed zero mirth.

"Well before Comrade Brezhnev apparently misplaced his balls this morning, I was expecting there to be a helpful trawler transmitting in the clear twenty miles behind one of their light carriers," Misha said. "Alas, based on the briefing I received at our embassy an hour ago, it would appear that the Americans sailing through a typhoon shed them of their tattletales. One was attempting to regain contact this morning when President Ford made his declaration."

Misha laughed again.

"Of course, a 'weapons demonstration' just five miles away convinced the trawler captain he needed to be elsewhere."

"Coward," Bay spat.

"Comrade, if you were in an unarmed trainer, would you attempt to dogfight a fully armed MiG?" Misha chided, drawing a glare from Bay. "While I may demonstrate otherwise in forty-five minutes or so, I am well aware of the dividing line between bravery and stupidity."

That and there are other ways of acquiring general locations, Misha thought. *Such as the radio direction battalion that is currently triangulating the Americans' flight radios and radars as we speak.* Feeding several highly trained intelligence personnel to the Pacific's sharks was pointless and unable to help worldwide Communism's cause. Despite the obvious logic, Bay looked unmoved.

"Sacrifices must be made to demonstrate resolve to the Americans," Bay said.

"It is entirely possible that all of us will die," Misha snapped, gesturing to where his men were checking over their bombers. "I think there will be more than enough *demonstration* today, comrade."

I also do not pretend to know Comrade Brezhnev's will, Misha thought. *Perhaps our bloody sacrifice will be how he rallies or shames the Chinese into allowing bombers to transit their air space.*

Misha glanced around before continuing.

"In any case, I would advise you to consider when and where you complain more carefully," he said conversationally. "Last night, I noticed the political officers paying particular attention to your comments."

Bay scoffed, leading to Misha glowering at him. They were interrupted by Alexei walking from the command building, a pair of Czechoslovakian bombardiers whose name Misha could never remember behind him. The other two men moved off to their aircraft in animated conversation while Alexei strode towards Misha.

I know he was up until one this morning drinking and rutting, yet he looks as fresh as if he slept nine hours, Misha thought, envious of his bombardier's constitution.

"The Vietnamese People's Navy requested Comrade Popov attempt to coordinate any strike with the sortie of their torpedo and missile boats," Alexei snapped, face reddening. "That fucking idiot agreed."

Misha pointedly ignored Bay's mirthful look in response to Alexei's indiscreet outburst as the bombardier continued.

"So now we will *not* be launching in a half-hour but instead have to wait for those thrice-cursed *podonoks* to get their vessels prepared and await a target," Alexei said.

"How are they going to cross *hundreds of miles of ocean* to get towards the Americans?" Misha asked, incredulously. "Even if the Americans sent an invitation, it will only be so they know around what time waves of their attack aircraft can swarm the boats and sink all of them!"

"That may be the point," Bay said, smiling. "It is brilliant. The capitalist running dogs will have to decide whether they want to strike at us or the boats, for surely they cannot do both."

I think you have a misunderstanding of how bombs work, Misha thought uncharitably. *Unsurprising for a fighter pilot.*

"Wouldn't you want the Americans to strike here?" Alexei asked with a quizzical expression. "You have been preparing your new defenses for almost a decade. Your pilots cannot operate outside of your controller envelope."

"That is not true!" Bay spat. "We are completely capable of operating outside of our network."

"You would be the first Second Wo...*fraternal* pilots I have seen that could do that, comrade," Alexei observed drily.

He's been drinking, Misha thought, fighting down annoyance. *Not just last night, recently. He usually doesn't talk this much, and he's certainly not rude when he does so.*

"No matter," Misha interjected before Bay could respond. "We have our orders, now we awai..."

"*Comrade Sorokin!*" a panicked female voice boomed from multiple loudspeakers in Vietnamese. "*Comrade Sorokin! Report to the central command post immediately!*"

"You know, at this point I almost hope that's a firing squad," Misha snarled, looking towards the distant command post near Phuc Yen's tower a half-mile away.

"Not almost for me," Alexei said, slapping his friend on the back. "After all, I cannot fly if you do not."

Bay snorted at that comment as Misha glared at his bombardier.

"I hope she gave something that penicillin will not fix," Misha replied, then started looking for a vehicle.

"You there!" Bay shouted at a passing North Vietnamese enlisted man. The individual stopped, turned, and then came to attention when he saw Bay's rank.

"Go fetch a vehicle immediately!" Bay ordered. "If you are not back here in five minutes, I will see you shot."

"Yes, sir!" the man said, then ran away.

"I think you just sent that man on a fool's errand," Alexei grumbled, then pointed. "It looks as if someone is coming to fetch you."

Misha's response was cut off by yet another pair of *Floggers* roaring down the runway. As their noise faded, he could hear the distant warbling of air raid sirens. This was followed shortly thereafter by Phuc Yen's own sirens beginning to sing their song.

"It is Comrade Ngo," Bay said, squinting. Misha and Alexei both looked at the man in shock.

Damn fighter pilot eyes, Misha thought, turning to look at the jeep careening towards them. Another pair of *Floggers* got airborne, joining the ever-growing flock above Phuc Yen. Misha took a few moments to count, reaching twenty-six before the jeep's horn told him that Ngo was close.

"Get in!" the North Vietnamese colonel shouted, gesturing towards the canvas-covered rear seat. "You, too, Comrade Bay!"

"What?" Bay asked, raising an eyebrow. "My regiment is next to depart!"

"Not anymore! There is a report of an American battleship! Your mission has changed!"

U.S.S. Missouri
45 miles east of Haiphong
0615 Local

Captain White snatched the falling grease pencil out of midair as it vibrated off the mapboard in *Missouri*'s CIC. The crash of ceramic behind him indicated someone else had not been as attentive to their coffee mug, making it the fourth one to break in the last thirty minutes.

Has to be hell in the galley, he thought grimly. *Been a long time since the old girl has stretched her legs like this for so long.*

Task Group 64.2, as the *Missouri*, *Des Moines*, and their escorts were designated, had conducted underway replenishment (UNREP) operations in the early morning darkness far from prying Communist eyes. The UNREP, to include the offloading of *Missouri*'s nuclear warheads, had occurred under the watchful eye of an E-2B *Hawkeye* AWACS aircraft off *America* and eight F-110 *Spectres* off the *Midway*. Callsign Heimdall, the AWACS still maintained her guard from sixty miles behind the battleship. White noticed six more unknown aircraft designated "Flight 300" had joined the radar aircraft and its escorts.

The problem with having so much operational security is I'm not totally clear what is going on, he thought. *Even naming us Task Group 64.2 is a trick.* Although nominally the *Missouri* and half of her escorts were Sixth Fleet vessels, they were under the control of Seventh Fleet, which meant the rump task force White commanded should have been TG 74.2, not 64.2.

Of course, the fact they have me, a captain, acting as a commodore is even more trickery, White thought. *Oh well, "death or a peerage" and all that. I'll either get my star a little early or end up getting mentioned with Daniel J. Callaghan as "admirals who fucked up their first combat command."*

White yawned as he looked at the tactical board, forcing himself to focus on the present.

"Captain, we've confirmed that Soviet freighter saw us and reported our position," Lieutenant Commander Harold Farrell, CIC's officer of the deck, stated. "Multiple channels."

White looked across at his gunnery officer, Commander Abner McCampbell.

"You called it," he said mournfully, gesturing at the map. "That's what I get for trying to get a little bit more reach for the *Talos*. Guess our friends know we're here now; pass word to light off all the radars."

"Aye, aye," Farrell said.

"We've got two of those radar hunting *Talos* on the rails right now, sir," McCampbell reported. "Two more behind them. Just need our brownshoe friends to give us the okay to shoot them."

"Understood," White replied, watching as more hostile aircraft were added to the plot vicinity of Vinh. After a few moments, the board was updated to indicate they were a flight of MiG-21s.

The loudspeaker above White's head squawked as the E-2B began reading off what sounded like a bunch of gibberish. After a few moments, White turned and looked at the smiling McCampbell.

"From your mouth to God's ears, sir," McCampbell said, gesturing to a talker for the sound phone to the *Missouri*'s electronic warfare office. "We've got four radars, two long-range surveillance radars near Hanoi and two ship radars that just lit off around Haiphong. I think those are our targets."

The man looks positively feral, White thought. *Far be it from me to keep him from killing things.*

"Sir, the *Des Moines* reports she is assuming duties as Blue Crown."

Whomever thought about having two fighter control cruisers for this operation was brilliant, White thought, acknowledging the report with a nod. *There's way too much going on for one vessel's crew to handle things, especially with us getting ready to start pummeling things.*

"Sir, the *America* sends 'Elmer Fudd.' I say again, 'Elmer Fudd.'"

A-hunting we will go, indeed, White thought. *Here goes nothing.*

"You may fire when ready, Mr. McCampbell," White quipped.

"Aye, aye, sir," McCampbell replied, then began speaking rapidly into his microphone. White looked at the plot and began assessing the situation, thankful once more for a competent XO that he could trust on the bridge.

We're still twenty miles out from the reference buoys, White thought. *This is going to be a long forty minutes.*

The eight reference buoys had been deployed by the submarine *Halibut* the night before, with timers counting down on when to initiate their radio beacons. Now broadcasting, the chain of buoys would serve as loose geographical reference to assist in the *Missouri* and *Des Moines*'s gunfire raid on various targets within Haiphong proper.

Don't know if it's true that the dockyards are stacked high with ammunition and fuel that the Soviets just dumped before running out last night. But if they are, we're about to light one hell of a fireworks display.

"Bird away!" McCampbell shouted, followed by the roar of the RGM-8H *Talos* coming off its rail. The gunnery officer reported his cry a few moments later as the second weapon departed. On the *Missouri*'s stern, the twin launcher rotated to await the next pair of radar-seeking missiles.

Not quite as loud as the guns, White noted, *but the guns can't smack someone over 80 miles away.*

"Red Crown reports they've launched their own missiles."

I'm sure the Chicago *and* Albany *are about to make a mess of things up by Hanoi way.*

Each RGM-8H weighed in at over 8,000 pounds complete with its booster, with a length over thirty feet. While not returning the radar signature of an aircraft, the missiles were more than large enough to show up on every search radar from Hanoi to Vinh as they arced up on its outbound path. Misreading what their intended targets were, air defense controllers called out rapid warnings to the MiGs awaiting the USN's building strike.

It was only after the missiles reached apogee and began plunging downwards that Alexei's most recent lover, Helga, recalled an intelligence warning passed by Stasi agents a couple weeks before. Unfortunately, the East German controller did not have time to pass the warning to any of her Vietnamese compatriots, issue a radio call or, for that matter, even attempt to save herself. The *Talos'* 465-pound warhead would have been more than enough to shred the antenna, the radar van, and most of its occupants. The almost 1,000 pounds of aviation fuel that spewed out in an incandescent circle ensured not even dental records would help identify any of the controllers inside.

The process was repeated six times in a little under five minutes, as the U.S.S. *Albany* and *Chicago* contributed four more *Talos* missiles to the initial attack from north and east of Hanoi. Like a flurry of spears at the eyes of several cyclops, the attacks swiftly blinded the North Vietnamese air defense system's ability to detect strikes far out to sea. Almost as critically, the salvos served to discombobulate the already airborne MiGs, a process that was accelerated by the *Albany* and *Chicago* beginning to engage fighters at long range.

"Well, that has to be an unpleasant surprise," McCampbell laughed, looking over a radar operator's screen at the plot. "Sir, we'll have a gunnery solution for Haiphong in ten minutes."

Speaking of unpleasant surprises, White thought to himself, *these super long-range shells are going to be a very big one.*

The fine folks at the Bureau of Ordinance had found themselves with a large supply of brand-new 12-inch shells at the conclusion of World War II. Originally intended for the *Alaska*-class, the scrapping of the *Guam* and *Hawaii* had provided an abundance of relatively large shells. Since it was unlikely the *Alaska* was ever going to be restored from her status as a museum ship, BuOrd had decided to convert the rounds to something the *Iowa*-class could use. By virtue of a saboted jacket and some minor machining, the *Missouri* and her sisters had a weapon that could reach up to forty miles.

Those bastards are going to expect us to have to get close enough so their brand-new missile boats can snipe at us from within the harbor, White thought, smiling as he imagined the look on some North Vietnamese "admiral's" face. *Instead, we're going to start walking rounds up and down your docks like a cat on the piano.*

The current shells that *Missouri* had taken on from the *Mount Baker* were a mixture of special rounds, the space for which had been created by the artillery bombardment the night before. First in the chute were roughly fifty cluster munition variants, dispensing a mixture of white phosphorus, high explosive, and delayed timing bomblets. Behind them in *Missouri*'s were three dozen airburst high explosives, intended for use against Cat Bi airfield's open-air revetments and anti-aircraft positions. By the time all the rounds were expended, White expected to be in range for both the *Missouri* and *Des Moines* to begin wreaking havoc with their normal weapons.

"Blue Crown, Blue Crown, you have four bandits, speed four-oh-oh knots, heading one-oh-five true, relative bearing three-five-oh, altitude one-oh-oh-oh, range one-oh-oh from HAVOC."

Heimdall's radio transmission caused White to jerk his head around. The AWACS had detected a flight of four aircraft, likely jets, heading southeast across North Vietnam at very low altitude. The hostile jets were so low that they were currently below the radar horizon for TG 64.2's own radars, which is why the AWACS had given the *Missouri*'s current daily codename in its range report.

Somehow, I do not think they're just going on a joyride, White thought as the *Missouri*'s crew began to prepare to engage aircraft. The talkers and the OOD spoke rapidly and moved smoothly around the air plot to update the task group's position. White braced himself as the *Missouri* began a sharp turn to present her bow towards the threat.

"Heimdall is vectoring *Spectres* towards the incoming contacts."

"The *King* and *Waddell* are requesting permission to engage once in range."

Those are two reports that don't go well together, White noted. *Need to let the flyboys do their thing.*

"Tell the *King* and *Waddle* to hold fire—there's going to be plenty of targets for their missiles later, I suspect," White barked.

"Sir, ESO reports we have multiple *Square Tie* radars, range four-oh miles, bearing three-five-five true."

"That would be the missile boats," McCampbell said, gulping down the last of his coffee.

"Do you think they'll come out of the harbor, Guns?" White asked, once more noting the changing plot.

"Not until we demonstrate we can hit from outside their range," McCampbell replied.

"Holy shit," someone shouted. All eyes turned towards the radar operator who had uttered the expletive, and the electronics seaman had the decency to look embarrassed.

"Spit it out, son," White said gently, waving off the petty officer going towards the young sailor.

"*Something* just came across my screen and splashed all four of those bandits, sir," the young man replied.

"That was Chevy Flight, sir," another talker informed White, then continued as the captain glanced at the plot, then the callsign list.

Flight of F-14s off the America, White thought. *But where's their orbit?*

"Why aren't they on the plot?" he asked.

"Sir, you said to limit the plot to sixty miles for friendly forces," McCampbell replied, shock creeping into his voice. "They're well out of range for *Sparrow*."

"Well, however they did it, that was pretty impressive," White replied, then looked at the clock. "Guns, I believe it's about time for your second curtain-raiser."

"Yes, sir, it certainly is," McCampbell said, smiling.

"You may fire once we are in range."

3

PILUMS, BEAGLES, AND WASPS

No plan survives first contact with the enemy, Damon thought to himself, leaning into the lazy turn Spinster had put their *Tomcat* into. *First Skull Two's radar goes to shit, then Connor can't get the damn strike organized, and now the damn Chinese are getting frisky.*

Technically, the Chinese weren't getting "frisky" yet. All thirty fighters they had launched had pointedly remained in Chinese airspace. Indeed, if the USN hadn't had a pair of *Hawkeyes* orbiting forty miles in Hainan's direction, they probably wouldn't have even known the MiGs were airborne. However, electronic surveillance systems accompanying the E-2Bs indicated the fighters had been joined by twelve Chinese bombers. Rear Admiral Lang had thus reinforced the northern combat air patrol (CAP) with six "Bounty Hunter" F-14s and a flight of *Spectres*.

There's honoring the threat, Damon thought uncharitably as Spinster once again reversed his turn and began climbing, *then there's being scared of past ghosts.* In his opinion, the *Albany* and *Chicago* were more than capable of gunning down a dozen bombers before any of them got close to hitting range. It was a big ocean and, as decisively demonstrated to the North

Vietnamese Air Force, the USN owned the skies above it. There was definitely no reason to take twenty-four *Phoenix* missiles and park them *away* from where they were about to be needed.

"How we looking over there, Rigger?" Keg asked. He and Skull Two were orbiting thirty miles off the *Hawkeye's* starboard wing, with the two sections "figure eights," ensuring there was a pair of *Tomcats* facing towards North Vietnam at all times. While the *Spectres* were nominally protecting Heimdall, in reality Combat Tree could see four times as far as the older fighter's radar.

Damon glanced down at the notepad strapped to his knee and did some quick math. For at least the twentieth time, he made sure Skull Three's radios were set on their lowest power setting that limited their ability to be intercepted much past twenty miles.

"We've only accounted for roughly half of the demons," he replied, referring to the code name they'd established for speaking of *Floggers* over the radio. "They're arch demons, but still only half."

Always makes me nervous when we're talking about the Tree on the radio, Jigger thought, shaking his head. *Especially when we're pointing out we can tell Soviet and NVAF* Floggers *apart.*

The Soviet *Floggers* used a different transponder than either the J-6 / MiG-19 *Farmer* or MiG-21 *Fishbeds*, with the NVAF's "export" *Floggers* using yet another type of signal. As the Flight 300 *Tomcats'* powerful AWG-9 radars were currently in standby mode, all four F-14s had appeared as just another flight of *Spectres* to the recently deceased North Vietnamese radar controllers. This had allowed Damon to feed data from the Tree to his radar display without drawing attention that there was a flight of F-14s south of the now advancing USN strike. In conjunction with the controllers on Heimdall, he designated all airborne *Floggers* with a "700"-series contact.

If the Soviets are able to pick up and record our comms, they're going to figure out that something's strange about our contact numbers, Damon thought. *It'll be unfortunate, but I'll let someone with a higher pay grade than mine figure out what disinformation they're going to spread about this ambush.*

"Connor needs to hurry the hell up," Spinster muttered from the front seat. "Those *Crusaders* off *Oriskany* don't have all the fuel in the world."

"I just hope we clear the *Floggers* for them," Damon replied, glancing for a moment at their fuel state. "Gonna be a waste carrying all these missiles up here to still have them end up dancing with MiG-23s."

"It's like carrying six goddamn bombs," Spinster agreed. "But holy shit, glad to see they worked just like test runs on those four *Fishbed*s."

Yeah, that felt almost like an execution rather than an engagement, Damon thought. *Helluva lot more reliable than the Sparrows, even if those idiots made it a simple math problem.*

Not that Damon really blamed the *Fishbed* pilots. Flying overwater was hard, and he doubted they'd had a really good read on where the *Missouri* had been. They'd likely not even realized death was coming for them unless their radar warning receivers had picked up the *Phoenixes'* onboard radars going active.

"Blue Crown, Blue Crown, be advised you have six more contacts heading your direction, angels one-oh-oh, speed four-two-oh, bearing oh-four-oh relative, heading one-seven-oh true, range six-oh miles," Heimdall warned.

Those gents, on the other hand, will have a much better idea now that Missouri's *sending high-explosive hurt to all the Communist boys and girls in Haiphong*, Damon thought. *Christmas comes early, assholes.*

His casting a battleship as a malevolent Santa's sleigh was interrupted by Captain Connor's voice.

"All fighters, all fighters, this is Courage CAG," the man drawled. "Pilum, I say again, pilum."

About goddamn time, Damon thought as *Spinster* pulled a hard reversal and advanced the *Tomcat*'s throttles. Glancing back between the fighter's twin tails, Damon watched as Skull Four matched the maneuver and slid into line abreast formation.

The skull and crossbones is fitting for what we're about to do, he thought, grinning evilly. *Guess we'll have to just take what the Commies are giving us, and that's about to be a bunch of Soviets on a platter.*

"Heimdall, you're going to have to let the black shoes take those contacts," Damon stated. "All fighters, Skull Three, stand by for target assignations."

"Skull Flight, check in!" Keg ordered on the Flight 300 net as the *America*'s air group net became very busy with acknowledgment.

"Skull Two, radar still tango uniform, missiles armed."

Rampage and Argo have to be going nuts, Damon thought. *Good thing the Tree will still feed target information even without a functional radar.*

"Skull Three, six ready to fire and radar ready to go hot."

"Skull Four, same."

Okay, Gilligan, calm down, Damon thought. *Sound like you're a high school freshman getting ready to go into a state championship game.* He glanced to his right at Skull Four and got a wave from Sunburst, Skull Four's RIO. The experienced lieutenant was likely talking to his excited pilot as he prepared to fire their six *Phoenixes.*

Thank God no one changed their minds about this plan at the last minute, Damon thought, busying himself in the cockpit. Their F-14s, in their current configuration of six AIM-54 *Phoenixes* apiece, could not have landed aboard the *America* without jettisoning at least two of the large missiles. Damon had been terrified some higher-level idiot would have gotten even colder feet than they had about restricting the F-14s from getting too close to the North Vietnamese coast.

Whether worried about some AIM-54 going stupid and giving the Soviets a working copy, Damon thought, *or concern about us about to straight up murder some Soviet pilots, it would track with the bullshit so far.*

"Skull Leader, Hickok Leader, we have contacts one-oh-oh through one-two-four," Commander O'Kane called out. Damon turned to look out the starboard side of the cockpit as Spinster accelerated to keep up with Keg.

Warlock has to hate that they're going to burn through all those AIM-54s on old fighters, he thought. *But we've got to sell the fire distribution.*

"Roger, Hickock leader," Keg replied. "Skull Leader, gate."

Damon was pushed back into his seat as Skull Flight engaged their afterburners as one, pointing their noses upward to gain altitude as they closed with the North Vietnamese coast.

"Hickock Leader, Fox Three," Warlock stated. His call was followed by several more as the five other F-14s accompanying him all released their payload of four missiles apiece. Damon paid little attention to the acknowledgment, busy locking up their first victims.

"Skull Leader, Fox Three."

"Skull Two, Fox Three."

Satisfied with his target, Damon took a deep breath, then pressed the launch button on his console in front of him. Skull Three lurched upwards as the first big *Phoenix* was ejected from the belly weapons station, gaining separation before its massive rocket motor ignited. The next thirty or so seconds was mayhem as each *Tomcat* repeated the process six times, accelerating to give the missiles good initial velocity. As the last *Phoenix* came off the jet, Damon looked up out of his cockpit just in time to see Skull Four's sixth missiles come off their wingman.

"Sonofabitch," Spinster snarled as the big missile just kept plunging towards the Pacific below them. "Four, your last missile didn't ignite."

"This is Skull Leader, I had one failure also," Keg said. "Break starboard on my mark...*break, break, break*."

In perfect synchronization, all four F-14s reefed around into a hard starboard turn, pivoting exactly on a line at fifty-one miles from the North Vietnamese coast. Turning his head against the gs, Damon tracked the twenty-two AIM-54s arcing off towards what was hopefully going to be a merge with some very surprised *Flogger* pilots.

Forty-two AIM-54s successfully launched from the four Flight 300 and six Bounty Hunter *Tomcats*. Whereas Flight 300 had given their *Phoenixes* maximum initial energy and launched at high altitude to maximize the odds they'd destroy their intended *Flogger* prey, the Bounty Hunters' missiles' targets were more correctly addressed "to whom it may destroy." As such, the Bounty Hunters continued to close the North Vietnamese coast with their AWG-9 radars illuminating at maximum power.

With most of their experienced radar operators dead and the remainder scrambling to regain control of the sixty airborne MiGs, no one tracked the relatively small contacts arcing in from the ocean at over 80,000 feet. For their part, the North Vietnamese, East German, and Yugoslavian pilots currently airborne in their *Fishbeds*, *Farmers*, and *Floggers* received no warning of their impending doom before the AIM-54s' own active radars illuminated during their terminal maneuvers. Six of the *Phoenixes* suffered their final, ignominious malfunctions at this point and became incredibly expensive, inaccurate rockets.

The remaining thirty-six AIM-54s, on the other hand, ended their existence as instruments of abject terror. The first to die was a North Vietnamese regimental commander at the head of twenty-three MiG-21s. One moment the man was barking orders for his subordinates to climb and begin heading north in preparation of vectors to the rear of the American strikes just at the edge of the surviving North Vietnamese radars. The next, his *Fishbed* was a puff of black and orange, followed in quick succession by the rest of his flight. Twenty miles away to the southeast, this process was repeated with a flight of hapless MiG-19s, but this time with the sudden onset of debris snuffing out the engines of four more *Farmers*. So it went as the Bounty Hunters lived up to their name, collecting a total of twenty scalps between their targets and those aircraft that crashed due to foreign object ingestion or collisions with falling debris.

Far, far worse was what befell the Soviet "volunteer" regiment. In one of warfare's quirks that occurred due to different ranges, angles, and speeds, the *Floggers* had roughly twenty seconds to observe the deaths of their erstwhile North Vietnamese brethren. Even worse, in a handful of cases the MiG-23s' *Sirena* radar warning systems functioned. Unfortunately for those pilots, the *Phoenixes'* massive warheads and high speed just meant these men mostly died aware of what killed them. In a flurry of expanding rod warheads, disintegrating aircraft and, belatedly, screams over the radio, twenty-six MiGs became eight. That number swiftly dropped to six as frightened, shocked pilots collided trying to evade missiles that had already wrought their havoc.

Dodging at unseen, undetected assailants suddenly became the norm in the skies over North Vietnam. With no word from their controllers, limited internal radar capability, and poor cockpit sight lines, many *Farmer*, *Fishbed*, and *Flogger* pilots jumped at ghosts that were either not there or, in a few cases, were piloted by their comrades. All the while, actual *Spectres*, surging ahead of the incoming *America*, *Oriskany*, and *Midway* strikes against targets around Hanoi, began to select targets.

"There go their jammers," Damon noted over the intercom. The North Vietnamese had belatedly activated several electronic warfare systems, the interference starting to cloud the edges of their *Tomcat*'s AWG-9 radar set.

"Not our problem," Spinster said, mirth in his voice. "Right now, the only thing I'm looking forward to is getting some damn fuel, then landing back aboard *America*."

Damon laughed.

He's in a much better mood, Damon thought. *Scoring kills will do that.*

"Why, Spinster, don't you feel a little bit of remorse for what we've done?" Damon asked mockingly. "Hardly fair to blow a bunch of folks out of the air without so much as a 'by your leave.'"

"Fair fights are for suckers, Jigger," Spinster replied. "If I wanted to fight by rules, I'd have been born back in the Middle Ages."

"Texaco's ready with gas, folks," Keg said. "State fuel."

As Skull Squadron rattled off their fuel states, Damon glanced at the radar screen again.

I'm thinking that static has to be messing with the Missouri *and her friends. I mean, I don't recall the North Vietnamese having any strike assets, but I'd be concerned if they did.*

"Skull Leader, Skull Leader, this is Blackbeard Lead," a familiar voice came faintly across Damon's headphones. He jerked up at the radio call, glancing at his radar just in time to see four friendly IFF come up at the edges.

What the hell?

"Blackbeard" was the callsign of VF-84's second flight, led by Lieutenant Commander Connor "Poison" Barrett. That the four F-14s were on his radar, much less showing up ready to take station, meant the nuclear-powered carrier had not only kept rushing at flank speed through the night, but launched her fighters a couple hours earlier.

"Glad to hear you, Blackbeard!" Keg replied, joy clear in his voice. "First round back at Subic's on me. Let's get you on Heimdall's net."

U.S.S. Missouri
35 miles east of Haiphong
0700 Local

"Sir, we can't spot our fall of shot effectively," Commander McCampbell stated, clearly exasperated.

"Can we triangulate any of the jammers?" Captain White asked, looking at the plot. "We've still got a couple of those homing *Talos* left, don't we?"

McCampbell looked thunderstruck as the *Missouri*'s main battery roared once more.

"Sir, gotta be honest, I'm not sure anyone's tried that with the *Talos*," the gunnery officer replied.

"I'm just a dumb electronics major," White replied with a shrug, "but I'd have to think that those things are transmitting on known frequencies."

McCampbell nodded, clearly chewing on the problem.

"Sir, we're down to our last dozen long-range shells."

White turned around at the talker's report.

Surely we haven't been firing that long, he thought, looking up at the bulkhead clock. *Oh, wait.*

"Skunk contacts!" a different talker reported, his voice rising a couple of octaves. "Bearing two five oh relative, range three oh miles, speed four oh knots!"

"*What?*" White asked, surprised. "Where in the hell did those come from?"

"Sparks reports that the Skunks were probably lost in the jamming," Lieutenant Commander Farrell reported. He held a sound powered phone to his ear, eyes narrowed as he studied the map.

"Bring the task group to course oh two oh true, speed thirty knots," White barked. He could feel cold sweat starting to run down his back as he continued the ramifications of what was occurring. "Stand by to repel missile attack."

"Sir! More skunks, bearing two oh oh relative, range two five miles!"

The jamming is wreaking havoc with our radar range, White realized.

"Vampire! Vampire! Vampire! Bearing two oh oh, range two five miles!"

The squawking call from the speaker momentarily silenced the CIC. "Vampire" meant that at least one or more anti-ship missiles were inbound, with follow on information due to follow. White blinked rapidly at the news, his pulse loud in his ears. Then training kicked in.

"Prepare to fire chaff!" he barked. "AA batteries cleared to engage once in range."

"Sir, permission to engage skunks with main battery," McCampbell queried.

Fuck it, they're in range of the new shells…

"Granted!" White barked.

Shit, the rest of the task group…

"All task group vessels clear for anti-air action! Fire at will," White barked, gesturing towards the talker to relay his order.

As McCampbell began passing orders to the director, White moved rapidly to the radar display. Eight bright white dots were advancing rapidly towards the center of the screen, coming right for the *Missouri* and her escorts.

Only eight missiles?

"Sir, Frisco flight reports they are attempting to jam missiles!"

Who the hell is Frisco… Wait, the Prowlers.

White had no idea why the EA-6Bs were dubbed Frisco flight, but quickly stowed his curiosity as he tried to think through the geometry before him. Coming back to his previous internal question, he tried to remember how many missiles the missile boats carried. His recall was interrupted by the firing gong, then the *Missouri* shuddering as her main guns fired. A moment later, there was the roar of a *Terrier* leaving the stern, followed all too soon thereafter by the secondary battery opening rapid fire.

Oh shit...

Unbeknownst to Captain White or, for that matter, any American, the *Missouri*'s initial broadside was the reason for the discombobulated counteroffensive by the Vietnam People's Navy's missile corvettes. Three of the battleship's first rounds had been short, exploding two hundred yards away from the intended dockyards. Unfortunately for the NVN's chief admiral, the head of the missile squadron, and their Soviet advisors, that distance had placed the one of the modified high explosives shells right through the bridge of *Special Missile Vessel No. 1*. In addition to decapitating the NVN, the resultant explosion had sparked a mass exodus by the NVN's seven remaining *Osa*, four *Komar*, and eight P4 torpedo boats.

It was the four *Komar*, under the control of an intrepid but ultimately insubordinate commander. Ignoring increasingly strident orders from the senior captain attempting to rally the captains southwest of Haiphong, the small flotilla had flung all eight of their missiles at the large contact just barely on their radar screens. In a stunning display of what good maintenance could accomplish, every one of the weapons successfully launched as the *Komars* continued closing.

Based on a failed experimental jet fighter, the *Styx* were relatively simple weapons. Initially fired along the range and bearing provided by the *Komars'* radar, the missiles were halfway along their journey when they activated their onboard seekers. Once more, proper care for the missiles meant that each weapon smoothly adjusted their course to head towards what was by far the largest radar return ahead of them.

Unfortunately, this singlemindedness sent every missile on the same relatively linear, easily predicted path. It was only the inherent shortcomings of the *Terrier* missile systems and TG 64.2's multipurpose guns that limited the *Styx*'s casualties to the trailing pair of missiles. Fortunately for the United States Navy, active defenses were only part of the equation, and simple systems required only simple countermeasures. From the missiles' perspective, the single *Missouri* return suddenly became three as the battleship fired her Mark 33 chaff countermeasure system. Four missiles dutifully followed the reflections without hesitation, passing through the reflective clouds to thunder harmlessly into the ocean. Another, presented with far too many targets for its seeker to handle, opted to simply continue along its current path out into the Pacific where it, too, harmed nothing but fish.

It was the sixth missile, opting for "all of the above," that brought a sudden stop to Operation Hammerhead. Passing astern of the *Missouri*, the last *Styx*'s seeker head sought a new target. Getting a return off the *Turner Joy* to the battleship's starboard, in accordance with its programming and purpose, the *Styx* decided the destroyer would do as prey. Before onlookers' horrified eyes, the missile made an adjustment, suffered a near-miss from the *Turner Joy*'s anti-aircraft guns that caused its nose to dip, and hit the 4,000-ton destroyer under her bridge at the waterline.

The *Styx*'s warhead had been designed with large carriers or heavily armored surface combatants as its expected prey. A shaped-charge design, it was strangely mounted behind the missile's fuel tank rather than at the weapon's front. Against a heavy opponent, this was expected to allow the missile's momentum to pierce a flight deck, an outer hull, or superstructure before the charge detonated against armor plating. For the *Turner Joy*, it meant that the first problem presented to her crew as a massive fireball of unspent liquid rocket fuel burst through the compartments adjacent to the impact point.

This impromptu crematorium was still creating a large body of work for Western Union when the half-ton warhead detonated at its sharp down angle. In no particular order, the detonation sent a hot white jet aft that severed the destroyer's keel, blast and spall upwards that eliminated her bridge and CIC as functional entities, and more fragments fanning outwards for fifty feet.

The last damage would have been horrific wherever it occurred. That it was a mere thirty feet to the thinly protected 5-inch magazine turned the damage to catastrophic. The *Turner Joy*'s death would initially manifest as a brilliant, white hot horizontal deflagration spewing through the destroyer's starboard side. Then before anyone aboard or around her could react, a massive brown and black eruption quickly obscured all but the *Turner Joy*'s bow from view. Even this lasted for maybe five seconds before the bow whipsawed backwards into the massive cloud, jackknifing from the conflicting forces of forward momentum, sudden separation from the rest of the ship as the keel snapped, and the blast.

. . .

"Sir, the *Turner Joy* has been hit!"

White had just enough time to turn towards the talker before the young sailor, his face suddenly turning white as a sheet, gave an amplifying report.

"Sir, the *Turner Joy* blew up," the young sailor said, his voice quiet from shock.

Missouri shook as her 16-inch battery fired for the third time since the missiles had been reported.

That all happened so fast, White thought, trying to wrap his mind around what they had just witnessed. Then gripping the table and taking a deep breath, he forced the shock away.

"Task force to course oh-nine-oh true," he barked. "Tell the *Maddox* to stand by to rescue survivors.

"Sir, ESO reports there are Square Tie radars bearing one-nine-five relative and closing."

That's right, the damn group to the southeast, White thought, glancing back at the plot.

"Guns, we need those jammers gone now!"

"Working on it, sir," McCampbell replied, holding his hand over a handset's mouthpiece. "We think we can get *Talos* off in five minutes."

We might not have five minutes, White thought.

"How much chaff do we have left?" he asked, the compartment vibrating once more from *Missouri*'s main battery.

"We have four more volleys left, sir," the talker replied after a quick query to the bridge.

"Got the bastard!" McCampbell exclaimed, drawing White's gaze.

The gunnery officer sheepishly amplified his report a second later.

"Hits on Skunk 12, sir," McCampbell said. "We're almost out of the long-range shells."

We can't trade a destroyer for a single missile boat. Need some help.

"Sir, Hangman Actual is asking for a status report."

Speak of the Devil, White thought, gesturing for the radio.

"Hangman Actual, this is Hammerhead Actual," White began. He quickly ran through the situation, ending with, "Request immediate attack support, my location."

"Sir, Skunks 10, 11, and 13 are fleeing," Lieutenant Commander Farrell reported.

"I can get you six attack planes off the deck in ten minutes," Rear Admiral Lang replied. "Can you keep the range open until then?"

"No, sir," White replied grimly. "I need to rescue survivors."

"You can come back for survivors, Commodore," Lang responded. "Frisco will keep jamming those boats chasing you. I need you to keep from getting shot full of missiles."

White exhaled heavily, bile rising in his throat.

Hope the Turner Joy *doesn't have five brothers from Iowa on it*, he thought grimly. *Here, that goes badly for your career when you leave those in the water.*

"Yes, sir, understand my orders are to keep enemy boats at range," he stated.

"On my authority, yes," Lang replied, indicating he knew exactly what White was thinking about. "We'll get you help as soon as we can."

"Sir! Heimdall reports many, many bogeys! Bearing one-seven-oh true, range four zero miles!"

Koschei Wing
0710 Local

It has been a terrible day, Misha thought as the coast of North Vietnam disappeared behind him. *But perhaps now we go and make it better for us all.*

His IL-28 shook as the lead flight of NVAF MiG-23 *Floggers* hurtled past barely fifty feet above him. Wings swept back, engines glowing, the four fighters put their noses up and rapidly gained altitude, drop tanks shimmering as they dropped behind them. Five more flights streaked by in pursuit of their leader, also climbing towards where fighter control was certain the Yankee jammers and electronic aircraft were.

"Comrades, maximum speed!" Misha ordered, advancing his own throttles. "Assume line abreast formation, altitude five hundred feet!"

"Holy fuck," Alexei said, his voice in awe. "The suitcases..."

Misha looked up and saw what had startled his bombardier. Eight of the MiGs had just ceased to be, with another two falling as flaming comets from the sky.

The radio! Why do I hear nothing on the radio but static? Misha wondered.

"We are being jammed," Alexei stated as if he'd read his mind. "It is all right, the rest of the wing is with us."

Well, thirty-five of them, he thought bitterly. Thirteen of the IL-28s had suffered various maintenance issues. As he watched the debris that had formerly been high-performance fighters falling from the sky, Misha had the terrible feeling that number was about to rapidly dwindle.

Prayer is talking to an empty sky, he thought, feeling as if he was going to void his bladder at any moment. *But I would certainly engage in it right now.*

"Three minutes to target!" Alexei reported from the bomber's nose. "Do you see the smoke?!"

"No, not yet," Misha replied, squinting.

Wish I could use binoculars right now, he thought, envious of his bombardier.

"Come left, come left, maybe ten degrees!" Alexei replied.

Misha began the slight correction, hoping his regiment would follow him.

Is that the smoke? he pondered, squinting at the horizon. *Where are their fighters?*

The answer came moments later in the form of several blurred, hurtling forms falling like arrows all around the formation. Happening so quickly that Misha did not have time to process what was occurring before it was over, five IL-28s were blotted from the sky.

"That nearly hit us!" Alexei screamed from the bomber's nose.

"*What* nearly hit us?" Misha responded, glancing back to see that their bomber was suddenly alone. Their flight had simply vanished, the aircraft no longer anywhere in sight.

"A goddamn missile, Misha! We were nearly hit by a goddamn missile!" Alexei cried. Misha's hands began to shake on the controls. He glanced to starboard just in time to see another black-and-brown explosion just in front of an IL-28. The explosion shredded the bomber's front end, almost certainly killing the pilot and bombardier but somehow not igniting the aircraft's wing tanks. Misha tore his eyes away from the tumbling mass of wreckage, scanning the sky to see where the missiles were coming from.

Misha would have required both the vision and mental acuity of a god to decipher the myriad threats firing at his approaching bombers. The *Floggers'* acceleration had carried them forward like a legion of their namesakes right at the E-2 *Hawkeye* and accompanying *Spectres*. Even with the rapidly accelerating Blackbeard flight lobbing sixteen AIM-54s, the *Spectres* firing AIM-7 missiles, and even TG 64.2 lobbing a handful of SAMs, over twenty-five MiG-23s managed to launch a pair of AA-7 *Apex* missiles as they closed.

In the end, the volley was largely sound and fury signifying little. Between Frisco flight's jamming, the *Spectres'* own internal countermeasures and evasive maneuvers, "Heimdall's" pilot shutting off the radar and diving hard away, and shaken NVAF pilots forgetting steps in missile preparation, only three missiles hit their target. While a tragedy for the pair of *Spectres* hit, in and of itself the attack was not the NVAF's finest moment.

This changed as Colonel Bay, howling in frustration at his inability to communicate with his men, closed to visual range with his USN counterparts. The *Flogger* had never been intended as a dogfighter, especially at medium altitude. Unfortunately for the surviving USN fighters, the *Spectre* was allegedly proof that "even a brick could fly with sufficient thrust." With two-to-one odds, the Americans were immediately defensive, freeing up a flight of *Floggers* to pursue the rapidly descending *Hawkeye*, while another pair of keen-eyed MiG-23s spotted the distant Frisco flight. Desperately calling for assistance, the *Prowlers* also dived from altitude.

In the end, the USN's electronic aircraft would suffer split fates. Colonel Bay would increase his score by placing two heat-seeking missiles into the *Hawkeye*...and promptly get smashed from the sky by a *Standard* from the *Waddell*. The *Prowlers* would be similarly saved, as missiles from the *King* convinced the four MiG-23s to break away. Still, the damage was done as Frisco flight shut off their jammers as a precautionary measure.

"Clear the network! Remember your training!" Misha roared. "I will shoot the next man who gives a spurious report!"

The cacophony of radio traffic and frantic cries that assailed his ears had startled Misha so badly, he nearly crashed. With the enemy ships on the horizon, he was desperately attempting to regain control of his subordinates.

"Missiles! Missiles to starboard!" Alexei warned. Misha turned and felt his heart swell with joy.

"The missile boats! They are from the missile boats!" he replied, slamming his seat arm with joy. There were at least a couple dozen of the weapons, hurtling from his right side.

The Americans will have to decide who they want to shoot at! he thought.

"Attack pattern Bear!" Alexei snapped over the radio. "Go! Go! Go!"

Attack pattern Bear was the code for the regiment's first two squadrons to attack the largest target, while the third squadron attacked the next largest. As soon as he'd set it, Alexei had a revelation.

What if there's nothing left from one of the squadrons? he thought, pushing his nose down. *Oh, well, then we... Chekist bastards!*

The skies in front of his bomber had suddenly erupted in black puffs of smoke and explosions. He recognized the *Missouri* in front of him, the battleship's stern towards him at roughly ten miles. A large missile roared from the launch rail on the vessel's stern, heading towards the North Vietnam even after another, smaller missile streaked off the rail towards the six *Styx* missiles heading towards the vessel. To the battleship's starboard, a smaller vessel was hit by one, then two more *Styx*. Geysers suddenly sprang up all over the American formation from anti-ship missiles slamming into the waves for various reasons.

Oy! Misha thought, his mind struggling to process the insanity of what was before him.

"Four thousand yards!" Alexei shouted, jerking him out of his reverie. "Opening the bomb bay doors!"

The *Missouri* was hit by a *Styx* forward, the missile striking at an angle as it detonated. Misha did not have time for more than a brief moment of joy before the IL-28 was starting to pitch and yaw from the disturbed airflow of the bomb bay doors. He glanced at the altimeter and airspeed.

Three hundred feet, five hundred and fifty knots, he thought. *I hope the drogue chute works.* The American battleship looked like she was wreathed in flames, with all of her secondary guns firing. Her bow, ablaze from the missile hit, began to turn to starboard, wake rooster tailing behind her.

"Torpedo away!" Alexei shouted.

The IL-28 lurched upwards as their weapon dropped away...then the world came apart. Misha did not hear the blast, merely felt the hot stab of steel fragments down his left side and the rush of wind against his face as his canopy was shattered. Glass and metal slammed past him as he realized that the bomber's nose was shattered.

Alexei, he thought. Then suddenly there were orange flames licking past his head, and he realized the IL-28 was afire even as it arced upwards. Another blast and shudder to his rear told him that it was definitely time to abandon the aircraft. Misha reached for the left seat handle, shoulder screaming in agony as he used his right arm to desperately keep the IL-28 from rolling to the side. Pulling upward, Misha let go of the stick and braced backwards in his seat. His vision blurred as the canopy's remnants blew away.

I am sorry, Alexei, he thought helplessly. *I failed...*

The seat firing briefly knocked all possibility of thought from him as his spine compressed. Misha screamed into his oxygen mask as he was thrust into the IL-28's slipstream. Barely able to move his limbs, he quickly found himself hanging underneath his parachute at roughly eight hundred feet. His bomber was rolling and corkscrewing down, its entire aft end on fire before hit slammed into the Pacific.

You bastards, Misha thought, glancing to where the *Missouri* was going into a port turn. With a start, Misha realized that there were no other bombers near him. Spotting at least three spreading pools of fire and two other parachutes, Misha surmised several of his bombers had not made it.

How many dropped?

The answer to Misha's question was six IL-28s, including his, had released their heavily modified "wake homing" torpedoes at the *Missouri*. Of these, two had been dropped at the outer edge of the weapons' 4,000-yard range. Despite the best efforts of the finest Soviet naval engineers, the weapons' sensor suites simply were not up to the task of attempting to determine the *Missouri*'s wake in the confusing acoustic chaos of exploding *Styx*, falling aircraft, secondary explosions from the sinking *Maddox*, and other distractions. Another weapon, dropped at optimal range, had its drogue chute shredded by a missile pursuing its carrying aircraft. Lastly, one weapon's warhead, for reasons that would never be known to a living soul, simply decided to prematurely detonate as it began to zigzag up the *Missouri*'s wake.

That left Misha's and an Ethiopian crew's weapon with any chance to catch the American battleship. Resembling hungry eels in their pursuit pattern, both weapons rapidly accelerated to their fifty-knot speed, established the parameters of the *Missouri*'s wake, then began chasing the radically maneuvering battleship. Lacking sonar herself and with seemingly more pressing problems such as the six remaining North Vietnamese torpedo boats attempting to close within range of their far less sophisticated weapons, the *Missouri* had no idea of the danger approaching.

Come on, come on... Misha thought, spotting the wake that seemed to be cutting across the American battleship's. *Wait, is she... Oh no, OH NO!*

The *Missouri* had completed its turn to unmask her main battery. Unfortunately for Misha, the bearing to what he could only assume was approaching craft of some sort meant he was looking almost directly down the bore of six 16-inch rifles. His stomach clenching, Misha tried to shrink himself in a ball...to no avail. The broadside's roar deafened him, the blast wave physically shoving him and his parachute straight backwards. The punch to the cloth collapsed it, and Misha fell the last forty feet to the Pacific like a sack of stunned potatoes.

No sooner had the *Missouri* fired than the first torpedo hit her. Striking just above her No. 1 screw where her torpedo protection system tapered to almost nothing, the weapon's 1,000-pound warhead functioned exactly as designed. One moment the battleship's crew was going about their desperate task of fending off the approaching torpedo boats. The next, over two thousand men were thrown about as if they'd been in the back of a pickup truck that hit a ditch doing fifty miles an hour. The quicker and luckier managed to either grab something or tuck as they fell to the ground. The vast majority were tossed into bulkheads, tables, or other furniture with enough force to cause massive bruising, break bones, or rend flesh on sharp edges. The supremely unlucky joined their comrades directly above the explosion in death as their skulls smashed into unyielding steel or, in two cases, the fall down ladders snapped their necks.

The crew had just enough time to realize they'd been struck when the second weapon, its sonar damaged by the blast, struck the port rudder. Although not as violent as its predecessor, the second fish was arguably more damaging. Instantly shuddering the port rudder, the water hammer from the detonating fish slammed the starboard rudder hard enough to jam it and warp its posts. Already damaged by the first torpedo, the *Missouri*'s stern was ripped further open. The always relentless ocean began to pour into her port aft spaces, immediately threatening the fire and engine rooms on that side from progressive flooding.

Misha coughed into his oxygen mask, tasting blood as his ribs and shoulder screamed in agony. Although not close enough to be killed by the twin torpedo explosions, the twin blows had exacerbated the damage from his forty-foot fall. Thanking whomever had decided that ejecting pilots might need their own oxygen supply after ejecting from an aircraft, Misha tried not to think about the fact he was under the water and starting to sink.

You have time, Misha, he thought. *Just not much of it.*

Fighting against his left arm's attempts not to function, he first released his chute and struggled away from the sodden lines. Free at last, his life vest carried him upwards and to the surface. Breaking into a noisy, chaotic bedlam, Misha immediately began to search for his survival pack, hoping that it had functioned as designed. Showing that the day had not turned wholly against him, he spotted the olive-green dinghy floating roughly fifteen yards away.

Now if only I don't get killed by some random fragments, he thought as the *Missouri*'s main battery turrets roared again. An easy swim in normal times, getting to the raft was anything but with whatever was going on with his ribs, shoulder, arm, and leg. Similarly, hauling into the small raft exhausted him so that he nearly slipped back into the warm Pacific. Finally in, he rolled over on his back, screaming as he gasped for air. He struggled to unsnap his oxygen mask, finally ripping it off with the *hiss* of the emergency bottle pushing its contents into open air. The roar of jets passing overhead caused him to look up, and he saw a pair of MiG-23s rushing back towards North Vietnam with a pair of bigger, variable geometry American jets trying to gain on them.

They're going to run out of fuel if the Americans chase them much further, Misha thought disapprovingly, then laughed at himself. *Look at me, ever the flight instructor even as I'm looking dying of exposure dead in the face.*

Something bumped the bottom of his dinghy, hard. His mouth suddenly dry with dread, Misha rolled over and spotted one, then two large and lean shapes in the water beneath his raft. One of them came and nudged his small craft again with its long, pointed nose.

Oh no, please no, Misha thought, clawing for his Makarov. To his eternal relief, one of the creatures broached the surface, air escaping out of its blow hole as it rolled to look at him. Then spooked by a large explosion, both dolphins disappeared back into the depths.

"Comrade Sorokin!" a voice shouted from behind him. "Comrade Sorokin, the cruiser is blowing up!"

Misha gingerly and carefully rolled over to look at who was speaking to him. He struggled to see the fellow pilot roughly two hundred yards away. But he could see the direction the man was pointing, and once again gently turned in the dinghy. Just barely on his visible horizon, he could indeed see an American cruiser, its fore half a blazing ruin. There was a second, more massive explosion a moment later, the blast obscuring the vessel's entire front half.

Where is the Missouri? he wondered. *I saw the wasps stung her at least once. Maybe our fish finished her off.*

Rotating once again, Misha saw that his hope was misplaced. Clearly down by the stern and listing to port, the battleship continued to steam away from him. The missile boats' solitary hit continued to burn, but he doubted that the massive battlewagon was going to actually go down. Six aircraft flashed over the battleship, then passed over his head, clearly American.

Those look like they're about to go wasp killing, Misha thought grimly. *Well, that damnable cruiser and a couple of destroyers is much better than I expected this to go. Now if only someone remembers to come pick us up before the Americans do.*

4

LESSONS, SURVIVORS, AND PRISONERS

The bosun's whistle sounded its high, stringent tones as Rear Admiral Lang stepped out of the SH-3 *Sea King*'s starboard side. Coming to attention, his stomach doing flips, Captain White saluted the flag officer as Lang set foot on the *Missouri*'s titled deck.

Well, it was a nice command while it lasted, White thought, noting Lang had brought his chief of staff with him. *Wonder if he's even going to let me finish my report before I get shitcanned?*

The *Missouri* was currently steaming in a small patrol box southeast of Yankee Station. Under the constant, watchful eye of several P-3 *Orion* staging up from Subic Bay, a constant combat air patrol maintained by the four USN carriers now on Yankee, and a matching surface warfare patrol of at least four attack aircraft, *Missouri* was only awaiting the arrival of additional escorts to begin the slow, painful transition back to Mare Island.

"Welcome aboard, Admiral," White said. Lang returned the salute and then, to White's surprise, extended his hand.

"You fought a helluva fight, Nathan," Lang said as White took the pre-offered hand. "Let's head to your day cabin and talk about what the hell happened."

"Aye aye, sir," White said, somewhat surprised at the genial greeting.

"I've got folks from Pearl to D.C. panicking about 'the new missile threat,'" Lang said, making air quotes as they began heading for their destination. "Congressmen already talking about this shows the era of all big ships are dead like you didn't blow half those bastards out of the water and the *America*'s air wing get most of the rest."

That's a very...positive way to look at it, White thought, fighting to keep his face expressionless.

"Damn North Vietnamese are still putting out the fires you started, and your trick with the *Talos* and their jammers has them scared to turn the damn thing on," Lang continued, shaking his head. "Their army's running out of supplies now and the South Vietnamese are kicking their ass up around their shoulders because of it."

Cold comfort for my hundred and fifty dead, White thought. *Even less so for the* Des Moines *crew.* The heavy cruiser had taken three-quarters of her crew with her to the bottom of the Yellow Sea. From what the survivors had pieced together, three of the wake homing torpedoes had hit her, knocked out her power, and thrown the vessel into confusion just before the VPN's third *Styx* volley had arrived.

I'm not sure Missouri *would have survived four* Styx *hits,* White thought grimly. *Certainly not to the bunkerage and turrets.*

He fought back a sudden burning in his eyes.

So many friends gone.

They reached White's day cabin, the Marine guard outside coming to attention as Lang approached. The rear admiral waved the gunnery sergeant down.

"Watch the hatch, sir," White warned as he gestured for Lang to precede him. "The list throws everyone off until you get used to it."

Lang nodded, even as his chief of staff gave White a reproachful look... then promptly snagged his foot and stumbled as he passed through.

"You know, Rodney, I'm going to have to leave you back aboard the *America* if you can't heed simple warnings."

"Yes, sir," the commander replied.

"Sir, I can send down to the galley for some coffee," White stated. "My steward is currently assisting in the mess hall due to casualties."

Lang shook his head at the offer, then gestured for Rodney to shut the hatch.

"Nathan, we've got bigger things to worry about than a cup of joe," the flag officer stated. "Those damn missile boats were a nasty shock. From what I understand, a lot of folks in the surface warfare community have been telling BuOrd for years that the *Terrier* and *Tartar* weren't up to snuff."

"Yes sir, I've been keeping up with the debate in *Proceedings*," White replied. "I didn't think I'd be a practical example."

"I should have given in to my first impulse and given you an extra destroyer," Lang replied. "And air cover."

"Sir, I'll admit to also thinking we had plenty of assets," White replied. "I thought the new guns would be able to keep up with the missiles, since the *Styx* is subsonic."

White laughed bitterly.

"Apparently, it's still good for shooting down airplanes," he noted. "But not the missiles."

"Fleet intel is still trying to figure out who shit the bed about the damn commies having a new air-dropped torpedo," Lang replied. "You couldn't have done anything about that."

White laughed bitterly, then caught himself.

"Even if they'd known no one would have thought it was a wake homer."

He took a swig of water while he regained control of his emotions.

"We thought they'd lost their nerve and were jettisoning," White said.

"Some of them did," Lang replied. "At least, according to the radar tapes from the *Waddell*."

"Not surprised," White replied. "Lucky thing they did. Two more of those torpedoes on my starboard side and we'd be towing this ship back to Cavite."

He drank once again, thinking back to the CIC shaking like a bungalow in an earthquake.

"Pretty sure the commies have some sort of torpex equivalent," White observed. "There's no way, even at the stern, we should have had that much damage. Lucky it was a clear snap of the propeller shaft."

"Oh?" Lang asked, cocking his head.

"If the shaft had not snapped clean off, there's a possibility we would've had a runaway or it would have ovaled the opening. I think that might have been enough to kill her with progressive flooding, sir."

Lang nodded, turning to make sure his aide had captured White's thought.

I didn't even see that bastard break out a notebook, White thought. *I'm more tired than I thought.*

"We're going to need some sort of countermeasure for the torpedoes soon," White continued. "Damn countries throughout the Third World are going to consider them giant killers, and they're far cheaper than the *Styx*."

Pausing as Commander Rodney continued to scribble, White gathered his thoughts.

"Any surface ship operating in missile territory or around medium bombers will need a missile system that either operates independent of individual beams or something that can provide multiple beams at once," White continued. "Our missile unit was not able to service targets fast enough, plain and simple. If we hadn't had the *Prowlers* in support, this ship would likely be on the bottom of the ocean."

Lang nodded in agreement.

"The *Tomcats* validated every dollar we spent on their *Phoenix* missile over the last decade," Lang replied. "I think the bureaus can get together and rig something up for surface ships. That abomination with putting the *Sparrow* on tin cans has the same problem you brought up with the *Terrier* and *Standard*."

"A lot of this can be solved by putting electronic warfare systems aboard," White replied.

"Why do you think your 5-inchers didn't work as well as we'd hoped?" Lang asked.

"If we're going to have guns, we need something that shoots faster and a helluva lot more shells than the 5-inch," White replied. "I'm not sure proximity fuzing should be the biggest concern versus putting streams of shells on a target. I understand that mount is supposed to let the destroyers and frigates do shore bombardment, but we're not going to be able to get within twenty miles of a shoreline unless something radically changes, anyway."

Lang's next question was interrupted by the hatch opening to reveal Commander McCampbell.

"Gentlemen, we have traffic from the *Enterprise*," McCampbell stated. "Vice Admiral Stockdale is requesting Rear Admiral Lang's presence for a planning conference aboard the Big E."

"Thank you, Commander," Lang said, then turned back to White. "It would appear that my tour will have to wait."

"Yes, sir," White said, feeling as if a massive weight had been taken off his shoulders. One more, Lang showed almost preternatural understanding of his internal state.

"I've informed Pearl that I will testify as a friend of the defense if there are any attempts at a negative action against you," Lang said simply. "I can acknowledge that I was too aggressive with wanting to catch the North Vietnamese on the back foot after we disrupted their fighters. If what our radar telemetry and SIGINT tells us is true, those bastards are terrified of the *Tomcat* and the F-14s haven't even gone feet dry."

That's wonderful for the brown shoes, White thought bitterly.

"Still, I wanted to apologize to you," Lang said solemnly. "I overestimated your ability and underestimated the enemy's. It's my fault, and I don't want you to beat yourself up about it."

White could see McCampbell and Rodney's shock at Lang's frank words.

They always said Lang was a straight shooter, White thought. *I never realized how much integrity he had before now.*

"Our nation faces an existential threat," Lang said, his tone almost explanatory. "We're not going to preserve our way of life if people aren't trying to learn from things that happen. We'll talk again when I get an opportunity."

"Thank you, sir," White replied, turning to follow the admiral as he made his way out the hatch.

"My staff informs me that we'll be able to get you underway for Pearl in about seventy-two hours," Lang continued. "Godspeed, Captain White."

U.S.S. ENTERPRISE
VF-84 READY ROOM
1500 LOCAL
22 APRIL

"I'm just sayin', there's a point where it becomes murder," Spinster said, shaking his head.

"They're commies," Keg shot back, grinning. "Can't murder something that doesn't have a soul in the first place."

This, children, is how genocide happens, Damon thought to himself, keeping his face passive as he kept reading the Louis L'Amour hardback. He'd been waiting almost a year for his former brother-in-law to finish reading the book and get it in the mail to him. Of course it had arrived aboard a *Greyhound* the same day Flight 300 had left the Big E.

"What do you think, Jig...erm, Hoplite," Spinster asked.

Damon did allow himself a small smile at his new callsign. Keg, as squadron commander, had the authority to go through the process of giving him another callsign. He'd offered Damon the choice of "Bowman" or "Hoplite" in recognition of his planning the long-range ambush of the NVAF. Damon, for his part, had pointed out that there were literally people aboard the *Enterprise* with that former as a last name. On the other hand, as a fan of Homer, he'd been happy to take the second.

Guess I'm not getting any reading done today, he thought, looking at the clock then putting a bookmark in his novel.

"Every human being has worth and a soul, Spinster," Damon responded quietly. "We're no better than the reds if we start speaking blasphemy."

"Okay, but before the chaplain comes in here and files a complaint about you interfering with his mission," Keg said, rolling his eyes, "what about whether the kills should count?"

Damon laughed.

"You're asking a RIO whether we should count kills where I was the one who actually pressed the button?"

The two pilots looked at each other as if just realizing just how silly the question had been.

"Of course I think it should count," Damon continued. "That's like saying we shouldn't count any kills made with a heat-seeking missile. Whether they saw it coming or it just arrived, there's still MiG parts coming down like rain."

Keg slapped the table, startling the rest of Flight 300 where they sat around the Acey Deucy table.

"That's what we should have made your new callsign," he said. "Dammit."

"Um, boss, I don't think that would be a good plan," Spinster said.

Keg looked at Damon, then back at Spinster.

"Why not?" he asked.

"Just trust me, sir," Spinster replied.

The two men were interrupted by a familiar commander stepping into the hatchway.

Oh shit... Damon thought.

"Gentlemen, Rear Admiral Lang!"

The eight members of Flight 300 got on their feet as Lang entered the ready room. The admiral, for his part, waved them all down.

"Please, please, take your seats back," Lang said. "I know you all don't have long before you're taking off for your shift over the *Missouri*. I was just here for another skull session with Vice Admiral Stockdale and thought I'd take the opportunity to come thank you all personally."

That's the third meeting in the last three days, Damon noted. *There has to be something big in the offing.*

"You men did good work," Lang said. "Your efforts have made the NVAF largely ineffective, and they didn't even scramble any fighters against our latest strike."

Keg and Damon shared a knowing look, drawing a smile from Lang.

"No matter how beautiful she is, kick a man in the dick often enough and he stops trying to fuck your daughter," was how Keg had prophesied the NVAF's eventual reaction to getting killed from far beyond visual range. To their credit, the MiG drivers and the controllers had tried several countermeasures. Fortunately for the USN, it appeared that they remained ignorant to Combat Tree and the role their own transponders were playing in their demise.

"This is good news, as in about six hours the Air Force and we are going land what we hope will be a Sunday punch," Lang continued. "Our brothers in blue are committing three bomber groups from Guam to simultaneously striking Vinh, Haiphong, and Hanoi."

Holy shit, Damon thought. *B-52s? The Air Force is still pissed they couldn't buy as many of those bombers as they wanted over the last twenty years and now they're going to risk them in a conventional attack for the first time since Hainan?*

The shocked look on everyone else's faces told Damon that he was not alone in his surprise.

"If we shake the bastards hard enough, they'll probably ask for a ceasefire," Lang continued. "I imagine our friends in Hanoi are not pleased that the only other place even threatening problems is North Korea."

Which, to be fair, if they come into the party, things are going to get a lot less crowded here at Yankee Station, Damon thought grimly.

"In any case, that's a later problem," Lang finished. "Just know that your efforts are appreciated, and hopefully we'll all be meeting on the *Enterprise*'s flight deck back in Pearl when this is over."

Oh, wow, Damon thought, standing again as Lang turned to leave. It was naval tradition dating back to World War II for prominent medals to be awarded in front of a ship's company. The Medal of Honor, of course, was reserved for the White House. But everything from the Navy Cross down to the Bronze Star usually happened in front of the men that a recipient served with.

"Well, too bad your twins couldn't see reason," Keg observed, turning to Damon. "I think having you as their dad just might have made their lives even easier at Annapolis."

"Part of the reason they went to Colorado Springs," Damon replied ruefully.

Of course, Colorado is also a long way from Dixie. Much further than a city that was still segregated when I went to the Academy and hasn't improved much since.

"I'm a little concerned how those bomber escort missions are going to go, given our *Phoenix* situation," Damon said, changing tack. "Any word on us getting more missiles?"

"None," Keg stated. "Ran it up through the CAG and he got stonewalled by Vice Admiral Stockdale's staff."

"I guess having every *Tomcat* go down to two -54s is a technique," Damon stated. "But not one for long-term success."

"Reading between the lines on the intel briefings," Keg noted, "it appears the Chinese and Soviets are sitting this one out other than providing replacement aircraft."

"I can't imagine they've got a lot of pilots surviving getting smacked by a *Phoenix*," Damon noted. "Considering some of the telemetry is showing a single missile killing two bandits, it would appear that big-ass warhead is doing exactly what it's designed to."

"Like I said, *murder*," Spinster said from behind them.

"All right gentlemen, let's go make sure no one 'accidentally' sinks our battleship," Keg said, pointedly ignoring Spinster. "We'll..."

Keg was interrupted by Rear Admiral Lang's aide reappearing in the hatch.

Commander Rodney looks like he's seen a ghost, Damon thought, concerned.

"Commander Hanson, Vice Admiral Stockdale and Rear Admiral Lang request your presence on the flight deck," Rodney stated, stumbling slightly over his words. "Lieutenant Commander Peters will have to lead the CAP flight for the *Missouri*."

"What?" Keg asked, incredulously. "That's not going to work out really well."

"Nightmare got shot down by flak a half-hour ago," Rodney replied.

"Sounds like it hit him just as he was rolling in on the target. Unlikely there were any survivors, apparently the flak hit him and detonated his bombload. You're the senior squadron leader in the task force."

Connor is dead, Damon thought, sick to his stomach at the relief that washed over him. *Asshole or not, he had a wife and kids.*

"Can't exactly lead strikes if I can't get within fifty miles of the North Vietnamese coastline now, can I?" Keg asked.

"PACFLT has just rescinded that order for every F-14 but your squadron," Rodney replied. "For obvious reasons. There are still restrictions at the carriage of the AIM-54, but we can go over those once we get to *America*."

"I'm going to need a CAG bird," Keg said. "Preferably a Bravo, but I can make an Alpha work in a pinch."

"We're already working that for a Bravo," Rodney stated, clearly getting annoyed. "But we can talk about this as we're getting up to Rear Admiral Lang's bird."

Keg nodded, lips pressed together. He turned to Damon and extended his hand.

"It's been an honor, Hoplite," he said simply.

"Same, sir," Damon replied, taking the proffered hand.

Hope you don't get shot down, he thought grimly. *More than one way for the Tree secret to get out.*

Fraternal People's Hospital
Hanoi
1900 Local
5 May

Once more, the damnable air raid sirens brought Misha out of a fitful sleep. The combination of blackout curtains and a lantern on its lowest setting made it quite dim in the room, but he could make out two shapes sitting next to the bed. His usual nurse stood nervously near the door behind the two men, glancing repeatedly out into the hallway, as if waiting for help.

I must be having a hallucination, Misha thought. *For surely Leonid Brezhnev himself is not sitting in my hospital room.*

"Comrade Sorokin, it is good of you to join us."

This is the first time I have been under long-term drugs, Sorokin thought. *The hallucinations are so vivid.*

"Thank you, sir," he replied gingerly. "I hope you can forgive me for not standing up."

The large, barrel-chested man laughed, his beetle eyebrows moving up and down with the expression of mirth.

"From what the doctors have told me, you are lucky to even be alive," Brezhnev replied. "So yes, not standing for your Secretary General is completely excused."

"We do not have long, Lieutenant Colonel Sorokin," the other man said. He looked somewhat familiar, but Misha's drug-addled brain could not quite place him. "Indeed, I cautioned against coming here at all, but Comrade Brezhnev was insistent."

So he could kill me with his own bare hands? Misha thought despondently. *Sentence me to death himself? If so, shame to waste all the morphine.*

"I am told that your regiment was able to strike a great blow for the Soviet people," Brezhnev stated. "Indeed, for our fraternal brothers everywhere."

"I...I do not know, sir," Misha stated. "I can confirm we hit the battleship. But the Vietnamese..."

"Fought bravely," the second man interrupted, sparing a glance towards the nurse. "But it was your regiment that avenged Pusan."

What is he... Oh, wait, the cruiser, Misha thought. *So it* was *the* Des Moines.

"I am glad to hear that I will never buy my own drinks in Pyongyang," Misha joked, startled at how unsteady his own voice was.

A loud discussion began at the end of the hall. Misha recognized the Vietnamese voice, but not the men responding with truly atrocious pronunciation.

"Ah, I see that they have found your doctor," Brezhnev noted, looking at his companion. "Yuri, we should probably go introduce ourselves."

If this is because of the drugs, I really should get injured more often, Misha thought. *Nurse still looks like she was some provincial village's contestant in "good enough in bad light" contest, but having the two most powerful men in the Communist Bloc appear as conversational visions is rather amazing.*

Brezhnev reached into the pocket of his plain overalls. Taking out something, he reached towards Misha. Hands shaking, the older man affixed the medal to Misha's pillow.

He smells of cigarette smoke and high-end vodka, Misha thought. *Maybe I should have listened to those Ethiopian mystics who claim to be able to control dreams. At least then I'd be seeing my beloved Katarina when I'm clearly losing my mind.*

"I am sure the paperwork for this will catch up to you along with your promotion, *Colonel* Sorokin," Brezhnev rumbled. "Oh, and hopefully by the end of this week those drinks will be in *Seoul*, not Pyongyang. There are some surprises brewing for our capitalist friends."

Misha's brain lacked the horsepower to really understand what the Secretary General was saying.

Interesting, he thought. *But irrelevant...*

The brilliant sunlight streaming into the room was one indicator of passing time. The next was the somewhat sharper pain of whatever had gone wrong internally. The next was the sound of feminine laughter from the nurse's station.

Night shift never laughs, he thought, inhaling slowly. *Then again, if my city was getting bombed so hard the ground was shaking every evening, I'd probably be rather dour, also.*

He turned his head to the side and saw nothing but a bare pillow.

Well, that was indeed a vivid hallucination, he thought. *I'm almost scared to ask for more painkillers, but everything still hurts. Just less.*

The laughter was getting closer, the two women talking in rapid fire Vietnamese. In his addled state, Misha couldn't quite follow it, but he could have sworn one woman was talking about him being a lazy layabout.

That's rather ru...

"If he continues to lay in this bed much longer, I am going to have to hire someone to warm mine," the same woman said. "Do you have anyone you could recommend?"

Before Misha could fully react, a tall, familiar form was standing in the doorway. A wave of emotions crossed over the beautiful brunette's face as she brought her hand up to her mouth.

All right, I'm going to have to get different narcotics, he thought, feeling panic.

"Misha..." Katarina Sorokin breathed. Then in a moment she was across the room, going to hug him then stopping short. Taking a deep, shuddering breath, she instead reached out and touched his face. Misha jerked backwards.

"You're real," he breathed, seeing shock and hurt cross her face. "You're really here...and your hands are frigid, as always."

Katarina laughed, her tears coming then as she put both her hands on his cheeks.

"Is this too frigid for you, you idiot," she snapped in Russian, then kissed him.

"I remind you he is on bedrest, Madam," the nurse chided from the doorway. "Please do not set back his healing; his doctor is already in trouble."

The nurse closed the door before Katarina could turn back around to ask who had visited Misha before she had.

"Who came to visit you last night?" Katarina asked, raising an eyebrow.

Misha laughed, then immediately regretted it.

"I'm sorry," Katarina said, concerned.

Misha looked at her.

You're real...you're here. With that realization, his eyes started to burn.

"Misha," Katarina said, reaching out to touch his arm as he began to sob. The emotion caused his ribs to begin aching, which in turn made his breath catch.

"Alexei..." he gasped, then could not continue.

"I know," Katarina said, gingerly bringing his head to her chest. "I know."

For several long minutes, Misha let himself continue to be lost in the pain. Finally, gaining control of himself, he leaned back from her embrace.

"I had the craziest dream last night," he said, laughing. "To answer your question, I dreamed Comrade Brezhnev and Yuri Andropov were here."

Katarina looked at him, her face expressionless.

"They were here, Misha," she said, pulling a box out of her purse. "The nurses gave me this to give back to you. They changed your pillow and bedding while you were unconscious yesterday."

"Yesterday?"

"You've been unconscious for another day," Katarina said. "It's not important."

No, I guess it is not, Misha thought, taking the box. He opened it and was surprised to see a Hero of the Soviet Union medal laying on the interior white field.

"My brave husband," Katarina said proudly, running her hand over his face. "I would show you just how proud I am of you, but I think your doctor would kill me. He actually swung at the Secretary General."

"What?"

"Yes," Katarina said, laughing. "He'd apparently left directions that no one was to disturb you while you healed upon order of Van Dong himself."

She regarded Misha seriously for a moment.

"Honestly, I am surprised the man is still alive."

So am I, Misha thought. *Shame, as he is a good doctor.*

A wave of fatigue washed over him.

"My beloved, I fear I must rest," Misha said, then turned to look up at his wife. "How long are you here for?"

"As long as you are, my love," she replied simply. "As long as you are."

AUTHOR'S NOTE

This story is a continuation of "The Lightnings and the Cactus," "Mr. Dewey's Tank Corps," (both in *Dispatches from Valhalla*) and "Mr. Dewey's Fire Brigade" (which can be found in this work's sister anthology, *Thin Red Tales* and the forthcoming short story collection *Missives From the Green*). It is highly likely that I will step into this timeline again, but probably not until after I'm done with the fourth *Usurper's War* novel. But that's going to be at least a year, probably two...so sorry to tease on the "Hainan Incidents."

Folks familiar with 20th Century American History will catch a lot of the allusions in here. For military nerds, the U.S.S. *Columbia* is the U.S.S. *Forrestal*. Since Dewey wins in 1948, Truman does not have an opportunity to drive Secretary James Forrestal into a mental spiral, culminating in his suicide. McDonnell Douglas sells its missile interceptor to the Air Force, a service which is not wholly subsumed by Strategic Air Campaign due to no "Massive Retaliation" under the Eisenhower Administration. The *Spectre* moniker is a nod to the F-4 *Phantom's* short-lived "F-110" designation.

ABOUT JAMES YOUNG

James Young is an American author of science fiction, alternative history, and post-apocalyptic fiction. His primary series is the *Usurper's War*, which is set in an alternate history where Adolf Hitler is killed by an RAF bomb in November 1940. He is also the author of *The Vergassy Chronicles*, a military sci-fi universe set in the 3050s.

In addition to his own work, James has edited anthologies including bestselling authors Sarah Hoyt, S.M. Stirling, and David Weber. His non-fiction writing credits include *Eagles, Ravens, and Other Birds of Prey*, winning the United States Naval Institute's (USNI's) 2016 Cyberwarfare Essay Contest, and various articles in *Armor*, *The Journal of Military History*, and *Proceedings*.

LinkTree (i.e., one stop for everything - scan or click):
https://linktr.ee/jamesyoungauthor

Blog (i.e., the thing I wish I updated more often - scan or click the link):
Jamesyoungauthor.com

PER MARE PER TERRAM

Jan Niemczyk

1ST MAY 2005. HMS *BULWARK*,
TRONDHEIMSFJORD, NORWAY

"...Operation FISH HOOK was the first major NATO counteroffensive not mounted in direct response to a Warsaw Pact operation. In one form or another, the planners at HQ Allied Forces North had been working on something like FISH HOOK since almost the day Norway had joined NATO, so they had a lot of past experience to draw on when working on the final plan. FISH HOOK would also see the Striking Fleet Atlantic emerge from its fjord bastions to support the operation and hopefully provoke the Soviets into mounting a major attack against it rather than the assets of FISH HOOK itself.

"The timing of FISH HOOK was always going to be an issue—firstly the initial Soviet thrust had to be brought to a halt along the main defence line in Troms. Once that was achieved, it was hoped that Soviet combat troops could thoroughly locked into a battle and FISH HOOK would be launched once they were fully committed to breaching the line, by 1st May it was felt that this had been achieved and with the arrival of the balance of II Marine Expeditionary Force, 7 Canadian Brigade Group and the leading elements of 10th (US) Mountain Division, it was felt by Commander in Chief Allied Forces Northern Europe (CINCNORTH) that the initial phases of FISH HOOK could begin. To this end, the UK/NL Amphibious Force began to board British and Dutch ships which had been sheltering in the

Norwegian fjords and apart from 4 Marine Expeditionary Brigade, which was already ashore, the remaining portion of II MEF would remain aboard its ships.

"The paratroopers of 5th (UK) Airborne Brigade were also due to be relieved by 7 CBG, although some Paras would remain with the Canadians and continue to broadcast radio traffic that would suggest that the brigade was still in place. Two battalions of Norwegian infantry were also attached to the FISH HOOK force."

—Extract from *The Battle for the North—the Nordic countries and World War Three* by Generalløytnant Christian Stubø, Norwegian Army (retired) and Generalmajor Thor "Eeo" Eriksen, Royal Norwegian Air Force (retired).

Major Robert Williams, RM, O.C X Ray Company, felt happy to be back aboard HMS *Bulwark*, after the days of inactivity 45 Commando and the rest of 3 Commando Brigade had to endure. After the brief period of the war's first few days, "Booties" had been placed in Commander North Norway's (COMNON) reserve; they had continued to train and were occasionally mobilised to prepare to reinforce the Main Line of Resistance in Norway. However, the forces already in position had always managed to deal with Soviet attacks every time without their help. The fact that 3 Commando Brigade and its attached Dutch elements were being loaded onto British and Dutch amphibious ships suggested that something big was brewing. Williams's excitement was somewhat tempered by the fact that he had been summoned to a briefing aboard the flagship of the Commodore Amphibious Warfare (COMAW), Commodore Michael Ramsey; last time that had happened, he had ended up leading a dangerous company-sized raid to evacuate a Norwegian coastal fort under siege by Soviet forces; his ribs were still sore after being blown off his feet by a mortar round.

"Evening, Bob," Lt. Colonel Winchester, Williams' Commanding Officer, said in greeting. "I'm afraid we've been given a rather 'interesting' job by brigade."

"Why do I not like the word 'interesting,' sir?" Williams replied, rhetorically. Following Winchester to the Amphibious Operations Room, the Major was interested to see that along with the usual suspects— Brigadier Larkin, the Brigade commander, Commodore Ramsey, COMAW, several RN and RM staff officers and their liaison officer from the Norwegian Costal Rangers, *Kapteinløytnant* Petersen—there were also three officers from the Royal Fleet Auxiliary present. Williams recognised one of them as Captain Sam Duncan, master of RFA *Sir Tristram*. The other two he had not seen before, but guessed that they were the masters of the other two Round Table Class LSLs assigned to the UK/NL Amphibious Force.

Well, something is clearly afoot, he mused, feeling suitably intrigued that the masters of these three ageing ships and not their counterparts in command of the modern *Bay*-class were attending this meeting. Williams took his seat and waited for the briefing to begin.

"Good evening, ladies and gentlemen," Commodore Ramsey said, taking his place at a podium at the far end of the AOR. "No doubt you are wondering why you are all here; well, you people have been assigned a special task as part of Operation FISH HOOK."

Ramsey brought up a map of northern Norway on the screen behind him, and Major Williams got his first look at what he was going to be asked to do.

"Bloody hell," he muttered under his breath. "Looks like a good chance to earn a V.C. Posthumously."

4TH MAY. RFA SIR TRISTRAM,
LOPPHAVET, NORWAY

Captain Sam Duncan peered out from the bridge of the LSL into the gloom, trying to make out the village of Hasvik on the nearby island of Sørøya with no luck. Like all Norwegian settlements in Finnmark, it had been evacuated and subject to the "scorched earth" policy intended to deny the Soviet invaders any shelter. The Norwegians had also removed all the navigation markers at the mouth of the thirty-eight-kilometre-long Altafjord and liberally seeded it with mines.

Hope these ship pilots recall where they left all the "presents," Dunlop thought, thinking of the other four ships in this small convoy. *Or that none of them have a heart attack, seeing as only the Norwegians know where the minefields are.*

Ahead of his ship, Duncan could just make out the frigate HMS *Alacrity* carefully picking her way towards the strait between the island of Stjernøya and the mainland. Although he could not see them all astern, his experience allowed him to visualize the other ships in line: RFA *Sir Bedivere*, RFA *Sir Galahad* and HMS *Avenger*.

Every one of us is an old ship, Duncan thought. *Which, of course, makes us all expendable.*

Even if FISH HOOK was a complete success, there was a good chance that the LSLs, at least, would be Constructive Total Losses (CTL).

Thank goodness we can at least defend ourselves somewhat. For this mission, each of the three Landing Ship Logistics had been modified with steel plate and Kevlar armor. Moreover, in addition to the two 40mm Bofors the ships had been armed with at the beginning of the war, additional armament including 20mm cannon, 12.7mm Brownings, 7.62mm GPMGs, and even M134 Miniguns had been emplaced. Perhaps the most interesting modification had been a change to the LSLs paint scheme and pennant numbers, which were now Soviet in style. Furthering the ruse, each ship was now flying the Soviet naval pennant rather than the Blue Ensign of the Royal Fleet Auxiliary.

The additional weapons were manned by RN personnel attached to the ships. Rounding out the crews were all of the RFA sailors who had volunteered to remain with the ships. Duncan thought wryly of the intensive refresher training every RFA member, himself included, had received in both the use of the additional weapons as well as the personal arms they all now carried.

Feel like a bloody buccaneer, he thought. *The Marines are the ones supposed to be doing the fighting.*

The reason for the modifications to the ships were below decks—the Marines of 45 Commando with attached engineers, signals personnel and various support troops from its parent brigade, plus two troops from the Blues and Royals, and another two troops of Challenger 2s from 5 Royal Tank Regiment.

As part of FISH-HOOK, the Marines and sailors would seize Alta and its important airport in a *coup de main*. Once the airport was secure, more troops from 3 Commando Brigade could be flown in by helicopter to expand the beachhead. Simultaneously, at other points along the coast, troops from the U.S.M.C.'s II MEF would be coming ashore, whilst 5th Airborne Brigade would be making the first British combat drop since 1956 to secure an airhead for follow-on forces. The latter included two battle groups from the Norwegian Brigade North.

The operation's next phase would be the most delicate. Under command II MEF, the American, British, Dutch and Norwegian forces would expand and hold their bridgehead, which would cut-off the Soviet forces currently engaged in combat along the main NATO defensive line to the south from resupply.

It will be a thing of beauty if it works, total carnage if it does not, Duncan thought.

"Time to the next course change?" Duncan asked the Norwegian pilot.

"Two minutes, Captain."

"Good."

Duncan was satisfied that so far all was going well, as evidently their disguise was working. He knew there were several Observation Posts ashore and that the fjord was covered by a number of artillery batteries, all capable of blowing his ship and its sisters out of the water.

———

Below decks, Major Williams finished putting his rifle back together, having taken an opportunity during the voyage to clean it. The men of his company, seeing his example, had all begun doing the same. Satisfied that all was well, Williams put the last parts of the rifle back into place and loaded a magazine. Hearing some stirring towards the entry hatch, he looked up and spotted a messenger from the headquarters troops making his way towards him. The man stopped to speak to other sub-unit commanders as he made his way to Williams, leading towards the other impatiently drumming his fingers on his rifle.

"How long?" Williams asked the messenger, anticipating his message.

"Thirty minutes, sir," the sergeant replied.

"Right, I'll start to get my lads ready to move."

*USS Iwo Jima, off
Sørøya, Norway*

The Landing Forces Operations Centre of the LHD was crowded, filled, as it was, with the staff of II MEF, plus liaison staff from the UK/NL Amphibious Force and 5th Airborne Brigade. There were also personnel from the Striking Fleet Atlantic and the ASW Striking Force present.

Lieutenant-General Douglas S. Burns watched the amphibious "plot" as the situation developed. He could see that Marines from 2nd Marine Regiment had seized the airport at Hammerfest by vertical envelopment using MV-22B *Ospreys* and were now fighting their way through the town against troops from 77th Motor Rifle Division. Other troops from 2nd Marine Division had also landed successfully, either by *Osprey*, or LCAC and more men and equipment were now being ferried ashore.

The British and Dutch Marines also seemed to be doing well, having taken Hasvik and a few other small settlements around the entrance to Altafjord to secure for follow-on forces. However, these landings would only be worthwhile if the *coup de main* to seize Alta worked out. Burns could see that effort was now approaching the most dangerous phase as the group of British ships closed in on Alta.

The only fly in this very nice ointment might be the Brits' drop, Burns thought. Radio contact with the paratroopers had been fragmentary, but from what could be gleaned from them was that the wheels had come off this particular part of Operation FISH HOOK. It seemed as if there were far more Soviet troops in Lakselv than had been expected, with casualties amongst the NATO side had been heavy.

"We've sent them into another Arnhem," Burns muttered as he looked at the part of the display showing Lakselv.

"I hope not, sir," the liaison officer from 5th Airborne commented. "One Arnhem is quite enough for the regiment."

"I think you need to modify your plan, Colonel," Burns told him. "Clearly, your second lift can't be an air-landing insertion of engineers. You need infantry reinforcements in there now; what do you have available?"

"Two Royal Green Jackets and the Gurkhas both have a reinforced company's worth of airborne-qualified troops which we can send in right now. Our brigade commander has already been in contact with CinC-UK Land Command, and 1 Para is boarding aircraft as we speak."

The news that one of his British subordinates had gone outside the chain of command of AFNORTH, never mind II MEF, caught Burns by surprise. However, he gave the Brigadier full points for initiative and reacting so quickly.

"Wow, that was quick work, Colonel; pass on a Bravo Zulu to the Brigadier when you get a chance."

"Well, we always included them in our contingency planning; in fact, I believe they have spent the last few hours hoping there was a crisis that would call for their deployment. I'll make sure your 'well done' gets passed along, sir."

Burns chuckled.

"They missed the Falklands, didn't they?"

"Indeed they did, sir; got stuck in Northern Ireland, despite their best efforts to join the Task Force."

"So they won't have wanted to miss this op, then," Burns observed. "Glad we were able to oblige."

ALTA, NORWAY

Alta was garrisoned by troops from 131st Motor Rifle Division, who were currently the immediate reserve for the assault on the Lyngen Line. Much of the division was spread out between Alta and the Main Line of Resistance, leaving only one motor rifle battalion and elements of its tank battalion in Alta itself. Surrounding the town were additional forces consisting of mainly engineers, signals troops, artillery and a variety of other rear area troops. There were also a couple of Border Troops-manned *Grisha II*-class corvettes anchored off the town.

It was the corvette *Rubin* that first spotted the convoy of British ships approaching. As a resupply convoy was expected sometime in the next day or so, the watch currently on duty was not overly concerned, however, they did attempt to contact the ships by blinker light. The reply they received was a little confusing, even if it did seem to be in Russian, so the officer in charge decided to summon the captain. However, this all took time, and by the time he reached the bridge and realized that the signals were not in the code of the day, it was too late: the British frigates were within point-blank range.

114mm shells from HMS *Alacrity* tore into the corvette, blasting it apart and killing most of the crew. HMS *Avenger* engaged the second corvette, *Izmail*, the smaller ship blowing up spectacularly after half a dozen hits. The sound of gunfire could not be disguised and alerted every Soviet soldier in Alta. However, by now the three *Round Tables* ships were only a minute or so from their designated landing beaches.

To offer as much covering fire as possible, both frigates engaged targets in town. Knowing that they did not have to worry about collateral damage due to every Norwegian civilian having evacuated, the frigates' gunnery officers were able to be profligate with their ordnance. Both vessels' priority target was a battery of A-222 *Bereg* 130mm coastal defense guns. Mobile weapons, the *Bereg*s were more than capable of sending all five ships to the bottom within minutes.

Airborne reconnaissance had located the battery, and *Alacrity* and

Avenger blanketed the area with shells. The weight of the frigates' fire more than made up naval bombardment's inherent inaccuracy, as five of the guns were destroyed by this hurricane of high explosives. Unfortunately for the convoy, however, the now-deceased battery commander had decided, for reasons he took to the hereafter, to move one of the guns to a new location.

This remaining *Berg* engaged *Alacrity*, straddling the frigate twice within a few seconds. In less than a minute, the gun scored a hit, a 130mm shell exploding in the warship's funnel, blasting it apart. *Alacrity* rapidly reversed course, smoke and flames pouring from the area around her destroyed funnel. A second shell burst in her hangar as she attempted to withdraw. Fortunately, she was not carrying a helicopter and all of the aviation fuel had been landed, but the impact still killed over a dozen crewmembers.

Before the *Berg* could finish *Alacrity* off, two *Harrier* GR.9s dropped a load of RBL.755 cluster bombs on its location, the anti-tank bomblets destroying the gun, its crew, and its nearby ammunition. While the crew of *Alacrity* fought to put out the fires started by the pair of 130mm shells, the two *Harriers* climbed back to altitude and circled the town, allowing other aircraft to make attacks, attention being especially paid to any armoured vehicles. This far in the Soviet rear area, the only Surface-to-Air Missile threat came from man portable weapons, and by remaining above the effective ceiling of these weapons as much as possible, the NATO aircraft were able to get on with their jobs relatively unmolested.

While the *Harriers* were putting paid to the coastal defense gun, *Sir Tristram* grounded on a gravel beach only a few meters away from the edge of Havenevien airport. Located in an industrial estate on the edge of town, the beach was perfectly situated for the LSL to open her bow doors and drop her ramp. The added mixed armament of cannons and machine-guns engaged a variety of targets, to include a BDRM-2 that had unwisely got a bit too close to the LSL. Before the crew could get off a contact report, the reconnaissance vehicle was riddled by a mixture of 40mm and 20mm shells, which set it alight.

The *Scimitars* and *Challenger* 2s that the ship had carried raced off to secure the airport, followed closely by a company of Marines on foot. The final vehicles off the LSL were Trojan and Terrier engineer vehicles, part of the Royal Engineers team that would hopefully restore the airport.

Across the bay, *Sir Bedivere* and *Sir Galahad* were able to land their armoured vehicles and marines onto either a quay or the car park of a hotel, so that the men did not even get their feet wet. The troops and vehicles from *Sir Bedivere* moved rapidly down the E6 road towards Alta itself, forming a blocking position, while those from *Sir Galahad* moved into Elvebakken, to cover the flank of the troops securing the airport.

———

Major Williams ducked as several 82mm mortar bombs burst rather too close for comfort. He decided that establishing his company HQ this close to *Sir Tristram* was not one of his better ideas, as the ship was now attracting all manner of Soviet fire from mortar bombs and heavy machine-guns down to rifle fire. The sound of her guns returning fire was also somewhat distracting.

"Sooner she gets out of here, the better," he said to his assembled "O" Group. "Well, no matter, we can't stand around here all day, gentlemen, we've an airport to secure. Let's push on."

———

If I leave now, there's a good chance I'm going to end up looking like the Herald of Free Enterprise, Captain Duncan thought. *The damn crew has to get the hatch up manually before we get a hole we can't fix.* His vessel had already been struck by hundreds of small-arms rounds, most of which had punched through the hull with relative ease. If not for the *ad hoc* armor, there probably would have been dozens dead and wounded among his crew.

KABOOM!

The LSL shook and Duncan was briefly blinded by a flash. When his vision cleared, he could see that something, probably a mortar bomb, had burst on the upper deck, starting a fire.

Well, that tears it, we can't stay here regardless of what might *happen*, Duncan thought. *For those mortars will* certainly *destroy us.*

"I need that ramp closed now!" He barked. "Officer of the Watch, stand by to withdraw from the beach."

"But the ramp, sir?"

"I'll take my chances; besides, we'll be going astern. Tell the men below they have five minutes to get the ramp up."

USS WISCONSIN, OFF

SØRØYA, NORWAY.

BLAM!

The half-century-old battleship shook as another 16-inch salvo crashed out, throwing nine car-sized shells at a target onshore. The gun fire support that *Winsconsin* was providing to the 2nd Marine Regiment in Hammerfest was proving to be crucial in their fight against troops from the 77th Motor Rifle Division for control of the town. Every time the Soviet infantry had managed to form a cohesive defensive line against the advancing Marines, their positions had been blasted to pieces by a few salvos from the battleship. To the Soviets' horror, they had found the 16-inch shells powerful enough to throw even armoured vehicles through the air. What they did to men had led to several squads and platoons simply breaking and running despite their commissars' best efforts.

Wisconsin was now methodically demolishing all Soviet artillery batteries within her range. As with the British frigates, the battleship had started with A-222 *Bereg*s. Despite her best efforts, a handful of surviving guns were currently preventing any amphibious ships from landing heavy equipment directly to the quay. Indeed, the 130mm guns were even making the transit of fast vessels like the LCAC somewhat perilous, as well as preventing destroyers and frigates from closing with the coast to provide more responsive naval gun fire with their 5inch guns.

With not much to see from the bridge, Captain Craig Flack, USN, the battleship's captain, had decided that it was best to fight his ship from the CIC. It might be dark and claustrophobic, but at least he could watch the flatscreen TV that was currently displaying the footage being beamed back by one of the battleship's RQ-2 Pioneer UAVs. There was a brief flash on the screen as the latest salvo reached its destination, obliterating the target.

"Good shooting, Weaps," Flack remarked to the Weapons Officer, Commander Leverett. "Shame we don't have color on this thing like the chair farce's *Predators*."

"Thank you, sir, I'll pass that along," Leverett replied. "The new *Fire Scout* will have colour and much better cameras than the *Pioneer*."

"That's nice, Weaps, for whoever gets to have one on their ship, but it does squat for me now. Watching a black and white TV is like being back in the Seventies."

———

As the explosions from *Wisconsin*'s salvo began to subside, Staff Sergeant Dennis Novak, 1st platoon, A/1-2 Marines, rose from the temporary shell scrape that marked the furthest point of his platoon's advance into Hammerfest. Or at least the collection of rubble and charred wood splinters that marked where the town had once been. What structures had survived the Norwegian demolitions during the evacuation of Hammerfest had been destroyed by a combination of NGFS, CAS and the Soviet efforts to defend their positions.

We even got the damn chapel, and that thing survived the Germans, Novak thought sadly.

"Move, move, move!" Novak yelled to his Marines. "Do you want to live forever?"

The shells from the battleship had created some useful ready-made foxholes for the Marines to drop into once they had crossed the open ground between their positions and those of the Soviets. Novak dropped down into one of the holes, discovering that he was sharing it with a disembodied left leg. He fired a couple of short bursts from his rifle before dropping back into cover, finding that the platoon's commander, a young 2nd Lieutenant and his RTO, had joined him.

"Those battleship shells sure help a lot, Staff Sergeant," the platoon commander, 2nd Lieutenant Simon Young, commented.

"Amen to that, LT," Novak replied. "Without the 'Big W,' I doubt we'd have made any progress at all, especially since the Russkies have got armor and we don't. No way would we have been able to ship in heavy equipment, either."

"Any news on that?" Young asked. "I haven't been paying attention due to our friends up ahead."

"I heard on the battalion 'net that an artillery firebase is getting set up at the airport and we should have some tanks and LAVs on the ground pretty soon."

As if on cue, all three Marines heard the distant squeaking of tracks and the whine of gas turbine engines. The first of a platoon of four M1A1 Abrams tanks from Company C, 2nd Tank Battalion, hove into view.

"Now that sure is a sight for sore eyes," Novak commented approvingly.

ALTA, NORWAY

Captain Duncan could see that for some reason RFA *Sir Bedivere*, which was now ablaze, had failed to back off from the quay that she had landed her vehicles and troops on. In a scene reminiscent of Bluff Cove, flames were licking up her superstructure. Duncan's own ship, *Sir Tristram*, was damaged but operational, as was the other LSL, *Sir Galahad*, so he decided that he might just still be able to do some good.

"Take us alongside the *Bedivere*'s stern," he ordered the helmsman. "We'll see if we can take off some of her crew."

"Aye, aye, sir," the helmsman replied. Swallowing hard, the man put the *Tristram*'s helm over. Duncan had five long minutes to think about his decision as they headed towards the blazing LSL. Then there was the sound of metal scraping against metal as *Sir Tristram*'s bow rubbed up against the stern of *Sir Bedivere*. Damage control parties from the former directed firehoses onto the fires burning just forward of the latter's superstructure.

"Hold her there!" Duncan told the helmsman as he watched members of *Sir Bedivere*'s crew leap from the burning LSL onto *Sir Tristram*. Rather fortunately for both vessels, the surviving Soviet defenders of Alta were now too occupied with the attacking Royal Marines and tanks to pay much attention to the two LSLs still close to the shore. The third LSL, RFA *Sir Galahad*, was making her way back up the fjord with the damaged HMS *Alacrity*. Duncan turned from watching the departing vessel to see one of *Sir Bedivere*'s surviving officers, a Second Officer, a rank equivalent to a naval lieutenant, managed to make his way to the bridge of *Sir Tristram* to report.

"How bad is it, son?" Duncan asked.

"We've lost her, sir, she's beyond saving," the man replied. "Only reason she hasn't sunk is because she's beached; engineering spaces and the tank deck are partially flooded, and the fires are likely to burn everything that is not underwater."

Duncan winced at the news.

"Most of the reserve ammunition is in the flooded holds," the man continued. "Captain Batten is getting the last of our crew off at the moment; he'd appreciate you keeping your bow where it is for as long as you can."

"I've no intention of going anywhere," Duncan said. "Do you need any help getting crew off?"

"It would be appreciated, sir."

"Speak to Chief Officer Masters, he's down on the tank deck; tell him I've ordered that he is to give you any help you need."

"Thank you, sir."

The smoke-blackened officer ducked out of the bridge and hurried back down to the tank deck. Duncan turned his attention back to events forward. He could see that while his damage control parties were not bringing the fires under control, they were at least preventing them from spreading aft.

"Not sure how long I can hold her here before we start to damage the bow doors, sir," the helmsman reported.

"Do your best; we'll shore up the doors if we need."

———

I feel like I'm looking at Ypres, Major Williams thought to himself. *Wait, no, Passchendale*. Between the initial Soviet attacks, Norwegian demolition, and now what FISH HOOK had done, Alta looked like a moonscape. At least the lack of civilians meant that there was no need to worry about collateral damage, something demonstrated very well by a Challenger 2 fitted with a dozer blade. Having had a Soviet stronghold pointed at it, the tank shrugged off machine gun fire and a lone RPG before firing a HESH round into the already badly damaged building.

Poor bloody bastards, Williams thought as the structure imploded. His horror increased as the MBT used its dozer blade to bury any surviving occupants alive, then followed that up by driving over the wreckage on the way to its next objective.

The treadheads seem to be a bit more ruthless than I expected, Williams thought.

The Royal Marines did not often work with heavy armor, so they were taking the opportunity to use the advantage the tanks gave them to the full. The combination of surprise, speed, aggression and firepower meant that 45 Commando had very quickly secured a lodgement, allowing more Marines from 42 Commando and an artillery battery from 29 Commando Regiment, RA to be flown in to Alta Airport by helicopter to reinforce them.

There was the sound of ship's horn from the harbour. Williams turned to see that more reinforcements had entered the fjord. With the Soviet coastal batteries eliminated, a second convoy of landing craft, this time belonging to the army, set off from the amphibious holding area. Consulting his notes, Williams realized this was probably the remainder of the 5 RTR coming ashore. Smaller RM manned LCU and LCVP also set off down the fjord as 3 Commando Brigade began to build up its strength in the Alta beachhead.

We're about to be a very large bone choking off the Soviets' throat. With that pleasant thought, Williams turned back to leading his company.

A FEW HOURS LATER

The Lynx AH.7 helicopter carrying Brigadier Robert Larkin, the commander of 3 Commando Brigade, touched down by the Brigade forward HQ. The landings were going well enough that Larkin felt that he could transfer from HMS *Bulwark* to ashore.

"How are things going, Dick?" he asked his Chief of Staff, who had established the forward H.Q.

"Doing very well, sir," Major Richard Capewell replied. "Forty Commando and the Dutch 1st Marine Combat Group are now ashore. 42 and 45 Commando have captured most of their initial objectives. The balance of 29 Regiment and its guns should be ashore soon.

"The really good news is that the first Norwegian troops have arrived at the airport. I watched them raising their flag; got me rather emotional, I can tell you.

Brigadier Larkin smiled. "Looks like we are in good shape, Dick."

———

Major Williams took a moment to look back at the harbour. He could see smoke coming from the beached RFA *Sir Bedivere*, her surviving crew had been evacuated to *Sir Tristram*, which had now departed the fjord. It was a stark reminder that success had been bought at a price, which was still being paid.

Williams' company was advancing up the E6 towards the village of Nerskogen, following three Challenger 2s from 5 RTR. The Marines had come to appreciate the tank's support and firepower. It had been a nice change to put armor before flesh and have three 120mm cannons at their disposal. One tank in particular had proven especially helpful; it had clipped a garden shed, which had against all the odds survived intact, causing it to topple over. To the Marines' delight, they had found a number of almost brand-new shovels, spades and picks which they would be able to use to dig in.

The tanks advanced slowly through Nerskogen while the Marines cleared the village—not that it took very long given there were no intact buildings. However, evidently some Soviet troops had managed to find a place to shelter as an RPG round suddenly shot out and slammed into the side of the turret of one of the Challengers. Rather like shooting a rhino with a pellet gun, all the rocket did was make the tank mad. The turret traversed round and, after a moment, the coax began to spit fire. Under cover of tank's fire, the Marines "pepper potted" their way towards the source of the RPG round. Once in range, grenadiers placed several 40mm grenades into the position.

Williams' attention was drawn from the counterattack by the "pop, pop" of small-arms fire as his Marines engaged other fleeing Soviet troops whose positions had become untenable.

That anti-tank ambush didn't go quite the way they had planned, obviously, he mused with a grim smirk.

A waving hand drew his attention, and he turned to where his radioman, Marine Paul Young, had sought a position to obtain better reception. Whatever the man was now hearing, his facial expression said he did not like it.

"Boss, battle group has just passed a message to go firm." Young said.

"What? We've got them on the run," Williams replied incredulously. "Another few hours and we could link up with the *Septics*.

"Give me that," he said, taking the Bowman's handset. "This is X-Ray One Sunray; repeat your previous message, over."

"X-Ray One Sunray, you are to go firm at your present location until further orders, over."

"I've got the enemy on the run, what the hell is going on, over?"

"Do as you're told, X-Ray One Sunray," the voice of Lt. Colonel Winchester said, irritation clearly evident, even over the radio. *"This is not a Chinese Parliament, out."*

Williams handed back the radio handset, absolutely mystified. On the face of it, the order went against all military logic—once an enemy was on the run, he should not be given a chance to rest, or regroup. All Williams could think of was that something had happened elsewhere that had affected the brigade as a whole.

"Well at least we'll get to use those spades and shovels now," he commented to his radioman.

SKAIDI, FINMARK, NORWAY

The MV-22B *Osprey* landed almost precisely on the intersection between the E6 and Highway 94 (Rv94). Staff Sergeant Novak sprinted down the rear ramp and took cover in the trees while the *Osprey* off-loaded the remaining Marines, who joined him in the trees, sheltering while other MV-22Bs landed to drop off the rest of the battalion.

Novak took a good look around him. The small village, like all settlements he had come across in Finmark, had been very effectively razed. Across the intersection, he could see what might have once been a shop and small gas station.

The briefing given to Novak's platoon had been that they were to secure the intersection between the E6 and Rv94. The use of the word "intersection" had given them the impression that it would be something much grander.

"Intersection, now there's a joke," the Senior NCO grunted under his breath.

"Well, it looked more important on the map," Lieutenant Thomas Dewey, Novak's platoon commander, remarked. The man pointed in one direction. "The E6 is the most important north-south road in Norway and the west coast of Sweden."

"Looks like a two-lane back home to me," Novak said. "But if it's this big all the way up, it means the Soviets can't move much on it."

"Well, we got to get a move on," Dewey said. "The Brits have been told to hold up so the flyboys can concentrate on supporting us."

―――――

1st Battalion, 2nd Marines had the task of securing the intersection to allow other Marine units to advance both north and south, linking up with the other elements of FISH HOOK. Once relieving forces arrived, the battalion would join the advance north to relieve 5th Airborne Brigade.

―――――

Novak and Dewey's conversation was suddenly interrupted by the squeaking of tracks and the rumble of diesel engines that announced the approach of a Soviet column. The first vehicle, a BTR-90, was followed by a pair of MTLBs. Behind them was a long line of trucks, indicating that this was a supply convoy.

"Contact!" Novak shouted, his cry simultaneous with several others down the line.

There was no time for any finesse or to call in any outside support, as one of 1st Platoon's anti-tank gunners immediately engaged the BTR-90 with a *Predator* SRAW. The rocket hit the APC at the base of its turret, cooking off the 30mm cannon's secondary ammunition in a large fireball.

As Russian infantry began abandoning the APC, Novak threw a pair of smoke grenades to blind the MTLBs' drivers. With both the sudden obscuration and the demise of the BTR-90 in front of him, the first MTLB's driver instinctively slammed on the brakes. Half-asleep, his counterpart in the next MTLB did not see the manoeuvre, thus causing a chain reaction that saw both MTLBs and a truck piling up.

"Go, go, go!" Dewey shouted, operating under the principle that attack was the best defense. The Marines pushed forward, destroying the stalled MTLBs with grenades rather than use valuable anti-tank missiles or their AT-4s. With the slight rise interrupting the convoy, the two MTLBs and BTR-90 of the rear escort were able to disgorge their infantry. Unfortunately for the Soviets, when the BTR-90 tried to maneuver around the stalled trucks, it found that the road was too narrow, while the truck drivers attempting to escape the now-attacking Marines did not make the motor rifleman's job any easier. The BTR-90 finally managed to bump across a grass verge onto a minor village road that ran parallel to the E6 and opened fire on the Marines.

"Get that dammed BTR!" Novak yelled as 30mm shells shot over his head.

"We've got incoming choppers!" another Marine yelled.

"Ours or theirs?" Novak wondered.

The answer to Staff Sergeant Novak's question was "both." Almost simultaneously, a pair of Soviet Mi-24VM *Hinds* and two Marine AH-1Z *Vipers* arrived over the battlefield; rather than providing Close Air Support to either side, they instead engaged each other.

The Marine *Vipers* had the advantage. Not only were they faster and more agile than the *Hinds*, but they were also armed for air-to-air combat and their crews regularly practiced for helicopter-versus-helicopter engagements. One *Hind* was brought down by a couple of bursts of 20mm cannon fire, while the second was felled by an AIM-9M *Sidewinder*.

With the immediate threat to them eliminated, the two Marine *Vipers* pulled back and circled, awaiting directions from the FAC on the ground. These were not long in coming, and the troublesome BTR-90 was blasted to bits by a *Hellfire* missile and the two remaining MTLBs riddled with cannon fire. Since the Marines on the ground could handle what was left, the FAC ordered the *Vipers* to fly up the E6 and attack any other Soviet troop columns that posed a threat.

———

Staff Sergeant Novak got to his feet and slowly made his way down the line of trucks, some of which were now on fire. A few of the drivers had not made it out of their vehicles and he could smell the sickly sweet odour of burning human flesh. For a moment, it looked as if all the Soviet troops were either dead, or fled. However, a figure holding a rifle with a banana-shaped magazine suddenly popped out from between two trucks; Novak brought up his rifle and put a three-round burst into the soldier, felling him.

"Now what was the point of that you stupid bastard," Novak muttered as he loaded a fresh magazine into his rifle.

With no further threats the marines spread out, taking up defensive positions to protect the intersection. Two hours later they had the satisfaction of seeing their handiwork bear fruit as a column of M1A1s and AAV-7A1s approached down Highway 94; part of the column joined the marines already in place, while the majority headed south down the E6 to link up with the British and Dutch marines.

· · ·

5TH MAY. SITREP FROM
COMNON *to* CINCNORTH

From: COMNON
   To: CINCNORTH
   For information: CO II MEF, COMSONOR
   Subj: Op FISH HOOK

FISH forces now all but fully landed, Forward HQ 3 Cdo Bde now established ashore. Secure perimeter in place, landing of supplies continues. Armored battle group formed from troops of Brigade North now landing.

4 MEB now established ashore; has pushed south to link up with 3 Cdo Brigade, forming continuous beachhead.

Position of HOOK forces rather more precarious. Most airborne-capable elements of 5 AB Bde are now on the ground. However, the perimeter of the air-head is not large enough to allow air-landing elements to be inserted. Supplies are being landed by parachute and LAPES.

Brigade commander believes he can expand air-head enough to allow rest of brigade to be inserted if he is given sufficient air support. If not forthcoming, his brigade will need to wait for arrival of FISH forces.

Air reconnaissance suggests that major Soviet counterattack will be launched against HOOK forces in the next 24-48 hours. Troops currently on the ground will have difficulty in holding any major attack, especially if it includes armor. Therefore, it is requested that majority of available air support be assigned to HOOK forces. Will assign majority of suitable aircraft under my command to HOOK.

6TH MAY. INDRE BILLEFJORD,
FINNMARK, NORWAY

The US Marines were using their air mobility to leap forward again; this time, 1/2 Marines were being dropped on the small village of Indre Billefjord. A fishing village once home to around 256 people, Indre Billefjord had been lain waste by the retreating Norwegians, like so many other villages and towns in Finnmark. Only the church remained standing amongst the devastation.

The Marines had been warned not to enter any buildings that had been left intact, or to pick up any object they spotted on the ground, no matter how interesting or enticing it looked. The Norwegians had been very thorough when it came to boobytraps.

———

Staff Sergeant Novak made sure that the magazine was seated properly in his rifle as the *Osprey* he was traveling in made its final approach to the Landing Zone. On emerging from the aircraft, he was surprised to find that the LZ had already been secured by members of Force Recon and Norwegians from the Finnmark Landforsvar; the latter had been operating covertly behind enemy lines, but had emerged into the open when the first Marines had arrived.

"Spread out, guys!" Novak shouted to his Marines. "We don't know if there are any Russkies in town, but we should assume that there might be!"

The Marine infantrymen spread out, clearing any possible hiding places before pushing further out to form a defensive perimeter. Once the perimeter was secure, *Ospreys* and *Super Stallions* began to lift in more troops and heavy equipment.

The only Soviet troops they encountered were a group of Traffic Directors and a couple of lorry drivers whose vehicles had broken down. Unsurprisingly, they rapidly surrendered to the heavily armed Marines and were soon evacuated by *Ospreys* bringing in reinforcements.

"Okay, Marines good work," Novak told his men once they had dug in.

Satisfied that all was well, he reported to his platoon commander, who was speaking to the company commander.

"We're all squared away, LT. No more hostiles within our part of the perimeter."

"Good work, Staff Sergeant," Lieutenant Dewey replied.

"Those Traffic Directors give you any trouble, Staff Sergeant?" the Company commander asked.

Novak smiled and shook his head.

"They all but crapped their pants when they saw us coming, Captain. I think that directing traffic is supposed to be a cushy billet in their army."

———

Within an hour of the first Marines arriving, a battery of M777 howitzers from 1/10 Marines was in position and Marine engineers were busy constructing a FOB for aircraft. Initially, it would only be for helicopters and *Ospreys*; however, it was intended that it would soon be able to take Marine and RAF Harriers.

While the Marines at Indre Billefjord could not yet quite support the British and Canadian troops, they could engage Soviet forces on the other side of the fjord, and the howitzer battery was soon engaging armored vehicles advancing towards the Anglo-Canadian positions. Once the FOB was operational, they would also be able to provide almost constant air support.

The HOOK forces had not quite been relieved, but an important step among many had been taken towards that ultimate goal. At best, friendly forces should reach them within the next 48 hours; at worst, the Marines had established a safe line of retreat.

7TH MAY. SIGNALS BETWEEN
FISH-HOOK AND CINCNORTH

From: Com FISH-HOOK
   To: CINCNORTH
   Copied: COMNON, SHAPE

FISH forces now all ashore and have consolidated their beachhead; Marines from 2(US) MEB and 3 (UK) Cdo Bde now form a single lodgement. If possible, would like troops from COMNON or CINCNORTH reserve to be released for garrison duty within the lodgement. Also request transfer of 4 (US) MEB from COMNON to own command to reinforce advance north as soon as 10th (US) Mtn Div is operational. If 4 (US) MEB cannot be released, would instead request that balance of Brigade North be assigned to my command.

HOOK forces continue to hold out against weak Soviet attacks and are no longer in danger of being overrun. Advance forces from 2 (US) MEB have established a FOB close to HOOK perimeter and are now able to provide support with artillery and aviation. Once additional battalion is airlifted into FOB, I am confident that an expanded lodgement can be made with HOOK forces in advance of link-up with ground column.

For reasons not fully understood to me, Commander 3 (UK) Cdo Brigade has requested that a token unit from his force be included in troops that link up with 5 (UK) Abn Bde;I have given permission for X-Ray Company, 45 Cdo to be detached for this reason. Neither Cdr 3 Cdo nor senior liaison officer from 5 Abn have responded in detail when requested to explain importance of this, but felt that if British forces wished to be involved in relieving their countrymen, I could see no problem with that.

X-Ray Company will be attached to US Marine battalion due to fly into the FOB and be included in force making link-up within the next 24 hours.

From: CINCNORTH
To: Com FISH-HOOK
Copied: COMNON, SHAPE

COMNON cannot currently release 4 (US) MEB, as it is holding an important part of the Lyngen Line. It is also currently the only major non-Norwegian formation in the front-line; therefore, it is important politically that it remains where it is. COMNON intends to use the brigade as part of the spearhead of an eventual counterattack.

However, COMNON is willing to release the balance of Brigade North to your command. A significant armored force may be of more use to you than another brigade of Marines, especially if the Soviets mount a major counterattack from the Kola.

I endorse decision to detach X-Ray Company, 45 Cdo to take part in link-up with HOOK forces. RM and Parachute Regiment have important historic relationship, it will be important to former that they take part in relief of latter.

For your information, Swedish/Finnish force in Finnish Lapland is making good progress against Soviet troops. This makes it likely that our troops along Lyngen Line will be able to mount offensive sooner rather than later, as Soviet troops opposite them are now effectively cut off. Will need your forces to act as anvil to the hammer of COMNON's troops; does make counterattack from Kola much more likely. With effective elimination of Soviet Northern Fleet, the Striking Fleet Atlantic will be available to provide air support for the foreseeable future. However, be aware that a major operation about to be launched in Germany may temporarily restrict the availability of transport aircraft. Please advise if this will affect ability of HOOK force to conduct combat operations.

. . .

From: Com FISH-HOOK
   To: CINCNORTH
   Copied: COMNON, SHAPE

Have enough organic rotary and fixed-wing assets to continue to supply HOOK force if number of C-130 aircraft is reduced or eliminated altogether. Expect full link-up with ground column to take place within the next 48 hours, in any case.

Have enough troops from FISH force to act as anvil when COMNON launches a counterattack. Very pleased to hear of good progress in Finnish Lapland; anything that keeps the Soviets occupied is good, in my book. Similarly hope that operation in Germany is successful.

9TH MAY. OUTSIDE IGLEDAS, FINNMARK, NORWAY.

Major Williams always felt slightly claustrophobic when riding in an armored vehicle; as a Marine Commando, he always had visions of being trapped in an APC after it had been hit by an ATGW or RPG. He did make an exception when it came to the Bv-206S and BvS-10 *Viking*s used by 3 Commando Brigade, but only because he knew a lot about the capabilities of those vehicles. However, he could not help but think this American vehicle was a deathtrap.

"You doin' okay, Major?" the vehicle commander asked.

"Fine, thanks, Sergeant," Williams replied. "How long till we get to the RV?"

"About ten minutes," the sergeant replied.

"Okay," Williams said, thinking that it was ten minutes too long.

―――

Sergeant Lee, a member of the Canadian Merville Company attached to 5th Airborne Brigade, had been snoozing when the sound of approaching armored vehicles woke him up. As with most combat soldiers, he was able to go from fast asleep to full wakefulness almost immediately.

"Weapons tight, repeat weapons tight. Friendly armor approaching," the radio headset in his left ear said.

"Gents! Weapons tight!" he yelled to his section. "Friendly armor approaching!"

Knowing that he was about to witness a historic moment, Sergeant Lee sat up on the lip of his rifle pit. The first two vehicles to appear out of the gloom were a pair of LAV-25A1s, followed closely by a quartet of M-1A1 tanks. AAVP-7A1 Amtracks followed next, cheerful Marines waving to the Canadian and British paratroopers as they passed by. Most of the vehicles passed through without stopping, heading to the other side of the perimeter to take up their positions. However, Lee was intrigued to spot a group of Amtracks halt by 2 Para's battalion HQ.

———

Major Richards, the Acting CO of 2 Para, was also slightly puzzled as to why the group of Amtracks had halted beside his Command Post. He guessed that perhaps the American column commander wanted to talk to him for some reason. His puzzlement soon turned to dismay, and he groaned audibly as he saw the camouflage pattern of the Marines who debussed from the vehicles.

"Better contact brigade," he sighed to the battalion adjutant. "We've just been relieved by the 'Booties.'"

"*Our* Booties, sir?" the adjutant queried as he emerged from the tent.

"I'm afraid so," Richards confirmed. "We're never going to live this down."

———

Major Williams stretched his back to get all the kinks out of it once he had stepped off the rear ramp of the AAVP-7A1. He looked around and spotted the two Para officers watching the arrival of his company.

Should be good payback for Stanley, he thought to himself as he strode towards the two men.

"Major Williams, Officer Commanding X-Ray Company, Four-Five Commando," he stated as the two men glanced up. "I'm looking for the CO of 2 Para."

"You've found him," the senior of the two Paras replied. "Major

Richards, acting CO, 2nd Battalion, The Parachute Regiment. Welcome to Lakselv, Major Williams."

"Thank you, Major Richards," Williams said. "My orders were to report to you before heading to brigade HQ."

I'll bet they were; somebody wants to make sure as many people as possible know we were relieved by the "Booties," even if it was only a single company, Richards thought.

"Well, I suppose I should say something like 'I stand relieved' before passing you on to brigade, Major Williams," he said with more friendliness than he felt.

"Thank you, Major Richards; always a pleasure to work with the Paras."

*NYBY, FINNMARK,
NORWAY*

While he had often worked with British Marines, Staff Sergeant Novak had never worked with British airborne troops. However, they seemed like professionals, at least for "army pukes." His platoon of A Company, 1/2 Marines was dug in just to the rear of the forward positions of 3 Para, having moved in hopefully unobserved by the Soviets. When the expected Soviet attack came, the Marines had been given strict instructions not to engage until ordered.

Doesn't make a lot of sense to me, Novak thought. *Standoff is our friend. I guess someone has a plan.*

———

Where are the enemy helicopters and jets? Colonel Anatol Sokolov thought. Sokolov kept his face impassive as his regiment advanced, but he kept glancing nervously into the skies.

"Comrade Colonel, we have reached Phase Line Moskva," his lead battalion reported. *"Continuing to advance."*

As he monitored the division command net, Sokolov felt strangely reassured about the lack of airpower.

They are all concentrating on the 115th Guards Motor Rifle Division over on E6 Highway, Sokolov thought. *To be fair, they likely seem like a larger threat. No matter, we will achieve penetrat...*

The first sign of the enemy were anti-tank missiles that reached out to destroy some of his leading recce vehicles, tanks, and MTLBs. Sokolov cursed at the contact reports, immediately ordering the regimental artillery and supporting divisional rocket battalions to conduct a "hurricane" artillery bombardment.

"All battalions push through!" he barked into his radio. "We do not have time for a methodical attack."

The artillery seemed to have done its work, as to his satisfaction forward troops soon reported seeing the enemy beginning to drift back. The general smiled.

Looks like we will beat the 115th into Lakselv, after all.

———

"All right, mates?" the British Para sergeant said as he dropped down into the foxhole that Novak and another Marine were occupying. "Never thought I'd be glad to see Marines," he added with a grin that showed several missing teeth, confirming what Novak thought about the Brits and dental hygiene.

"Always happy to save airborne from themselves, buddy," Novak replied. "Now it's time for us to kick some Commie ass."

As the Soviets passed over the now-abandoned British positions, Nowak's radio crackled with the order to open fire. Javelin and TOW missiles flashed out from the Anglo-American positions, while mortar and artillery fire lashed the Soviet rear. The surprise volley caused the lead Soviet battalion to stagger to a stop, burning vehicles blocking the roadway and the unswept surrounding terrain seeming an unsafe proposition. As the lead Soviet units were sorting themselves out, 1st/C/2nd Tank and two platoons of LAV-25s from 2nd LAR Battalion joined in the execution. The artillery and mortar fire briefly lifted to allow attack helicopters and fixed-wing aircraft to join in the attack.

Colonel Sokolov lived just long enough to realize that he had been drawn into an ambush. He was trying to think of a way to get out of it when a salvo of MLRS rockets fired by O Battery, 5/10 Marines obliterated his command vehicle and the accompanying headquarters.

———

A short distance away, the lead regiment of the 115th Guards Motor Rifle Division also ran into an ambush. As at Nyby, the British defenders appeared to retreat after a short initial engagement. Again, the Soviet troops shortly after ran into the massed firepower of USMC units; then, with the lead units stopped, had their follow-on forces engaged by attack helicopters, fixed-wing aviation, and long-range artillery. With the confined road and total supremacy, the massacre was almost complete.

In less than an hour, the NATO defenders had effectively destroyed the equivalent of two Soviet divisions, sending the survivors retreating east towards the border. The Soviets did have other troops available in the Kola, but these were lower readiness formations and it would take time for them to be made available for another attack.

*USS Iwo Jima, off
Søroya, Norway*

"We've done it, sir! We've done it, sir!" Major Andrew Rawson, USMC, said excitedly as he burst into the stateroom of the Commander of II MEF.

"What have we done?" a groggy Lieutenant General Burns replied, swinging his legs out of his bunk.

"We've met all of our objectives, sir—our forces now form a single lodgement. We've also defeated the last Soviet forces that pose an immediate threat."

A now-fully awake Burns got to his feet, grabbing his uniform jacket. He exited the stateroom, heading towards the amphibious operations room, Rawson following in his wake.

"Any news from CINCNORTH or COMNON?" he asked.

"While we were completing our operations, 4 MEB, Norwegian troops from their 6th Division and the Army's 10th Mountain Division mounted an attack on Skibotn. They took the village and are now sitting astride the road out of Finnish Lapland."

"So there goes the Soviet's last land-based supply lines," Burns commented.

———

"Well, ladies and gentlemen, I go away for a couple of hours' sleep and you complete FISH-HOOK," Burns said to the Operations Room staff. "A very well-deserved Bravo Zulu to you all; I'm sure we'll all be getting one from CINCNORTH and the Supreme Allied Commander Europe soon, too.

"Now to serious matters: where is the Soviet air force? We've been damned lucky that our air cover had been able to protect us from what they've sent against us."

"The Soviet Northern Fleet is out, sir," the senior naval officer on the staff, Captain David Garcia, USN, replied. "Intelligence suggests that the Soviets have been saving their air assets to go after the Striking Fleet, Atlantic."

Burns *harrumphed* in disapproval.

"Damn fools. With half of what they probably plan to use against the carriers, they could have caused us very real problems. Still looks like the *Airdales* will be in for a tough fight."

The general turned to Major Rawson.

"How long has it been, Major?"

"Sir?" a puzzled Rawson wondered.

"Since the war started, Major."

"Ah...thirteen days, I think, sir...yes, thirteen days," Rawson confirmed. Burns smiled.

"Then it has taken NATO thirteen days to win its first major victory of the Third World War. It won't be our last."

———

Author's note

This story is an adapted extract from my continuing web novel, *The Last War*. Readers who have read the original story will notice some differences; these have been necessary to make the story work as a standalone work.

I want to thank all those who helped with making both this story and *The Last War* a better story than it would otherwise be.

ABOUT JAN NIEMCZYK

Jan Niemczyk was born and brought up in Scotland, where he currently lives. He has long had an interest in military history, aviation, naval warfare, cats and horses. He also has an interest in the Cold War.

Mr Niemczyk is the author of the web novel The Last War, an alternative history where the USSR has survived into the early 21st Century. He is currently employed in the public sector.

IN THE END

Whoa boy, *this has been a trip*. There are a lot of emotions at the conclusion of any endeavor, be it a singular book or a group of them. That is true whether an endeavor is initially powered by malevolence ("I can accomplish all things through the power of *spite*, which strengthens me...") or sustained by the power of friendship. This trilogy has been a combination of both. There are way too many folks to thank, so I'm gonna hit the highlights.

First and foremost, I'd like to thank my lovely wife, Anita. In the little over 18 months this project has taken Anita has filled several roles. First, she provided wise counsel ("Okay, and what does that accomplish?") that helped shape the plan for execution. Second, even though she didn't exactly agree with the "side quest," once I decided to make the trilogy happen the only person working harder on it was me. In everything from patiently explaining why the latest successful mauling by the "good idea fairy" wouldn't really fit on the back cover to conceptualizing branding "in stride," Anita has epitomized the concepts of "helpmate" and "partner." Ye Olde Artwife has often held the opinion that "someone could do this [insert task she was working on] better." Carly Simon has sung a whole damn song about my response to *that*. *pause* No, not the song everyone thinks is about them, the one she did for "The Spy Who Loved Me." Jeez.

Speaking of the covers, I want to give a huge shout out to the man who painted all three, Wayne Scarpaci. He took the "Hey Wayne, I'm going to need three paintings, quickly..." and ran with it like a world championship was on the line. As those of you who have seen my art book *Days That Never Were* are aware, Wayne has been involved in many of my projects. From that first email asking, "Can you paint the U.S.S. *Arizona* at sea getting attacked by the Japanese?" to "Okay, so I'm going to need a P-80 in AVG colors with Viet Minh markings...", I've never been disappointed and regularly amazed.

A book with a great cover and bad content is just a nice art piece, however. Every author who gave me a story did exceptional work, and if I thanked everyone appropriately this postscript would be longer than my own "allegedly 10,000 words" additions. That being said, I want to first recognize Philip Wohlrab for raising the rights issue that prompted me to seek some legal advice in the first place. Next, I'd like to give a shout out to Justin Watson for much wise counsel and encouragement. There's a reason two of the three covers belong to these gentlemen, and if I ever do a project like this again, they're definitely getting an invite. Last but not least, I want to thank "The Blogmother," Sarah Hoyt. Indie publishing is a game where everyone needs a wise mentor and cheerleader. Sarah has been the Qui Gonn to my Anakin. You know, minus the whole "killed by a Sith Lord" thing.

Speaking of practitioners of dark arts, indie publishing also teaches you there are a lot of folks who are critical to a book even existing yet are never listed in the acknowledgments. Sarah Clithero, the editor for all three of these, mentioned in front of an entire roomful of people she wanted to collaborate with me on a project at Libertycon. I'm all about making ~~nightmares~~ dreams come true, and I'd like to thank her for all the work she did. Candice Gilmer handled all of the interior arrangements, soldiering on even though I never had the foresight to figure out a common template for all the authors to use. Finally, a huge *thank you* to my agent Stephanie Hansen of Metamorphosis Agency and Maggie Marr of Maggie Marr Legal. Stephanie could negotiate a favorable deal with Lucifer himself, while Maggie's going to make sure "in the details" works wholly in her clients' favor. [**Note: No deals with agents of infernal powers were made with *these* anthologies. No, I will not explain any further.**] If you do the indie thing long enough you realize amateurs draw up agreements on Word, *professionals* "lawyer up" and ask for help. I'm just glad help answered the emails in all of these cases.

Anyway, I hear the next project politely clearing its throat. It takes a village to get things done. Even if I failed to name "the butcher, the baker, and the candlestick maker" by name in the preceding paragraphs, the meat, bread, and blunt objects ("Wait, what?") were appreciated. Even if it sometimes felt like I should have invoked Atlas instead of Ares thanks to all the mountains that had to move, you hold in your hands the proof the rocks got shifted. The view of the sunset is great from this height, and I'm looking forward to the sunrise that heralds the next day's labor. See ya on the next ridgeline.

The Slinger, January 2026

EXCERPT FROM WONDER NO MORE

James Young

Turn the page for an excerpt

A SAMURAI ASSUMES COMMAND

IJNS YAMATO
1600 LOCAL
24 OCTOBER 1944

"Sir, what are we going to do?"

Vice Admiral Matome Ugaki took a deep breath.

What do we do indeed? he considered, looking out the flag bridge's shattered windows. He could see a vessel, one of the Center Force's heavy cruisers, smoking profusely and listing hard to port. Without his binoculars and in the deteriorating visual conditions, he could not make out what ship it was for certain.

"Assemble the staff, Lieutenant Commander Ryuunosuke," Ugaki replied. "I will issue my orders once we have a full damage report."

Ugaki could almost feel Vice Admiral Kurita's's presence still, even in the chaos that was the battleship's shattered flag bridge. The stench of explosives permeated the structure, fighting its own battle with the smell of blood, loosed bowels, and still smoldering fires.

Damn the Americans, Ugaki thought. He was still not sure how he'd survived the direct hit. One moment he'd been struggling against the *Yamato*'s heeling over from a sharp turn. The next, he'd been on the deck, gasping for breath amid his comrade's screams. He looked down at the sword clutched tightly in his hands.

Once again, it appears that you and I have survived, he thought, glancing over at the sheet-covered body arranged in a neat row with several others. *While yet again, my admiral is dead.*

For one moment Ugaki's mind turned to another disastrous afternoon, off the coast of Bouganville. He shook his had to clear those thoughts.

This time I am not struggling to escape a sinking bomber, he thought. *No, this time I am in my rightful place.* Turning, he saw that Ryuunosuke still stood beside him.

"Do you need further instructions, Lieutenant Commander?" he asked sharply.

"Sir, Vice Admiral Kurita's orders…"

"I know what Vice Admiral Kurita said," Ugaki said lowly. His grip tightened on the samurai sword. The junior officer, after a moment, bowed quickly in acknowledgment. Ugaki watched the man leave the ruined flag bridge.

The Americans have battered us, but if this weather gets much worse we may yet get to our objective, Ugaki thought. *The nation is counting on us. The fleet will not fail.*

It was ten minutes before Lieutenant Commander Ryuunosuke returned, six men following solemnly behind him.

Has this been so terrible that all I have left are junior officers? Ugaki wondered, before quickly recalling the previous two days. He sighed.

First the submarines, now the American carrier aircraft. Perhaps I should thank my lucky stars that we have anything left at all.

"Situation report," Ugaki said. The men all looked at one another, then back at him.

"The *Musashi* is almost certainly lost," one of the men, a lieutenant (j.g.) stated. "She is down by the bow and the water is almost over her forward deck."

"Instruct two of the destroyers to stand by her," Ugaki said. "They'll take off the wounded while the rest of our force comes about."

"*Mutsu*, *Nagato*, and *Kongo* all report bomb damage," a different man, this one a lieutenant, offered. "But thankfully no torpedoes, in part because of *Noshiro*'s bravery in putting herself between a torpedo squadron and *Mutsu*."

Mutsu is indeed lucky, Ugaki thought. *First that the fire that started in Hiroshima Bay last year didn't set off her magazines, then that they were able to get her ready for this battle.* What had caused the fire to start in the battleship's magazines was still unknown. Whether sabotage, as some whispered, or the instability of the special anti-aircraft shells she'd been carrying, the blaze had nearly ended the vessel's career in a ball of fire.

It looks like Fate determined her guns were necessary to help save us all.

"Tell Captain Morishita to bring the *Yamato* about," Ugaki said. "Take us back to the west, back into the squall line."

"Hai!" the staff answered in unison, even as they exchanged confused glances.

"We cannot continue to get pummeled by the American carriers," Ugaki explained. "The bad weather is our cloak, at least for the next couple of hours."

"But sir, what of the Southern Group?" Ryuunosuke asked. "If we turn back to the west, won't Vice Admiral Nishimura be their only target?"

Ugaki pinned the man with a hard look. After a moment, Ryuunosuke broke his gaze and looked down at the deck.

"Sorry sir, I did not mean to question you," the junior officer stated quietly.

"Nishimura will have to see to his own devices," Ugaki replied.

Nishimura is a sacrificial lamb, Ugaki thought. *Which is why he is trying to force Surigao Strait with two ancient battleships. I am envious of his opportunity.*

A few moments after Ryuunosuke left, Ugaki felt the *Yamato* begin to heel over in a turn.

Good, good, hopefully this will give us some respite, he thought.

USS GAMBIER BAY
1800 LOCAL

"Halsey's boys are fucking crazy," Lieutenant Aaron Mackenzie said as he walked into the *Gambier Bay*'s ready room. "They actually tried to get another raid off in this slop."

"Yeah, well, I'm more concerned about the damn Japs' ability to fly in it," his friend, Lieutenant Mason Murdock, replied. The man was puffing contentedly on a cigarette as he played chess with one of composite squadron (VC) – 10's FM-2 *Wildcat* pilots. The ensign's brow was furrowed as he contemplated Murdock's last move.

Wow Mason, you could have just killed the kid quickly rather than dragging it out, Aaron thought, looking at the board. It was clear to him that Murdock was toying with the more junior pilot.

Guess we all have our ways of dealing with nervous energy.

"Tough luck for the *Princeton*," someone said from the back of the room.

"Better her than us," Murdock replied. "Those yahoos get all the best equipment and get to fly off a huge deck. Meanwhile, I'm sitting here in a glorified merchant ship."

Gambier Bay, as an escort carrier, was under no obligation to try and fly off her paltry air group in the worsening weather outside. Designated as a "CVE" officially, the *Gambier Bay*'s purpose was to provide air support to a landing beachhead until either the Marines or Army could seize an airfield. Unofficially, the diminutive carrier's crew called her a "Kaiser coffin" due to the shipyard that built her and the sheer fragility of her hull. A single bomb or torpedo could, in an instant, kill every man aboard.

Happened to those poor bastards on the **Liscome Bay,** Aaron thought. He'd been aboard the escort carrier *Coral Sea* when their sister ship had caught the tin fish from a Japanese submarine. Several of his friends from flight school had been aboard the doomed vessel. The four men, along with over two thirds of the *Liscome*'s crew, had not survived.

*Good ol' **Coral Sea**. Can't believe she's the **Anzio** now.*

"You look like you've seen a ghost, Aaron," Murdock said, moving a chess piece. "Checkmate, Ensign Rhodes."

"Shit," the young officer muttered, clearly annoyed.

"Just thinking about Derek, Connor, and Jim," Aaron said. Murdock grew somber.

"Yeah, it's been a helluva war," Murdock replied, running his hands through his hair. The ensign looked between both men as if expecting an explanation. Seeing he wasn't going to get one, Ensign Rhodes opened his mouth to say something right as the sound of rain on the deck intensified.

"Yep, that tears it," Aaron said. "I don't think we're getting in that last anti-submarine patrol."

"With the way the small boys have been tearing up the India boats lately, I'm not sure how many of the Japs are left," Murdock replied, stubbing out his cigarette. "You hear about that destroyer escort that sank six of them all by herself a few months back?"

"Yeah, the *England*," Aaron said. "Meanwhile, we haven't even sighted a Japanese ship, even a small one, in months."

The *Gambier Bay* was part of Task Unit 77.4.3, a subunit of Vice Admiral Kinkaid's Seventh Fleet. With six escort carriers and a handful of escorts, "Taffy 3" was perhaps as powerful as a single one of Third Fleet's larger vessels...if one squinted really hard.

"Keep talking like that and you're going to get transferred over to Halsey's carriers as a replacement pilot," Murdock said. "You're going to wish you were back here in a jiffy when you're having to drop a fish on some carrier."

*That'd be a lot more funny if I were Rhodes or another **Wildcat** pilot*, Aaron thought. The FM-2s, while faster than their predecessors, were far too obsolescent to even be considered for using on Halsey's fast carriers. His *Avenger*, on the other hand, was almost exactly the same model flown off the larger *Essex* and *Independece*-class vessels.

"Not that there will be anything left when you get there from what the radio shack eavesdropped on," Murdock continued.

Aaron briefly looked around the ready room, drawing a short laugh from Murdock.

"What, worried someone here might be a Japanese spy?"

No, but one of us might get shot down tomorrow or the next day over land, Aaron thought, then paused. *Okay, fine, that's ridiculous. Pretty sure the Japanese know how much damage they suffered.*

"Insane how long this war's been going on," Murdock said after a moment. "I wonder if those yellow fuckers are regretting Pearl Harbor now."

Aaron shrugged.

"If so, probably just until the sharks show up," he replied. "Hope they don't give the fish indigestion."

"I hope they don't give those fish a hankering to try international cuisine," Murdock said.

Aaron saw Rhodes look at both of them nervously.

"Don't worry Rhodes, we haven't had anyone go into the drink for at least three weeks," Aaron pointed out. "The mechanics are good, especially with those *Wildcats*."

Murdock laughed.

"Besides, just think about what a sympathetic pick up line that will be when you get back home," the man said, then struck a mock, solemn pose. "'My dear, I'll have you know that I fought off savages, sharks, and simians for this country. Now let me buy you a drink."

Rhodes looked puzzled for a second.

"Simians?" the younger man asked, puzzled.

"What is the school system coming to?" Murdock asked, feigning shock.

"Apes," Aaron said. "Lieutenant Murdock regularly compares our opponents to apes."

Murdock shrugged, clearly unapologetic.

"It might be my good Louisiana upbringing," he stated. "Or it might just be I'm pissed off being here in the middle of the Pacific while my parents are back home living out their golden years without me nearby to help."

"You know, there's six of you kids," Aaron replied, shaking his head. "I'm sure they've got plenty of help from the younger ones."

"Dewayne just shipped off for Europe about a month ago," Murdock said, referring to his younger brother. "Got mail the last time you all did as well. Kinda glad he's going someplace civilized rather than these hell holes."

"You have any family Rhodes?" Aaron asked.

"I had two brothers," Rhodes said quietly. "My oldest brother didn't make it back from Italy."

Well, that took a turn, Aaron thought, looking over at Murdock.

"They still sent you out here?" Murdock asked incredulously.

"I wanted to do my part," Rhodes replied defensively.

"No offense, but your poor mother might feel differently," Aaron said. "I mean, I'm glad that my younger brother might just miss this thing."

"If the Japanese had a lick of sense, it'd already be over," Murdock said angrily. "You can look at a map and see that it's past time to throw in the towel for them."

A mess steward poked his head into the room.

"Gentlemen, do any of y'all want some sandwiches?" he asked. "I've got a tray."

"Are they going to serve a meal in the wardroom tonight?" Aaron asked.

"No sir," the steward said. "Captain Vieweg is expecting us to remain at Condition Zebra even if we secure from General Quarters."

Oh for fuck's sake, Aaron thought, sharing a look with Murdoch. *Always a pain in the ass opening, then closing, then opening every. fucking. hatch.* While he could understand the captain's caution given the Japanese Fleet being out in strength, it didn't change the fact it made simple shipboard functions annoyingly difficult.

"I'll grab a sandwich," Aaron said. He grabbed one then, after a second's thought, another half. The steward smiled for a moment at his decision, then immediately became stone faced as Murdock glared at him.

"Something amusing?"

"Yeah, I'm a greedy pig," Aaron responded. Murdock looked about to say something else when he realized Aaron was not about to let him pick at a mess steward for being human.

I don't care how you folks treat him down in the South, Aaron thought. *He's stuck out here just like the fucking rest of us.*

Before the mess steward could say anything else, a familiar form stood in the hatchway behind him. Turning, the mess steward recognized VC-10's commander, Lieutenant Commander E.J. Huxtable, and quickly moved out of the man's way.

"Mackenzie, Rhodes, you've got first ASW patrol in the morning," Huxtable said.

"Aye aye, sir," Aaron responded, looking over at the *Wildcat* ensign. The young man nodded, then stood up from the table.

"I'm going to go get a shower then turn in, sir," he said to Aaron. "Unless you want to go over anything."

"By this point, I think you've flown enough patrols I don't have to babysit you," Aaron said with a wry smile. He could see that Lt. Commander Huxtable was not impressed with his decision, but the senior officer let it slide.

Tomorrow is probably going to be just another boring day in the Pacific, he thought. *While complacency can kill us dead, over preparation just leads to fatigue...which also kills us.*

"In any case, I'm probably not far behind you," Aaron said. "Might as well write the wife."

"Still apologizing for knocking her up again?" Murdock teased.

Aaron glared at him.

"What?" Murdock said, putting up his hands in mock innocence as Rhodes and Huxtable both grinned. "Just thinking maybe we *should* send you over to Third Fleet to see if you're as accurate with a *tor*pecker. War would be over next week."

Aaron started to smile despite himself.

"I swear, Murdock, there's a reason you're still single," he said. "A gentleman. The second half of the sentence is '...and a gentleman.'"

Huxtable was shaking his head as he walked back out of the compartment, Rhodes right behind him. Murdock watched him go, then turned back to Aaron.

"I'm some ROTC filler who would've been lucky to get promoted if war hadn't broken out," Murdock replied. "Maybe if I was from Canoe U like you are, I'd be a little less couth. Simple fact is, I'm going to be unemployed about ten days after this war is over. Which is fine by me, I just want to get back to Baton Rouge in one piece."

Hadn't thought about what I'll do after the war, Aaron thought. *Way too much water between here and Tokyo to start doing that, honestly. Plus it's not like I need any more motivation to get home than Meredith and the kids.*

USS W*ASHINGTON*
0200 L*OCAL*
25 O*CTOBER 1944*

"You know, if those idiots on *New Jersey* fuck around much longer, we're going to have *South Dakota* three hours astern of us with just a couple of destroyers for a screen," someone muttered the *Washington*'s in darkened flag plot.

Figures it would be **South Dakota** *that had an engineering casualty*, Lieutenant Commander Hank Orrick thought, but he kept a poker face while regarding the coterie of officers standing around the map board. Vice Admiral Willis Lee, currently the USN's most experienced surface combat commander, stood at the head of the table. Of average height and build, with a round face and dark eyes, Lee did not have the same dashing aura as Third Fleet's commander, Vice Admiral Halsey. Still, having recently been reassigned from the *New Jersey* to Lee's staff due to a washing machine incident, Orrick was already preferring Lee's calmness to Halsey's fits of temper. Thinking of the circumstances that had brought him to this point, Orrick had to shake his head once more.

Pretty sure that's the third time it's happened, Orrick thought. *Or maybe just the second, but I'm going to go out on a limb and say this is why men should not try to do laundry.*

"Sir, we can't get anything besides a 'roger' off the *New Jersey*," Commodore Thomas Jeter, Lee's chief of staff, stated from the senior officer's left. An aviator, Jeter was looking at the map with obvious concern as the staff adjusted the position of the Third Fleet ever further north.

"How long did Captain Riggs say he expected repairs to take again?" Vice Admiral Lee asked, rubbing his temples.

How long has he been up? Orrick wondered. *I mean, I know he just caught a couple of hours, but this is getting insane.*

"He's two hours past his estimated time, sir," Jeter replied. "The *South Dakota* can still cruise at twenty-two knots, but he believes that's his current maximum."

"He can't keep running the powerplant at maximum power," Lee observed. "Especially as long as it's been since she's been back to Pearl or the West Coast."

Jeter nodded in agreement.

"Sir, with all due respect, I think we make Third Fleet staff wake the old man up or live with our decision," Jeter snapped. "We're one hundred miles ahead of the *South Dakota*, and I don't like her being back there by herself."

None of us do, Jeter, Orrick thought. A former aide to Ernest King, Jeter had been the captain of the U.S.S. *Bunker Hill* before being assigned to Lee's staff. To say the two men had not gelled was an understatement.

Lee doesn't feel like he needs an aviator to babysit him as chief of staff, Jeter feels like this is keeping him from commanding a task group, Orrick thought. *Meanwhile, the rest of the staff is just trying to keep us all from getting killed.*

"So what do you propose we do for air cover, Commander Jeter?" Lee asked gently. "Because if your compatriots are to be believed, they've reestablished that battleships without air cover are sitting ducks."

Lee said the last with very little sarcasm, but the fact it was there at all would have been dripping for any other officer. Jeter pressed his lips together and was clearly debating how to respond.

I mean, how many times have aviators claimed to have sunk every Japanese battleship? Orrick thought. *Hell, starting with that Kelly kid back in '41, the Army alone swears they've bagged at least five more **Kongo**s than the Japanese ever built.*

"Sir, Vice Admiral Halsey's staff will have to figure out what they'll do at daylight," Jeter began evenly. "With the *Independence* damaged, no one has done a night search. Like you, I don't have a good feeling about those Japs coming through San Bernadino Strait."

"I'm not in the habit of conducting gross insubordination, Commander," Lee stated.

"Sir, Vice Admiral Halsey was going to form Task Force 34," Jeter said. Orrick could see the man was barely able to contain his frustration. "Then he canceled it. Or *someone* did."

He's not wrong, Orrick thought.

"At a minimum, if we don't turn some of our ships around we'll have the *South Dakota* all by herself in the morning," Jeter continued, his words coming fast. "I think the Royal Navy tried a couple capital ships with only a handful of destroyers right after Pearl Harbor. You know what happened to both of those vessels."

"Who is here from intelligence?" Lee asked.

Everyone shifted around the crowded flag plot.

Fuck, guess that's me, Orrick thought.

"Here, sir," Orrick replied. He pressed towards the map, parting the press of officers.

"What's your best guess on what the Japanese started with versus what they have now?" Lee asked. "Just the heavy ships."

Just thousands of men's lives hanging on my next few words, Orrick thought. *No big deal.*

"Sir, the reports stated there were six battleships," Orrick said. "That's already one more than we were expecting, especially with the crews saying there were *two* of the *Nagato*-class."

"I thought there were always two," Jeter interrupted.

"Yes sir, there were," Orrick said. "But allegedly General MacArthur's boys captured a prisoner who said *Mutsu* blew up at dockside. There are other sources that corroborated this."

Funny thing about breaking someone's codes, he thought. *At times you may get something slightly off.*

"Could she have sank and they refloated her?"

"Could have, yes," Orrick replied. "But how she got here is irrelevant, she's clearly here."

"So two of those new super ships they have with the 16-inch guns, two *Kongo*, two *Nagato*," Lee said. "Two more in the south, but Seventh Fleet is dealing with those."

"Yes, sir," Orrick said.

"And the strike claims they sank three of the ones outside of San Bernandino, which is where the rest of them turned tail?"

"Yes sir," Orrick said.

In for a penny, in for a pound.

"But I personally doubt that the Japanese commander would turn around in these circumstances," Orrick continued in a rush. "This is their last throw of the dice, sir. If we were all that stood between the Japanese and San Francisco, there's not a single one of our commanders that would turn around just because of a little battle damage."

"Does anyone know what Seventh Fleet has in the north?" Lee asked.

There were a few long moments of silence.

"Okay, does anyone know how to get a hold of Seventh Fleet?"

Again, there was silence. Lee shook his head.

"Damn MacArthur and Kinkaid," he muttered. He looked up at the clock.

"Commodore Jeter, issue the following order: We will form Task Force 34.2 in order to support the *South Dakota* and prevent her from getting caught by herself at daylight. Go with the *South Dakota*, *Washington*, *Alabama*, *Massachusetts*, and *Alaska*."

Well, looks like it's a good thing that "large cruiser" got here a couple months early, Orrick thought. He wasn't quite sure on what had happened, as apparently the *Alaska* wasn't supposed to have arrived for another thirty days. He suspected some chicanery on the part of her captain and crew, but that was well above his pay grade.

Just hope them being green doesn't make this any harder, Orrick thought. *Already going to be a nightmare for those ships detaching from the carriers and forming up in the dark."*

"Sir, we'll set the rendezvous point once we issue the initial order," Jeter replied. "Do you have any preferences?"

"No," Lee replied. "Just keep us from having any collisions if you could."

"Aye aye, sir," Jeter said. Lee turned to Orrick.

"As far was we know, the Jap carriers only have those two hermaphrodites with them, correct?" Lee inquired, referring to the "battle carriers" *Ise* and *Hyuga*.

"Yes, sir," Orrick replied.

"Well if the *New Jersey* and *Iowa* can't handle the two of them, their captains should be hanged," Lee said simply. "Same cruiser line up as planned. Courtesy copy the *Intrepid*. If anyone is going to break ranks and follow us, it's Rear Admiral Bogan."

Jeter nodded.

I hope the Japanese don't make a fool of me in the morning, Orrick worried. *Oh well, if I'm wrong what are they going to do to me? Send me thousands of miles from my wife?*

"Gentlemen, we had a chance to finish this in June and I talked Vice Admiral Spruance out of it," Lee said, looking around the room. "That's why we trained in September, and I'm confident we'll shoot the shit out of some Jap battleships tomorrow if we have to."

Orrick looked at the map as Lee continued.

"But let's make sure we don't give Seventh Fleet a heart attack when we show up," Lee continued. "I was with Vice Admiral Kinkaid around Guadalcanal. He's an excitable sort, doesn't like surprises. So make sure we send a dispatch plane off at first light."

"Aye aye," Jeter said.

"I'm going to bed," Lee said. "You don't take 'no' for an answer unless it's Vice Admiral Halsey himself. I'm not going to have his damn staff end up with us leaving some baby carriers and destroyers out to dry. We'd never hear the end of it from the damn Army."

That brought a slight chuckle around the room. With a last nod, Lee turned and left the flag plot.

Orrick did some quick math as he measured distance.

We'd be near the escort carriers by around seven tomorrow morning if the **South Dakota** *fixes her boilers soon*, he thought. *Couple hours after dawn. At least it won't be another night fight.*

USS JOHNSTON
0250 LOCAL
24 OCTOBER 1944

"Jesus, it sounds like someone is getting pounded," Ensign Jack Murphy said, looking up from a letter home to his mother. The young officer was referring to the speaker mounted on the U.S.S. *Johnston*'s radio shack bulkhead. The *Fletcher*-class destroyer was cutting through the waters just off Samar Island, her compartments mostly blacked out to prevent giving away Taffy Three's position.

"Not someone, the damn *Japs* are getting their asses handed to them," his companion, Lieutenant (j.g.) Dennis Schuler stated, voice filled with awe.

Technically, the little destroyer should not have been able to pick up the radio transmissions from far to their south. Furthermore, the two officers were nominally supposed to be standing watch and assisting the officer of the deck, Lieutenant Hagen, *Johnston*'s gunnery officer. However, once the senior officer realized the freak in atmospherics that was allowing them to pick up Vice Admiral Oldendorff's ambush, he'd released both junior officers to listen.

Mom can wait, Jack thought. *She'll forgive me later.*

"Is that the destroyers going in?" Jack asked, barely able to discern the call sign. "Wonder who that is in charge of them. Seems to have a definite hold on things."

"Captain Coward, I imagine," a familiar voice said from behind them. Both officers and the three sailors in the compartment jumped up from their seat as Commander Ernest Evans walked into the radio shack.

"Sit down, sit down," Evans said genially. "I take it you all forgot that I have a speaker piped into my day cabin?"

Jack and Lieutenant (j.g.) Schuler shared a look of pure terror, as did all the sailors.

"No worries," Evans said, yawning. "If we've got a front row seat to a radio drama, might as well see how it plays out."

"Aye aye, sir," Schuler replied. At the point, Lieutenant Hagen poked his head in.

"You guys need to keep it down in...oh. Hello sir, sorry to wake you."

Evans waved him off, focusing intently on the radio. He grinned, and Jack felt a slight sense of disquiet at the look.

The only reason that's not how Crazy Horse probably looked at Custer right before the scalping started is because the Old Man is Cherokee, not Sioux, Jack thought.

"Gentlemen, what you're hearing is a textbook destroyer attack," Evans said. "I imagine our boys are going in with radar and actually just using their torps rather than firing back at that Japanese screen."

With Evans giving them a description, Jack could just imagine things in his head.

Dark as hell out there, with cloud cover to boot, he thought, thinking about the worsening weather.

Evans looked at his watch.

"Now listen to see what you hear in about seven minutes or so," he said, tone almost wistful.

"If the torps work," Hagen said grimly. Evans nodded at that comment.

"We've done a lot to fix the fish," Evans replied, then saw the blank look on the younger officers' faces.

"Beginning of the war we had a lot of duds," he explained. "Everyone did, from the submariners to the aviators. How many torpedoes did you bounce off that Jap battleship during the Friday Night Massacre?"

A pained look crossed Hagen's face even as Jack wondered what the captain was talking about.

"I think the *Aaron Ward* should have hit her at least three times from that range," Hagen replied.

That's right, Lieutenant Hagen was at Guadalcanal, Jack thought to himself. *First Guadalcanal, as I recall.*

"Why didn't the torpedoes work, sir?" Schuler asked.

"We didn't test them prewar," Evans said. "Too expensive. Too bad the man who made that decision went on to become an admiral rather than getting shot for it."

Jack saw the same shocked expression on Schuler's face he was sure was crossing his own.

"Shame the fly boys took care of the other Jap fleet earlier today," Hagen said. "Would have loved another crack at them."

Evans turned from the speaker and smiled.

"Be careful what you wish for, Robert," Evans chided with a smile.

"Sir, I think you're being a bit hypocritical," Hagen replied with a broad grin. "Something about 'I intend to take this ship into harm's way' comes to mind."

Two of the sailors laughed before they could stop themselves. Schuler favored them with a hard look.

I feel like I missed something, Jack thought. *I guess that's what I get for getting aboard as a replacement.*

His predecessor had been "washed overboard" in the middle of the night. No one had seen the man go, and allegedly there'd been a note the captain had ordered burned.

Not sure I'd jump off a ship in the middle of the Pacific over a dame running off with another man, Jack thought. *But that's also one of those decisions you don't get to reconsider, unfortunately.*

"I meant what I said in that speech, gentlemen," Evans said, his tone firm. "If this vessel sighted a Japanese battleship tomorrow, I would only hope we would have an opportunity to..."

The radio was suddenly a cacophony of conversation, the voices distorted by distance and atmospherics. All of the men in the compartment listened intently, but Jack had little clue what was going on until Evans deciphered it for him.

"Sounds like a good spread of fish," he observed. "At least two large vessels blown up, one of them maybe a battleship. Of course, everyone thinks they've sunk a battleship at night."

"You never forget one when you see it up close," Hagen said. "Even worse in daylight though."

"Is it true your last captain tried to duck behind a bulkhead when that *Kongo*-class fired at you the next dawn?" Evans asked, raising an eyebrow.

"Sir, if I could've clicked my heels together and disappeared up my own asshole, I would have done it," Hagen said earnestly. "At least if it happens again I'll hopefully have some guns to shoot back with."

He looks positively haunted, Jack thought. His uncle had once sworn he'd seen Jack's long dead grandmother Christmas Eve night. While Jack was sure that had more to do with the half bottle of whiskey than any maternal afterlife visits, Hagen's face bore almost the exact same expression Uncle Hank's had that December morning.

"The battleline just opened up," Schuler remarked. Evans was about to reply when the radio abruptly went dead. The sailors immediately began tending to it, checking wiring.

"Sir, looks like whatever was letting us hear the fight we moved out of," one of them said apologetically after five minutes.

"Well, looks like we go back to being carrier escorts rather than spectators," Evans sighed. "Speaking of which, you'd best get back on the bridge, Robert."

Lieutenant Hagen nodded, heading forward out of the radio shack.

"As for you two, there's no reason for you both to get no sleep," Evans said. "Between Third Fleet and Oldendorff, I don't think there's a whole lot of ships left to shoot. But we'll probably have to deal with more of those damn planes in the morning."

"Third Fleet didn't have a good time of it yesterday, sir," Schuler said. "Sounds like the Japanese carriers got the *Princeton* and put a couple of bombs into the *Independence*."

Evans shook his head.

"Well there goes that night carrier experiment," he muttered.

"Sir?" Schuler asked.

"Nevermind," Evans said. "Just a conversation I had with one of my classmates when I was last in Pearl."

A runner poked his head into the radio room.

"Sir, Lieutenant Hagen says the visibility is getting worse," the sailor said. "Down to eight thousand yards due to haze."

Evans looked as if he was pondering something for a moment.

"Tell him to make sure to set a good radar watch, but we don't need to wake up any more lookouts," Evans replied. "I suspect Rear Admiral Sprague will have a plan he'll pass along, and we've got plenty of sea room."

"Aye aye, sir," the sailor replied, then was gone.

"Murphy, you finish your letter to your mother then get to bed," Evans said with a smile.

I guess it's true what they say about the captain sees all and know all, Jack thought, feeling his face flush.

"Sir, someone has to do it," Jack said sheepishly. "She claims she never hears from the other three. Something I intend to fix if we ever are in Ulithi at the same time as *Alaska*."

Evans shook his head.

"Not surprised she hasn't heard from your brother if he's on her," Evans noted. "Scuttlebutt is her captain was lucky he didn't 'accidentally fall over the side' as hard as he worked that crew. She's out here six months earlier than expected."

Jesus, Jack thought. *Okay, maybe I'll go easier on Tommy when I see him next.*

"Still, it only takes ten minutes a night," Evans continued. "Just don't get yourself thrown in the brig for beating your brother's ass."

"Yes sir," Jack said, smiling. "I would never strike a superior officer."

Evans shook his head with a smile as he walked out the aft hatch. Hagen watched him go, then turned back to look at Jack.

"I didn't know you were related to Tommy 'Gun' Murphy," Hagen replied. "You don't look anything like him."

That's a long story we just don't talk about in the family, Jack thought, shrugging.

"We get that a lot, sir," he replied.

———

Want to read more? You can find the rest of the book either as a standalone novella or as part of my short story collection **Dispatches From Valhalla***, both available at booksellers everywhere.*

ALSO BY JAMES YOUNG

USURPER'S WAR SERIES

ALTERNATE WORLD WAR II | HAS AUDIOBOOK

COLLISIONS OF THE DAMNED | MULTIPLE BOOK SERIES

AN USURPER'S WAR NOVELLA

ALTERNATE HISTORY ART

Hardcover | Soft Cover

ALTERNATE HISTORY SHORT STORY COLLECTIONS

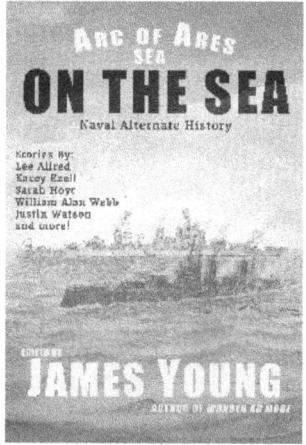

Navel Alternate History

Arc of Ares: Sea - On the Sea

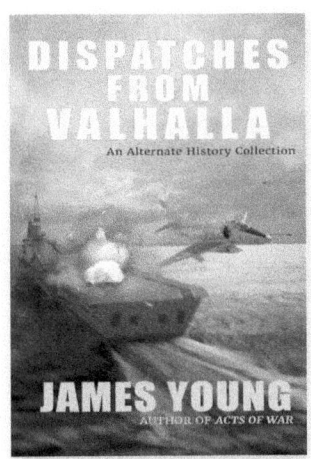

Short Story Collection

Dispatches from Valhalla

Ground Alternate History

Arc of Ares Land: Thin Red Tales

Barren SEAD

Eagles, Ravens, and Other Birds of Prey

Works Previously Published in Those In Peril (2019) by Chris Kennedy Press

"Far Better to Dare" by Rob Howell

"A Safe Wartime Posting" by Joelle Presby

"For Want of A Pin" by Sarah Hoyt

"Beatty's Folly" by Philip Wohlrab

"Martha Coston and the Farragut Curse" by Day Al Mohammed

"Per Mare Per Terram" by Jan Niemczyk

"Corsairs and Tenzans" by Philip Bolger

"Naked" by Kacey Ezell

www.ingramcontent.com/pod-product-compliance
Lightning Source LLC
Chambersburg PA
CBHW060805030726
47503CB00002B/340